D1320107

A
Garland Series

VICTORIAN FICTION

NOVELS OF FAITH
AND DOUBT

A collection of 121 novels
in 92 volumes, selected by
Professor Robert Lee Wolff,
Harvard University,
with a separate introductory volume
written by him
especially for this series.

THE NEMESIS OF FAITH

SHADOWS OF THE CLOUDS

James Anthony Froude

Garland Publishing, Inc., New York & London

1975

Library of Congress Cataloging in Publication Data

Froude, James Anthony, 1818-1894.
    The nemesis of faith.

    (Victorian fiction : Novels of faith and doubt ;
v. 68)
    Reprint of 2 works, the 1st originally published in
1849 by J. Chapman, London; the 2d originally published in 1847 by J. Ollivier, London.
    I. Froude, James Anthony, 1818-1894. Shadows
of the clouds. 1975. II. Title. III. Series.
PZ3.F939Ne15 [PR4706]   823'.8   75-1519
ISBN 0-8240-1592-4

Printed in the United States of America

THE NEMESIS OF FAITH

Bibliographical note:

this facsimile has been made from a copy in the
Beinecke Library of Yale University
(Ip.F939.849N)

THE

NEMESIS OF FAITH.

LONDON:

GEORGE WOODFALL AND SON,
ANGEL COURT, SKINNER STREET.

THE

NEMESIS OF FAITH.

BY

J. A. FROUDE, M.A.,

FELLOW OF EXETER COLLEGE, OXFORD.

" Καὶ μὴν ἔργῳ γ᾽ οὐκ ἔτι μύθῳ
Χθὼν σισάλευται·
. . . . σκιρτᾷ δ᾽ ἀνέμων
Πνεύματα πάντων, εἰς ἄλληλα
Στάσιν ἀντίπνουν ἀποδεικνύμενα."
PROMETHEUS.

LONDON:
JOHN CHAPMAN, 142, STRAND

MDCCCXLIX

NEMESIS OF FAITH.

LETTER I.

I PROMISED so long ago to write to you, dear Arthur, that by this time, if you have not already forgotten me, you will at least have begun to think it desirable to forget me as soon as possible, for an ungrateful, good-for-nothing fellow; but I am going to be very just, and pay heavy interest—and I think letter debts are like all other debts. If you pay them when they are due, they are taken as a matter of course, and without gratitude; but leave them till your poor creditor leaves off expecting, and then they fall in like a godsend. So I hope you are already delighted at the sight of my handwriting, and when you get to the end of these long sheets, which I am intending to fill to you, I shall be quite back again in my old favour. Perhaps, though, I am too sanguine; I have nothing

B

but myself to write about, no facts, no theories, no opinions, no adventures, no sentiments, nothing but my own poor barren individualism, of considerable interest to me, but I do not know why I should presume it will be so to you. Egotism is not tiresome, or it ought not to be, if one is sincere about oneself; but it is so hard to be sincere. Well, never mind, I mean to be, and you know me well enough to see through me when I am humbugging. A year has gone since we parted; I have had nothing all this time to tell you, except that I was unsettled and uncomfortable, and why should I trouble you with that? Now you will see I want your help, so now I come to you. It is not that I have had any positive grievance, but I seem to have had hold of every thing by the wrong side. My father is very anxious to see me settled into some profession or other, and here have the three black graces alternately been presenting their charms to me, and I can't get the apple delivered; I turn from one to the other, and the last I look at seems always the ugliest, always has some disagreeable feature I cannot reconcile myself with. I cannot tell why it is, Arthur, but I scarcely know a professional man I can like, and certainly not one who has been what the world calls successful, that I should the least wish to resemble. The roads they have to travel are beaten in by the unscrupulous as well as the scrupulous; they are none of the cleanest, and the race is too fast to give one time to pick one's way. I know men try to keep their private conscience distinct from their professional conscience, but it does not always do. Their nature, like the dyer's hand, is subdued to what it works in; and you know a lawyer when you see him, or a doctor, or a professional clergyman. They are not simply men, but men of a particular sort, and, unfortunately, something not more but less than men — men who have sacrificed their own selves to become the paid instruments of a system. There may be exceptions where there is very great genius; but I am not a genius, and I cannot trust myself to hope I should be an exception, and so I go round and round, and always end where I began, in difficulties. I believe you know something of my father—a more upright, excellent man never breathed; and though not very clever, yet he has a breadth of solid understanding which, for such creatures as we men are, is far better furniture to be sent into the world with than any cleverness; and I am sure there must be something wrong in my fastidiousness when he so highly disapproves of it. He was contented to laugh at me, you know, as long as I was at college, because my dreaming, as he called it, did not interfere with my succeeding there; but it is quite another thing now, and he urges me again and again, almost with a severity of reproof which is bitterly distressing to me. I have shown talents, he says, of which it is my duty to make use; the common sense of mankind has marked out the best ways to use them, and it is worse than ridiculous in a young man such as I am to set myself up to be dif-

ferent from everybody else, and to be too good to
do what many of the best and wisest men he knows,
are doing. My brothers were all getting on honour-
ably and steadily, and why was not I? It was
true, he allowed, that unscrupulous men did sometimes succeed professionally, but it was not by their
faults but by their virtues, by activity and prudence,
and manly self-restraint . . . . . . He added something which made a deeper impression upon me
than this; for all this I had said often and often to
myself. I had told him that as I had a small independence, I thought I might wait at least a year or
two, and give myself time to understand my own
wishes clearly before I committed myself. "You
say you wish to be a man, Markham," he answered,
" and not a professional man. I do not propose to
control you. At your age, and with your talents,
you must learn what life is now, not from me, but
from life itself; but if you will hear an old man's
opinion, I will give it you. If you think you can
temper yourself into manliness by sitting here over
your books, supposing you will grow into it as
a matter of course by a rule of necessity, in the
same way as your body grows old, it is the very
silliest fancy that ever tempted a young man into
his ruin. You cannot dream yourself into a character; you must hammer and forge yourself one.
Go out into life, you will find your chance there,
and only there. You ask to wait. It is like a
timid boy waiting on the river bank to take his
plunge. The longer he stands shivering the harder

he finds it. At the year's end you will see more difficulties than you see now, because you yourself will have grown feebler. Wait one more, and then you will most likely go on to the end, into your second childhood of helplessness."

What shall I do, Arthur? It is so true every word of this. I feel it is. I know it is; and it is shameful, indeed, to rust into nothingness. Yet what to do! Surely it were kinder far, to train us out from our cradles into a course which should be chosen for us, and make us begin our crawling on the road we are to travel, with spelling-books of law and physic, and nursery courts of justice, or diseased dolls to lecture or to doctor. All would be so easy then; we should form each about our proper centre, and revolve calmly and surely in the orbit into which we were projected. It is a frightful business to bring us up to be only men, and then bid us choose for ourselves one of three roads which are to take us down again. For they do take us down. Unless we are in Fortune's best books, and among those same lucky sons of genius, for law or physic, we must learn a very dirty lesson, and train our lips into very smooth chicanery, or it is slow enough her wheel will move with us. Speak the truth, and the truth only, and in the first you are a fool, and in the second you are a brute. "Ah, well, but at least the Church is open to you," you will say, and that is what my father says. There the most fastidious person will find the purest course he could mark down for himself fall infinitely short

of what is required of him. And you believe I
always intended to be a clergyman; yes, and it is
true. I always did intend it; and if you could tell
the envy with which I watch my friends passing in
within the precincts of its order into what ought to
be the holiest and happiest of lives; alas! here too
I seem to be barred out, and one of my worst
sorrows is that I cannot tell my father why I am.
I will tell you, Arthur, but not now. I must think
well over what I am to write on that subject, and
you shall have another letter about it. But, oh,
what a happy life that is! I cannot understand
why, as a body, clergymen are so fatally uninteresting; they who through all their waking hours
ought to have for their one thought the deepest
and most absorbing interests of humanity. It is
the curse of making it a profession— a road to get
on upon, to succeed in life upon. The base stain
is apparent in their very language, too sad an index
of what they are. Their "*duty*," what is it? – to
patter through the two Sunday services. For a
little money one of them will undertake the other's
duty for him. And what do they all aim at?—getting livings! not cures of souls, but *livings;* something which will keep their wretched bodies living
in the comforts they have found indispensable.
What business have they, any one of them, with a
thought of what becomes of their poor wretched
selves at all? To hear them preaching, to hear the
words they use in these same duties of theirs, one
would suppose they really believed that getting on,

and getting rich, and getting comfortable, were quite the last things a Christian should propose to himself. They certainly say so. Alas! with the mass of them, the pulpit keeps its old meaning, and is but a stage. Off the stage there is the old prate of the old world stories, the patronage of this rich man and that, the vacant benefice or cathedral stall. So and so, lucky fellow, has married a bishop's daughter, and the bishop himself has the best dressed wife and the best equipage in London; and oh, bitterest satire of all! the very pulpit eloquence with which they can paint the better life, the beauty of Christianity, is valued only but as a means of advancing them into what they condemn. Yet this need not be, and this is not what I shrink from. The Church is an ill-paid profession, and so of the men who make a profession the main thing in this life of ours, it must be contented with the refuse of the educated. Not more than one in fifty takes orders who has a chance in any other line; but there is this one in each fifty, and so noble some of these units are, that they are not only enough for the salt of their class, but for the salt of the world too. Men who do indeed spend their lives among the poor and the suffering, who go down and are content to make a home in those rivers of wretchedness that run below the surface of this modern society, asking nothing but to shed their lives, to pour one drop of sweetness into that bitter stream of injustice: oh, Arthur, what men they are! what a duty that might be! I think if it is true what they say who profit by this modern system; if there is indeed no help for it, and an ever increasing multitude of miserable beings must drag on their wretched years in toil and suffering that a few may be idle and enjoy; if there be no hope for them; if to-morrow must be as to-day, and they are to live but to labour, and when their strength is spent, are but to languish out an unpensioned old age on a public charity which degrades what it sustains; if this be indeed the lot which, by an irrevocable decree, it has pleased Providence to stamp upon the huge majority of mankind, incomparably the highest privilege which could be given to any one of us is to be allowed to sacrifice himself to them, to teach them to hope for a more just hereafter, and to make their present more endurable by raising their minds to endure it. I have but one comfort in thinking of the poor, and that is, that we get somehow adjusted to the condition in which we grow up, and we do not miss the absence of what we have never enjoyed. They do not wear out faster, at least not much faster, than the better favoured; that is, if you may reckon up life by years, and if such as we leave them may be called life. Oh what a clergyman might do! To have them all for an hour at least each week collected to be taught by him, really wishing to listen, if he will but take the trouble to understand them, and to learn what they require to be told. How sick one is of all sermons, such as they are! Why will men go on thrashing over and again the old withered straw that was thrashed out centuries ago, when every field is waving with fresh, quite other, crops craving for their hand? Is it indolence or folly? What is it? I could linger on for hours over an employment I so much long for. It seems to be mine, as I dwell upon it; so entirely it is all I crave for; I have not talent enough to create fresh thought for strong cultivated men; but it has always been my delight to translate downwards what others have created; and I have been so much about among the poor, and with all their faults and all their ignorance, I love their simple hearty ways so much that I could say with all my heart I felt myself *called*, as the Prayer Book says, to be their teacher; and yet, and yet . . . . well, good bye, and bear with me.

Your affectionate
M. SUTHERLAND.

LETTER II.

September 6.

"WHAT possible reason can I have for not taking orders?" you may well ask. I promised to tell you, and I will; yet I know not what you will think of me when I have done so. Wherever as yet I have even dared to hint my feelings, I have been met by looks so cold and withering that I tremble at exposing them even to you. O, Arthur, do not—do not make my trial harder—do not you leave me too—do not make me lose my

oldest, my only friend. Do not be frightened, I
have committed no crime, at least nothing which I
can conceive to be a crime; and yet they say it is
one. Arthur, before I can be made a clergyman, I
must declare that I unfeignedly believe all "the
canonical writings of the Old Testament;" and I
cannot. What does it mean—unfeignedly believe
it all? That all the actions related there are good,
and all the opinions true? Not that, of course;
because then all that Job's friends said would be as
true as what Elihu said, and Lot's actions as good
as Abraham's. But, I suppose, we are to believe
that all those books were written by men immediately inspired by God to write them, because He
thought them good for the education of mankind;
that whatever is told in those books as a fact is a
real fact, and that the Psalms and Prophecies were
composed under the dictation of the Holy Spirit.
Now I am not going to weary you with all the
scientific difficulties and critical difficulties, and,
worse than all, metaphysical difficulties, which have
worn the subject so threadbare; though I think but
badly of this poor modern sophistry of ours, which
stumbles on between its two opinions, and, when it
is hunted to its death, runs its head into the sand
and will not see what it does not like to see. If
there were no difficulties but these, and only my
reason were perplexed, I could easily school my
reason; I could tell myself that God accommodated
His revelations to the existing condition of mankind,
and wrote in their language. But, Arthur, bear

with me, and at least hear me; though my head
may deceive me, my heart cannot. I will not, I
must not, believe that the all-just, all-merciful, all-
good God can be such a Being as I find him there
described. He! He! to have created mankind
liable to fall—to have laid them in the way of a
temptation under which He knew they would fall,
and then curse them and all who were to come of
them, and all the world, for their sakes; jealous, passionate, capricious, revengeful, punishing children for
their fathers' sins, tempting men, or at least permit-
ting them to be tempted into blindness and folly, and
then destroying them. O, Arthur, Arthur! this is not
a Being to whom I could teach poor man to look
up to out of his sufferings in love and hope. What!
that with no motive but His own will He chose out
arbitrarily, for no merit of their own, as an eastern
despot chooses his favourites, one small section of
mankind, leaving all the world besides to devil-worship and lies; that the pure, truth-loving Persian of
the mountains, who morning and night poured out
his simple prayer to the Universal Father for the
good of all His children; that the noble Greeks of
Marathon and Thermopylæ, the austere and stately
Romans, that then these were outcasts, aliens, devil-
worshippers; and that one strange people of fanatics
so hideously cruel that even women and children
fell in slaughtered heaps before their indiscrimi-
nating swords, that these alone were the true God's
true servants; that God bid them do these things,
and, exulting in their successful vengeance as a
vindication of His honour, compelled the spheres

out of their courses to stand still and assist the murdering! . . . . And why all this murdering? Sometimes for sins committed five centuries past; while, for those five centuries, generation was let go on to follow generation in a darkness
out of which no deliverance was offered them; for
Israel monopolized God. It is nothing to say these
were exceptive peculiar cases. The nation to whom
they were given never thought them peculiar cases.
And what is Revelation if it is but a catalogue of
examples, not which we are, but which we are not,
to follow? No, Arthur! this is not God. This is
a fiend. Oh, surely this is not the faith of men who
worshipped the Father of mankind, but rather of
the followers of a god who was but one of many a
god among gods—the God of Israel, as Baal was
the god of the nations; and I cannot think the
disputes and jealousies of Heaven are tried and settled by the swords of earth. No! If I may believe that the Jews were men like the rest, and
distinguished from the rest not by any difference in
kind in the nature of their relations with Heaven,
but by their own extraordinary character; that,
more than any set of men who ever lived, they
realised the life and active energy of God upon
earth—that *they believed* they were the favourites
of Heaven—and that, in spite of the savage fanaticism into which it sometimes plunged them, their
faith did in a way make them what they professed
to be, and produced fruits of a most wonderful kind
—all is easy to me then. Winning Canaan by
strength, it was natural they, or at least their

children, should think that God had given it them ;
and in those fierce and lawless times many dreadful
things might be done, which at least we can understand and allow for, though in sorrow. But that
the unchanging God should have directly prompted,
should have interfered to assist in what humanity
shudders at while it reads—oh, I would sooner perish
for ever than stoop down before a Being who may
have power to crush me, but whom my heart forbids
me to reverence. It runs through the whole Old
Testament this feeling, with but a few great exceptions, and it is little use to make particulars. David
may have been the man after God's heart if the
Israelites were His peculiar people; and the furious
zealots in the last desperate wars in Palestine were
the same people as their fathers who slaughtered
Amalek. David himself is the great type of the
race in his savageness and in his piety! Who could
believe that the same man who wrote the *De pro-
fundis Domini* could have craved to wash his footsteps in his enemy's blood? The war of good and
evil is mightiest in mightiest souls, and even in
the darkest time the heart will maintain its right
against the hardest creed. Bear with me, Arthur,
we read the Bible with very different eyes. For
myself, the most delightful trait in the entire long
history is that golden thread of humanity which
winds along below the cruelty of the exclusive
theory, and here and there appears in protest, in
touches of deeper sympathy for its victims, than are
ever found for the more highly-favoured. Who are

those who most call out our tears? Is it not the outcast mother setting down her child that she may not see it die, the injured Esau, the fallen Saul, Aiah's daughter watching by her murdered children, or that unhappy husband who followed his wife weeping all along the road as David's minions were dragging her to his harem?

If the Church is a profession, I know all this is very weak and very foolish; one might enter it then, accepting what it insists upon, in the same way as the lawyer takes the laws as he finds them, not perhaps as he would have them if he had to choose, but as facts existing which it is not his place to quarrel with. And many sensible people do accept the Bible in this way, they take it as it stands; they are not responsible, and they are contented to draw reasonable doctrines from it, gliding over what is inconvenient. I know, too, there are some excellent, oh, most excellent people, deep and serious people, who do not find the difficulties there at all which I find, and accept it all with awe and fear, perhaps, but still with a real, serious conviction that it is all true. Perhaps it is. And then I . . . I . . . am . . . am . . .

And then there is another thing, Arthur, which seems to be taught, not in the Old Testament but in the New, which I should have to say I believed; a doctrine this, not a history, and a doctrine so horrible that it could only have taken root in mankind when they were struggling in the perplexities of Manicheeism, and believed that the Devil held a divided empire with God. I mean that the largest portion of mankind, these very people who live about us, feel with us, act with us, are our daily companions—the people we meet at dinner or see in the streets, that are linked in with us with innumerable ties of common interests, common sympathies, common occupations—these very people are to be tortured for ever and ever in unspeakable agonies. My God! and for what? They are thrown out into life, into an atmosphere impregnated with temptation, with characters unformed, with imperfect natures out of which to form them, under necessity of a thousand false steps, and yet with every one scored down for vengeance; and laying up for themselves a retribution so infinitely dreadful that our whole soul shrinks horror-struck before the very imagination of it; and this under the decree of an all-just, all-bountiful God—the God of love and mercy. O, Arthur! when a crime of one of our fallen brothers comes before ourselves to judge, how unspeakably difficult we find it to measure the balance of the sin; cause winding out of cause, temptation out of temptation; and the more closely we know the poor guilty one, the nature with which he was born, the circumstances which have developed it, how endlessly our difficulty grows upon us!—how more and more it seems to have been inevitable, to deserve (if we may use the word deserve) not anger and punishment, but tears and pity and forgiveness. And for God who knows all! who not only knows all but who determined all—

who dealt us out our natures and placed us as it
pleased Him! "what more could have been done to
my vineyard that I have not done?" Alas! then, if
Omnipotence could not bring but wild grapes there,
why was the poor vineyard planted? It never asked
to be. Why fling it out here into these few miserable
years; when it cannot choose but fall to ruin, and
then must be thrown into hell-fire for ever? . . . .
I cannot tell. It may be from some moral obli-
quity in myself, or from some strange disease; but
for me, and I should think too for every human
being in whose breast a human heart is beating, to
know that one single creature is in that dreadful
place would make a hell of heaven itself. And
they have hearts in heaven, for they love there.
Justice! what justice! I believe that fallen creatures perish, perish for ever, for only good can live,
and good has not been theirs; but how durst men
forge our Saviour's words " eternal *death*" into so
horrible a meaning? And even if he did use other
words, and seem to countenance such a meaning for
them (and what witness have we that He did, except that of men whose ignorance or prejudice
might well have interpreted these words wrongly as
they did so many others?) . . . . But I am on dangerous ground; only it seems to me that it would be
as reasonable to build a doctrine on every poet's
metaphor, or lecture on the organic structure of the
Almighty because it is said the *scent* of Noah's
sacrifice pleased Him, as to build theories of the
everlasting destiny of mankind on a single vehe-

ment expression of one whose entire language was a figure.

I know but one man, of more than miserable intellect, who in these modern times has dared defend eternal punishment on the score of *justice*, and that is Leibnitz; a man who, if I know him rightly, chose the subject from its difficulty as an opportunity for the display of his genius, and cared so little for the truth that his conclusions did not cost his heart a pang, or wring a single tear from him. And what does Leibnitz say? That sin, forsooth, though itself be only *finite*, yet, because it is against an Infinite Being, contracts a character of infinity, and so must be infinitely punished. It is odd that the clever Leibnitz should not have seen that a *finite punishment*, inflicted by the same Infinite Being, would itself of course contract the same *character of infinity*. But what trifling all this is, Arthur! The heart spurns metaphysics, and one good honest feeling tears their shrivelled spider webs to atoms. No, if I am to be a minister of religion, I must teach the poor people that they have a Father in heaven, not a tyrant; one who loves them *all* beyond power of heart to conceive; who is sorry when they do wrong, not angry; whom they are to love and *dread*, not with caitiff coward fear, but with deepest awe and reverence, as the all-pure, all-good, all-holy. I could never fear a God who kept a hell prison-house. No, not though he flung me there because I refused. There is a power stronger than such a one; and it is possible

to walk unscathed even in the burning furnace.
What! am I to tell these poor millions of sufferers,
who struggle on their wretched lives of want and
misery, starved into sin, maddened into passion by
the fiends of hunger and privation, in ignorance
because they were never taught, and with but enough
of knowledge to feel the deep injustice under which
they are pining; am I to tell them, I say, that
there is no hope for them here, and less than none
hereafter; that the grave is but a precipice off which
all, all of them, save here one and there one, will
fall down into another life, to which the worst of
earth is heaven? "Why, why," they may lift up
their torn hands and cry in bitter anger, "why,
Almighty One, were we ever born at all, if it was
but for this?" Nay, I suppose the happiest, the
most highly favoured, of mankind looking back over
a long unchequered life, where all the best and
highest which earth has to give her children has
been scattered at their feet, looking back and
telling over their days, might count upon their
fingers the hours which they had lived, which were
worth the pains it cost their mother to bear them.
And all for this! No, Arthur, no! I never can
teach this; I would not so dishonour God as to
lend my voice to perpetuate all the mad and foolish
things which men have dared to say of Him. I
believe that we may find in the Bible the highest
and purest religion . . . . . most of all in the history of Him in whose name we all are called. His
religion—not *the Christian religion,* but *the religion*

of Christ—the poor man's gospel; the message of forgiveness, of reconciliation, of love; and, oh, how gladly would I spend my life, in season and out of season, in preaching this! But I must have no hell terrors, none of these fear doctrines; they were not in the early creeds, God knows whether they were ever in the early gospels, or ever passed His lips. He went down to hell, but it was to break the chains, not to bind them. Advise me—oh, advise me! I cannot stand by myself—I am not strong enough, without the support of system and position, to work an independent way; and my father and my friends too, it would be endless bitterness with them. Advise me! No, you cannot advise me! With what absurd childishness one goes on asking advice of people, knowing all the while that only *one's self* can judge, and yet shrinking from the responsibility; only do not hate me, Arthur—do not write me cold stuffy letters about my state of mind. For Heaven's sake, if you love me, if you ever loved me, spare me that. Show me if I am wrong. It is easy to be mistaken. But do not tell me it is wicked of me to have thought all this, for *it is not* —I am certain it is not.

M. S.

LETTER III.

September 11.

I DID not say half I wished to say, Arthur: ever since I wrote I have been thinking how confusedly and stupidly I expressed myself. Somehow one never has one's thoughts in the right place when they are wanted, either for writing or for talking; and it is only after, when they can do no good, that the stupid helpless things come poking up into one's mind. "This is what I wanted; this is what I ought to have said," you think; you catch him, and he is a Proteus in your fingers, and you have only got a monster, half human and half beast. Ah, well, it is ill laughing with a heavy heart. I will try again. At any rate you will be clever enough to see what I mean. I suppose most people would allow they found some difficulties at any rate with the Old Testament, when I find insuperable ones, only they cannot feel them as I do. To believe, for instance, that God worked miracles to plague a nation for their ruler's sins, ought to make their lives intolerable. Perhaps if it all really is as they say, a certain apathy of heart is one of the rewards of their implicit faith to save them from its consequences.

But why do they believe it at all? They must say because it is in the Bible. Yes, here it is. Other books we may sit in judgment upon, but not upon the Bible. That is the exception, the one book which is wholly and entirely true. And we are to believe whatever is there, no matter how monstrous, on the authority of God. He has told us, and that is enough. But how do they know He has told us. The Church says so. Why does the Church say so? Because the Jews said so. And how do we know the Jews could not be mistaken? Because *they said* they were God's people, and God guided them. One would have thought if this were so, He would have guided them in the interpreting their books too, and we ought to be all Jews now. But, in the name of Heaven, what is the history of those books which we call the Old Testament? No one knows who the authors were of the greater part of them, or even at what date they were written. They make no claim to be inspired themselves; at least only the prophets make such claim; before the captivity there was no collection at all; they had only the Book of the Law, as it is called, of which they took such bad care that what that was none of us now know. The Pentateuch has not the slightest pretensions to be what Moses read in the ears of all the people, and Joshua wrote upon twelve stones. There is no doubt at all that it was written, or at least compiled into its present form, long long after. All we can make out is, that in the later and fallen age of the Jews, when their imaginative greatness had forsaken them, when they were more than half Chaldaicized, and their high enthusiastic faith and passionate devotion to their God had dwindled down into intolerant arrogance and barren fanaticism, wishing to console themselves for their present degradation by the glory of the past, they made a collection out of the wreck of the old literature.   Digests, like the Books of Chronicles were compiled out of the fragments of the old Prophets; the whole was then cast together in one great mould, where of course God was the founder; the number of books, sentences, words, syllables, letters, were all counted, and sealed with mystical meanings, and behold the one complete entire Divine Revelation of the Almighty, composed, compiled, and finished by Himself.   Were ever such huge pretensions hung upon so slight a thread? And the worst is, that by this tinsel veil we have hung before it, the real splendour of the Bible is so entirely hidden from us; what with our arbitrary chapter readings cutting subjects into pieces, our commentaries and interpretations, built not on laboured examination of what the people were for whom and by whom the books were written, but piled together hap-hazard out of polemic lucubrations as if they were all prophecies, and their meanings fixed by after history; with the unfathomed dulness of our Service, in which the *Venite Exultemus* is followed by the *Miserere mei Domine* in the same dull, stupid, soulless tone, as if it was a barrel organ that was playing them, and not a human voice speaking out of human heart.   Oh, what are we doing but making a very idol of the Bible, treating it as if we supposed that to read out of it and in it had mechanical virtue, like spells and charms—that it worked not as thought upon thought, but by some juggling process of talismanic mate-

rialism. Oh, Heavens! how our hearts bleed with
the poor mourners by the waters of Babylon; how
we exult with them, and share their happiness in
the glorious hymns they poured out on their return,
if we may believe that it was they themselves whose
souls were flowing out there in passionate simplicity.
But how are we flung back upon ourselves perplexed, confused, and stupified, when we are told
that all this is, as Coleridge calls it, but a kind
of superhuman ventriloquism—that the voice and
the hearts of the singers no more made this music
than the sun clock makes the hours which it marks
upon the dial-plate! And then all David's prayers
in his banishment. What, were they not prayers
then? Not his prayers as his broken spirit flung
itself upon God, but model prayers which God was
making for mankind, and using but David's lips to
articulate them into form? Ah, well! The Maho-
metans say their Koran was written by God. The
Hindoos say the Vedas were; we say the Bible was,
and we are but interested witnesses in deciding
absolutely and exclusively for ourselves. If it be
immeasurably the highest of the three, it is because
it is not the most divine but the most human. It
does not differ from them in kind; and it seems to
me that in ascribing it to God we are doing a
double dishonour; to ourselves for want of faith in
our soul's strength, and to God in making Him responsible for our weakness. There is nothing in it
but what men might have written; much, oh much,
which it would drive me mad to think any but men,

and most mistaken men, had written.   Yet still as
a whole, it is by far the noblest collection of sacred
books in the world; the outpouring of the mind of a
people in whom a larger share of God's spirit was
for many centuries working than in any other of mankind, or who at least most clearly caught and carried
home to themselves the idea of the direct and immediate dependence of the world upon Him.   I
is so good that as men looked at it they said this
is too good for man: nothing but the inspiration
of God could have given this.   Likely enough men
should say so; but what might be admired as a
metaphor, became petrified into a doctrine, and perhaps the world has never witnessed any more grotesque idol worship than what has resulted from
it in modern Bibliolatry.   And yet they say we are
not Christians, we cannot be religious teachers, nay,
we are without religion, we are infidels, unless we
believe with them.   We have not yet found the
liberty with which Christ has made us free.   Infidels, Arthur!   Ah, it is a hard word!   The only
infidelity I know is to distrust God, to distrust his
care of us, his love for us.   And yet that word!
How words cling to us, and like an accursed spell
force us to become what they say we have become.
When I go to church, the old church of my old
child days, when I hear the old familiar bells, with
their warm sweet heart music, and the young and
the old troop by along the road in their best
Sunday dresses, old well-known faces, and young
unknown ones, which by and by will grow to be so

like them, when I hear the lessons, the old lessons, being read in the old way, and all the old associations come floating back upon me, telling me what I too once was, before I ever doubted things were what I was taught they were; oh, they sound so sad, so bitterly sad. The tears rise into my eyes; the church seems full of voices, whispering round me, Infidel, Infidel, Apostate; all those believing faces in their reverent attention glisten with reproaches, so calm, they look so dignified, so earnestly composed. I wish—I wish I had never been born. Things grow worse and worse at home. Little things I have let fall are turned against me. The temperature is getting very cold, and our once warm and happy family, where every feeling used to flow so sweetly together in one common stream, seems freezing up, at least wherever I am, into disunited ice crystals. Arthur, Arthur, the sick heart often wants a warm climate as well as the sick body. They talk in whispers before me. Religious subjects are pointedly avoided. If I say anything myself, I am chilled with frosty monosyllables, and to no one soul around me can I utter out a single thought. What! Do they fancy it is any such wonderful self-indulgence, this being compelled to doubt what they stay trusting in? That it is a license for some strange sin? No, no, no. And yet they are right too—yes, it is very good, and very right. They are only following the old lesson, which I followed too once, that belief comes of obedience; and that it is only for disobedience that it is taken from us. My father says

c

before them, that I am indolent and selfish; and the
rest seems all of a piece and a part of the same
thing . . . . . Yet God is my witness, nothing
which I ever believed has parted from me, but it has
been torn up by the roots bleeding out of my heart.
Oh! that tree of knowledge, that death in life.
Why, why are we compelled to know anything,
when each step gained in knowledge is but one
more nerve summoned out into consciousness of
pain? Better, far better, if what is happier is better,
to live on from day to day, from year to year, caring
only to supply the wants each moment feels, leaving
earth to care for earth, and the present for the present, and never seeking to disentomb the past, or
draw the curtain of the future. Suppose I was to
write a book, Arthur, and say I was inspired to
write it—like Emmanuel Swedenborg—a madhouse
would be the best place for me, because common
sense would at once pass sentence on the pre-
tension, and if it did not, the poor book would be
its own sentence. But no one dreams that there
is anything improbable in the Jewish writers having been inspired; and they will not let us try
the books by their contents. No, it is written,
they say, and so we must believe. Was there
ever such a jumble of arguments? The Bible
is its own evidence, because it is so pure and holy.
This and that thing we find in parts of it seems
neither pure nor holy; but because it is there, we
must believe it—on some other evidence therefore
—on what, then? on the witness of the Church.

The Church proves the Bible, and the Bible proves the Church—cloudy pillars rotating upon air—round and round the theory goes whirling like the summer wind-gusts. It has been the sacred book by which for so many centuries so many human souls have lived, and prayed, and died. So have the Vedas, so has the Koran, so has the Zenda Vesta. As many million souls day after day have watched the sun rise for their morning prayer, and followed its setting by committing themselves to God's care for protection in the darkness from the powers of night, have lived humble, God-fearing lives, and gone to their graves with the same trust of a life beyond waiting all who have been faithful to those books—as many, or more, perhaps, than the Christians—no, there is no monopoly of God's favour. The evidence of religion—ah, I know where the true evidence lies, by the pleadings of my own heart against me. Why, why must it be that all these alien histories, these strange theories and doctrines, should be all sown in together in the child seed-bed with the pure grain of Christianity? so that in after years it is impossible to root them out without trampling over rudely on the good. And we must do it. They may be harmless, growing there unrecognised; but known for what they are, their poison opens then, and they or we must die. Arthur, is it treason to the Power which has given us our reason, and willed that we shall use it, if I say I would gladly give away all I am, and all I ever may become, all the years, every one of them

which may be given me to live, but for one week of
my old child's faith, to go back to calm and peace
again, and then to die in hope.   Oh for one look of
the blue sky as it looked then when we called it
Heaven!   The old black wood lies round the house
as it lay then, but I have no fear now of its dark
hollow, of the black glades under its trees.   There
are no fairies and no ghosts there any more; only
the church bells and the church music have anything of the old tones, and they are silent, too,
except at rare, mournful, gusty intervals.   Whatever
after evidence we may find, if we are so happy as to
find any, to strengthen our religious convictions, it
is down in childhood their roots are struck, and it is
on old association that they feed.   Evidence can
be nothing but a stay to prevent the grown tree
from falling; it can never make it grow or assist
its powers of life.   The old family prayers, which
taught us to reverence prayer, however little we
understood its meaning; the far dearer private
prayers at our own bedside; the dear friends for
whom we prayed; the still calm Sunday, with its
best clothes and tiresome services, which we little
thought were going so deep into our heart, when
we thought them so long and tedious; yes, it is
among these so trifling seeming scenes, these, and
a thousand more, that our faith has wound among
our heartstrings; and it is the thought of these
scenes now which threatens me with madness as I
call them up again.

LETTER IV.

Sept. 13.

I CAN do nothing but write to you, dear Arthur. You must bear with me—I am sure you will; it is so inexpressible a relief to me. My feelings have begun to flow to you, and it is unsafe to check an opening wound. I find little pleasure enough in being at home: all day in the beautiful autumn I wander about by myself, and listen to what my heart is saying to me; and then in the evening I creep back and hide myself in my little room and write it all down for you. I wonder whether I am serious in wishing to die. I certainly am in wishing I had never been born; and at least it seems to me that if I was told I was to go with this summer's leaves, it would do more to make me happy for the weeks they have got to hang upon the trees, than any other news which could be brought to me. I love the autumn. I love to watch my days dropping off one by one before the steady blowing time. You and I, Arthur, are but twenty-four, and your life is just beginning and mine seems to be done. It is well for me that I was never very hopeful; and the sweetest moments I can have now are when I stray at evening alone along the shore and watch the sea-birds as they sweep away after the sun on their gilded gleaming wings, or when the swallows are gathering for their long flight to bright smiling lands one knows not where. Some hope there is in their parting beauty, even when they seem to leave us desolate; and as the sweet planets come out above the purple

twilight, they are opening glimpses into some other
world to which peace has flown away, and I, perhaps,
may follow. There is a village in the wood, two or
three miles from here—there was an abbey there
once. But there is nothing left of the abbey but
its crumbling walls, and it serves only for a burying-
ground and for sentimental picnic parties. I was
there to-day; I sat there a long time, I do not know
how long—I was not conscious of the place. I was
listening to what it was saying to me. I will write
it down and look at it, and you shall look at it: an
odd enough subject for a Christian ruin to choose—
it began to talk about paganism. " Do you know
what paganism means?" it said. Pagani, Pagans,
the old country villagers. In all history there is no
more touching word than that one of Pagan.

In the great cities where men gather in their
crowds and the work of the world is done, and the
fate of the world is determined, there it is that the
ideas of succeeding eras breed and grow and gather
form and power, and grave out the moulds for the
stamp of after ages. There it was, in those old
Roman times, that the new faith rose in its strength,
with its churches, its lecture-rooms, its societies. It
threw down the gorgeous temples, it burnt their
carved cedar work, it defiled the altars and scattered
the ashes to the winds. The statues were sanctified
and made the images of saints, the augurs' colleges
were rudely violated, and they who were still faithful
were offered up as martyrs, or scattered as wanderers over the face of the earth, and the old gods

were expelled from their old dominion—the divinity of nature before the divinity of man. . . . Change is strong, but habit is strong too; and you cannot change the old for new, like a garment. Far out in the country, in the woods, in the villages, for a few more centuries, the deposed gods still found a refuge in the simple minds of simple men, who were contented to walk in the ways of their fathers—to believe where they had believed, to pray where they had prayed. What was it to these, the pomp of the gorgeous worship, the hierarchy of saints, the proud cathedral, and the thoughts which shook mankind? Did not the sky bend over them as of old in its calm beauty, the sun roll on the same old path, and give them light and warmth and happy sunny hearts? The star-gods still watched them as they slept—why should they turn away? why seek for newer guardians? Year by year the earth put on her robes of leaves and sweetest flowers—the rich harvests waved over the corn-fields, and the fruit-trees and the vineyards travailed as of old; winter and summer, spring and autumn, rain and sunshine, day and night, moving on in their never-ending harmony of change. The gods of their fathers had given their fathers these good things; had their power waxed slack? Was not their powerful hand stretched out still? Pan, almighty Pan! He had given, and he gave still. Who watched over the travail pangs of the poor ewes at the breeding time? Pan, almighty Pan! Who taught the happy shepherd to carve his love-notes in the invisible air, and fill the summer nights with softest, sweetest flute music? Pan, almighty Pan! Had the water-nymphs forsaken their grottoes where the fountains were flowing as of old? Were the shadows of the deep woods less holy? Did the enchanted nightingale speak less surely the tale of her sorrow? As it was in the days of their fathers so it was in theirs—their fathers had gone down to the dust in the old ways, and so would they go down and join them. They sought no better; alike in death as in their life, they would believe where they had believed, though the creed was but a crumbling ruin; sacrifice where they had sacrificed; hope as they hoped; and die with them too! Who shall say that those poor peasants were not acting in the spirit we most venerate, most adore; that theirs was not the true heart language which we cannot choose but love? And what has been their reward? They have sent down their name to be the by-word of all after ages; the worst reproach of the worst men—a name convertible with atheism and devil-worship.

"And now look at me," the old ruin said; "centuries have rolled away, the young conqueror is decrepit now; dying, as the old faith died, in the scenes where that faith first died; and lingering where it lingered. The same sad sweet scene is acting over once again. I was the college of the priests, and they are gone, and I am but a dead ruin where the dead bury their dead. The village church is outliving me for a few more generations; there still ring, Sunday after Sunday, its old reverend bells, and there come still the simple peasants in their simple dresses—pastor

and flock still with the old belief; there beneath its
walls and ruins they still gather down into the dust,
fathers and children sleeping there together, waiting
for immortality; wives and husbands resting side by
side in fond hope that they shall wake and link again
the love-chain which death has broken; so simple,
so reverend, so beautiful! Yet is not that, too, all
passing away, away beyond recall? The old monks
are dead. The hermit-saints and hallowed relics are
dust and ashes now. The fairies dance no more
around the charmed forest ring. They are gone,
gone even here. The creed still seems to stand; but
the creed is dead in the thoughts of mankind. Its
roots are cut away, down where alone it can gather
strength for life, and other forms are rising there;
and once again, and more and more, as day passes
after day, the aged faith of aged centuries will be
exiled as the old was to the simple inhabitants of
these simple places. Once, once for all, if you would
save your heart from breaking, learn this lesson—
once for all you must cease, in this world, to believe
in the eternity of any creed or form at all. Whatever grows in time is a child of time, and is born
and lives, and dies at its appointed day like ourselves. To be born in pain and nursed in hardship,
a bounding imaginative youth, a strong vigorous
manhood, a decline which refuses to believe it is a
decline, and still asserts its strength to be what it
was, a decrepit old age, a hasty impatient heir, and a
death-bed made beautiful by the abiding love of
some few true-hearted friends; such is the round of

fate through nature, through the seasons, through
the life of each of us, through the life of families, of
states, of forms of government, of creeds.   It was
so, it is so, it ever shall be so.   Life is change, to
cease to change is to cease to live; yet if you may
shed a tear beside the death-bed of an old friend,
let not your heart be silent on the dissolving of a
faith."

   This is what the old ruin said to me, Arthur.
Arthur, did the ruin speak true?

LETTER V.

Sept. 20.

THINGS grow worse and worse with me at home;
my brothers are all away, lucky fellows, happy and
employed.   Oh, how I envy them.   Letters come
home, such bright sunny letters.   They are getting
on so well, Henry has just got his epaulets, and his
captain took the occasion of writing a most polite
letter to my father about it.   He said he promised
to be one of the most excellent officers in the service, and so much more than merely a sailor, nice
fellow, that he is; and his highest pleasure seems to
be the pleasure he knows his success will give my
father.   Then for James and Frederick; you know
they are both younger than I am, yet James is
already a junior partner in the house, and Frederick
tells us he is intending to strike for wages, as all
the hardest cases in his master's office are handed

over to him; they seem born to get on, and when they come here, it is such an entire happy hearty holiday with them, riding, hunting, shooting, balls, and parties; they are the life of everything about us; while poor I—I, who was once expected too to be a credit to myself, am doing nothing and can do nothing. I cannot work, for there is nothing I can work upon, and yet I never have a holiday, my wretched thoughts cling about me like evil spirits. I have no taste for what is called amusement. I suppose I do not like hunting and shooting, but I say to myself that I think it wrong to make my pleasures out of helpless creatures' pain; and for the party-going, one had better have a light heart to like parties, or to be liked by them. Books nauseate me; I seem to have learnt all that I can learn from books, or else to have lost the power of learning anything from them; and of all these modern writers there is not one who will come boldly up and meet the question which lies the nearest, or ought to lie the nearest, to our hearts. Carlyle! Carlyle only raises questions he cannot answer, and seems best contented if he can make the rest of us as discontented as himself; and all the others, all, that is, who have any power at all, fight beside religion, either as if it were not worth saving, or as if it had nothing to do with them. Every day five columns of the *Times* are full of advertisements of new books, most of them with enough of flashy cleverness to let us endure them through a single reading; but then there is an end of them. A really serious, open-minded, single-hearted man—there is not one in the whole fraternity; and the impudent presumption of these reviewers, critics and all; well, at any rate, I am flung utterly upon myself, on my own resources, sufficiently miserable ones. My sisters work hard in the parish, if not in the best way, yet with strong enough sense of their duty, and with no lack of industry; they sometimes ask me to join them, but it is in the patronising unpleasant sort of way which reflects upon my helplessness, as if they partly pitied and partly despised me; not that I should care for that; but somehow everything they do is in the formal business style, as if " the poor" were a set of *things* with which something had to be done, instead of human beings with hearts to feel and sufferings to be felt for and souls to be reverenced ;—and so I wander about mostly my own way. I go a good deal among the poor too, but at a distance from here; and there are many pleasant cottages where I am sure of a smile and plenty of affection from the children. This is all very helpless, I know it is; but there is no mending it, it must be. I wait for guidance, and my soul must have it, if I give it time.

M. S.

LETTER VI.

Oct. 10.

WELL, Arthur, we are come to a crisis now. Here I am at the parting of the ways; I look down one, and I see a bright flowery road, with friends and fortune smiling, and a happy home, and the work I longed for, all which promise to make life delightful: down the other and I see—oh, I will not look down the other; if I do I shall never dare to choose it. Do you not think that sometimes when matters are at the worst with us, when we appear to have done all which we ourselves can do, yet all has been unavailing, and we have only shown we cannot, not we will not, help ourselves; that often just then something comes, almost as if supernaturally, to settle for us, as if our guardian angel took pity on our perplexities, and then at last obtained leave to help us? And if it be so, then what might only be a coincidence becomes a call of Providence, a voice from Heaven, a command. But I am running on as usual with my own feelings, and I have not told you what it is which has happened—after all it is nothing so very great—the bishop has offered my father a living for me; it was done in a most delicate way, and with a high incidental compliment paid to myself. My father, before he spoke to me, had at the first mention of it reminded the bishop I was not yet in orders. The bishop said that in my case it did not matter, from the high character which I had borne at college, and from the way I had distinguished myself there. I had been spending my time, he had no doubt, to the very best advantage at home; and he thought it was a good sign in any young man when he took a longer time for study and moral preparation, instead of rushing at once into his profession. It was odd to see how flattered my father was, and how immediately his own opinion of me began to alter when he saw great people disposed to make much of me. He was embarrassed, however, in telling this to me, and he evidently had more doubts how I should take the information than he had liked to tell the bishop. Both the ordinations could be managed within a short time of one another, so there was no escape that way; my face did not brighten and my father's consequently fell; I saw he had set his heart upon it. I could not bring myself to mortify him with the peremptory *no*, which my conscience flung upon my lips; I said I would think about it and give him my answer in two days. In justice to him as well as myself, I felt I could not act any more entirely on my own judgment; I could not open myself to him, no matter why, I could not . . . . . but the next day I rode over to ——— to talk to the dean, my uncle. I made no mystery of anything with him; I told him exactly how it was with me, my own difficulties and my embarrassment at home. It relieved me to see how little he was startled, and he was so kind that I could ill forgive myself for having so long shrunk from so warm a mediator. He said he was not at all surprised, not that he thought there was anything particularly wrong about myself which should have led me astray, but my case he said was the case of almost all young men of talent before they passed from the school of books into that of life. Of course revelation had a great many most perplexing difficulties about it; but then he said, just as my father said before, I must remember that the real discipline of the mind is *action*, not speculation; and regular activity alone could keep soul or body from disease. To sit still and think was simply fatal; a morbid sensitiveness crept over the feelings like the nervous tenderness of an unhealthy body, and unless I could rouse myself to exertion, there would be no end at all to the disorder of which I complained. It was odd he treated it simply as a disorder, like one of the bodily disorders we have once in our lives to go through, which a few weeks' parish routine and practical acquaintance with mankind would dissipate as a matter of course. I felt I was sinking, but I made another effort: would it not be better, I asked, if I was to make trial first, and take work as a layman under some sensible and experienced rector. He thought not; it would be difficult to find a person with a mind which could influence mine, and it would not do to risk a failure. The really valuable lessons were the lessons we taught ourselves, and as this opportunity had offered, it would be wrong, he fancied, to reject it: my father's feelings ought to weigh with me. Then surely, I said, I ought to tell the bishop, at any rate, something of which I had told him; but my uncle said *no* again. At present, at

least, there was no occasion; *of course* it was all
nothing, as my own good sense in a very short
time must show me; and though a person in high
authority might know things privately without any
inconvenience, yet a public or official communication
would be an embarrassing challenge upon him to
take a part, for which in reality he might be quite
sure there was no necessity. Well, I need not tell
you what I felt; it was something like a sentence of
death, and yet I had determined to abide by his
opinion. It seemed at any rate as if the responsibility was not mine, though in my heart I knew it
was. I set my teeth and galloped home, and to
carry my fate through, and give myself no time to
quarrel with it, I went at once to my father and
committed myself to an assent. The heartfelt pleasure I saw I was giving him went far to relieve my
own heart; at any rate the sacrifice was not for
nothing. Life is more than a theory, and love of
truth butters no bread: old men who have had to
struggle along their way, who know the endless bitterness, the grave moral deterioration which follow
an empty exchequer, may well be pardoned for an
over-wish to see their sons secured from it; hunger,
at least, is a reality, and when I am as old as he is,
and have sons of mine to manage for, I shall be
quite as anxious I dare say about the "*provision.*"
He was delighted, you may be sure he was;
we seemed to forget that there had been any cool-
ness or difference between us; in a little while we
were talking over my income, the condition the

house was in, and the furniture he was going to provide for me: a good wife was to be a serious advantage to me, and even more ambitious prospects were already beginning to dawn over the horizon; and now here I am dismissed to my own room and my own reflection. What have I done? After all, only what many do under a lower temptation. I have consented for the sake of others, while they do it only for their own; and after all perhaps what my uncle says is true, and by and by I shall find it so; and then one remembers the case of Synesius, who when he was pressed to take a bishopric by the Alexandrian metropolitan, declared he would not teach fables in church unless he might philosophise at home. But Synesius made his conditions and got them accepted; while I . . . Arthur, I cannot cheat myself with sophistry: it is not too late; I ought not, I think I ought not. Oh, curses on this old helpless theological fanaticism which encumbers us with a clumsy panoply of books and doctrines before it will trust us with our duties.

Surely the character of the teacher, his powers, and the culture he has given them, the heart that there is in him, is what should be looked for in a clergyman; not the readiness of servility with which he will plod along under chains, and mutter through the Sunday ritual. I believe in God, not because the Bible tells me that He is, but because my heart tells me so; and the same heart tells me we can only have His peace with us if we love Him and obey Him, and that we can only be happy when we each love our neighbour better than ourselves. This is

what the clergyman's business is to teach: when the
Bible says the same, let him use the Bible language.
But there are many other things, besides what
are in the Bible, which he ought to learn if he would
assist the people to do what he tells them to do, if
he would really give them rest from that painful
vacancy of mind which life spent in routine of never-
ending work entails upon them; he should study
their work, and the natural laws that are working in
it; he should make another version of the Bible for
them in what is for ever before their eyes, in the corn-
field, in the meadow, in the workshop, at the weaver's
loom, in the market-places and the warehouses. Here,
better far than in any books, God has written the
tables of His commandments; and here, where men's
work lies, their teacher should show them how to read
them.   Let every flower have a second image to their
eyes; let him bring in for witness to the love of the
great Creator, every bird, every beast, every poorest
insect; let the teeming earth tell of Him as in her
unwearied labour-pangs she fashions up the material
elements into the great rolling flood of life which
ebbs and flows around them.   They might do something, these clergy, if they would go to work over
this ground; labouring in good earnest they would be
for the souls of mankind.   But they will not do it,
and I long to do it; and yet, and yet, Arthur, my
conscience shrinks from those melancholy articles.
It seems to say I should not trifle with my own
soul; and the guilt, if guilt there be, in all the sorrow
which may follow on my exclusion, will rest not on me

who shrink from them, but on those who compel submission to them as the price at which we are to be admitted.

But if I decline this living, what is to become of me? I shall finally offend those whose happiness I value far more than I do my own. I shall condemn myself to an inert and self-destroying helplessness. Educated as I have been, there is no profession, except that of an author, which would be tolerable to me; and to be an author, I fear, I fear I have too little talent. The men that write books, Carlyle says, are now the world's priests, the spiritual directors of mankind. No doubt they are; and it shows the folly and madness of trying still to enforce tests, that you do but silence a man in the pulpit, to send his voice along the press into every corner of the land. God abolished tests for all purposes, except of mischief and vexation, when he gave mankind the Printing Press. What is the result of sustaining them, but that we are all at the mercy now of any clever self-assumer? and while our nominal teachers answer no end for us, except the hour's sleep on Sunday, the minds of all of us, from highest lords to enlightened operatives, are formed in reading-rooms, in lecture-rooms, at the bar of public-houses, by all the shrewdest, and often most worthless, novel writers, or paper editors. Yet even this is better than nothing—better than that people should be left to their pulpit teachers, such as they are. Oh! how I wish I could write. I try sometimes; for I seem to feel myself overflowing with thoughts, and I cry out to be relieved of them.   But it is so stiff and miserable when I get anything done.   What seemed so clear and liquid, comes out so thick, stupid, and frost-bitten, that I myself, who put the idea there, can hardly find it for shame, if I go look for it a few days after.   Still, if there was a chance for me!   To be an author—to make my thoughts the law of other minds!—to form a link, however humble, a real living link, in the electric chain which conducts the light of the ages!   Oh! how my heart burns at the very hope.   How gladly I would bear all the coldness, the abuse, the insults, the poverty, all the ill things which the world ever pays as the wages of authors who do their duty, if I could feel that I was indeed doing my duty so—being of any service so. I should have no difficulty about this living then, Arthur.   I should know my work, and I would set about it with all my soul.   But to do nothing; to sit with folded hands, and the rust eating into my heart ; or, because I cannot do the very best, to lie down and die of despair!   Oh! yes ; this life of ours is like the deep sea-water, when with bold exertion we may swim securely on the surface, but to rest is to sink and drown.   Tell me, Arthur, tell me, what I ought to do.

LETTER VII.

Oct. 20.

THANK you a thousand times, my dear, dear friend, for your most kind, most wise letter. I will try, as you tell me, to have done with these inane speculations. The world is a mystery; and if the Bible be the account which God has been pleased to give us of it, we may well be content if we find no fewer difficulties in the Bible, as Butler says, than we find in the world. I am no better than the wise and admirable men who have found deepest rest and happiness there, and I think I can do what you say is the least I ought to do—subdue my doubts, if I cannot satisfy them, and try the system which wise men say can only be known in trying. I will taste and see, and perhaps God will be gracious to me. At any rate, believing, as I do, in Providence with all my heart, I cannot doubt that it *has* been the way in which God has chosen to have His people taught; and what am I, that I should dare to fancy that I know better now? I will take it in submission; and as I am to teach with authority, so I will endeavour to learn under authority. At any rate, there can be no doubt what one ought to teach. With the Bible for a text-book, there is no doubt what, in the main, is the drift of its teaching, whatever one may think of parts of it. The best which can be said to individuals to urge them to their duty, is in that book; and we have our conscience, too, and the Bible of universal history too; and, more than all,

experience—the experience of our own hearts—each
of which falls in with the great Bible to the moulding
of our minds.   They do as a fact mould them; they
must do it; and therefore it is God's will that they
should; so that between them all there is no lack
of matter, without breaking debated ground.   Well,
then, I will try; and if I am wrong, if I am indeed sin-
ning against light, I am at least led astray by no unworthy motive in wishing to do something for God's
service, and to spare distress to those who are most
dear to me.   For the rest—for advancement in the
world, for the favour and the smiles of men, for
comfort, and ease, and respectability, and position,
and those other things for which so many men in
these days sell their souls, God is my witness they
have not weighed so much in the balance with me,
as to put me on my guard against their influence.
Oh, no! It were easy to go without all these things;
far easier than to bear them.   Oh! what a frightful
business is this modern society; the race for wealth
—*wealth*. I am ashamed to write the word. Wealth
means well-being, weal, the opposite of woe.   And
is that money? or can money buy it? We boast
much of the purity of our faith, of the sins of
idolatry among the Romanists, and we send mis-
sionaries to the poor unenlightened heathens, to
bring them out of their darkness into our light, our
glorious light; but oh! if you may measure the
fearfulness of an idol by the blood which stains its
sacrifice, by the multitude of its victims, where in all
the world, in the fetish of the poor negro, in the

hideous car of Indian Juggernaut, can you find a monster whose worship is polluted by such enormity as this English one of money! You must pardon me, my heart is bleeding. I have made a resolution which has cost me more than tears, and now it is my best relief to flow out to you at random.   Yes, if God adapts His revelation to the capacities of mankind, and the fierceness of His rule over them to the depth of their abasement, then, indeed, there is a cry in heaven for something darker than the darkest discipline of the old idolaters.   Riches!   I suppose, at the smallest average, for the making of a single rich man, we make a thousand whose life-long is one flood-tide of misery. The charnel-houses of poverty are in the shadow of the palace; and as one is splendid, so is the other dark, poisonous, degraded.   How can a man grow rich, except on the spoils of others' labour?   His boasted prudence and economy, what is it but the most skilfully availing himself of their necessities, most resolutely closing up his heart against their cries to him for help?   In the homes of the poor, Arthur, I have seen—oh! I will not appal your ears with what I have seen—hunger, and vice, and brutal ignorance, and savage rage, in fierce consciousness of what they suffer.   Poor wretches struggling home from their day of toil, to find their children waiting for them with a cry for food, when they have none to give, and the famished mothers in broken-hearted despair.   Ah, Heaven! and our beautiful account-books, so cleanly written,   the polished persiflage of our white-gloved rulers, and the fair register of the nation's prosperity, what does it look like, up in heaven, in the angel's book, Arthur? No; God has saved me, at least, from that bad service; there is no danger of my falling down before that monster; and the one lasting comfort which is left me now, is that I shall be able to pay back something of my own long debt for my easy life, and use this money they tell me I shall have, to clean my hands against the long account. Well, I will not bore you any more; we cannot get on for ever with nothing but gloom and sulkiness, and I have bothered you enough. It is night and day (or it ought to be) with all of us, if we want to keep in health. To be sure, now and then there will come a North Pole winter, with its six months' frost and darkness and mock suns: but Nature is still fair, and pays them off with their six months of day. I have had my share of the shadow, so I hope I am not going to be cheated. It is marvellous the importance I find I have stepped into. There has been an expedition over to see my house that is to be; and my sisters have settled the drawing-room paper, and the colour of the curtains, and promised to set up my penny club for me. I never told you, by the by, where this said establishment was to be. It is one of the suburbs of Morville, so I shall have a fashionable audience. And I hear there is already a schism at the tea-parties; one side have settled that I am a Puseyite, and another, that that is impossible, because I have such beautiful eyes. My eccentricities, which used to be my shame, have now become "so interesting." One young lady says Selina will do for me, she is so like me—so enthusiastic; another thinks that a good little plain common-sense, brisk, practical body, is what I want, and so Clara was exactly made for me. My sisters do not particularise names, but one thinks, and the other thinks, and they look knowing, and say, "Well, we shall see." "As long as thou doest well unto thyself, men will speak good of thee;" what a word is there! It is hard, though, that the kind words won't come, when one most wants them. But it is a shame of me to be grumbling now.

My father has prescribed a good body of Anglican divinity. By the by, how coolly we appropriate that word, Arthur. Go into a picture gallery, and ask whose that rosy full-fed face may be, looking out from those rounded and frilled canonicals, and you are told it is Bishop So-and-So, an eminent *divine;* and then one thinks of the Author of the Revelation, the only person, I believe, besides our own Anglicans, who has been thought worthy of that title. Well, any how, I am to have the divinity; though I cannot say that in any one of those worthy writers, except in Butler and in Berkeley, I could ever take much pleasure. But I will try—by and by, not now; I have closed up my books, much to my father's dismay, who is in alarm for my examination. The Bishop has formed a high opinion of me, and should not be disappointed. But, since my degree, I have read almost nothing but church

D

history, and criticism, and theology, of all sorts, and in all languages; and as I am gorged with it to the full, and as it has but left me where I am, or where I was, it is wiser, perhaps, to leave it. And now that every thing is settled, dear Arthur, write me a nice bright letter. I have a fountain of cold water playing inside my own heart, which all but extinguishes me—don't visit me with any more. It is but smoking, my flax; do not quench it; and when you come to see me, either soon, or in after years, you shall find me—not with six children and a pony carriage, and rosy cheeks, and much anxieties on my turnip crop—not pale with long watchings over folios, nor with oiled hair inditing hymnbooks for the pious children of the upper classes—not correcting the press of my last missionary sermon—but, I hope, a happier and a better man than I am now—and always your dear friend, Arthur.

LETTER VIII.

Morville, Jan. 1.

WELL, my dear friend, it is over; for good or evil I am committed finally to my calling, and I must abide by it. With three-fourths of what I have undertaken it will be with all my heart—with the remaining fourth—with   .   .   .   .

I do not console myself with the futile foolishness which whispers to me that so many do the same; for, with such self-contradictory formularies as those to which we bind ourselves, with Articles insisting on our finding one thing in the Bible, and a Liturgy insisting on another, yet the Articles committing themselves to the Liturgy, while notwithstanding they tell us, too, that the Bible is the only rule of faith; it is impossible for any one who has ever thought or read to take them all without straining his conscience one way or another; I dare say this is true; yet what others may have to do is nothing to me: I am only concerned with myself. In theory it is a thorny road enough; but practically it is trodden in by so many sorts that I shall make shift to get along. I was ordained deacon privately a fortnight before Christmas, and priest yesterday—the Sunday after it. Exquisite satire on my state of mind!—I was complimented publicly on my examination, as having shown myself possessed of so much well-digested information, and on being so prudent in avoiding extremes. In spite of my protestations I was chosen to assist in the service yesterday, and I was told privately that I had only to persist in such sensible moderation, and that with my talents, in these trying times, I should be an ornament to the Church, and that its highest places might be open to me. But, above all, my admonition concluded—" Be extreme in nothing—you do not require me to remind you of Aristotle's caution. Puseyism is the error on one side, German rationalism on the other. Walk steadily in the position which our own admirable

Church has so wisely chosen, equidistant between these two. Throw yourself into her spirit, and, with God's grace, you may rise hereafter to be one of those strong lights which it is her highest honour and her highest witness to have nurtured." I felt so sick, Arthur. So, I may live to be like Burnet. or Tillotson, or Bishop Newton, or Archdeacon Paley—may I die sooner! I had nearly said so; but it was all so kind and so good, and there was such a sort of comfortable dignity about it, that in spite of myself I was awed and affected. Oh why, why, is there no confessional among us— no wise and affectionate friend with a commission to receive our sorrows, and with a *right* to guide us? It is the commission we should have, Arthur; anybody may advise us, but we want some one to order. I dare say the Bishop, if I had spoken out to him, would have been shocked enough, and would have ordered me not to undertake the office; only it would not have been because I thought as I did, but because of the scandal in a candidate for orders saying he thought so. It would have been nothing but a " You must not." He would defend the place against me as an enemy; but of my own soul might become what I could myself make of it; he would have been troubled enough to have known what to do with that. Well, now for my duties (I suppose I may be extreme in them), and the blue chintz curtains, and the Penny Club; and may God guide me!

A year's interval elapses now between the date of this last letter and of the events to which we must now pass forward.   Sutherland was busy, and wrote less frequently than before ; and when they did come, his letters had lost something of that passionate truthfulness of tone which made them so telling even in their weakness.   They were mostly of the self-blinded sort, and, as his power was but scanty in that line, they were poor of their kind.   It appeared as if he was endeavouring to persuade himself that he was contented and happy ; when it was too clear that all was still wrong with him, that he had but silenced himself, not replied to himself ; and that the wound which, had it continued open, might have made progress towards healing, or, at worst, continued but itself, being now closed over was corrupting inwardly, and the next outbreak might be far worse than the first.   No censure shall be passed upon his conduct here ; and the casting of stones shall be left to those who are happy in a purer conscience than I can boast of.   Some persons may find it easy and obvious to condemn him ; others may wonder at the foolishness of so much excitement over such a very trifle, and regard such excessive sensibility as a kind of moral disease.   But I, who was his friend, am unequal to either, and consider myself happy in having but to tell the story as it was ; to relate the facts as they grew into their consequences ; the judgment which Providence passed upon him—on the whole, perhaps, a judgment as just as that Power's judgments usually are found to be. We had kept our misgivings to ourselves; but from the first we had felt all of us a painful conviction that Sutherland's was not a mind to compose itself as he proposed and expected; and that the ideas which were disturbing him were of a kind which would grow; whatever his own will liked to say about it. Again, his occupation was sure to prove less agreeable than he hoped to find it. To be enthusiastic about doing much with human nature is a foolish business indeed; and, throwing himself into his work as he was doing, and expecting so much from it, would not the tide ebb as strongly as it was flowing? It is a rash game this setting our hearts on any future beyond what we have our own selves control over. Things do not walk as we settle with ourselves they ought to walk, and to hope is almost the correlative of to be disappointed. Moreover, for the practical work of this world (and a parson's work is no exception), a thinking man is far more likely to require the support of a creed to begin with, than to find the quarry in his work out of which he can sculpture one. Let his uncle the dean say what he pleased, it is no such easy matter after all to believe that all the poor unhappy beings we have left to rot in ignorance and animalism, with minds scarcely so well cultivated as the instinct of a well-trained brute; that the fashionable loungers of the higher classes, and the light, good-tempered, gossip-dealing, ball-going young ladies, have really and truly immortal souls, which God came down from heaven to re-

deem, and for which He and the Devil are contending.   It is easy to talk largely of the abstract
dignity of humanity, and to take Socrates or Shakespeare for a type of it.   One can understand something of spirits such as theirs continuing, because
we see they do continue; but really, with the mass
of us, one would think the most reasonable as
well as the kindest thing which could be done
would be to put us out.   The stars want no snuff-
ing; but I fear, if we are all to be kept burning,
whoever has the trimming of us will have work
enough.   Neither good enough for heaven, nor bad
enough for the other place, we oscillate in the tem-
perate inertia of folly; answering no end whatever
either of God or Devil; surely, one would think,
we should be put out.

At any rate, for this unfortunate normal state
of the mass of mankind, Markham was not calcu-
lating; he was, he thought, to be teaching men
to love good and hate evil, and hardly any one of
those he came in contact with would have power
really to do either one or the other.   Love and hate
of such matters are intellectual passions, with whose
names we must not dignify the commonplace self-
ishnesses or respectabilities of common people, who
may like and may dislike, but cannot love and cannot
hate.   He fancied he was going to make the lot of
poverty more tolerable: as far as giving away money
went, no doubt he succeeded; but it was unlucky for
him that his parish lay on the outskirts of a large
town.   His poor were the operative poor, whose

senses were too keenly quickened to let them sink
into contentment, while they lived side by side with
luxury which they knew was trampling them under
foot while it was feeding itself upon their life juices;
living, as they were, for the most part in filth and
vice, yet without that torpor of faculty which helps
the agricultural poor through their sufferings;
without the sense of home either which these have,
or of the feudalism which secures the most ill-
deserving landlord something of their respect and
of their hearts. It was ill-dealing for Markham
with such as they; he was one of the hated order.
They would take his money with a kind of sullen
thanks, as if they knew very well they were but
receiving a small instalment of their own rights;
but it was impossible to make them learn from him;
and their hard stern questions often wrung from
him the bitter self-confession, that the doctrinal
food which the Church had to offer to men of
stamp like that was but like watered chaff for the
giant dray-horse of the coal-yard. He could have
more easily touched them if he had spoken out
what once had been his own feelings; but he had
consented to be a declaiming instrument. He
could only speak now—not as man to man, but as
thing to thing; and when he found a man who
would speak his own old doubts to him, he discovered that he had not been rewarded for his submission with any enlightenment to answer them.

LETTER IX.

My dear Friend,

Something very uncomfortable has befallen me: a fool can fire a powder magazine as well as the wisest of us; and in spite of the mournful absurdity which hangs about the story, I cannot tell in what disaster it may not conclude. However, I will not anticipate; you shall have it all *ab initio*. You know, in all large towns, there are those very detestable things, religious tea-parties. In this place, where there are such a number of business people, who have either retired from business themselves, or have withdrawn their families out of its atmosphere to make idle ladies and gentlemen of them, they are particularly rife; all people want some excitement, and as they are in too uneasy a position in this world, and common ordinary intercourse with one another is too vulgar to suit their ambition, they flit about in the shadow of the other world; and with wax lights, and psalm singing, and edifying conversation, entertain one another with evening soirées, in imitation, as they fancy, of the angels. I hate these things, and as I have never cared to avoid saying so, I have of course made myself innumerable enemies, partly because I ought to be shining among them as the central figure, and partly for the reason I have given for my dislike. I fear the main element of angel tea-parties is seldom there. These people can really have very little love for one another from the

delight with which they mourn over each other's
failings; and when, unhappily, no such topic has
newly presented itself, the edifying talk consists in
the showing up of the poor Puseyites; or, if the
party happen to be Puseyite, in the sort of self-
satisfied sham business-like we-are-the-wise assump-
tion, which is even more intolerable. I suppose the
angels do not stimulate the monotony of their lives
by half-envious stories of the unlawful words or unlawful enjoyments of the other place, do they Arthur? Well, my place on the occasion has been
commonly supplied by the town curates and rectors,
who have done the honours, no doubt, far better
than I could do them; and I was contented to let
it be so, and think no more about the matter. But
it seems I must have made myself the occasion of a
great deal of talk. I didn't marry any of them—
that was the first great sin. I patronised no societies, and I threw cold water on philanthropy
schemes. The clergy! I hope it is not wrong of
me, but I cannot like them. Though I have not
avoided their acquaintance, we have never got
on; and after one or two ineffectual attempts, we
have tacitly given up all hopes of intimacy. I
never saw the clouds gathering. The Bishop cau-
tioned me against party, and here it has been my
sin that I am of none. What is not understood is
suspected; and, what is worse, it is for ever talked
about.   It is one of the oddest of men's infirmities,
that no talk of what they do understand, is spicy
enough to interest them. Well, never mind, I must

tell my story.   About a fortnight ago I was asked
to dine with the Hickmans.   They are one of the
few families that I really like here.   Miss Hickman and I often meet in the dark staircases and the
back alleys; and, though the least trifle in the world
given to cant, they have enough good sense and active
conscience about them to be saved from any serious
harm from it.   I had often been there before, and
yet I felt a strange reluctance on this unhappy
evening.   I think there is a spiritual scent in us
which feels mischief coming, as they say birds
scent storms.   I felt somewhat assured on entering
the drawing-room.   I was the last; and of the six
or seven people present, there was only one I did
not know at all, and one more with whom I was not
intimate—this last, a young lady, a Miss Lennox,
a niece of Mrs. Hickman, who had been for some
weeks staying with them.   The other was the newly-
arrived rector of a parish in the neighbourhood,
who, I understood, had brought with him a reputa-
tion of cleverness, and was shortly to be married
to the young lady.   No one was coming in the
evening: alas! who could have guessed from the plain
unthreatening surface of that quiet little assembly,
what a cunning mine had been run below it,—that
I had been brought there to be dragged into an ar-
gumentary examination in which this new-found
chymist was to analyse me, to expose my structure
for his betrothed's spiritual pleasure, his own vanity,
and the parish scandal.   Well, unsuspecting, I went
on tolerably well for some time: I rather liked the

fellow. He was acute, not unwitty, and with a *savoir faire* about him which made his talk a pleasing variety to me. Once or twice the ladies made serious remarks; but he, as well as I, appeared to shrink from mixing more religion with our dinner than the grace which went before and which succeeded it; and in the half-hour we were left together after the ladies were gone, there was nothing to make me change my mind about him, except that I felt I could never be his friend; he knew too much and felt too little.

In the evening the conversation turned on a projected meeting of the Bible Society, where they were all going. There was much talk—what such talk is you know. Nothing at first was directly addressed to me, so I took no part in it. The good rector came out with really some tolerably eloquent discoursing; and the poor ladies drank up his words; oh, you should have seen them. I fancy the fair *fiancée* drank a little too much of them, and got rather spiritually intoxicated—at least I hope she did—as some excuse for her. As he went rolling on for an hour or more, he described the world as grinding between the nether millstone of Popery and the upper millstone of Infidelity, and yet a universal millennium was very near indeed through this Bible activity. At the end he turned sharp upon me. Of course Mr. Sutherland would feel it his duty to take the chair on so truly blessed an occasion?

Now, conceive societies, with chairmen, dragging at the poor world from between two such millstones!!

" I believe you need not ask Mr. Sutherland," the
young lady said, in a tone of satiric melancholy:
" he never preaches the Bible."

I didn't laugh. I was very near it; but I luckily
looked first at Mrs. Hickman, and saw her looking
so bitterly distressed—and distressed, too, (how
much a look can say!) from her partly sharing her
niece's feeling, that I gathered up as much gravity
as I could command. " I believe I read it to you
twice every day," I said, " and my sermons are a
great deal better than my own practice, perhaps
than the practice of most of us." She coloured, because she thinks daily service formal and superstitious. I do not know what indignation would
not have bubbled out of her lips, when the rector
heroically flew in to the rescue, and with sufficient
tact only noticed her with a smile, and repeated his
own question.

" I fear not," I said. " I shrink from meetings
where a number of people are brought together,
not to learn something which they are themselves
to do, but to give money to help others in a remote employment. There is a great deal of talking and excitement, and they go away home fancying they have been doing great things, when
they have, in fact, only been stirring up some un-
profitable feeling, and giving away a few shillings or
pounds, when all their active feeling and all the
money they can spare is far more properly required
at home. Charity is from person to person; and it
loses half, far more than half, its moral value when

the giver is not brought into personal relation with those to whom he gives."

"Mr. Sutherland is general enough, and perhaps vague enough," was the answer. "Permit me to keep to my subject. The Bible Society in the course of each year disperses over the world hundreds of thousands of Bibles in many different languages. The Word of God is sent into lands of Egyptian darkness, and souls at least may come to saving knowledge who else were lost without hope."

I said coldly, I was sorry. I found my own duties far beyond my powers both of mind and money. I had only expressed my own feelings to explain my own conduct. I passed no opinion about others.

"I fear you cannot defend yourself on so general a ground without reflecting upon others, Mr. Sutherland," he said. "I could understand you, in a manner sympathise with you, if you took the ground of objection so many good churchmen take, in declining to act with a mixed body; but in this case, I fear, pardon me, I think you have some other reason. I do not fancy the objects of the society can entirely meet your approbation, or you would not have spoken so coldly."

Miss Lennox was looking infinitely disagreeable; the Hickmans as much concerned. The vulgar impertinence of such offensive personality disgusted me out of temper. Partly, too, I was annoyed at feeling he had heard, or she had been cunning enough to

see, I had some particular feeling on the point beyond what I had spoken out.

"Yes," I said, "it is true I have particular
feelings. I dislike societies generally; I would join
in none of them. For your society in particular, as
you insist on my telling you, I think it is the very
worst, with the establishment of which I have been
acquainted. Considering all the heresies, the enormous crimes, the wickednesses, the astounding follies
which the Bible has been made to justify, and which
its indiscriminate reading has suggested; considering
that it has been, indeed, the sword which our Lord
said that he was sending; that not the Devil himself
could have invented an implement more potent to
fill the hated world with lies, and blood, and fury; I
think, certainly, that to send hawkers over the world
loaded with copies of this book, scattering it in all
places among all persons—not teaching them to understand it; not standing, like Moses, between that
heavenly light and them; but cramming it into their
own hands as God's book, which He wrote, and they
are to read, each for himself, and learn what they
can for themselves—is the most culpable folly of
which it is possible for man to be guilty."

I had hardly spoken before I felt how wrong, how
foolish, I had been; and that a mere vulgar charla-
tan, as I felt the man was, should have had the
power to provoke me so! I had said nothing which
was not perfectly true, in fact; but I ought to have
known it was not true to the ignorant women who
were listening with eyes fixed and ears quivering, as

if the earth was to open and swallow a blasphemer
—What did they know of the world's melancholy
history?

I saw Mr. ——'s eyes sparkle as he felt the triumph I was giving him, and his next word showed
me it had been a preconcerted plan.

"It is as I told you," he said, turning away from
me; "the enemy is among us." The ladies gathered together for mutual protection in a corner.

"What do you mean, Sir?" I said; "this is
most unwarrantable language. With what purpose
did you come here?"

"Language! Sir," he sighed, "unwarrantable!—
I might ask you, Sir, what you mean—with what
purpose you are come a wolf among these sheep?
They know you now, Mr. Sutherland. I knew what
you were before, but your disguise had been too
cunning for their eyes."

Mrs. Hickman looked the picture of despair;
quite wretched enough to disarm any anger I might
feel at her.

"Really, Madam," I said, rising, "if you have
connived at this scene, you must be sufficiently
punished at its results. I will not add to your pain
by continuing my presence." The miserable young
lady was flushed with exultation; the rector had
smoothed himself into an expression of meek triumph in a successful exorcism. I had been too
much in the wrong myself to enable me to say *then*
what might have to be said. I would wait till the
next morning, which I supposed must bring my

hostess's apology, and so bowed coldly and departed. The whole thing was so very insufferably bad that I could not even let myself think of what I was to do till I had considered it coolly. I went home and went to bed. The next morning came, but no note, and the day passed without any; and I began to feel, as a clergyman, in a most embarrassing position indeed. As a man, it was far too contemptible to affect me; but as I thought it over, I saw that it was a seriously concerted design, whether from dislike or suspicion—what I do not know—to attack my position, and I had not heard the end of it. I called once or twice at the Hickmans, but they were not at home to me; long faces began to show about the parish. It was evident tongues had been busy, and last Sunday the church was half empty. I was at a loss what to resolve upon, and had been thinking over various plans, when something came this evening which is likely to resolve it all for me and save me the trouble. My folly has bred its consequence; the word flies out and has a life of its own, and goes its own way and does its own work. Just now a note was brought me, a very kind one, from the Bishop, requesting me to take an early opportunity of calling on him: if I were not engaged, fixing tomorrow morning. The sooner down the better with all nasty medicine, from the first magnesia draught to the death finish. I shall present myself at the first moment. I can have no doubt of the occasion.

LETTER X.

WELL, it is over, this interview; and a great deal else is over, I believe. He is a good man, a really good man, and a great one. Would to God I had been open with him before! however, it is idle lamenting now. You shall hear: I found him alone of course; I was shown into his study; he was good enough to remember that the moments we are kept waiting for such interviews are not the very sweetest, and he joined me almost immediately. There was a grave kindness in his manner, which told me at once I had been right in looking for unpleasantness, and his good sense kept him from hanging on the edge of what was inevitable. He said he was very sorry, &c., and that I was not to regard what he was going to say to me as in the least official; whether anything of that kind might have to follow, would depend very much on what he heard from me. In the mean time he wished to speak to me, as a friend, on some very serious matter which had been communicated to him. I bowed. He said he concluded from my manner that I was prepared for what was coming; and then he went on, that I was said to have used certain very incautious language, to say the least of it, at a private party in my parish, on the subject of the Bible Society. Perhaps in itself it was not a thing which he could formally notice. With the society in question he had as little sympathy as I could have; and he could easily under-

stand that a young man of strong feelings might
have been led to express himself with an unwise
vehemence.   But I must be aware how strongly inclined foolish people were to misunderstand and
misrepresent, and how extremely cautious in my position I was bound to be.   He stopped there; so, as
well as I could, I thanked him for his kindness.   I
said I knew I had been very unwise, and, as nearly
as I could remember them, I repeated the exact
words which I had used.   He answered very truly,
with a sort of a smile, that words like those, unexplained, were quite as dangerous as anything I could
find in the subject of them.   But then, he went on,
that this was not all he had to say to me.   There
was another matter, and a more serious one, he was
sorry to tell me, of which he hoped I could give explanation.   I had now been a year at my parish, and
on all, except on one point, he was happy to tell me
that if I had not exactly pleased my people, it was
their fault, not mine.   But a very serious complaint
had been made to him on the nature of my sermons.
He need not go into detail; but he had been in-
formed generally that during that entire season I
had not preached a single one which might not have
been a Socinian's.   He did not charge me with having taught Socinianism; on the contrary (and perhaps, as a general rule, I had done wisely), I had
steadily avoided all doctrine; but that I had not
said a word to prove that I held opinions which So-
cinians did not hold, on the points on which they
differed from us; neither on the incarnation nor on

the atonement, as such, had I ever directly spoken. I was silent. "I presume it is true," he continued, "and from your present manner, that it has been purposely so." "Yes," I said. He waited for me to go on. "If the Catholic doctrine be true," I said; he started; "if the Catholic doctrine be true," I repeated, "it is so overwhelming a mystery, that I cannot think of it without its crushing me. I cannot bring myself to speak in public of it, before such a mixed assembly, or lend myself to the impiety (I can use no other word) with which the holiest secret of our faith is made common and profane. I think there is no one in my parish to whom, even in private, I should feel it possible to speak upon it."

"Then you have not spoken in private either?"

"I have never been sought. If I had, however, I should probably have been still silent."

"You said *if* the Catholic doctrine be true—you observed that I remarked your words, and you desired that I should do so, from your repeating them. Am I to suppose that you have any doubts about it?"

"My lord," I said, "you were good enough to tell me you were speaking to me as a friend, and I will show you my thanks by being entirely open with you. Many times I have been on the point of volunteering a confession to you; I have only been withheld by an unmanly fear; a doubt of how you might receive it. However, I will speak now. I owe my situation to your goodness, and perhaps I have hitherto made a bad return to you. Now I put myself without reserve in your hands, and whatever you think I ought to do, I will do. Never, either by word or action, until this *if*, have I given reason to living man to suppose I did question it. But that in these times every serious person should not in his heart have felt some difficulty with the doctrines of the incarnation, I cannot believe. We are not as we were. When Christianity was first published, the *imagination* of mankind presented the relation of heaven to earth very differently from what it does now. When heaven was one place, and earth was another, imaginatively coextensive, extended under it—with, in every nation, a belief in a constant intercourse between them, shadowing itself out in legends of God's appearing upon earth, and mortals elevated among gods—it cannot but have seemed far simpler then that this earth should have been the scene of a mystery so tremendous, than it can now seem to us, knowing what we know of this little earth's infinite insignificance. But as this is but an imaginative difficulty, so it has not been on this, but rather on the moral side of the doctrine, that I have found my own deepest perplexity. I will be candid. I believe God is a just God, rewarding and punishing us exactly as we act well or ill. I believe that such reward and punishment follow necessarily from His will as revealed in natural law, as well as in the Bible. I believe that as the highest justice is the highest mercy, so He is a merciful God. That the guilty should suffer the measure of penalty which their guilt has incurred, is justice. What we call mercy is not the remission of this, but rather the remission of the extremity of the sentence attached to the act, when we find something in the nature of the causes which led to the act, which lightens the moral guilt of the agent. That each should have his exact due is *just*—is the best for himself. That the consequence of his guilt should be transferred from him to one who is innocent (although that innocent one be himself willing to accept it), whatever else it be, is not *justice*. We are mocking the word when we call it such. If I am to use the word *justice* in any sense at all which human feeling attaches to it, then to permit such transfer is but infinitely deepening the wrong, and seconding the first fault by greater *injustice*. I am speaking only of the doctrine of the atonement in its human aspect, and as we are to learn anything from it of the divine nature or of human duty. To suppose that by our disobedience we have taken something away from God, in the loss of which He suffers, for which He requires satisfaction, and that this satisfaction has been made to Him by the cross sacrifice (as if doing wrong were incurring a debt to Him, which somehow must be paid, though it matters not by whom), is so infinitely derogatory to His majesty, to every idea which I can form of His nature, that to believe it in any such sense as this confounds and overwhelms me. In the strength of my own soul, for myself, at least, I would say boldly, rather let me bear the consequences of my own acts myself, even if it be eternal vengeance, and God requires it, than allow the shadow of my sin to fall upon the innocent."

I stopped. He said, quietly, "You have more to say, go on."

I continued. "I know that in early ages men did form degraded notions of the Almighty, painting Him like themselves, extreme only in all their passions: they thought He could be as lightly irritated as themselves, and that they could appease His anger by wretched offerings of innocent animals. From such a feeling as this to the sense of the value of a holy and spotless life and death—from the sacrifice of an animal to that of a saint—is a step forward out of superstition quite immeasurable. That between the earnest conviction of partial sight, and the strong metaphors of vehement minds, the sacrificial language should have been transferred onwards from one to the other, seems natural to me; perhaps inevitable. On the other hand, through all history we find the bitter fact that mankind can only be persuaded to accept the best gifts which Heaven sends them, in persecuting and destroying those who are charged to be their bearers. Poetry and romance shadow out the same truth as the stern and mournful rule under which Heaven is pleased to hold us, that men must pay their best to it as the price of what they receive. I understand this— I can understand, as I can conceive, that as the minds of men grew out into larger mould, these two ideas united into one, in such a doctrine as that which we are now taught to hold.

"But if I am to believe that in plain prose it is true as a single fact—not which happens always, but which has happened once for all—that before the world was made it was predetermined so, and we must obey the Bible, and allow that this is justice and this is mercy; then in awe and perplexity I turn away from the Bible, not knowing, if it use our words in a sense so different, so utterly different, from any which we attach to them, what may not be the mystical meaning of any or every verse and fragment of it. It has but employed the words which men use to mock and deceive them.   A revelation!   Oh, no! no revelation; only rendering the hard life-enigma tenfold harder.   I thank you very much for bearing with me.   I will but say, in conclusion, that I do not disbelieve that in some mysterious transcendental sense, as involved in the system of the entire universe, with so vast an arc that no faculty of man can apprehend its curve, that in some such sense the Catholic doctrine of the atonement may be true.   But a doctrine out of which, with our reason, our feeling, our logic, I at least can gather any practical instruction for mankind—any deeper appreciation of the attributes of God, any deeper love for Him, any stimulant towards our own obedience—such a doctrine I cannot find it.   I bury what I am to think of it in the deepest corner of my own heart, where myself I fear to look."

It was said and over.   And oh! what a relief I felt.   A weight which had been sinking me to the earth was taken off. I was an honest man again, with nothing more to conceal, and follow now what might, I had done my duty, and I was not responsible.

He said my convictions seemed deeply thought— were they altogether new? formed since the time of my taking orders?

I said I would be frank with him again. I had had very great difficulty in taking orders. At that time my feelings were far less defined than they were at present; but even then I had anxiously desired an explanation with him, and it had only been the advice of others, (which I had never sufficiently regretted having followed,) which had deterred me. I was told, and I partly believed it, that my uncomfortable feelings were the result of want of employment, of my mind being so entirely flung in upon itself; that they were but symptoms of a disease which required only exercise for its cure. I determined, for myself, that I would submit absolutely, in all I said and did; in no way hint a doubt even to myself; and, in, I believe, a spirit of real humility, I did endeavour with all my heart to see the truth as the Church sees it. It had pleased God to govern my mind in His way, not in mine. I had bitterly repented my orders, for I felt my uneasiness not pass away, but deepen into conviction. I was now more grateful for this opportunity which he had given me of speaking out, than any words could tell him. I had not come prepared to make so full a confession; but I had been forced on by an impulse which I could not, if I had wished, control. And now I threw myself on his hands, to do with me as he thought right.

He said nothing for some time. He sat silent. His thoughts appeared to have left me, and travelled off on some abstracted interest. I had no more to speak. I did not interrupt him. After perhaps a quarter of an hour, he seemed to make an effort to collect himself, and said sharply, " Of course I have but one duty." But the tone showed it was to himself he was speaking, not to me. Presently he turned to me, and said with a voice of mournful kindness, "May God help you, my son! It is a terrible trial. Only He who is pleased to send such temptation can give you strength to bear it. You shall have my prayers . . . and my blessing . . . not as your bishop, Markham. I cannot bless you as your bishop. But as an old man and an old friend, who can still love you and feel for you, yes, such a blessing you shall not want, my poor, poor boy." There were tears in his eyes. I was prepared for any thing but this; for ny rebuke, for any harshness. I could not contain myself. I burst into tears too. I caught his hand and kissed it. He did not take it from me; but his eyes were seeking heaven and God, and his lips were fast moving. Was it for me, was it for himself, that he was praying? I knew not, I might not, I would not, hear. But his overflowing heart poured out its secrets. Broken words fell in upon my ears which I could not choose but catch. He was praying to be taken away from the evil day, that last dreadful time of terror, when the Devil should have the power for a season over hearts not sealed with the Devil's mark, when even the elect would be tempted to deny their Lord.

Well I cannot tell you more of this, how kind he was, how much I was overcome. He thanked me for my candour, as he called it, while he allowed how bitterly it distressed—it embarrassed him : once there was a passionate burst. "You, too, of whom I had heard so much, and formed so many hopes . . . I knew more of you than you supposed, and sympathised more with you; yours is a mind of no common order, and I had looked, yes I had looked to you, I had hoped that you, with a knowledge of the power of that spirit of antichrist which is now working in this world, so different from anything which we knew, or now at our age can ever learn, that you might have been a chosen champion of the Church. God's will be done—and our duty; of course I cannot (I would not if I could) take any public steps in consequence of what you have disclosed to me; and I am sure you yourself are too high-minded to take advantage of your situation or mine; what I advise you, you will do. You cannot remain where you are; give your mind time, and try other scenes; go travel, see what men are; see what all men are or must become who allow their faith to glide out of their hearts, as you have allowed yours; and you may yet by God's grace. . . . . . I cannot tell—I have little hopes, they have all gone; yes, there is not one, not one in all these many years which I have seen upon the earth, not one man of more than common power who has been contented to abide in the old ways." He was half speaking to himself, half to me. He took down a book from his shelves; it was the confession of the Vicar of Savoy; he saw I knew it. "This does not content you," he said; "you cannot—you are too honest far, to take his terms for yours, and continue on in your position as he held on in his. No! you will go; I will find some one to supply your place in your absence, and you will be generous in what you will leave him. If at the end of three years your mind is not changed, I think you will leave the service for ever which is not yours, and you will not shrink from what you will lose by it."

I answered at once my benefice was in his hands; what changes my mind might pass through I could not tell; but that if—if I ever came to feel that I had been walking in a delirious dream, and that the old way was the true way, it would be with far too deep humiliation to permit me ever again to dare to become its minister. A few words, he did not mean of common-place advice, against over haste, against imprudence, was all the weak opposition which he made to this. My living is resigned—my employment gone. I am again free—again happy; and all the poor and paltry net-work in which I was entangled, the weak intrigues which like the flies in the summer irritate far worse than more serious evils, I have escaped them all; and if the kind good people who have brought all this about, can find any miserable pleasure in what they will suppose their victory; each one of the thousand pluming himself or herself on the real secret—the exact story—the only true, full, perfect and sufficient account of Mr. Sutherland's disgrace, let them have it, I can afford it; they gain their pleasure, I do but lose, what perhaps it is our best credit to be without, the world's good opinion. All I really grieve for is my father. He, they, all of them, will never forgive me; the old feelings, or far worse than the old, will flow back now into the old channel, and my small measure of affection will turn sour in the thunder storm, and curdle into contempt. It must be so, I shall go away and they will forget me when they do not see me. Perhaps if I live beyond their eyes, and my vexing presence is not by to irritate, I may be at least endured—tolerated . . . . and in after years when what now they most value has proved its hollowness; when the world passes by them and through them, and they learn at last that they cannot take it with them, cannot gain from it one kind smile they do not pay for; that the world with all its power, splendour, caresses, promises, for all the love we waste upon it, cannot love us, for it is heartless; perhaps then . . . . But I will not dwell upon so melancholy a picture.

N.

It is an easy way to get rid of the difficulties of this world, to say, in the off-hand way in which it is commonly said, that if a man cannot get along with it, it is all his own fault; that the world is a looking-glass which gives every man his own image;

that he has no one to blame but himself; that he is not active enough; that he is not sensible enough; not enough of any thing that he should be, and too much of every thing he should not be; that he expects what he cannot find, and does not choose to be contented with what he can; anyhow to shift the responsibility of his failure off Nature's shoulders upon his own. And yet I think Nature, if she interests herself much about her children, must often feel that, like the miserable Frankenstein, with her experimenting among the elements of humanity, she has brought beings into existence who have no business here; who can do none of her work, and endure none of her favours; whose life is only suffering; and whose action is one long protest against the ill foresight which flung them into consciousness.

I cannot understand why the worst sentence which could be pronounced against the worst man that ever lived, should be nothing more than that it were better for him if he had never been born. Surely it were better for half mankind if they had never been born, considering the use they make of themselves; and then the stage would be left clear for the other half, and both sides would be such infinite gainers. The vicious, the foolish, and the passionate, would escape a service which is torture to them; and the others would be spared the nuisance of such disagreeable companionship. There is already a fear the earth is growing overpeopled, and this matter might really be taken into consideration.

Μηδὲν ἄγαν should be the maxim, and, in future, no colonists should be sent into this world who have too much or too little of any thing.

The class of persons who get on best here, who understand nature, and whom nature understands, are the good sort of prudent people, who push their way along the beaten track, neither loving very strongly, nor loved very strongly. Allowing the heart to have a voice when it does not plead against understanding, they do not exactly love their neighbours, but they keep on broad terms of reasonable good-will with them; liking such as do not stand painfully in their way, and sympathising as far as they can feel sympathy with all sensible persons like themselves. They form their attachments, connubial and otherwise, for mutual convenience and comfort; and in the routine of profitable occupation, intermittent like night and day with their hours of pleasant relaxation, they pass through their seventy years with no rest disturbed by any more painful emotion than what might arise from an infirm digestion, or a doubtful pecuniary speculation. They love, they fear, they hope, they pray, they fulfil all their duties to earth and heaven on the broad principles of moral economy; and having walked as the world judges them with unblemished integrity, and lived prudently within their incomes, money income and soul income, and never permitted themselves in extravagance in either, they entertain well-grounded hopes of continued prosperity beyond the grave. And most likely ·they will find them

realised; they have the monopoly of this world's good
—they form the world's law and the world's opinions,
as the favourites and the exponents of the will of the
higher Powers; and "coming in no misfortune like
other folk, neither being plagued like other men,"
wherever they are they will be still themselves; and
carrying with them the elements of their prosperity
in their own moderation, it is difficult to conceive a
state of being in which they could be less happy than
they are.

Why need any other sort be compelled into
existence, besides these? What use are fools?
What use are bad people? What use are dreamers
and enthusiasts? Surely it cannot be necessary to
have them as foils to the excellence of the others,
and to indulge these in Pharisaic self-laudations
that they are not as the publicans. I know that
a holy father of the Church defines one mode of
the happiness of the blessed to be the contemplation of the torments of the damned; and I know
that those who succeed in life do now and then
make pleasant comparisons of themselves with their
less fortunate neighbours: but one would hope, if
they were asked, they would not say it was essential to them; and, unless it be, it is a large price to
pay for what could be dispensed with. I should
be sorry to think there was so much favouritism in
Providential government; and I would sooner believe there is some impracticable necessity in the
nature of things than accept the holy father's de-
finition, and allow him to have seen clearly into

the conditions of happiness either upon earth or in heaven.

Yet, whatever be the cause why things are as they are, still to be conscious of nothing is better than to be conscious only of pain; and to do nothing than to do what entails pain. So that whether this earth be all, and this little life-spark of existence flicker but its small time and then expire for ever; or whether there be, as we are taught and we believe, some mysterious fuel which will still feed it through the silence of eternity; doubtless it would be better for half of us never to have been at all. *Les méchants*, Jean Jacques says, *sont très embarrassants*, both in this world and in the next; and if we are compelled to doubt so much what just destination to assign to the wicked, infinitely harder it is to know what to do with natures which fail from excess of what we must call rather a kind of good than of evil, and from a delicacy of sensitive organization, to which their moral energy of character bears too small proportion; men who are unable to escape from themselves into healthy activity; because they want the strength to carve out their own independent road, and the beaten roads offend their sensibility; and are therefore engaged their lives long in a hopeless struggle with elements too strong for them; falling down from failure to failure, and either yielding at last and surrendering their souls to what they despise, or else lying down to die of despair over a barren past and a future without a prospect.

E 3

Whether it was a misfortune to himself or to the world that Markham Sutherland was born into it; beyond question it was a very great misfortune both to himself and to his family that his lot was cast among them. Upright and conscientious, their tempers, as we have partly seen, were of the broad, solid, sturdy kind; which, as they never know the meaning of a refined difficulty, so never experience any which it is not easy for them to overcome.

He was quite right in his anticipation of the way in which this last break-down would be received; they did not mean to be unkind, but as it was clear the success by which they were accustomed to measure their fellow creatures now never could be his, and as he was the only one of a large family who had failed to find it, their minds being all constructed on a common type, to which his formed the only exception, their affections circulated round and round among themselves, and he lay outside the circle which was complete without him. You cannot reason people into loving those whom they are not drawn to love; they cannot reason themselves into it; and there are some contrarieties of temper which are too strong even for the obligations of relationship. Unhappily, too, they let themselves despise Markham, and where the baneful glance of contempt has once fallen, love is for ever banished. The feeling was not returned, although, perhaps, it might as deservedly have been so. Markham still saw much in them to love; still struggled, perhaps, to make up their short-comings by his own fulness.

His mind was wider than theirs, little as they thought it was; and he could understand and make allowance for the unkindness which was wounding him, while they could make none for his disappointing their hopes, and being so unlike themselves. Well, he was quite wise in deciding to keep away from them. It would have been better, perhaps, if he had gone at once abroad; but he was anxious, he told me, to spend some time at least in severer study than hitherto he had been able to pursue, and try if he could not calm his mind, instead of drowning it in the excitement of motion. He was going to try what philosophy would do for him, and at least for a time it appeared to answer. "One of two things one must have," he wrote to me, "either sufficient respect for oneself to take whatever comes, *æquo animo*, even it be what is called damnation, I mean so great an honouring of oneself, or confidence in oneself, that nothing external can affect one ——, or else, sufficient faith in an all-powerful, external Being, of qualities which ensure His preserving us on both sides of the grave. It is a question, I think, whether we can have both; but, though we may go without houses, carpets, horses, carriages, one of these two we cannot go without, under penalty of madness or suicide, or, the common fate of mankind, of becoming machines for the decomposing of dinners." He proposed the question fairly to himself; it remained to be seen what he would make of it. I confess I had serious misgivings. I am not going to follow his pilgrimage along the road with any detail; externally his life had now, for the next year, little variety, and a few specimens of the thoughts he left behind him will be enough to indicate the direction, and generally the sort of view of nature, of the world, of human life, and its conditions, which are likely to be the goal of men who go astray from the old way as he went.

Why is it thought so very wicked to be an unbeliever? Rather, why is it assumed that no one can have difficulties unless he be wicked? Because an anathema upon unbelief has been appended as a guardian of the creed. It is one way, and doubtless a very politic way, of maintaining the creed, this of anathema. When everything may be lost unless one holds a particular belief, and nothing except vulgar love of truth can induce one into questioning it, common prudence points out the safe course; but really it is but a vulgar evidence, this of anathema.

Genuine belief ended with persecution. As soon as it was felt that to punish a man for maintaining an independent opinion was shocking and unjust, so soon a doubt had entered whether the faith established was unquestionably true. The theory of persecution is complete. If it be necessary for the existence of society to put a man to death who has a monomania for murdering bodies, or to exile him for stealing what supports them; infinitely more necessary is it to put to death, or send into exile, or to imprison those whom we know to be destroying weak men's souls, or stealing from them the dearest of all treasures. It is because—whatever we choose to say —it is because *we do not know, we are not sure* they are doing all this mischief; and we shrink from the responsibility of acting upon a doubt.

Sometimes it is a spot of sunlight travelling over a dark ground—sometimes it is the black shadow of a single cloud, the one speck in the great ocean of light; one wonders which, after all, human life is.

Where was ever the teacher who has not felt, at least, if not said, "No man cometh to the Father except through me?"

The end of all culture is, that we may be able to sustain ourselves in a spiritual atmosphere as the birds do in the air. This is what philosophy teaches. Men sustained by religion, take a creed for a substitute, and hang, or believe that they are hanging, suspended by a golden chain from the throne of God. It is happy for mankind that they are able to do this. For mankind—not for philosophers. I confess it sickens me to see our philosophic savans, as they call themselves, swinging in this way mid-air among the precipices of life, examining a flower here, a rock there; analysing them and cutting them in pieces, and discovering the combination of elements which went to their making, and calling this *wisdom*. What is man the wiser or the happier for knowing how the air-plants feed, or how many centuries the flint-stone was in forming, unless the knowledge of them can be linked on to humanity, and elucidate for us some of our hard moral mysteries.

––––––

In Christianity, as in every thing else which men have thrown out of themselves, there is the strangest mixture of what is most noble with what is most . . . . . . I shrink from the only word. A man is born into the world—a real man—such a one as it has never seen; he lives a life consistently the very highest; his wisdom is the calm earnest voice of humanity; to the worldly and the commonplace so exasperating, as forcing upon them their own worthlessness—to the good so admirable that every other faculty is absorbed in wonder. The one killed him. The other said, this is too good to be a man—this is God. His calm and simple life was not startling enough for their eager imagination; acts of mercy and kindness were not enough, unless they were beyond the power of man. To cure by ordinary means the bruised body, to lift again with deep sympathy of heart the sinking sinner, was not enough. He must speak with power to matter as well as mind; eject diseases and eject devils with command. The means of ordinary birth, to the oriental conception of uncleanness, were too impure for such as he, and one so holy could never dissolve in the vulgar corruption of the grave.

Yet to save his example, to give reality to his sufferings, he was a man nevertheless. In him, as philosophy came in to incorporate the first imagination, was the fulness of humanity as well as the fulness of the Godhead. And out of this strange mixture they composed a being whose life is without instruction, whose example is still nothing, whose trial is but a helpless perplexity. The noble image of the man is effaced, is destroyed. Instead of a man to love and to follow, we have a man-god to worship. From being the example of devotion, he is its object; the religion of Christ ended with his life, and left us instead but the Christian religion. The afflictions which by an act of his own will, as being himself the source of all power, he inflicts upon himself—what afflictions are these? The trial of humanity, which gives dignity to the persevering endurance through life for truth's sake, and which gives death its nobleness, is the constancy of the mind to good, *with uncertainty of the issue*, when it does but feel its duty, and does not know the consequences. The conviction of the martyr that the stake is the gate of Paradise, diminishes the dignity of the suffering in proportion to its strength. If it be absolute certainty, the trial is absolutely nothing. And that all-wise Being who knew all, who himself willed, erected, determined all, what could the worst earthly suffering be to him to whom all the gates which close our knowledge were shining crystal? What trial, what difficulty was it all to him? His temptation is a mockery. His patience, meekness, humility, it is but trifling with words, unless he was a man, and but a man.

And yet what does it not say on the other side *for* mankind, that the life of one good man, which had nothing, nothing but its goodness to recommend it, should have struck so deep into the heart of the race that for eighteen hundred years they have seen in that life something so far above them that they will not claim a kindred origin with him who lived it. And while they have scarcely bettered in their own practice, yet stand, and ever since have stood, self-condemned, in acknowledging in spite of themselves that such goodness alone is divine. This is their ideal, their highest.

People canvas up and down the value and utility of Christianity, and none of them seem to see that it was the common channel towards which all the great streams of thought in the old world were tending, and that in some form or other when they came to unite it must have been. That it crystallized round a particular person may have been an accident; but in its essence, as soon as the widening intercourse of the nations forced the Jewish mind into contact with the Indian and the Persian and

the Grecian, such a religion was absolutely inevitable.

It was the development of Judaism in being the
fulfilment of the sacrificial theory, and the last and
purest conception of a personal God lying close
above the world, watching, guiding, directing, interfering.   Its object was no longer the narrow one of
the temporal interests of a small people.   The
chrysalis had burst its shell, and the presiding care
extended to all mankind, caring not now for bodies
only but for souls.   It was the development of Par-
sism in settling finally the vast question of the
double principle, the position of the evil spirit, his
history, and the method of his defeat; while Zoroas-
ter's doctrine of a future state was now for the first
time explained and justified; and his invisible world
of angels and spirits, and the hierarchies of the
seven heavens, were brought in subjection to the
same one God of the Jews.

It was the development of the speculative Greek
philosophy of the school of Plato, of the doctrine of
the Spirit, and the mysterious Trinity, the ἕν καὶ πᾶν,
the word or intellect becoming active in the primal
Being; while, lastly, the Hindoo doctrine of the incarnation is the uniting element in which the other
three combine, and which interpenetrates them with
an awful majesty which singly they had not known.

So these four streams uniting formed into an
enormous system, comprehending all which each
was seeking for, and bringing it all down home,
close to earth, human, direct, and tangible, and sup-

plying mankind with full measure of that spiritual support with which only minds most highly disciplined can afford to dispense.

———

[These fragments require no comment. They are their own. I will but add one more, one which I think really remarkable in itself.]

———

The source of all superstition is the fear of having offended God, the sense of something within ourselves which we call sin. Sin, in its popular and therefore most substantial sense, means the having done something to gratify ourselves which we knew, or might have known, was displeasing to God. It depends, therefore, for its essence on the doer having had the power of acting otherwise than he did. When there is no such power there is no sin. Now let us examine this. In reflecting upon our own actions we find that they arise from the determination of our will, as we call the ultimate moral principle of action, upon some object. When we will, we will something, not nothing. Objects attract or repel the will by the appearance of something in themselves either desirable or undesirable. And in every action, if analysed, the will is found to have been determined by the presence of the greatest degree of desirableness on the side towards which it has been determined. It is alike self-contradictory and contrary to experience, that a man of two goods

should choose the lesser, knowing it *at the time* to
be the lesser.   Observe, I say, at the time of action.
We are complex, and therefore, in our natural state,
inconsistent, beings, and the opinion of this hour
need not be the opinion of the next. It may be
different before the temptation appear; it may return
to be different after the temptation is passed ; the
nearness or distance of objects may alter their relative magnitude, or appetite or passion may obscure
the reflecting power, and give a temporary impulsive
force to a particular side of our nature.   But, uniformly, given a particular condition of a man's nature,
and given a number of possible courses, his action is
as necessarily determined into the course best corresponding to that condition, as a bar of steel suspended
between two magnets is determined towards the
most powerful. It may go reluctantly, for it will
still feel the attraction of the weaker magnet, but it
will still obey the strongest, and must obey. What
we call knowing a man's character, is knowing how
he will act in such and such conditions.   The better
we know him the more surely we can prophecy.   If
we know him perfectly, we are certain.

So that it appears that at the stage first removed
from the action, we cannot find what we called the
necessary condition of *sin*.   It is not there; and we
must look for it a step higher among the causes
which determine the conditions under which the
man acts.   Here we find the power of motives depends on the character, or the want of character.   If no character be formed, they will in-

fluence, according to the temporary preponderance
of this or that part of the nature; if there be formed
character, on the conditions, again, which have
formed it, on past habits, and therefore on past
actions. Go back, therefore, upon these, and we
are again in the same way referred higher and still
higher, until we arrive at the first condition, the
natural powers and faculties with which the man has
been sent into the world.

Therefore, while we find such endless differences
between the actions of different men under the same
temptations, or of the same man at different times,
we shall yet be unable to find any link of the chain
undetermined by the action of the outward circumstance on the inner law; or any point where we can
say a power lay in the individual will of choosing
either of two courses,—in other words, to discover
sin. Actions are governed by motives. The power
of motives depends on character, and character on
the original faculties and the training which they
have received from the *men* or *things* among which
they have been bred.

Sin, therefore, as commonly understood, is a
chimera.

If you ask me why, then, conscience so impera-
tively declares that it is real? I answer, conscience declares nothing of the kind. We are conscious simply of what we do, and of what is done
to us. The judgment may come in to pass sentence; but the judgment is formed on instruction
and experience, and may be as wrong in this matter

as in any other: being trained in the ordinary theory of morals, it will and must judge according to it; but it does not follow that it must be right, any more than if it be trained in a particular theory of politics, and judges according to that, it must be right. Men obey an appetite under present temptation, to obey which they have before learned will be injurious to them, and which, after the indulgence, they again learn has been injurious to them; but which, at the time, they either expected would, in their case, remit its natural penalty, or else, about which, being blinded by their feelings, they never thought at all. Looking back on their past state of mind, and finding it the same as that to which they have returned when the passions have ceased to work, it seems to them that they knew better, and might have done otherwise. They wish they had. They feel they have hurt themselves, and imagine they have broken a law. It is true they have broken the higher law, but not in the way which they fancy, but by obeying the lower law, which at the time was the stronger. Our instinct has outrun our theory in this matter; for while we still insist upon free will and sin, we make allowance for individuals who have gone wrong, on the very ground of provocation, of temptation, of bad education, of infirm character. By and by philosophy will follow, and so at last we may hope for a true theory of morals. It is curious to watch, in the history of religious beliefs, the gradual elimination of this monster of moral evil. The first state of mankind is the unreflecting state. The nature is undeveloped, looking neither before nor after; it acts on the impulse of the moment, and is troubled with no weary retrospect, nor with any notions of a remote future which present conduct can affect; and knowing neither good nor evil, better or worse, it does simply what it desires, and is happy in it. It is the state analogous to the early childhood of each of us, and is represented in the common theory of Paradise—the state of innocence.

But men had to grow as we grew. Their passions developed rapidly, their minds slowly; but fast enough to allow them in the interval of passion, to reflect upon themselves, to generalise, and form experience; and, acquiring thus rudimental notions of laws from observing the tendency of actions, men went through what is called the Fall; and obtained that knowledge of good and evil which Schiller calls " ein Riesen Schritt der Menscheit." Feeling instinctively that the laws under which they were, were not made by themselves, but that a power was round and over them greater than themselves, they formed the notion of a lawgiver, whom they conceived they could please by obedience to the best they knew, and make angry by following the worse. It is an old remark, that as men are, such they paint their gods; and as in themselves the passionate, or demonic nature, long preponderated, so the gods they worshipped were demons like themselves, jealous, capricious, exacting, revengeful, the figures which fill the old mythologies, and appear partly in the Old Testament. They feared them as they feared the powerful of their own race, and sought to propitiate them by similar offerings and services.

Go on, and now we find ourselves on a third stage; but now fast rising into a clearing atmosphere. The absolute worth of goodness is seen as distinct from power; such beings as these demon gods could not be the highest beings. Good and evil could not coexist in one Supreme; absolutely different in nature they could not have a common origin; the moral world is bipolar, and we have dualism, the two principles, coeternal, coequal.

By and by, again, the horizon widens. The *ultimate* identity of might and right glimmers out fully in the Zenda Vesta as the stars come out above the mountains when we climb out of the mist of the valleys. The evil spirit is no longer the absolute independent Ahriman; but Ahriman and Ormuzd are but each a dependent spirit; and an awful formless, boundless figure, the eternal, the illimitable, looms out from the abyss behind them, presently to degrade still farther the falling Ahriman into a mere permitted Satan, finally to be destroyed.

Such a position could not long continue: after two hundred years of vague efforts after Pantheism, which would have leapt the chasm, not bridged it, out came the great doctrine of the atonement, the final defeat of the *power* of sin; the last stage before the dissolution of the idea.

Finally rises philosophy, which after a few monstrous efforts from Calvin to Leibnitz to reconcile contradictions and form a theodice, comes out boldly in Spinozism to declare the impossibility of the existence of a power antagonistic to God; and defining the perfection of man's nature, as the condition under which it has fullest action and freest enjoyment of all its powers, sets this as a moral ideal before us, toward which we shall train our moral efforts as the artist trains his artistic efforts towards his ideal. The success is various, as the faculties and conditions which God has given are various; but the spectre which haunted the conscience is gone. Our failures are errors, not crimes—nature's discipline with which God teaches us; and as little violations of his law, or rendering us guilty in His eyes, as the artist's early blunders, or even ultimate and entire failures, are laying store of guilt on him.

It could not last with Markham, this philosophising, I knew it could not. It was but the working off in a sort of moral fermentation of the strong corruption with which his mind had become impregnated. Markham's heart had more in it than blood, and his nature was either too weak or else too genuine to find its cravings satisfied, when he had resolved the great life of humanity, these six thousand years of man's long wrestle with the angel of destiny, into a cold system in which he could calculate the ebb and flow as on the tables of a tide. Doubtless, some such way of reading it there is; but wo to him to whom it is given to read it so; more than man ever was, he must be, or far less, not such a one at any rate as poor Markham. The spell broke; one day I had a letter from him of the old sort, of which his heart, not his head, had had the making. ,He was unwell, and the philosophising spirit which had possessed him, thinking a failing tenement no longer worth its occupying, had flung it off again to its old owner.   Whether it was that the unclean thing was but making a brief absence for some pro- cess of sweeping and garnishing to take place against a fuller possession, whatever it was, it was gone; and he himself, for the better comforting of soul and body, was going off to spend a winter at Como. He was going alone; one of his sisters offered to ac- company him, but it was an offer of duty rather than affection; and as those very dutiful people are so punctiliously scrupulous in keeping both sides of the equation equal, and as, poor fellow, he felt he would have to pay for what he received on one side by a yet further reduction of the little stock he had remaining upon the other, he thought it would be better for himself, for her and all of them, to hold himself under his own keeping and trouble them no further.   He was not ill enough to be alarmed or to alarm us; . . . . so only the seven devils were kept away, which seemed the only danger.

Well, Markham went.   Over the few centre pages of his life, while this fermenting was at its worst, we have till now been turning; what follows wilt complete it from its beginning, and we shall see what he was before, and whither, by and by, he was determined. Scepticism, like wisdom, springs out in full panoply only from the brain of a god, and it is little profit to see an idea in its growth, unless we track its seed to the power which sowed it. Among other matters with which he entertained himself in this Italian winter was a retrospective sketch, which to me, as I read it, appeared of a value quite unspeakable as an analysis of a process through which in these last years so many minds besides his own have been slowly and silently devolving. I had intended to mutilate it, but that each page pleaded with so much earnestness to be the one that I was to choose, that I could only satisfy all by taking all. It is not long, it was broken off abruptly, we shall see by and by how broken; but it is carried down to a point, when we can link it on with no too serious aposiopesis to those first letters which have already caused in us feelings which I will not endeavour to analyse, lest I find in myself more sympathy with them, than I wish to think I feel.

CONFESSIONS OF A SCEPTIC.

THAT there is something very odd about this life of
ours, that it is a kind of Egyptian bondage, where
a daily tale of bricks must be given in, yet where we
have no straw given us wherewith to burn them, is
a very old confession indeed. We cry for something we cannot find; we cannot satisfy ourselves
with what we do find, and there is more than cant
in that yearning after a better land of promise, as
all men know when they are once driven in upon
themselves and compelled to be serious. Every
pleasure palls, every employment possible for us is
in the end vanity and disappointment—the highest
employment most of all. We start with enthusiasm
—out we go each of us to our task in all the brightness of sunrise, and hope beats along our pulses:
we believe the world has no blanks except to
cowards, and we find, at last, that, as far as we ourselves are concerned, it has no prizes; we sicken
over the endless unprofitableness of labour most
when we have most succeeded, and when the time
comes for us to lay down our tools we cast them
from us with the bitter aching sense, that it were
better for us if it had been all a dream. We seem
to know either too much or too little of ourselves—
too much, for we feel that we are better than we can

F 2

accomplish; too little, for, if we have done any good
at all, it has been as we were servants of a system
too vast for us to comprehend. We get along
through life happily between clouds and sunshine,
forgetting ourselves in our employments or our
amusements, and so long as we can lose our consciousness in activity we can struggle on to the end.
But when the end comes, when the life is lived and
done, and stands there face to face with us; or if
the heart is weak, and the spell breaks too soon, as
if the strange master-worker has no longer any work
to offer us, and turns us off to idleness and to ourselves; in the silence then our hearts lift up their
voices, and cry out they can find no rest here,
no home. Neither pleasure, nor rank, nor money,
nor success in life, as it is called, have satisfied
or can satisfy; and either earth has nothing at all
which answers to our cravings, or else it is something different from all these, which we have missed
finding—this peace which passes understanding—
and from which in the heyday of hope we had turned
away, as lacking the meretricious charm which then
seemed most alluring.

I am not sermonizing of Religion, or of God,
or of Heaven, at least not directly. These are often
but the catchwords on the lips of the vulgarly disappointed; which, like Plato's Cephalus, they grasp
at as earthly pleasures glide out of their hands;
not from any genuine heart or love for them, but
because they are words which seem to have a meaning—shadows which fill up the blank when all else

is gone away. But there is one strong direction into which the needle of our being, when left to itself, is for ever determined, which is more than a catchword, which in the falsest heart of all remains still desperately genuine, the one last reality of which universal instinct is assured.

When my eyes wander down the marble pages on the walls of the church aisles, or when I stray among the moss-grown stones lying there in their long grassy couches in the churchyard, and spell out upon them the groupings of the fast crumbling names, there I find the talisman. It is home. Far round the earth as their life callings may have scattered men, here is their treasure, for here their heart has been. They have gone away to live; they come home to die, to lay their dust in their fathers' sepulcre, and resign their consciousness in the same spot where first it broke into being. Whether it be that here are their first dearest recollections of innocent happiness; whether the same fair group which once laughed around the old fireside would gather in together and tie up again the broken links in the long home where they shall never part again; whether there be some strange instinct, which compels all men back to the scene of their birth, to lay their bodies down in the same church which first received them, and where they muttered their first prayer; whatever be the cause—like those cunning Indian weapons which, projected from the hand, fly up their long arc into the air, yet when their force is spent glide back to the spot from which they were flung—the spent life travellers carry back their bodies to the old starting point of home.

The fish struggle back to their native rivers; the passage birds to the old woods where they made their first adventure on the wings which since have borne them round the world. The dying eagle drags his feeble flight to his own eyrie, and men toil-worn and careworn gather back from town and city, from battle-field or commerce mart, and fling off the load where they first began to bear it. Home—yes, home is the one perfectly pure earthly instinct which we have. We call heaven our home, as the best name we know to give it. So strong is this craving in us, that, when cross fortune has condemned the body to a distant resting-place, yet the name is written on the cenotaph in the old place, as if only choosing to be remembered in the scene of its own most dear remembrance. Oh, most touching are these monuments! Sermons more eloquent were never heard inside the church walls than may be read there. Whether those hopes, written there so confidently, of after risings and blessed meetings beyond the grave, are any more than the "perhaps" with which we try to lighten up its gloom, and there be indeed that waking for which they are waiting there so silently, or whether these few years be the whole they are compelled to bear of personal existence, and all which once was is reborn again in other forms which are not there any more, still are those marble stones the most touching witness of the temper of the human heart, the life in death protesting against the life which was lived.

Nor, I think, shall we long wonder or have far to look for the causes of so wide a feeling, if we turn from the death side to the life side, and see what it has been to us even in the middle of the very business itself of living. For as it is in this atmosphere that all our sweetest, because most innocent child memories are embosomed, so all our life along, when the world but knows us as men of pleasure or men of business, when externally we seem to have taken our places in professions, and are no longer single beings, but integral parts of the large social being; at home, when we come home, we lay aside our mask and drop our tools, and are no longer lawyers, sailors, soldiers, statesmen, clergymen, but only men. We fall again into our most human relations, which, after all, are the whole of what belongs to us as we are ourselves, and alone have the key-note of our hearts. There our skill, if skill we have, is exercised with real gladness on home subjects. We are witty if it be so, not for applause but for affection. We paint our fathers' or our sisters' faces, if so lies our gift, because we love them; the mechanic's genius comes out in playthings for the little brothers, and we cease the struggle in the race of the world, and give our hearts leave and leisure to love. No wonder the scene and all about it is so dear to us. How beautiful to turn back the life page to those old winter firesides, when the apple hoards were opened, and

the best old wine came up out of its sawdust, and
the boys came back from school to tell long stories
of their fagging labours in the brief month of so
dear respite, or still longer of the day's adventures
and the hair-breadth escapes of larks and black-
birds. The merry laugh at the evening game;
the admiring wonder of the young children woke
up from their first sleep to see their elder sisters
dressed out in smiles and splendour for the ball
at the next town. It may seem strange to say
things like these have any character of religion;
and yet I sometimes think they are themselves religion itself, forming, as they do, the very integral
groups in such among our life pictures as have been
painted in with colours of real purity. Even of the
very things which we most search for in the business of life, we must go back to home to find the
healthiest types. The loudest shouts of the world's
applause give us but a faint shadow of the pride
we drew from father's and sister's smiles, when we
came back with our first school prize at the first
holidays. The wildest pleasures of after-life are
nothing like so sweet as the old game, the old
dance, old Christmas, with its mummers and its
mistletoe, and the kitchen saturnalia. Nay, perhaps, even the cloistered saint, who is drawing a
long life of penitential austerity to a close, and
through the crystal gates of death is gazing already
on the meadows of Paradise, may look back with
awe at the feeling which even now he cannot imitate, over his first prayer at his mother's side in the
old church at home.

Yes, there we all turn our eyes at last; the world's glitter for a time blinds us; but with the first serious thought the old notes come echoing back again. It is as if God, knowing the weary temptations, the hollow emptiness of the life which yet we needs must lead, had ordained our first years for the laying in an unconscious stock of sweet and blessed thoughts to feed us along our way. We talk much of the religious discipline of our schools, and moral training and mind developing, and what more we will of the words without meaning, the hollow verbiage of our written and spoken thoughts about ourselves; yet I question whether the home of childhood has not more to do with religion than all the teachers and the teaching, and the huge unfathomed folios. Look back and think of it, and we cannot separate the life we lived from our religion, nor our religion from our life. They wind in and in together, the gold and silver threads interlacing through the warp; and the whole forms together then in one fair image of what after-life might and ought to be, and what it never is. No idle, careless, thoughtless man, so long as he persists in being what he is, can endure the thought of home any more than he can endure the thought of God. At his first return to himself, it is the first thought which God sends . . . well for him if it be not too late. If we could read the diary of suicide, and trace the struggles of the bleeding heart, in suspense yet between the desire and its execution, yet drawing nearer and ever nearer, and gazing with more fixed intensity on the grave as the end of its sorrow, ah, will not the one fair thought then on which it will last rest be the green memories of home! The last deep warning note either filling up and finishing the measure of despair with its maddening loveliness, or else, if there be one spot not utterly wasted and destroyed where life and love can yet take root and grow, once more to quicken there, and win back for earth its child again.

The world had its Golden Age—its Paradise—and religion, which is the world's heart, clings to its memory. Beautiful it lies there—on the far horizon of the past—the sunset which shall, by and by, be the sunrise of Heaven. Yes, and God has given us each our own Paradise, our own old childhood, over which the old glories linger—to which our own hearts cling, as all we have ever known of Heaven upon earth. . . . . . And there, as all earth's weary wayfarers turn back their toil-jaded eyes, so do the poor speculators, one of whom is this writer, whose thoughts have gone astray, who has been sent out like the raven from the window of the ark, and flown to and fro over the ocean of speculation, finding no place for his soul to rest, no pause for his aching wings, turn back in thought, at least, to that old time of peace—that village church—that child-faith—which, once lost, is never gained again—strange mystery—is never gained again—with sad and weary longing! Ah! you who look with cold eyes on such a one, and lift them up to Heaven, and thank God you are not

such as he,—and call him hard names, and think
of him as of one who is forsaking a cross, and pursuing unlawful indulgence, and deserving all good
men's reproach! Ah! could you see down below
his heart's surface, could you count the tears streaming down his cheeks, as out through some church-door
into the street come pealing the old familiar notes,
and the old psalms which he cannot sing, the
chaunted creed which is no longer his creed, and
yet to part with which was worse agony than to lose
his dearest friend; ah! you would deal him lighter
measure. What, is not his cup bitter enough, but
that all the good, whose kindness at least, whose
sympathy and sorrow, whose prayers he might have
hoped for, that these must turn away from him, as
from an offence, as from a thing forbid?—that he
must tread the wine-press alone, calling no God-
fearing man his friend; and this, too, with the sure
knowledge that coldness, least of all, he is deserving,
for God knows it is no pleasant task which has been
laid upon him! Well, be it so. You cannot take
my heart from me. You cannot take away my
memory. I will not say, would to God you
could, although it is through these that I am
wounded, and, if these nerves were killed, I should
know pain no longer. No, cost me what it will,
I will struggle back, and reproduce for myself
those old scenes where then I lived—that old faith
which, then, alas! I could believe—which made
all my happiness, so long as any happiness was possible to me.

You will never have perfect men, Plato says, till you have perfect circumstances. Perhaps a true saying!—but, till the philosopher is born who can tell us what circumstances are perfect, a sufficiently speculative one. At any rate, one finds strange enough results—often the very best—coming up out of conditions the most unpromising. Such a bundle of odd contradictions we human beings are, that perhaps full as many repellent as attracting influences are acquired, before we can give our hearts to what is right. Yet, as a whole, my own childhood found as much favour as any one can fairly hope for; and, as I look back, I can see few things which I could wish had been otherwise. I say this, neither in shame for what I am not, nor as refusing credit for what I am. I am concerned only with the facts—what I was, and what has resulted out of me. We were a religious family—I mean a sober, serious family—not enthusiastically devotional— very little good comes to children from over-passionate straining in this matter. Grown men, who have sinned, and who have known their sin, whose hearts have shed themselves in tears of blood, who can feel the fulness of the language of religion from their own experience of their failings and their helplessness, and have heard the voice of God speaking to them in their despair, *they* may be enthusiastic if they will—pour themselves out in long prayers, and hymns, and psalms, and have His name for ever on their lips—they may, because it will be real with them. But it is not so with child-

ren; their young bright spirits know little yet of
the burden of life which is over them. They have
hardly yet sinned—far less awakened out of sin—
and it is ill wisdom, even if it be possible, to train
their conscience into precocious sensitiveness. Long
devotions are a weariness to healthy children. If,
unhappily, they have been made unhealthy—if they
have been taught to look into themselves, and made
to imagine themselves miserable and fallen, and
every moment exciting God's anger, and so need
these long devotions—their premature sensibility
will exhaust itself over comparative trifles; and,
by and by, when the real occasion comes, they will
find that, like people who talk of common things
in superlatives, their imagination will have wasted
what will then be really needed. Their present
state will explain to themselves the unreality of their
former state; but the heart will have used out its
power, and thoughts, which have been made unreal,
by an unreal use of them, will be unreal still, and
for ever. This was not our case. We, happily,
were never catechised about our feelings; and so
our feelings, slight as they were, were always
genuine. Religion, with us, was to do our duty;
that is, to say our lessons every day; to say our
prayers morning and evening; to give up as many
as we could of our own wishes for one another;
and to earn good marks, which, though but slips of
blue paper, were found, at the end of the month, to
be good current paper of sterling value, and convertible into sixpences, which we stored up to make

presents to our kind governess, and kinder aunt.
Our own little prayers we said always by ourselves,
at our bedside; the Lord's Prayer out loud, and
small extempore ones, which we kept under a whisper, because they were commonly small intercessions
for some dear friends; which we shrunk from letting
those friends hear; for fear they might be grateful to
us, and that would be stealing so much of our pleasure in ourselves. Then, besides these, we had family
prayers in the school-room, which were far from
being so pleasant or so easy to attend to.   They
were read out of a book by the governess, and we
did not know them; they were in long words which
we did not understand; I always counted them
among the unpleasant duties, and I longed for them
to be over. Two long words particularly, that came
in the middle, I used to watch for, as I knew then
that half the time was past.   If I had been asked
whether I did not know that this was very disre-
spectful, and that I ought to have had the same
reverence in the school-room as in the silence of
my own sleeping place, I suppose I should have
answered quite satisfactorily; but I should not have
answered truly.   Whatever may be the case with
men, children, at any rate, only feel; they do not
know; I did not feel the same, and that was
enough.   I had said what I wanted; this was a
form which I might respect generally, but could not
enter into. Well, and after that came the Psalms and
chapters.   The Psalms we used to read verse and
verse; and here again I was very imperfectly what I

ought to have been. I could make nothing of them read in this way; I could not understand how anybody could; and very early then, I made an observation which I have never seen reason to alter, that nothing short of special interference with miracle will enable any heads ever to understand them, into which they have been beaten in the popular English fashion. I got a general reverence for them, as for the rest of the service, because they were treated reverentially by those I reverenced; but, for anything they taught me, they might have been kept in the old Hebrew: far better, indeed, as I should not then, as I do now, have known them all by heart, finding still their meaning sealed to me under the trodden familiarity of sound. To this day I can make nothing of the Psalms, except when I see a verse or two quoted, and the meaning so held out before me, or else when I read them in a less familiar language. Yet even so they will translate into the old jingle, and the evil reproduces itself. It fared no better with the Prophecies and Epistles. But all this was compensated by the stories in the Old and New Testament, which were the most intense delight to me. With a kind of half-fear I was doing something wrong, I used to transform my person into those I read about. I was Abraham, Isaac, Jacob. Joseph I liked best of all; I believe because he had such a pretty coat, and because he was good and ill-treated. Benjamin never took my fancy; everything went too well with him. I was always sorry at leaving off at the ends of chapters; I should have liked better to have had the stories complete; but I believed it was all right; that there was virtue in verses and chapters, as in everything else in the Bible. Whatever I may think at present of all this, and of the good and ill effects on the whole of our mechanical treatment of the Bible; still, I am sure that it is in this early unreasoning reverence that the secret lies of our all believing it as we do; and that it is here, and not in authenticities, and evidences, and miracles, and prophecy fulfilments, that our faith is rooted. We start on our reasonings with foregone conclusions; and well for us that we do so, or they would lead us certainly a very different road.

Well, so went on our lives. The horizon of our little home valley was not very wide; and our moral horizon was no wider; yet inside them lay all our world. We visited little; and what company came was always *company;* not nice pleasant friends, but a set of alien beings, only made to be looked at when we came in to dessert, and hardly known to be our fellow-creatures. They might have come from the stars for all we cared; and they took notice of us in ways we did not like in the least. The people of the village, our own family, and the servants, were all we recognised as *people.* They were the inhabitants of our own world. In the school-room lay our duties; outside, in the garden, or in the copses beyond, where the brook ran and the violets grew, was our pleasure place, while round it all lay the great wood with its dark trees and gloomy under-paths, into which we gazed with a kind of awful

horror, as the ghost and robber and fairy-haunted
edge of the world which closed it in. We were like
an old camp in the wilderness, on some Arabian oasis,
in which we lived as the old patriarchs lived. We
had our father, our mother, brothers, sisters; and the
old faces of the old servants, and the sheep and the
cows in the meadow, and the birds upon the trees,
and the poultry in the bushes, and the sky, and
God who lived in it; and that was all. And what
a beautiful all! My delight, in the long summer
afternoons, was to lie stretched out upon the grass,
watching the thin white clouds floating up so high
there in the deep æther, and wondering how far it
was from their edge up to the blue, where God was.

I have often thought it is part of the inner
system of this earth that each one of us should
repeat over again in his own experience the spiritual condition of each of its antecedent eras; and
surely we at home in this way repeated over again
the old patriarchal era in all its richness. Here
were we in our little earth. There above was our
Father in heaven—not so far away. He heard us
when we prayed to Him—His eyes were ever upon
us—He called us His children—He loved us and
cared for us. The imagination is too true to discriminate great distances of time. God had been
down on this earth of ours; and talked to the patriarchs and to Moses. They were very old; but then
papa was very old too, and I used to look at his
silver hair, and wonder whether he had ever seen
Abraham—whether he perhaps had seen God. Nay

once I remember, in an odd confusion of the name of father, the thought crossing me that he might be something very high indeed.

Well, to such children as we were, Sunday was a very intense delight. First of all, there were no lessons; then we had our best clothes; we had no employment which we liked, that Sunday interfered with. We might not dig in the gardens; but we did not complain of that if we might still look at the flowers and smell them. Every thing was at rest about us. The school-room was shut up. The family dined between churches, so that that day we were admitted to the parlour, and going to church was delightful. The day was God's own particular day, and church was God's own house. He was really there we were told, though I rather wondered we did not see him; and to go there was the happiest thing we knew. I thought the services rather long, and I did not much understand them; but I always liked all except the sermon. I liked evening service best because it was shorter; but I remember thinking it was not wisely shortened: and I would gladly have compounded to take back litany and communion to get off sermon. It was long words again; and I felt towards it much as I did to school-room prayers. As Goëthe says of Gretchen, when we were at church it was—

" Halb Kinderspiel halb Gott im Herzen."

Yet we loved God in our child's fashion, and it was the more delightful that neither feeling absorbed us.

The singing was very pleasant; but best of all it
was when a poor, too-curious robin had strayed into
the aisles, and went wandering in alarmed perplexity up and down among the long arches, beating its little beak against the window glass, or
alighting on the shoulder of one of the little
painted cherubims, with its shrill note lending a
momentary voice to the stone harp which hung
stringless in those angel-fingers. After church we
said our catechism, at which I was always best able
to answer my duty towards my neighbour; but
neither I nor my sister, who said it with me, could
ever make much of our duty towards God. We had
our own feelings, which this somehow interfered
with; it was not in easy enough language, and, as
we knew the routine of it very tolerably, we took
turns to begin, that we might escape. Yet there
was always this compensation, that whichever got
off that had the two long answers. But best of all
were the Sunday evenings,—alas, how unlike our
experience of later Sunday evenings,—for one of
two delights was always sure to me; either dear
Miss H—— read me the Fairy Queen, which then
was only second to the Bible with me, or else the
older ones of the party would play with us young
ones at animal, vegetable, and mineral—that first
intrusion of philosophy into the holy place; which
by and by would play work there we little enough
dreamed of then. Infinite was the glee with which
we strained our memory for the oddest stories, and
the oddest things in them, to be hunted down the

scent which the questions drew from us. The head of the floating axe was a great favourite; so was Jael's nail; or, harder still, the lordly dish in which the butter was presented. Kind elder ones, as then we thought, to trifle so with us; but my since experience of Sunday evenings in England has taught me that they were not so altogether losers, and I would gladly, as I grew up, have exchanged my devout sermon readings for the smallest game with the smallest child. Unhappily we fell, after a time, under another régime; we lost our games; my Fairy Queen, too, was sent to sleep upon her shelf; a profane poet was thought unfit for Sunday's serious perusing. In truth the allegory was not thought much of; Una was a fair damsel in distress—the lion a real, good, grand, noble lion, such as we saw at the menagerie; how I hated that Sansfoy for killing him. I am tempted to say here how serious a mistake we grown Protestants make with these modern Sundays of ours. I was after taught no book not strictly religious might be read. Sermons! who can go on reading sermons? I was called naughty if I went to sleep; and, at that time, " Wharton's Deathbed Scenes" was the only book in our library which sweetened the dull medicine with a story. I learnt these by heart, and then I was destitute; and my only comfort in thinking that heaven was all Sunday was the hope that at least there would be no long winter evenings there.

Grown people coquet with their consciences so ridiculously in this matter. They will talk and think all day of the foolishest of follies; young ladies will wear their best bonnets, thinking only how pretty they look in them: but to read a book of foolishness, or to act out the gay dress into a pleasure party, is sin. Some people will read letters, but not write them; but generally both are permitted, as well as newspapers. A magazine is a debateable point—questionable; though many degrees better than a book. A book, if you will have a book, must be a volume of sermons; or, at least, of commentaries. But to return to my healthy young Sundays; they were all bright. It seemed as if on Sunday it never rained; and one way or another, at least at home, it has never lost its calm, quiet beauty. The flowers wear a less business-like colour; the fields catch the colour of our spirits, and seem to lie in obedient repose. I cannot think the cattle do not feel it is not as other days; the lambs have a kind of going to church frisk about them; your dog, on every other day your faithfullest of companions, lies out before the hall-door, and never thinks of following you till after evening service; and your horse, if you have him out in the morning, looks a sermon full of puritan reproaches at you. The sacredness of Sunday is stamped on the soil of England, and in the heart of every Englishman; and all this by the old Sundays we remember of the first ten years of our lives.

So it was that, without any notion of the mystery of Christianity, I grew up in the intensest reverence for it; the more intense because I had no notion of its meaning. I cannot say what the Bible was not to me. I remember once in a fit of passionate bravado, when I was required to do something I did not like, saying " I swear I will not." I meant nothing except a great expression of my resolution. My sister told me I had taken God's name in vain; and my conscience burnt in what I had done upon my heart as if with a branding iron, and there lies its memory—uneffaced and ineffaceable.

Alas, alas, for the change! as I write, I seem for a moment to feel the old pulsations: but it is all gone away—gone like a dream in the morning— gone with the fairy-peopled world where then I thought we had our dwelling. " The things that I have felt, I now can feel no more;" when God gave them to me I felt them. He gave them— he has taken them away. The child is not as the man, and heaven lies all round our lives; in our young years we gambol upon its shores, and gather images from the shapes of light that sparkle there; and those light beings hover round us in our after wanderings, to hold our souls true in faith: that as the child was so in the end the man may be; and better far than that.

I am not going to trouble further the old vexed question of home and school education; but as I have been speaking of the religious sensibilities which form themselves at home, and as I have found that home and the thoughts connected with it are the elements out of which these are wrought, and the food upon which they feed; so I am sure that these

sensibilities are the strongest among those who remain longest in this home nursery garden, and,
whatever may become of the others, their roots at
least will never strike in a foreign soil. Character,
vigour, independence, these may best form when
there is most occasion for independent action, and
the boy thrown upon himself in the hard world
atmosphere of school, having to make his way and
push himself and take his own position, will be
better formed by far, perhaps, to elbow along in after-
life by practice of elbowing among schoolboys.
And, till we know something (at present we know
nothing at all) of the form after which it is most
God's will man should most shape himself, it is idle
to lay down laws for the *best* way of forming him.
Here I am concerned with religious sensibility, which
unquestionably is weakened in every school as it is
in the world. It leads to no results does religion, in
the first, any more than in the last; the forms of religion may be kept up, the outside praying and the
chapel going, some instruction too for decency's
sake; Greek Testament classes, article classes and
such like. But I will appeal to every boy's experience, whether all this has anything to do with his
real religion, or whether it looks to much advantage
by the side of the prayer-book his mother gave him,
or the Bible his sisters subscribed to buy for him.
I will ask him whether the tenderest form in which
his divinity is taught at school, has not seemed to
him worldly and irreverent; whether there, it is not
lessons, business, discipline—not love, heart and

pleasure ; and whether passing from the school Sunday to the first Sunday at home in holidays has not
been passing from earth into heaven. The older we
grow, the more surely we each feel our own sincere
experience to be the type of all sincere experience,
and I make my appeal without any fear at all.
. . . . . . The same feelings, if I know anything
of human nature, we shall all recognise : the same
voice in which God has spoken to our hearts. Once
for all, religion cannot be *taught* to boys.—Not till the
man is formed, not till the mind has been drawn out
of itself and forced to read, with its own eyes and not
with the eyes of books, the world and the men that
move and live in it ; not till the strangeness of their
own nature has broken upon them, till they have
looked fairly at this strange scene on earth here,
" this huge stage," and all its shows on " which the
stars with silent influence are commenting," not till
they have felt the meaning of history, have come to
feel that in very deed the actions of which they read,
the books in which they read them, were done and
made by beings in all points like themselves—in the
same trials, mysteries and temptations—not till then
can religion in its awfulness come out before men's
minds as a thing to be thought of ; not till the
question is asked will reason accept the answer. It
is the last, not the first, scene of education. It
cannot, try how you will, it cannot come before ; till
then it can be but a feeling—and so with this writer ;
God knows whether all his teaching weakened his
feeling : it certainly could not deepen it—yet at any

rate, ill obeyed as it was, the old faith he had learnt to love still held its place next his heart, till the time came for the change when the reason must assume its own responsibilities. I will step lightly over this period, long as it was ; I had been trained in rigid Protestantism—Faber on the Prophecies, Southey's Book of the Church, had been the pet books into which I had been directed. The Devil was at the bottom, and the Pope, the unquestionable Antichrist, very near him; and if possible an improvement on his ugliness. And the fulfilment, the exact fulfilment, of the prophecies, in the matter, for example, of the scarlet robe, the forbidding to marry, and the meat fasting, had always struck me, not as proofs of the truth of Christianity—Heaven knows I never thought of that—but as the most wonderful instances of the exactness with which the courses of the world were marked out for it.

So I was at about sixteen. Young boys take what they are told with readiest acquiescence, and difficulties are easily put away by a healthy mind as temptations of the devil. Cruelties said to have been committed by God's order in the Old Testament never struck me as cruelties; I glided on without notice over the massacres of women and children, much as good sensible people nowadays slide over the sufferings of " the masses;" condensing them into the one short word, and dismissing them as briefly as the lips dismiss the sound. . . . . . If misgivings ever for a moment arose, I had but to remember they were idolaters; and what was too bad

for a people so wicked as to be that? I remember
thinking it odd that I should be taught to admire
Hector, and Æneas, and Ulysses, and so many of them,
when all they were idolaters too. What had we to
do with the wisdom of Cicero, when he was as great
a sinner as these Canaanites? But I readily laid
the blame on the defects of my own understanding,
I was sure it was all right; and, though I read Hume
and Gibbon, I hated them cordially, only doubting
whether they were greater fools or greater knaves.
. . . . . . Why an all-knowing God, too, should require us to pray to Him, should threaten to punish us
if we did not, when He knew what we wanted better
than we knew ourselves; why we should put our
wishes into words when we even felt ourselves how imperfectly words expressed our feelings, and He could
know them without; nay, more, why, when as I began
to be taught we could not pray without He gave us
Himself the wish to pray, and the words to pray in, He
yet should be angry with us when we did not do it,
when He had not made us wish—this, too, seemed
very odd to me, ... but I dismissed it all as it came,
as my own fault, and most likely as very wrong.

Just as I was leaving off being a boy, we fell
under a strong Catholicising influence at home, and
I used to hear things which were strange enough to
my ear. Faber was put away out of my studies;
Newton was forbidden; and Davison, that I thought
so dry and dull, put in his place. Transubstantiation
was talked of before me as more than possible;
celibacy of the clergy and fasting on the fast days

were not only not wrong, but the very thing most needful . . . . our own dinners indeed did not suffer diminution . . . . but even to raise the question was sufficiently alarming, and I sat by in silence, listening with the strangest sensations. The martyrdom of Cranmer had always been a great favourite with me; the miracle of the unconsumed heart was a real miracle; at least I had been told so. The fulfilled prophecies about the Pope were real Scripture prophecies, of which I thought the verification almost terribly exact; and, what was worse, the interpretation was made sacred to me by early association . . . . and how to unlearn all this? I believe I may date from this point the first disturbance my mind experienced, and, however long I went on laying the blame upon myself, I never recovered it. I said to myself, if this miracle was not a miracle, how do I know there ever were miracles? This was easily answered, because one sort were in Scripture, and the other only in Southey's book. But as to fulfilment of prophecy, if this was not fulfilment, then what was? we could never be sure of any of it. Davison was no help; for his double sense was the wrong sort of double—double-minded. I went to the New Testament for old prophecies fulfilled there, and I was still more bewildered; for, in no one case that I could find, would it have been possible to conceive without the interpretation that there had been any prophecy at all intended. So I was forced altogether to give up prophecy till more inspiration came to explain it for us. . . . . . .

Alas! how little we understand the strange mystery of the heart. Thoughts come and go—float across our minds like the cloud shadows on a sunny day; the sun follows out, and no track is seen upon the earth when they have passed—all is bright as before. But the heart lies out under the breath of Providence like the prepared mirror of the photogenic draughtsman; the figure falls there, it rests but a few moments, and then passes away, and no line is seen; but the rays have eaten in and left a form which can never be effaced. . . . . . By and by the acid touches it, and there lies the image, full and faithful as the hand could paint it. The first doubt of the affection of one who is dear to us, how angrily we spurn it from us, how we despise and hate ourselves for entertaining a thought so detestable; one stone crumbled off a battlement, how little it affects our sense of its strength, our faith in its duration. Yet the same cause which flung down that one may fling down another and another, and what can begin to perish will at last perish all. I am not speaking of Christianity as it is in the eternal purpose of Almighty God; but of that image, that spiritual copy of it, which grows up in the human microcosm. The first is older than the universe—is coeval with its Maker; but the second is frail as the being in whom it is formed.

Wo to the unlucky man who as a child is taught, even as a portion of his creed, what his grown reason must forswear. Faith endures no barking of the surface; it is a fair, delicate plant

transported out of Paradise into an alien garden,
where surest care alone can foster it. But wound
the tenderest shoot—but break away one single
flower, and though it linger on for years, feeding
upon stimulants and struggling through a languish-
ing vitality, it has had its death-blow; the blighted
juices fly trembling back into the heart, never to
venture out again.

Nevertheless the mind of a young man is very
plastic. As personal affection lies at the root of
our first opinions, so the influence of persons whom
we love and venerate is for a long time paramount;
and, by a natural necessity, a mind falling in its
growth under the influence of a great man, great
alike in genius and in character, assumes the im-
print such a man will fix upon it, and most imitates
what it most admires. Only wider experience
flings us back upon ourselves; the experience
which shows us that men who, while they unite all
the greatest qualities in greatest measure, may yet
be as various in opinion as in the variety of their
gifts—as various as the million varieties of beautiful
objects with which God has ornamented the earth.
Painful, indeed, is the moment when this first breaks
upon us. It is easy to be decided so long as we
feel so sure that all goodness is on our side; and
only badness, moral badness, or else folly, can take
the other; but how terrible becomes the alternative
when we know men as they really are!

Well, the great men under whose influence I
now fell dealt tenderly with the imbibed preju-

dices even of Protestantism ; and, holding on by persons standing so firmly as they seemed to stand, I did not seem to have lost any thing—to have weakened my moral footing. They could make all allowance, sympathise with my sorrow such as it was, show how it was right and amiable that I should feel it; and, in the position which they had assumed, they seemed to have the antidote against the mischief from the transfer of allegiance from one set of teachers to another, in representing themselves not as speaking their own words, but those of the holy mother of us all—the Church. So a strange process began to form ; for, while it was in reality but their own great persons which were drawing us all towards them, they unwillingly deceived us into believing it was not their influence, but the body's power; and, while in fact we were only Newmanites, we fancied we were becoming Catholics.

Most mournful—for in the imagined security of our new position, as our minds were now unfolding, with deep faith in *one* great man, we began to follow him along the subtle reasonings with which he drew away from under us the supports upon which Protestant Christianity had been content to rest its weight; we allowed ourselves to see its contradictions, to recognise the logical strength of the arguments of Hume, to acknowledge that the old answers of Campbell, the evidences of Paley, were futile as the finger of a child on the spoke of an engine's driving-wheel; nay, more, to examine the logic of unbelief with a kind of pleasure, as hitting our adversaries to the death, and never approaching us at all. So, gradually unknowing what we did, to accept the huge bisection of mankind; to confine Christianity to the Church visible, and exclude those beyond its pale from the blessings of the covenant—to recognise the Catholic illustration of the ark—to continue the anathemas of the creeds, while we determined the objects on whom they rested—to allow the world outside to have all talent, all splendour, power, beauty, intellect, superiority, even the highest heroic virtues, and yet to be without that peculiar goodness which flowed out of the body of which the elect were members, and which alone gave chance of salvation.

It is true that we were defrauded of the just indignation with which our hearts would have rebelled against so terrible a violation of their instincts, by mysterious hints of uncovenanted mercies, of grace given to the heathen in overflowing kindness; and gentle softening of the more consistent theology of the fathers, which flung infants, dying unbaptised, into the everlasting fire-lake. They would not let us see what they perhaps themselves shrunk from seeing, that in the law of Divine Providence there is none of this vague unreal trifling; that, if they believed their histories and their illustrations, they must not flinch from the conclusions. The sucking children of the unchosen were not saved in Noah's flood. The cities of the Canaanites were deluged with the blood of hundreds of thousands whose innocence appeals to outraged humanity. What had those poor creatures done to justify their fate more than the Christians beyond the pale, or the heathen whose virtues plead to have intercession made for them?

The Catholics must not trifle with their theory, and on this twilight of uncovenanted mercies they must allow me to ask them these questions.

Was the Christian sacrifice necessary, or was it not? That is, could mankind be saved without it? You will answer, at least Catholics always do answer, They could not.

To derive the benefit of that sacrifice, is it necessary to be within the Church, and receive it through the sacraments? If Yes; then all beyond derive no benefit, and so are lost. If No; then what do you mean? There is no such thing as " partially necessary;" a thing is necessary or it is not. You will say then—Not necessary; but necessary in such and such circumstances—wherever God has made it possible. But if God had pleased it would have been universally possible; and with an attached natural penalty of eternal damnation, which can only be counteracted by a miracle, it is hard to conceive him leaving men without the one essential.

Well, then, do you mean these sacraments are essential to the living a saintly life? But others live saintly lives. If they do, you say that is by the extraordinary mercy. But the Catholics do not number a tithe of the human race—as a rule we do not find a larger proportion of good men among them than among others; and if, out of every age and nation, those who fear God are under the influ-

ence of His grace, and are in the other world to
become members of His Church, a larger number
by far will be taken from those beyond the pale
than from within it; *and, therefore, the Catholics
will receive by the extraordinary, the others by the
ordinary channels.* The extra-sacramental is the
common way; and how strange a system you make
the Almighty to have constructed, when it does but
answer a tenth of its purpose, and the rest is by
method of exception. Surely this is worse than
midsummer madness! The fathers are right—
you are ridiculous. It may be that sacramental
grace is essential; but the alternative is absolute—
it is, or it is not. Begin to make exceptions; bend
your line, here a little and there a little,—a curve
for the pious Lutherans, an angle for the better sort
of heathens,—and you will soon make your figure
a helpless, shapeless no-figure. Take *up the swim-
mers into the ark,* and they will soon outnumber
the good family there; and ark and all will go
down, and you will have to take common chance
in the water with the rest.

No! the earthly Canaan was given to the chosen
people without respect of virtue, as Jewish history
too painfully shows. So with your theory is the
heavenly. You need not come in with your text,
" Many shall come from the east and the west,"
giving it the human sense, which shall save the heathens in the next world. For you it means, and but
must mean, the call of the Gentiles under baptism.
If you recoil from this conclusion, then, in God's

name, have done with your covenant and your
theory; and do not in the same breath allow and
disallow human excellence as a title to heaven, or
the doctrine of the infinite divisibility of matter
must be called in to help you in your dividings.

A few words more shall be said to you, of which you
shall not like the hearing.   I will not prejudge you;
but, if you believe what you say, to allow us to go
on feeding ourselves upon the literature of those
old glorious Greeks and Romans, to think by Aristotle and Cicero, to feel by Æschylus and Sophocles,
to reproduce among ourselves by exclusive study
the early figures of those great kings, patriots,
poets, princes, is the most barbarous snare which
was ever laid before the feet of weak humanity.
And you do this—you who profess the care of our
souls !   Ah, if you did care for them, you would up
and gird yourselves, and cry—Leave them, leave
them, they are heathens !   Learn your Greek in
Athanasius, and your Latin in Augustine.   Those
were God's enemies whom He had not chosen, and
therefore has rejected.   The more dangerous because they look so like His friends; but splendid
sinners, as the wise fathers called them.

What, gentlemen, do you suppose that I am to
make friends with Socrates and Phocion, and believe that human nature is full of the devil, and that
only baptism can give chance for a holy life ?   That
I will hand Plato into destruction; that Sophocles,
and Phidias, and Pindar, and Germanicus, and Tacitus, and Aurelius, and Trajan were no better than

poor unenlightened Pagans, and that, where you not only permit me to make acquaintance with them, but compel me to it as a condition, forsooth, under which I may become a minister of the Christian faith!

You think, perhaps, that I shall draw healthy comparisons, and see what heathenism could *not* make of man. That I will place (I will not compare invidiously)—that I will place David above Leonidas, Eusebius above Tacitus, Jerome over Plato, Aquinas over Aristotle, and yourselves over . . . . . Ah, Heaven! where shall I find an antitype of you? You shall let me see and love whole generations of men who would live long lives of self-denial and heroic daring, for the love of God, and virtue, and humanity; asking no reward but in the consciousness that they were doing God's will; and persevering still, even with the grave as the limit of their horizon, because they loved good and hated evil; and you point me out in contrast the noble army of martyrs—men who knew how to die in the strength of the faith, that death was the gate of eternal Paradise; and which is the noblest, and which is the hardest task, I wonder? No, the world is mystery enough, no doubt of that, and your Catholic Christianity *may* be true; but, if you think so, you, who are our soul's shepherds, at your peril be it, close up the literature of the world; like that deeply believing Caliph, close, close our eyes in seven-fold blindness against all history except the Bible history, and mark out the paths of Christian teaching

in which you will have us walk within walls hard
and thick as the adamant round Paradise.

So much for the digressing upon an argument
which I have let fall here where it is lying, not as
what I felt at the time of which I speak, but as
what now, as I look back over it, appears the logical
account of the ill-satisfaction which I did feel.   It
is with argument as it is with the poetry of passion
—we feel before we can speak of what we feel; and
it is only on the return of calmness, when the
struggle is past and the horizon clear again, that
we can delineate and analyse our experiences.

Among all the foolish and unmeaning cries over
which party spirit has gone distracted, that of " private judgment" stands, perhaps, without parallel.
Whether, as the Protestant explains it, we take it as
a right, or as the Catholic, as a duty, the right of
judging for oneself, or the right of choosing one's
teacher, or the duty of doing both, or one, or neither, whatever we call it, never was so strange a
creature brought to birth out of our small but fer-
tile imaginings.

What is right or duty without *power?*   To tell
a man it is his duty to submit his judgment to the
judgment of the church, is like telling a wife it is
her duty to love her husband—a thing easy to say,
but meaning simply nothing.   Affection must be
won, not commanded.   If the husband and wife

both continue the same persons as they were when they did love each other (supposing it was so), the love will continue; but if the natures change, either of both or one of them, and become antipathetic, it would be as reasonable to lecture oxygen and hydrogen on the duty of continuing in combination when they are decomposed by galvanism. They may, indeed, be forcibly held together in juxtaposition by external restraint; but combined they are not. And, while they are as they are, they cannot be combined.

So it is with the church and its members. As long as the church has the power to mould the minds of her children after her own sort, in such a way that their coherence in her shall be firm enough to overcome whatever external attraction they may fall within the sphere of, so long she has a right to their hearts. While she has the power to employ the external restraints of hope and fear—so long as she can torture and scourge, or so long as she directs public opinion, and her frown can entail any practical inconvenience—so long she has a right to the external conformity of such individuals as are of a kind to be governed by such considerations. As soon as she loses both, the bereaved lady may still cry, "I have a right to your affections, it is your duty to submit to me;" but she will have lost her divine sanction, and would be about as reasonable as the last of the Stuarts whining over his rights to the duty of the English.

Again, for an individual, be he who he will, in a

world where faculties are so unequally distributed,
and some are weaker than others, to say he has a
right to be his own teacher, or to choose who he
will have for a teacher, is much as if a satellite of
Jupiter betrayed a disposition to set up on his own
account, or took a fancy to older ways and wished
to transfer his allegiance to Saturn. If Saturn left
his orbit, and came down for him, and by right of
stronger attraction could take him away in a struggle, then of course he would have a right to him.

So it is with us all. I use magnetic illustrations,
not because I think the mind magnetic, but because
magnetic comparisons are the nearest we have, and
the laws are exactly parallel. Minds vary in sensitiveness and in self-power, as bodies do in susceptibility of attraction and repulsion. When, when
shall we learn that they are governed by laws as inexorable as physical laws, and that a man can as easily
refuse to obey what has power over him as a steel
atom can resist the magnet? Take a bar of steel,
its component atoms cohere by attraction; turn off
the current of electricity, or find means to negative
it, and the bar becomes a dust heap. The earth's
attraction calls off this portion, the wind scatters
that, or another magnetic body in the neighbourhood will proceed to appropriate. So it is with belief: belief is the result of the proportion, whatever
it be, in which the many elements which go to
make the human being are combined. In some the
grosser nature preponderates; they believe largely in
their stomachs, in the comforts and conveniences

of life, and being of such kind, so long as these are
not threatened, they gravitate steadily towards the
earth.   Numerically this is the largest class of be-
lievers, with very various denominations indeed;
bearing the names of every faith beneath the sky,
and composing the conservative elements in them,
and therefore commonly persons of much weight in
established systems.   But they are what I have
called them : their hearts are where I said they
were, and as such interests are commonly selfish,
and self separates instead of unites, they are not
generally powerful against any heavy trial.   Others
of keener susceptibility are yet volatile, with slight
power of continuance, and fly from attraction to
attraction in the current of novelty.   Others of
stronger temper gravitate more slowly, but combine more firmly, and only disunite again when the
idea or soul of the body into which they form dies
out, or they fall under the influence of some very
attractive force indeed.   It may be doubted, indeed,
whether a body which is really organised by a
living idea, can lose a healthy member except by
violence.

If it be difficult to follow the subtle features of
electric affinity among the inorganic bodies or simplest elemental combinations, it may well be thought
impossible in organisms so curiously complicated as
that of the human being.   However, such as it is,
the illustration will serve.

The cry of private judgment meant simply this,
that the authority of the office was ceasing to influ-

ence, and was being superseded by the authority of
the gifted man—that the church had lost its power,
perhaps its life, and was decomposing. The talk of
the duty of determining to remain in her upon private judgment, was an attempt to inspire the atoms
which were flying off with salutary fear of consequences, which would submit them again to her
control.

Well, as we had none of us any very clear idea
to magnetize us, and as yet had not approached the
point when the other influences would come to bear
upon us, and we should begin to feel the gravi-
tation downwards in the necessity of getting on in
the world, the leader of the movement took us all
his own way ; all that is who were not Arnoldized.
And even some of these he contrived to draw away
by the nearness and continuance of his action upon
them, as the comet's attraction played the deuce
with Jupiter's satellites while it continued in their
neighbourhood. It is true we thought, yes, we
thought we were following the church : but it was
like the goose in the child's toy, which is led by
the nose up and down the basin by the piece of
bread .　.　. by the piece of bread .　.　. with the
loadstone inside it.

Well, everybody remembers the history of the
Tracts, and how the doctrine of development began
to show itself as the idea grew; threatening such
mighty changes; and how unsteady minds began
to grow uneasy ; and heads of houses to frown, and
bishops to deliver charges. Hitherto these Tracts

had represented pretty exactly Anglican Oxford. Though dangerously clever, and more dangerously good, they had never broken bounds, and the unenthusiastic authorities had found themselves unable to do more than warn, and affect to moderate. The world outside seemed partially to smile on the movement, as at any rate a digging over an unproductive soil. Rome was never spoken of as the probable goal of any but a few foolish young men, whose presence would be injurious to any cause, and who were therefore better in the enemy's camp than at home. And no worldly interests had as yet been threatened with damage, except perhaps the Friday dinner and the Lent second course; the loss of which, being not enough to be painful, became a piquant stimulant, and gave edge to appetite.

Now, to a single-minded man, who is either brave enough or reckless enough to surrender himself wholly to one idea, and look neither right nor left, but only forward, what earthly consequences may follow is not material. Persecution strengthens him; and so he is sure he is right, whether his course end in a prison or on a throne is no matter at all. But men of this calibre are uncommon in any age or in any country—very uncommon in this age and this country. Most of us are sent to universities or wherever it may be, not merely to be educated into men, but to get along in the world; make money, it may be called, in an invidious way; but it is not only to make money; it is that we may take up our own position in life, and support ourselves in the scale of society where we were born. We are placed in a road along which we have only to travel steadily, and the professions, as they are called, are trodden in by the experience of the common sense of mankind, making large advance and best success quite possible to average hack genius, which would make nothing of its across country. The world cares little about theology; and the worldly professions soon leave it out of account except on Sunday . . . But to the Oxford students, and particularly to such of them as form the opinion of Oxford, theology is itself the profession. Chosen as a profession, it is followed with professional aims, and, as the idea of the Tracts grew clearer and more exclusive, the time came when the angle at which the line of *its* course inclined towards the professional influence became obtuse instead of acute, and this last began to retard.

It became necessary to surrender tutorships, fellowships, and the hopes of them; to find difficulties in getting ordained, to lose slowly the prospects of pleasant curacies, and livings, and parsonage houses, and the sweet little visions of home paradises—a serious thing to young high churchmen, who were commonly of the amiable enthusiastic sort, and so, of course, had fallen most of them into early engagements . . . . . . and from this time the leader's followers began to lag behind. "They turned back, and walked no more after him." I am not blaming them. They did not know what was governing them, and, if they did, they would have had very much to urge for themselves. It is no light thing this mortifying the hopes of friends, who have, perhaps, made painful sacrifices to lift us forward. It is no light thing to encounter the hard words and hard facts of life, without sympathy, till the cause is won and it is not needed; rather perhaps with the coldness of those we love, the sneers of society, the three meals a-day never slacking their claims, and the wherewithal to provide them poorly forthcoming.

The idea drives a man into the wilderness before he comes to the land of milk and honey . . . . . . and little water and the scanty sprinkling of angel's food he must make shift to be content with. Speculation bakes no bread, and often, too, the sinking heart flags and fails to trust itself, and the moments of insight are short, and the hours of despondency are long, and the unsteady reason rises among vague misgivings, and points reproachfully back to the fleshpots of Egypt, which we have left to die in the desert. After all, too, is not the beaten road, a road which *men* have beaten, good men who had God's grace in them. Surely what presumption is it not for here and there a self-wise impertinent to refuse to listen to the old practised guides, and fly off, he knows not where, after a mirage he calls an "*idea*." . . . Peace, peace, perturbed spirits! Perfection in this world is a dream. . . . . Poor sheep! listen to the call of your shepherd; turn back before the sand overwhelm you . . . . . So reason with themselves the many half-worshippers of truth; and

they turn back and find their account in turning.
They find their account in the peace they sought.
Genius only has a right to choose its own way, for
genius only has the power to face what it will find
there.   There is a lion in the path . . . . . let the
common man keep clear of him.   So all men gravitate into their spheres; only wo to those who
swing suspended in the balance, and can follow
heartily neither earth nor heaven.

There is genius with its pale face and worn dress
and torn friendships and bleeding heart . . . strong
only in struggling; counting all loss but truth and
the love of God; rewarded, as men court reward,
perhaps by an after apotheosis, yet never seeking
this reward or that reward, save only its own good
conscience steady to its aim; promising nothing;
least of all peace—only struggles which are to end
but with the grave.

And there is respectability, with its sweet smiling
home, and loving friends, and happy family, a fair
green spring, a golden summer, an autumn sinking
fruit-loaded to the earth—the final winter rest following on the full finished course of gentle duty
done, and for the future prospects, easy and secure.
Choose between them, O man, at the parting of the
ways!   Choose.   You may have one; both you
cannot have.   Either will give you to yourself—
either *perhaps* to God.   Yet, if you do choose the
first, choose it with all your heart.   You will need
it all to bear what will be laid upon you.   No wistful lookings back upon the pleasant land which you

are leaving – no playing with life. You have chosen the heart of things, not the surface; and it is no child's play. Fling away your soul once for all, your own small self; if you will find it again. Count not even on immortality. St Paul would make himself anathema for the brethren. Look not to have your sepulchre built in after ages by the same foolish hands which still ever destroy the living prophet. Small honour for you if they do build it; and may be they never will build it. A thousand patriots go to the scaffold amidst the execrations of decent mankind. Out of these thousand, perhaps the after generation remembers one young Emmett; and his name finds honourable memory; and young ladies drop sentimental tears on the piano notes as they sing the sorrows of his broken-hearted bride.

Enough of this . . . . But once in our lives we have all to choose. More or less we have all felt once the same emotions. We have not always been what the professions make of us. Nature made us men, and she surrenders not her children without a struggle. I will go back to my story now with but this one word, that it is these sons of genius, and the fate they meet with, which is to me the one sole evidence that there is more in "this huge state" than what is seen, and that in very truth the soul of man is not a thing which comes and goes, is builded and decays like the elemental frame in which it is set to dwell, but a very living force, a very energy of God's organic Will, which rules and moulds this universe.

For what are they? Say not, say not, it is but a choice which they have made; and an immortality of glory in heaven shall reward them for what they have sacrificed on earth. It may be so; but they do not ask for it. They are what they are from the Divine power which is in them, and you would never hear their complainings if the grave was the gate of annihilation.

Say not they have their reward on earth in the calm satisfaction of noble desires, nobly gratified, in the sense of great works greatly done; that too may be, but neither do they ask for that. They alone never remember themselves; they know no end but to do the will which beats in their heart's deep pulses. Ay, but for these, these few martyred heroes, it might be after all that the earth was but a huge loss-and-profit ledger book; or a toy machine some great angel had invented for the amusement of his nursery; and the storm and the sunshine but the tears and the smiles of laughter in which he and his baby cherubs dressed their faces over the grave and solemn airs of slow-paced respectability.

Yes, genius alone is the Redeemer; it bears our sorrows, it is crowned with thorns for us; the children of genius are the church militant, the army of the human race. Genius is the life, the law of mankind, itself perishing, that others may take possession and enjoy. Religion, freedom, science, law, the arts, mechanical or beautiful, all which gives *respectability* a chance, have been moulded out by the toil and the sweat and the blood of the faithful; who, knowing no enjoyment, were content to be the servants of their own born slaves, and wrought out the happiness of the world which despised and disowned them.

So much for the sons of genius . . . . one of whom—perhaps one of three or four at present alive in this planet—was at that time rising up in Oxford, and drawing all men towards him. I myself was so far fortunate, that the worldly influence of which I spoke did not so immediately bear upon me. I was, as the phrase goes, moderately provided for; and, in my own reflectings upon the matter, it seemed to me that I in a way *ought* to take advantage of a fortunate position; and, without judging the motives of others who acted differently because I could not tell how I myself might have acted if I had been tempted in the same way, to follow on where the direct course seemed to lead me.

Life complete, is lived in two worlds; the one inside, and the one outside. The first half of our days is spent wholly in the former; the second, if it is what it ought to be, wholly in the latter—Pretty well till we have done with our educating theories are only words to us, and church controversy not of things but of shadows of things. Through all that time life and thought beyond our own experience is but a great game played out by book actors; we do not think, we only think we think, and we have been too busy in our own line to have a notion really of what is beyond it. But while so much of our talk is so unreal, our own selves, our own risings, fallings, aspirings, resolutions, misgivings, these are real enough to us; these are our hidden life, our sanctuary of our own mysteries. . . . . . It was into these that N.'s power of insight was so remarkable. I believe no young man ever heard him preach without fancying that some one had been betraying his own history, and the sermon was aimed specially at him. It was likely that, while he had possession so complete of what we did know about ourselves, we should take his word for what we did not; and, while he could explain *us*, let him explain the rest for us. But it is a problem heavier than has been yet laid on theologians to make what the world has now grown into square with the theory of catholicism. And presently as we began to leave the nest, and, though under his eye, fly out and look about for ourselves, some of us began to find it so. I was not yet acquainted with any of the modern continental writers, but I had read a great deal of English, and clouds of things began to rise before me in lights wonderfully different from those in which I used to see them. I will not go along the details, but I will lay down a few propositions, all of which were granted, with the conclusions I myself was tempted to draw, and those which I was taught to draw.

1. That, if the Catholic theory be true, it is not only necessary to *talk* of hating the Reformation, but

one must hate it with a hearty good-will as a rending of the body of Christ . . . . . and yet . . . . .

That in the sixteenth century the church was full of the most fearful abuses; that many of the clergy were unbelievers, and many more worldly and sensual; that to what we call an honest simple understanding, it had become a huge system of fraud, trickery, and imposture.   Granted.

2. That the after Reformation in the *Roman* Catholic church was, humanly speaking, a consequence of the great revolt from her, which had shamed her into exerting herself.   Granted.

3. That, ever since, the nations which have remained Catholic have become comparatively powerless, while the Protestant nations have uniformly risen; that each nation, in fact, has risen exactly as it has emancipated itself.   Granted.

4. That the Catholic church since the Reformation has produced no great man of science, no statesman, no philosopher, no poet.   Granted.

5. That historical criticism, that scientific discovery *have uniformly tended to invalidate* the authority of histories to which the infallible church has committed herself.   Granted.

6. That the personal character of the people in all Roman Catholic countries is poor and mean; that they are untrue in their words, unsteady in their actions, disrespecting themselves in the entire tenor of their life and temper.   Granted.

7. And that this was to be traced to the moral dependence in which they were trained; to the con-

H

science being taken out of their own hands and de-
posited with the priests; to the disrespect with
which this life is treated by the Catholic theory;
the low esteem in which the human will and character are considered; and, generally, to the condition of spiritual bondage in which they are held.
Not granted, but to be believed nevertheless.

Now if these things were facts, taken alone at
least, they were unquestionably serious. Happily I
had very early learned the fallacy of building much
on logic and verbal argument. Single sets of truths
I knew to be as little conclusive in theology as in
physics; and, in one as in the other, no theory to
be worth anything, however plausibly backed up
with Scripture texts or facts, which was not gathered
bonâ fide from the analysis of all the attainable phenomena, and verified wherever possible by experiment. " Here is a theory of the world which you
bring for my acceptance : well, there is the world ;
try—will the key fit ? can you read the language
into sense by it ? " was the only method; and so I
was led always to look at broad results, at pages and
chapters, rather than at single words and sentences,
where for a few lines a false key may serve to make
a meaning. . . . . . . So of these broad observations I only expected a broad solution. I did not
draw conclusions for myself, I never yet doubted;
but I wished to be told what I was to make of facts
so startling.

These answers which follow I do not mean to say
were given categorically to categorically asked ques-

tions, but on the whole they are such as were in various ways and at considerable intervals of time suggested to me.

1. Either it was true or it was not true, that man was fallen and required redemption; that from the beginning of time a peculiar body of people, *not specially distinguished for individual excellencies*, had nevertheless been the objects of peculiar care, the channels of peculiar grace; that their language was inspired, their priests divinely guided.

2. If this was true, we were not to demand at present results which never had been found.

3. That the Spirit worked not visibly, but invisibly.

4. That my arguments told not only against Catholicism, *but against Christianity, considered as historical and exclusive.*

5. That Protestant Christianity on the Continent had uniformly developed into Socinianism, and thence into Pantheism, and from a fact was becoming an idea merely.

6. That Catholicism altogether was a preternatural system, treating the world as a place of trial and temptation, and the Devil as the main director of what seemed greatest and most powerful in it; and, therefore, that we should least look among Christians for such power and greatness; and broken-hearted penitence was not likely to produce such effects as seemed to me so admirable.

7. The Bible everywhere denounced the world as the enemy of God, not as the friend of God; and by

the world must be meant the real world of fact, not a fantastic world of all kinds of vice and wickedness, which had no existence beyond our own imaginings. The world was always what the world is now—a world of greatness as well as pleasure—of intellect, power, beauty, nobleness. This was the world we forswore in baptism, and in our creed denounced. The temper of a saint was quite different from the temper of a world's great man; and we had no right, because we found this last attractive and beautiful, to assume that he was not therefore what the Bible warned us against. If man is fallen, his unsanctified virtues are vices.

9. That the hold of Christianity was on the heart, and not on the reason. Reason was not the whole of us; and alone it must ever lead to infidelity.

10. Finally, we were Christians, or we were not. Confessedly Christianity was mysterious; the mysterious solution of a mysterious world; not likely to be reasonable. If once we began accommodating and assimilating, shrinking from that difficulty, and stretching our creed to this, expanding liberalism would grow stronger by concessions. The Bible warned us sternly enough of what we were, and of the little right we had to place confidence in ourselves. Unbelief was a sin, not a mistake, and deserved not argument, but punishment.

It was enough for me to learn, as now I soon did, that all real arguments against Catholicism were, in fact, arguments against Christianity; and I was readily induced to acknowledge that the Reformation had been the most miserable infatuation. The world was an enemy dangerous enough without home feuds; and the Reformers, in allowing reason to sit in judgment in matters of faith, in appealing to common sense, and in acknowledging the right of personal independence, were introducing elements, no one of which could produce anything but falsehood, in a system which recognised none of them, which was divine, not human, and, being divinely founded, had the promise of divine sustaining. I saw that in denying the continual authority of the Church's witness, and falling back on individual experience, or historic testimony, they had, in fact, cut away the only support on which Revelation could at all sustain itself. That in the cry of "the Bible, and the Bible only" (setting aside the absurdity of the very idea, as if the Bible was not written in human language, and language not dependent for interpretation upon tradition; I say, setting aside this), men are assuming the very point at issue; for, if the Church was mistaken, why must the Bible be true? That is, why must it be wholly true? why not contain the same alloy of true and false to be found in all other books?

In fact, they had cut the roots of the tree; for a few years it might retain some traces of its old life; but they had broken off the supply, and they were but trading on what was left of the traditionary reverence for the Bible which the Church had in-stilled into mankind. Experience had shown, that the same reason which rejected the Saints' miracles

as incredible would soon make hard mouths at the
Bible miracles. The notion of inspiration was no
more satisfactory than that of the Church's infallibility; and if the power of the keys, and sacramental grace, and apostolic succession, were absurdities, the Devil was at least equally so. And with
the Devil fell sin, and the atonement fell, and all
revelation fell : and we were drifting on the current
of a wide ocean, we knew not where, with neither
oar nor compass.

And so I held on, with all my heart, in the power
of old association ; and, clinging fast to what I could
comprehend of our leader's views, for a time dreamed
they were my own. Hitherto, in considering the
existing unhappy state of Catholic countries, England,
unquestionably the strongest country in the world, we
had taken as a Protestant country. The tendency
of Catholicism we saw to be to depress the external
character of man; that, the deeper he believed it,
the more completely he became subdued. Protestantism, on the contrary, cultivated man outwards on
every side, insisted on self-reliance, taught every one
to stand alone, and depend himself on his own energies. Now, then, came the question of the Church
of England—was it Catholic, was it Protestant? for,
if this were Protestantism, surely the English, as a
nation, were the most Protestant in the world. Long
before the Reformation, the genius of independence
had begun to struggle for emancipation among them,
and the dazzling burst of the Elizabethan era was the
vigorous expansion of long-imprisoned energy, spring-

ing out in bounding joyous freedom. The poets, from
Chaucer to Milton, were, without exception, on the
reforming side; and the strong practical heart of the
country found its fullest and clearest expression in
Oliver Cromwell.   Unquestionably the English were
Protestants in the fullest sense of the word; yet,
in spite of this unhealthy symptom, the English
Church had retained, apparently providentially,
something of a Catholic character.   It had retained
the Succession, it had retained the Sacraments, it
had retained Liturgical forms, which committed it
to the just Catholic understanding of them.   The
question with the Tract writers was, whether, with the
help of this old framework they could unprotest-
antize its working character, and reinspire it with so
much of the old life as should enable it to do the
same work in England which the Roman Church produced abroad; to make England cease to produce
great men—as we count greatness—and for poetry,
courage, daring, enterprise, resolution, and broad
honest understanding, substitute devotion, endurance, humility, self-denial, sanctity, and faith.
This was the question at issue.   It might take other
names; it might resent the seeing itself represented
so broadly.   But this was, at heart, what it meant,
if it meant anything—to produce a wholly different
type of character.   It was no longer now a nice
dispute about authority.   Long-sighted men saw
now that Christianity itself had to fight for its life,
and that, unless it was very soon to die in England,
as it had died in Germany and France, something

else than the broad solid English sense must be inoculated into the hearts of us. We were all liberalizing as we were going on, making too much of this world, and losing our hold upon the next; forgetting, as we all had, that the next was the only real world, and this but a thorny road to it, to be trod with bleeding feet, and broken spirits. It was high time.

What a sight must this age of ours have been to an earnest believing man like Newman, who had an eye to see it, and an ear to hear its voices? A foolish Church, chattering, parrot-like, old notes, of which it had forgot the meaning; a clergy who not only thought not at all, but whose heavy ignorance, from long unreality, clung about them like a garment, and who mistook their fool's cap and bells for a crown of wisdom, and the music of the spheres; selfishness alike recognized practically as the rule of conduct, and faith in God, in man, in virtue, exchanged for faith in the belly, in fortunes, carriages, lazy sofas, and cushioned pews; Bentham politics, and Paley religion; all the thought deserving to be called thought, the flowing tide of Germany, and the philosophy of Hume and Gibbon; all the spiritual feeling, the light froth of the Wesleyans and Evangelicals; and the only real stern life to be found anywhere, in a strong resolved and haughty democratic independence, heaving and rolling underneath the chaff-spread surface. How was it like to fare with the clergy gentlemen, and the Church turned respectable, in the struggle with

enemies like these? Erastianism, pluralities, pre-
bendal stalls, and pony-gigging parsons,—what
work were they like to make against the proud,
rugged, intellectual republicanism, with a fire
sword between its lips, bidding cant and lies be still;
and philosophy, with Niebuhr criticism for a reap-
ing sickle, mowing down their darling story-books?
High time it was to move indeed. High time for
the Church warriors to look about them, to burnish
up their armour, to seize what ground was yet remaining, what time to train for the battle.

It would not serve to cultivate the intellect. All
over Europe, since Spinoza wrote, what of strongest
intellect there was had gone over to the enemy.
Genius was choosing its own way, acknowledging
no longer the authority either of man or docu-
ment; and unless in some way or other the heart
could be preoccupied—unless the Church could win
back the love of her children, and temper them
quite differently from the tone in which they were
now tempered, the cause was lost—and for ever.
So, then, they must begin with the clergy. To
wean the Church from its Erastianism into mili-
tancy, where it might at least command respect for
its sincerity – to wean the bishops from their palaces
and lazy carriages and fashionable families, the
clergy from their snug firesides and marrying
and giving in marriage: this was the first step.
Slowly then to draw the people out of the whirl
of business to thought upon themselves—from self-
assertion, for the clamouring for their rights, and

the craving for independence, to almsgiving, to endurance of wrong, to the confessional—from doing
to praying—from early hours in the office, or in the
field, to matins and daily service: this was the purpose of the Tract movement. God knows, if
Christianity be true, a purpose needful enough to
get fulfilled. For surely it is madness, if the world
be the awful place the Bible says it is, the Devil's
kingdom—the battle-field between good and evil
spirits for the eternal happiness or eternal perdition
of human souls—to go out, as we all do, clergy and
all of us—to go out into its highways and dust our
feet along its thoroughfares; to take part in its
amusements; to eat, and drink, and labour, and
enjoy our labour's fruit, and find our home and
happiness here. Madness! yes, and far worse than
madness! For once more, the world is not visibly
at least the hideous place our early religion dreams
it to be; it is not a world of profligates and pick-
pockets, and thieves and sensualists; it is a world
of men and women, not all good, but better far than
bad; a world of virtue as man's heart deems virtue;
of human feelings, sympathies, and kindness; a
world we cannot enter into without loving it . . . .
and yet, if we love it, we are to die.

Oh, most miserable example of disbelief in their
own precepts are the English clergy! Denouncing
the world, they yet live in it; speaking in the old
language against indulgence, and luxury, and riches,
and vanity in the pulpit, how is it that they cannot
bring themselves, neither they nor their families, to

descend from the social position, as they call it, in which they were born? Why must they be for ever gentlemen? Why is it that the only unworldliness to be found among them is but among those to whom poverty leaves no alternative?

It was a worldly Church; yes, there was no doubt of it; and, being so, it early began to scent danger, to cry out and anathematize the new teachers who prescribed a severer doctrine; who were trying to shame the clergy into a more consistent life by reminding them of the dignity of their office. Newman had dared to tell them that their armour was pasteboard; the oil dying out of their lamps; that a tempest was rising which would scatter them like chaff before it. Catholic feeling—Catholic energy—Catholic doctrine, exhibited in holy life, in prayer, and fasting, their own witness at least of their own fidelity, might save them. It was a chance, only a chance: but their last. Let them rouse themselves, and see what they did really believe, and why they believed; above all, let them come forward in deed as well as word, and prove that they were alive: with a faith really heart-rooted, they might yet stand in the storm; but their logic props were bruised reeds indeed. . . . . . . And what was his reward? He was denounced as a Cassandra prophet; bid, go get him gone, shake the dust from off his feet, and depart to his own place. He took them at their word, and left the falling house, not without scorn. A little more slumber, a little more sleep. It was the sluggard's cry, let them find the sluggard's

doom. But I had left him, too, before this. I
have outrun my own small history, and I must fall
back upon my own adventures. He was not the
only greatly gifted man then living in this England.
I think he was one of two. Another eye, deep-
piercing as his, and with a no less wide horizon,
was looking out across the same perplexed scene,
and asking his heart, too, what God would tell him
of it. Some one says that the accident of a ten
years' earlier or later birth into this world may
determine the whole direction and meaning of the
most powerful of minds. The accident of local
circumstances may produce the same result. Men
form their texture out of the atmosphere which
they inhale, and incline this way or that way as the
current of the wind in which they stand. Newman
grew up in Oxford, in lectures, and college chapels,
and school divinity; Mr. Carlyle, in the Scotch
Highlands, and the poetry of Goëthe. I shall not
in this place attempt to acknowledge all I owe to
this very great man; but, about three years before
Newman's secession, chance threw in my way the
" History of the French Revolution." I shall but
caricature my feelings if I attempt to express them;
and, therefore, I will only say that for the first time
now it was brought home to me, that two men may
be as sincere, as earnest, as faithful, as uncompro-
mising, and yet hold opinions far asunder as the
poles. I have before said that I think the moment
of this conviction is the most perilous crisis of our
lives; for myself, it threw me at once on my own

responsibility, and obliged me to look for myself at what men said, instead of simply accepting all because they said it. I began to look about me to listen to what had to be said on many sides of the question, and try, as far as I could, to give it all fair hearing.

Newman talked much to us of the surrender of reason. Reason, first of every thing, must be swept away, so daily more and more unreasonable appeared to modern eyes so many of the doctrines to which the Church was committed. As I began to look into what he said about it, the more difficult it seemed to me. What did it mean? Reason could only be surrendered by an act of reason. Even the Church's infallible judgments could only be received through the senses, and apprehended by reason; why, if reason was a false guide, should we trust one act of it more than another? Fall back on human faculty somewhere we must, and how could a superstructure stone be raised on a chaff foundation? While I was perplexing myself about this, there came a sermon from him in St. Mary's, once much spoken of, containing a celebrated sentence. The sermon is that on the development of religious doctrine—the sentence is this: "Scripture says the earth is stationary and the sun moves; science, that the sun is stationary and that the earth moves." For a moment it seemed as if every one present heard, in those words, the very thing they had all wished for and had long waited for—the final mesothesis for the reconciling the two great rivals, Science and Revelation; and yet it was that sentence which at once cleared up my doubts the other way, and finally destroyed the faith I had in Newman, after "Tract 90" had shaken it.   For to what conclusions will it drive us?   If Scripture does not use the word "motion" in the sense in which common writers use it, it uses it in some trans-cendental sense by hypothesis beyond our know-ledge.   Therefore Scripture tells us nothing except what may be a metaphysical unattainable truth. But if Scripture uses one word in such sense with-out giving us warning, why not more words?— Why not every word and every sentence?   And Scripture, instead of a revelation, becomes a huge mysterious combination of one knows not what; and, what is worse, seeming all the while to have a plain and easy meaning constructed purposely to lead us astray.   The very thing which Des Cartes, at the outset of his philosophy, thought it necessary to examine the probability of, whether, that is, *Deus quidam deceptor existat*, who can inten-tionally deceive us.   Nor is the difficulty solved in the very least by the theory of an infallible inter-pretation of Scripture.   For, by hypothesis, the interpretings are by the Holy Spirit; the same spirit which has played one such strange trick, and may therefore do it again; nay, is most likely to do it again and again.

This is carrying out the renunciation of the rea-son with a vengeance.   Perhaps it is consistent, the legitimate development of the idea; the position

which all defenders of Bible infallibility must at last
be driven to assume. Deepest credulity and deepest
scepticism have been commonly believed to be near
neighbours; but we have but to state it in its naked-
ness, and the strain so long drawn by the mystery
of revelation upon submission and distrust of our
own ignorance is overdrawn at last. . . . . . . We
may not know much, but we know enough to feel
that, if mankind were compelled to accept a doctrine
so monstrous, suicide and madness would speedily
make empty benches in the Church Catholic.

No; once for all, I felt this could not be. If
there were no other way to save Scripture than this,
then, in the name of plain sense and honesty, let
Scripture go.   Yet, here we had been brought at
last, amidst the noise and clatter of tongues, and
that by a man who had the deepest moral insight
into the human heart, and the keenest of logical
intellects.   It was enough to shake our confidence
in our own reason that his reason could accept and
be satisfied by such a theory ; and certainly, let passion adopt what view it will, that treacherous wit of
ours will contrive to make a case for it.

Here it was at any rate that I finally cast off.
Farther along that track I would not go.   I could
not then see the full force of the alternative, and the
compelling causes which were urging him.   I could
not believe all was indeed so utterly at stake.   I
would try for myself.   He went on to the end—to
the haven where sooner or later it was now clear he
must anchor at last.   The arguments for the Ca-

tholicity of the English church continued the same, but he on whom they were to tell was changed. He might have borne her supineness if he could have found the life in her for which he thirsted; but, as his desires deepened with his advances in the real feeling of Christianity, it was natural that his heart should incline where he could find them most fully gratified.

If there be any such thing as sin, in proportion to the depth with which men feel it, they will gravitate towards Rome.

If it be true that the souls even of holy men are as continually contracting infirmity as their bodies are; if absolution is as constantly necessary for the one as ablution is for the other; as men of cleanly habits of body are more sensitive to the most trifling dirt spot, so men of sensitive consciences are miserable under taints upon a surface which to a vulgar eye seems pure as snow . . . . add to this the conviction that the priest's voice and hand alone can dispense the purifying stream; and beyond question, where the fountain runs the fullest, thither they will seek to go.

And sin with Newman was real; not a misfortune to be pitied and allowed for; to be talked of gravely in the pulpit, and forgotten when out of it; not a thing to be sentimentally sighed over at the evening tea-party, with complacent feeling that we were pleasing Heaven by calling ourselves children of hell, but in very truth a dreadful monster, a real child of a real devil, so dreadful that at its first

appearance among mankind it had convulsed the
infinite universe, and that nothing less than a sacrifice, so tremendous that the mind sinks crushed
before the contemplation of it, could restore the
deranged balance. Unreasonable as it seemed, he
really believed this; and, given such an element
among us as this, one may well give over hope of
finding truth by reasonable analysis and examination of evidence. One must go with what haste one
can to the system which best understands this monster sin, which is best provided with remedies and
arms against it. To the dry mathematicizing reason, the Catholic, the Anglo-Catholic, the Lutheran,
Calvinist, the Socinian, will be equally unacceptable;
and the philosopher will somewhat contemptuously
decline giving either of them the intellectual advantage. But sin is of faith, not of mathematics. And
a real human heart, strong enough and deep enough
to see it and feel it in its enormity, will surely
choose from among the various religions that one
where the sacraments are most numerous and most
constant, and absolution is more than a name, and
confession is possible without episcopal interdict-
ings.

For myself I fell off; not because I had determined not to follow, but because I had not yet felt
this intensity of hunger and of thirst which could
drive me to accept the alternative, and consent to
so entire an abandonment of myself. I had learnt
enough of the reality and awfulness of human life

not to play with it; and I shrunk before what at least might be a sin against my own soul.

My eyes were opening slowly to see for myself the strangeness of this being of ours. I had flung myself off into space, and seen this little earth ball careering through its depths; this miserable ball, not a sand grain in the huge universe of suns, and yet to which such a strangely mysterious destiny was said to have been attached. I had said to myself, Can it be that God, Almighty God, He, the Creator himself, went down and took the form of one of those miserable insects crawling on its surface, and died Himself to save their souls? I had asked the question. Did ever man ask it honestly, and answer *yes?* Many men have asked it with a foregone conclusion; but that is not to ask it. I say, did ever man who doubted, find his own heart give him back the Church's answer?

I know not. I answered nothing; but I went down again upon my old earth home; and, with no anxiety for claiming any so high kindred for my race, I felt myself one among them; I felt that they were my brothers, and among them my lot was cast. I could not wish them to be children of heaven; neither could I make away their weaker ones to hell; they were all my fellows; I could feel with them all, and love them all. For me this world was neither so high nor so low as the Church would have it; chequered over with its wild light shadows, I could love it and all the children of it, more dearly, perhaps, because it was not all light.   "These many men so beautiful," they should be neither God's children nor the Devil's children, but children of men.

Here ends this manuscript, abruptly.   I know not what others may think of it . . . . . To me, at least, as I read it, it seemed as if my friend were working round, slowly perhaps, but surely, to a stronger and more real grasp of life; and, if he could only have been permitted some few months or years of further silent communing with himself, the reeling rocking body might have steadied into a more constant motion.   But unhappily the trials of life will not wait for us.   They come at their own time, not caring much to inquire how ready we may be to meet them . . . . and we little know what we are doing when we cast adrift from system.   "How is it," said Martin Luther's wife to him, "that in the old Church we used to pray so often and so earnestly, and now we can but mutter a few words a poor once a day, with hearts far enough away" . . . . Even superstition is a bracing girdle, which the frame that is trained to it can ill afford to lose.

Markham was beginning to find a happiness to which he had been long a stranger.   With his books and his pen he was making a kind of employment for himself; and, better perhaps than this, he was employing a knowledge of medicine, which at one time he had studied more than superficially, much to the advantage of many peasant families, with which he made acquaintance in his rambles. In this way passed along the winter. He had rooms in a small cottage close to the water; and with the help of a little skiff he had made for himself, as the spring came on, and the sky and the earth put on their beauty again, the fair shores of the lovely lake unfolded all their treasures to him, and reproached him into peace. . . . . A dreamer he was, and ever would be. Yet dreaming need not injure us, if it do but take its turn with waking; and even dreams themselves may be turned to beauty, by favoured men to whom nature has given the powers of casting them into form. "The accomplishment of verse" had not been granted to Markham; but music was able to do for him what language could not, and the flute obeyed him as its master. Many an evening the peasants wandering homewards along the shore had stood still to listen to sounds rising from the water which they little thought were caused by English breath; and the nightingales took their turn to listen to notes as sweet and more varied than their own. After all, it is no sign of ill health of mind, this power of self-surrender to the emotions which nature breathes upon us. We are like the wind harp under the summer breeze, and we may almost test how far our spirits are in tune with hers by the vagrant voices they send forth as she sweeps across their strings.

One evening late in May he was drifting lan-

guidly down the little bay which lay before his
window; the faintest air was slowly fanning him
towards the land; it was too faint even to curl the
dreamy surface of the lake; only it served to catch
the notes which were rising from off his flute and
bear them in fuller sweetness over the few hundred
yards of water to the shore.   He had been lying in
this way an hour perhaps or more, playing as the
feeling rose, or pausing to watch the gold and
crimson fading from off the sky, and the mellow
planets streaming out with their double image in
the air and in the lake.   His boat drifting against
the shore warned him at last to rise; he sprung out,
and drew it up beyond danger of the waves, and
then for the first time observed that he had another
listener besides the nightingales.   A lady was sitting on the grass bank immediately behind where
he was standing.   It was too dark to let him see
her face; but, as she rose hastily, he perceived that
she was young and her figure very elegant; and it
struck him that there was something English about
it.   He took his hat off as he made way for her to
pass him, and something seemed to pass between
her lips, as if her involuntary admiration was melting into a half-conscious acknowledgment.   He
returned home, and the next evening, on coming in
from a walk, he found on his table the card of a Mr.
Leonard.   He was the husband of the lady.   She
had sent him, it appeared, to make the acquaintance
of a countryman whom she had recognized by the
old English airs.

Mr. Leonard was an easy, good-natured, not very sensible English country gentleman, whose fortune more than whose person had some years before induced a certain noble family at home to dispose of an encumbrance to him . . . . . in the form of a distantly related young lady who had been thrown upon them for support. She only knowing neglect where she was, and what of duty she had ever been taught being the duty simply of marrying well and early to gain an independent position, had no courage, perhaps no wish, to decline Mr. Leonard's proposals. Her personal beauty had been his attraction. She had married him, and ever since had been tolerating a sort of inert existence, which she did not know to be a wretched one, only because her heart was still in its chrysalis, and she had never experienced another. It could not have been with any active pleasure that she found herself chained for a life to a person she was obliged to struggle not to despise, and glimpses now and then of some higher state would flash across her like a pang of remorse . . . . . but, rare and fleeting as they were, they had passed by her like the strange misgivings which from time to time flit about us all of some other second life we have lived we know not where, and had happily been without the power to wake her out of her apathetic endurance. The Leonards had gone to Italy, as English people do go there; she had longed to be taken there, because it was the land of art and poetry, and music and old associations—the land of romance and loveliest nature; he, because it was the right thing to have been there; because it would please his wife; and because he was promised a variety in the sporting amusements which were his only pleasure.

Ah! if those good world educators, who in early life crush the young shootings of the heart, and blight its growth in their pestilential atmosphere, would but innaturate it with their poison and make it barren for ever! how many a crime, as they are pleased to call it, would be spared . . . . But they only half do their work; they cut off the fruit, but they leave the life remaining; to wake at enmity with all it finds, and to speak only to betray. The Leonards were to go to Rome in the winter; but for the hot months, as the style of friends whom he liked best to visit were not the sort which best suited her, and as she found the shores of an Italian lake a more agreeable retiring place, they came to a kind of a compromise. He took a villa near Como, which she and her young child were to make their home; while he, who had many acquaintances, received a dispensation from constant attendance, and was allowed to relieve the monotony by frequent absence, leaving her in a solitude which, if the truth must be told, was more agreeable than his society, and only coming back to her now and then for a week at a time. He liked her very well, but a longer tête-a-tête after four years of marriage fatigued him. It was at one of these angel visits that she had seen Markham. They inquired who he was, and were told he was an Englishman, and

out of health. She had learned something more
of him in that evening music, which told her he
was not a common Englishman; and Leonard, who
had a theory of race, and believed with all his heart
in the absolute virtue of everything English, was
very happy to call upon him. The visit was returned. Markham was not quite a model Saxon,
and illness too was a drawback, a certain rude
health being part of the national idea; but Leonard
liked him well enough to make this week a fortnight; and, at the end of it, their new friend had
become so intimate with them, that under plea of
his requiring attendance, and with the excuse that
they had found out a number of common acquaintances at home which in Italy made them seem
almost to have claims upon one another, they had
begged him to leave his lodgings and make their
house his home.

It was the very thing for Leonard. He had an
excuse now for going away; while before he had felt
some compunction at leaving his wife so much
alone, however poor a companion he felt he could
be for her. But a nice pleasant fellow who played
the flute and talked poetry would far more than
supply his absence; and, with the honest English
confidence which is almost stupidity, he rejoiced for
his lady's sake at the friend which had been found
for her, and now stayed away as he pleased without
care or anxiety.

Women's eyes are rapid in detecting a heart which
is ill at ease with itself, and, knowing the value of

sympathy, and finding their own greatest happiness
not in receiving it, but in giving it, with them to be
unhappy is at once to be interesting. They never
ask for others' sympathy with them; they do not recognise their own troubles as of enough importance to any but themselves. But instinct teaches
them their power; they know what they can be to
others: they feel their gentle calling and they follow
it. . . . . It is curious too, whether it be that
people always admire most in others what they
have the least in themselves—whatever be the reason
—there is no kind of suffering in which they take
warmer interest, than the heart's sufferings over intellectual perplexities. Many women have died of
broken hearts, but no woman's heart ever broke in such
a trial . . . . yet it is just those into which they are
the least able to enter, that they seem most to sympathise in. Whether it be that such a case is a rare
exchange from the vulgar personal anxieties of common people, and they know that only a generous heart
can feel deeply on a question in which all the world
have as deep a stake as itself; whether, the danger
being said to be so great, a sceptic seems brave and
noble to risk it for the love of truth—I cannot tell
why it is, but I think no more dangerous person than
Markham could have been thrown in the way of Mrs.
Leonard. His conversation was so unlike any she
had ever heard before; his manner was so gentle; his
disinterestedness in sacrificing his home, his friends,
his fortune, as it seemed to her, was so truly heroic—
that he almost appeared like a being of another

I

world to her; and, long before she had dared to think
that her regard could be anything to him, she had at
the bottom of her heart resolved that she would be
all to him which others were not and ought to have
been; and, in intending to be his sister, had already
begun to love him more dearly than any sister.

Their worst danger lay in their security: neither
of them had ever loved before, so that neither
could detect the meaning of their emotions. If the
idea of the possibility of his loving a married
woman, as husbands love, had been suggested to
Markham, he would have driven it from him with
horror; . . . . and she in her experience of marriage
had had no experience of love; she did not know
into how false a life she had betrayed herself. She
did not know that she was unhappy with her husband; her unrest was but of the vague indefinite kind
that rises in a dreary heart which feels that it might
be happy, yet cannot distinguish what it requires to
make it so. Poor thing, she was only twenty-five!
Nature had sown the seeds in her of some of the
fairest of her flowers, but had taken no care for
their culture; and they were lying still in the emrbyo,
waiting for light and heart to wake them into life. . . .
It were better they had been left to die unborn than
that the light should have flowed in upon them from
Markham. How can we help loving best those who
first give us possession of ourselves? All the day
long they were together: living as they did, they
could not help being so; . . . . . only parting at
night for a few short hours to dream over the happy

past day, and to meet again the next morning, the happier for their brief separation.   It was a new life to him: what had often hung before him as a fairy vision—what he had longed for, but never found; and here, as if sent down from heaven, was what more than answered to his wildest dreams. Now for the first time he found himself loved for himself—slighted and neglected as he had been . . . . suddenly he was singled out by a fascinating woman, who made no secret of the pleasure his friendship gave her. All along his life he had turned with disgust from every word which was sullied with any breath of impurity; the poetry of voluptuous passion he had loathed. Alas! it would have been better far for him if it had not been so.   He would have had the experience of his fallen nature to warn him by the taste of the fruit which it had borne in others.

Mrs. Leonard's little girl, too, was not long in discovering that he was her most delightful companion. It was easy for children to love Markham ; he knew how to abandon himself; and there they sat these two, the child the third; the common element in which their hearts could meet ; Leonard seldom paid much attention to the little Annie, and she transferred her duty as well as her love to her friend : and when she would wind her fingers into his hair as she sat upon his knee, and kiss him and call him papa, he could meet her mother's sweet smiling eyes with a smile as innocent and unconscious as her own.   Through the heat of the day they stayed in the cool drawing-room. If Annie was sleeping, she would draw or work, and Markham would read. He read well, for he read generally his own favourites which he knew, so that, unless she looked at him, the words fell from him as if they were his own. Nor less happy was she when, instead of reading, he would talk to her, and, never having known a willing listener before, would now pour out the long pent-up stream of his own thoughts and feelings. Weak Markham! in the intense interest with which she hung upon his lips, he fancied he saw interest in the subject, which was only interest in himself.

In the evenings they would saunter down to the boat-house, and go out upon the lake. They seldom took a servant to row them; it was more pleasant to be alone: they felt it was, though they had not told themselves why it was; ah! how near are two hearts together when they understand each other without expression.

They were both passionately fond of music. He always took his flute, ... she would sing when he was tired of playing, and each soon learnt to feign fatigue for the pleasure of listening to the other.

It would be easy to linger over these scenes, yet they can give but small pleasure to us. Those two might. be happy in them, only feeling themselves gliding along a sunny stream between flowery meadow banks; but we, who hear the roar of the cataracts, can ill pardon the delirium which, only listening to the sweet voices of the present, holds its ears tight closed against every other . . . . So wise are we for each other . . . . while each one of us has his own small dream, too, over which he, too, is slumbering as foolishly as they, and is as much the mark of his wide-eyed neighbour's scorn.

Week hurried after week; when they met in the morning, they made their plans for the day, each sure that the other's pleasure was what each was most designing for. " Ils commençaient à dire *nous*. Ah, qu'il est touchant, ce nous prononcé par l'amour." . . . And it was par l'amour. The altered tone of their voices showed it; the hesitating tenderness of their glances showed it; the hand lingering in the hand when it had far more than said its morning greeting or its evening parting; and yet they did not know. . . . . They will soon know it now. . . . . The two metals are melting fast in the warm love fire; they are softening and flowing in and out, vein within vein, a few more degrees of heat, and then . . . . . A month had passed, still Leonard did not return. Letters came instead of Leonard. He knew his wife was happy, he said: and as nothing made him so happy as to know that she was so, and as he could not add to it, he was going with Count —— to a castle in the Apennines. He would be absent another six weeks, or perhaps two months; when he would return finally to stay till their removal to Rome; where Markham was to be persuaded to go with them.

Markham had not been very well again. His chest had been troublesome; he had caught cold from staying too late upon the lake, and, for a day or two, was unable to leave the sofa.   One very hot afternoon, Mrs. Leonard had been up-stairs for some little time with Annie; and, on her return, he was sleeping: she glided noiselessly to his side and sat down.   Some few intense enjoyments are given us in life; among them all, perhaps, there is none with so deep a charm as to sit by the side of those we love, and watch them sleeping.   Sleep is so innocent, so peaceful in its mystery and its helplessness; and sitting there we can fancy ourselves the guardian angels holding off the thousand evils imagination paints for ever hanging over what is most precious, most dear to us.   The long deep-drawn breathing; the smile we love to hope is called up over the features by our own presence in the heart; there are no moments in life we would exchange for the few we have spent by the side of these.   What thoughts, in that long half-hour, passed through the lady's mind, I cannot tell.   Markham felt that she was close to him; he was sleeping so lightly, that it was rather he would not than he could not rouse himself, to wake and break so sweet a charm. She was bending over him; he felt her breath tremble down upon his lips; her long ringlets were playing upon his cheek with their strange electric touches.   As she gazed down so close upon him, she forgot her self-command; a tear fell upon his face.   He opened his eyes, and they met hers full and clear.   She did not turn away; no confusion shook into her features.   She was but feeling how dear, how intensely dear he was to her; and there was no room for any other thought. One arm was leaning over the end of the sofa behind his head; the other had fallen down, and was resting on a cushion by her side. Her look, her attitude, those passionately tender tears, all told him the depth, the bewildering depth of her love. He caught the hand which lay beside him, and pressed it to his lips; and, as it lay upon them, he felt it was not only his own which held it there. Dear, dear Mrs. Leonard, was all he could say. How poor and yet how full! Not long volumes of love poetry and wildest passion could bear more of tenderness to the ear which could catch their intonation than these few words. Their lips formed no sound, only they trembled convulsively. They wished, and knew not what they wished; a minute passed, another, another, and still he lay there unmoving, and she was kneeling at his side. Her hand was still clasped in his, and they felt each other's beating hearts in their wild and wilder pulsations; from time to time the fingers closed tighter round their grasp, and thoughts they could not, dared not utter, thrilled through and through them. They did *not* utter them. It was something in the after-struggle to feel that at least no words, no fatal words, had passed. Their treacherous consciences cheated them into a delusive satisfaction that as yet, at least, they had not sinned. How long a time passed by they knew not, for time is only marked by change of thought and shifting feeling, and theirs was but one long-absorbing consciousness of a delicious present.

But the change came at last. Interruption, not
from within, but from the outer world which they had
forgotten. Ah, Heaven! that at such a moment
such a messenger was sent to break the spell. There
was a knock, and the door handle turned faintly;
she started. It was more, perhaps, from the in-
stinctive delicacy which would hide its deepest feelings from common eye, than from any sense of
guilt, and yet something, something shot through
her she would have ill liked to explain to herself.
She sprung up, and threw herself in a chair as the
door opened; and little Annie came tottering in,
came in bright and innocent, in there where the
two friends were she loved so dearly, to hide her
laughing face on the knees of mamma.

It was more than Markham could bear. Far better he could have faced her husband in his anger—
better have borne, perhaps, at that moment to have
heard his summons to the judgment bar, than that
bright presence of unsuspicious innocence. He
started from the sofa, and holding his hands before
his face, concealing himself from he knew not what,
only feeling how ill it all was now with him, and
seeming to meet the all-seeing Eye wherever his own
eye fell; he ran out of the room, and, hurrying to
his closet, flung himself in an agony upon his bed.
The child looked wonderingly at him. "Mamma,"
she said, "is Mr. Sutherland ill? go to him, mamma
—take me, and let us make him happy." Mrs.
Leonard's tears burst in streams over her little face,
from which she dried them off again with passionate

kisses; and, flinging herself upon her knees, she prayed that Heaven would strengthen her and forgive her if she was doing wrong.

And yet God helps not those who do not help themselves, and she had not the strength to fulfil her share of the condition. She hoped for strength to control her feelings, and yet she could not command herself to send the temptation from her. Twice she moved towards her writing-table: a note should go to Markham, and tell him, pray him, for both their sakes, to go away and leave her. Twice her heart failed. The third time the emotion rose, it was not strong enough to move her from her seat. And then insidious reason pressed up to urge a thousand arguments that it was far better he should stay. Both he and she knew themselves now: she knew him too well to fear that Markham was one of those men who, themselves yielding to every emotion, think less of the woman who is only as weak, no weaker, than themselves. No, he was too human to have withdrawn his respect from her; but they were on their guard now, and could never be in danger again. So sad, too, so lonely as he had been; and now his health so delicate; and she who had promised to be all to him which others should have been—she who, perhaps, alone understood him, and could sympathise with him. How could she, why should she, send him from her? Her husband, too, what reason could she give to him? Why need it be? Because she loved him —because he loved her. Surely that was a strange

reason; and, besides, they knew that before. Often
and often they had said how dear they had become
to one another. And now what difference? Because she would gladly have been more to him than
she could be—because she felt (she did not deny it
to herself) that she would sooner have been his
wife than Leonard's. But why? because they could
not be all to one another, must they be as nothing?
Dear friends they had been, and might still be, and
then—and then—there was something cowardly in
flying from temptation—mere temptation. How
far nobler to meet and overcome our feelings than
basely to fly from them! She had duties—dear
duties—to Markham as well as to her husband;
she would forget this afternoon, he would forget it,
and all would be as it had been.

There was something still which she had not explained—she had not satisfied: the last nerve of
conscience which she had failed to paralyse still
whispered it was all wrong—it was sophistry and
madness; but the dull unimpassioned voice was
unheard among the voluptuous melodies of her
wishes; and like the doomed city, which shrunk
from the voice of the prophetess, she pushed its
warnings from her as idle superstition.

When they met again at the tea table, all was not
as it had been; such as that it could never be again.
Markham, too, in his silent room had felt that there
was no safety for them but in parting; and the same
devil of sophistry had been at his ear whispering to
him. He had long left off writing, even thinking;

that was over when he had ceased to be alone.   He
had been in the trial of life since then, where the sun
and the wind had fallen upon his theories to test them.
Alas! where were they ?   Whirling like the sibyl's
idle leaves before the passion gust. . . . . Unequal to
the effort of a final resolution, yet still forcing himself to do something, he made a compromise with
his sense of duty.   He would do a little if he would
not do all, and he wrote to Leonard urging his return.   Unable to give the real reason, he invented
false reasons : he said his wife was delicate—he said
that for opinion's sake it was better her husband
should, by a more frequent presence, show, at least,
his approval of his own intimacy with her; that
he could not urge this upon her himself as an occasion for his own departure; and, therefore, he
had thought it better to write openly to him.   In
this way he satisfied himself that he had done all
he need do, and, let the future be what it would, he
had ceased to be responsible.

   Fools, and blind!   They might have read each
the answer to their delusive pleadings, each in their
common embarrassment.   They were uneasy when
alone ; their voices trembled as they spoke ; they
made no allusion to the past ; they could not speak
of it : it would have been far better if they could.
In open speaking and mutual confession *then*, there
would, at least, have been a chance of safety for
them ; their game would have been all upon the
board, and they would have taken counsel.   We are
often strong enough to persuade another against our

own wishes, when we have ceased to be able to persuade ourselves. But this neither of them dared to
begin to do. Perhaps it was impossible. Strange!
they fancied they intended to be less together, and
yet their outer lives went on as before. They left
off for a few days saying " *we*," but their eyes said
it with deeper tenderness than ever their lips had
done. They shrunk openly from each other's gaze,
yet each would catch the opportunity, when the
other's was turned away, to look as they had never
dared to look before; and now they could feel the
glances which they did not see, thrilling through them
like those on that memorable afternoon. Leonard's
answer came. It was what Markham knew it would be
when he wrote, though he had not confessed it to
himself:—" He was sorry his wife was out of health,
but Markham was a better sick-nurse than he was;
he would not hear of his leaving her. As to the
world, what had the world to do with him? He
knew them both, and could trust them too well to
let any such folly touch him ;"—and such other con-
fiding madness as so often in this world makes love
to ruin.

And Markham did not go. He never thought of
going now. His conscience was satisfied with what
he had done. Unsteady as it was, and without the
support which a strongly believed religious faith had
once provided for it, he experienced at last what so
long he had denied, that to attempt to separate morality from religion is madness; that religion, reduced to
a sentiment resting only on internal emotion, is like

a dissolving view, which will change its image as the passions shift their focal distances; that, unrealized in some constant external form, obeying inclination, not controlling it, it is but a dreamy phantom of painted shadow, and vanishes before temptation as the bright colours fade from off the earth when a storm covers the sun.

Rather, in a mind like Markham's, unsupported as his mind was, there is no conduct to which these vague emotions will not condescend to adapt themselves, and which they will not varnish into loveliness. If there be one prayer which, morning, noon, and night, one and all of us should send up to God, it is, "Save us from our own hearts!" Oh! there is no lie we will not tell ourselves. The enchanted Armida garden of love!—how like, how like it is to Paradise! Dreams, delusion, fantastic prejudice it may be called, which a strong mind should spurn from it as a fable of the nursery – ay, should spurn—if it can. Are not ashes bitter on the tongue, though you bring proof in all the logic figures that they are sweet as Hybla honey? And those pleasures which are honey-sweet to the first taste, is there not the sting with its venom-bag lying unseen? Ah! we know not; we know not; we know nothing. But something we can feel; and what is it to us what we know, when we are miserable? All men may not feel so. There are some who, as Jean Paul says, Mithridates-like, feed on poison, and suffer nothing from it; but all tender hearts, who remember the feeling of innocence, will try

long before they can reason away the bitterness out
of pleasure which once they have believed not innocent.   It is ill changing the creed to meet each
rising temptation.   The soul is truer than it seems,
and refuses to be trifled with.

Day followed after day, bringing with it what it
was God's great will should be.   I will not pause
over these sad weeks of intoxicating delirium.   If
they did not fall as vulgar minds count falling, what
is that to those who look into the heart?   Her promise of her heart's truth was broken; and he loved
her as he should not love; as once, he would have
loathed himself if he could have believed he could
ever love the plighted wife of another.   I will not
judge them.   Alas, what judgment could touch
them is past and over now!

It is strange, when something rises before us as a
possibility which we have hitherto believed to be
very dreadful, we fancy it is a great crisis; that
when we pass it we shall be different beings; some
mighty change will have swept over our nature, and
we shall lose entirely all our old selves, and become
others.—Much as, in another way, girls and boys
feel towards their first communion, or young men
to their ordination, which mechanically is to effect
some great improvement in them, there are certain
things which we consider sacraments of evil, which
will make us, if we share in them, wholly evil.   Yet,
when the thing, whether good or evil, is done, we
find we were mistaken; we are seemingly much the
same—neither much better nor worse; and then

we cannot make it out; on either side there is a weakening of faith; we fancy we have been taken in; the mountain has been in labour, and we are perplexed to find the good less powerful than we expected, and the evil less evil.

Only, long after, when the first crime has begotten its children, and the dark catalogue of consequences follows out to make clear their parent's nature; when in lonely hours we are driven in upon ourselves, and the images of our unfallen days come flitting phantom-like around us, gazing in so sadly, like angels weeping for a lost soul; when we are forced to know what then we were, and, side by side with it, stands the figure of what we have become, it is then that what has passed over us comes out in its real terrors. Our characters change as world eras change, as our features change, slowly from day to day. Nothing is sudden in this world. Inch by inch; drop by drop; line by line. Even when great convulsions shatter down whole nations, cities, monarchies, systems, human fortunes, still they are but the finish, the last act of the same long preparing, slowly devouring change, in which the tide of human affairs for ever ebbs and flows, without haste, and without rest. Well, so it was with Markham. This final fall of his was but the result of the slow collapsing of his system. His moral nature had been lowered down to it before he sinned; he did not feel any such mighty change; he was surprised to find how easily it lay upon him. Then, in the first delirious trance of happiness, he

seemed to laugh to himself at his old worn-out prejudices. He had been worshipping an idol, which
he had but to dare to disobey, to learn how helpless
the insulted Deity was to avenge itself. He could
still cheat himself with words. He had not yet heard
the voice of God calling him. His eyes were opened,
not as yet to evil, but only to find himself in a new
existence, which he could even dream was a higher
and a nobler one. And she—she—when a woman's
heart is flowing over for the first time with deep
and passionate love, she is all love. Every faculty
of her soul rushes together in the intensity of the
one feeling; thought, reflection, conscience, duty, the
past, the future, they are names to her light as the
breath which speaks them; her soul is full. Markham was all these to her; her life, her hope, her
happiness. Fearfully mysterious as it is, yet even
love, which should never be, yet does not lose its
nobleness; so absolutely it can enthral a woman's
nature, that self, that cunningest of demons, is deceived, and flies before the counterfeit. Her love
is all her thought, her care, her worship. To die for
Markham would have been as delightful to Helen
as the martyr's stake to a saint. I say it is a fearful
mystery that, if love like theirs be what all men say
it is, such heroism for it is possible. Yet, indeed, it is
but possible for woman, not for man; a man can
give his entire soul to an idea, not to a woman—
some second thought, even with the highest of us,
and in the most permitted relation, will always
divide his place with her; it is ever Abelard and

Eloise; Eloise loves Abelard all; Abelard loves intellect and the battle of the truth.

Well, on went the summer. They never looked forward, no thought of their guilt had yet intruded to disturb them. How could anything so beautiful be less than good? Even Annie, Markham could again bear upon his knee, and could laugh and tell her stories as he used to do. They took her with them in their rambles; she was their boat companion in their lovely evenings upon the water, and once, when the poor child was suffering from inflammatory fever, no father could have watched more anxiously, no physician more carefully put out his skill for her than he did.

At last September came. The finger of love is ineffectual on the wheel of Time; and, though the summer was deepening in loveliness, the changing tints betrayed that they were but purchasing their beauty at the price of decay; and now, as it grew clear that some change must come, something must happen soon, Markham began to grow uneasy. In one month at furthest Leonard would return, and what was to follow then? And his lips flagged in their eloquence, and the clouds began to gather again about his face—and she saw them, and dimly read the cause, which she feared to ask. It was a beautiful afternoon. They had gone, he, she, and Annie, to a distant island up the lake. They had taken a basket with them, and a few cold things, as they often did, and they were not going to return till the cool of the last daylight. The island was

several miles away, and they had overstayed the
time when prudence would have warned them homewards, in rambling about the place, and making
sketches of an old ruined chapel, which on certain
holidays was still a place of pious pilgrimage. It
wanted still an hour of dark, when they re-embarked,
and as a light warm air had sprung up, and Markham had taken a small sail with him, they still
hoped they would be at home before it. Their
anxiety was more for Annie than themselves. They
had often overstayed the sunset, and laughed to
find, when darkness came, how time had glided
by with them; but Annie had been ill, and was
still delicate . . . . Well, the skiff was shooting away
under the sunset; the purple sky above them, the
purple wave below them; they were sitting together in the stern, and Annie was scrambling about
the boat, now listening to the rippling music of the
water under the bow, now clapping her little hands
in ecstasy at the lovely light flashing and sparkling
with a thousand glorious colours in the long frothy
wake the thin keel had carved along the surface.
Markham told her to come over to them and sit
quiet; but they did not seem disposed to talk to
her, and at last, under condition of her promising
to be perfectly still, he consented to let her stay by
herself under the sail, fenced in with cushions.

They were sad those two, and, for a long time,
silent. A painful unexplained uneasiness was hanging over both of them. Thoughts were playing
across his mind which he feared to share with her,

for fear he might strike some unlucky chord. If, as has been said, it be true that things which concern us most nearly have an atmosphere around them, which we feel when we are entering; that, like birds before a storm, we are conscious of the coming change—perhaps it was another weight which was sinking down their spirits.

At last, as when after we have been some time in darkness, our eyes expand, and objects slowly glimmer out before them into form, so their words began to flow out of the silence, and for the first time Markham spoke of the future.

"Another month—and Leonard will return," he said, in a thick, half-stifled voice . . . . "and then?"

"I am yours, Markham," she said. "Dear Markham, you will never leave me?"

"Leave you! Helen," he answered; "never with my will; but it may not be mine to choose."

"Oh! yes, yes, it will, it shall. Do not think I have not thought of it. I know what I am going to do."

He looked inquiringly at her. "Leonard must know we love each other, Helen. We could not, if we would, conceal it from him."

"Conceal it? Deceive him?" she answered, proudly. "No, not if he was as base as he is noble-minded and generous. Never."

"Well!" he said, hesitating.

"Well," she answered; "well, I will tell him all. I will throw myself at his feet, and ask his forgiveness ; not for loving you, but for ever having been his. That was my sin ; to promise I knew not what, and what I could not fulfil."

Markham smiled bitterly.

" I will tell him," she went on ; " I will tell him I never loved him ; only till I knew you I did not know it. I will do my duty ; I will be his servant, if he wishes it. I have done everything for him at home ; I will do all that, and far more than all— only as he cannot have my heart . . . . I . . . . I . . . . Surely, if he cannot have it, my heart can be little to him if I give it to you."

Poor, poor thing, when she had lived in the world she had still lived out of it, and turned a deaf ear to its voices. She had no idea what she was doing. Ill instructed as she had been religiously, her instinct had recoiled from the worldly instruction which she might have learnt as a substitute ; and she had no notion of right and wrong beyond what her heart said to her.

" That is what you think, Helen," Markham answered. " Now, I will tell you what I think. When you tell him what I am to you, he will kill me, and for you . . . . ."

" For me ; if it were so, I would die with you, Markham ; we cannot live without each other. If we have broken this world's laws, and must die, then love will give us strength."

Markham shuddered. " We might fly," he said.

" Is it really certain that he will separate us, Markham, as soon as he knows ?"

"Certain," he answered. "Every man would feel it his duty; I should myself if I were as he is."

"Markham, Markham," she said, passionately, "in all the world I have not a friend—not one; till I knew you I never knew what love, what friendship meant. There is none but you on whom I can lean; there is none to whom I can turn even in thought. Teach me, Markham, teach me; what you tell me I will do."

"There is no hope except in flight," he answered, huskily; "if you will leave all for me, I can offer you a home, though but a poor one, and myself, in exchange for what you lose."

She was silent; her head hung down; he could not see the tears which were raining from her eyes.

"We shall do what the world forbids," he continued. "The world will punish us with its scorn. It is well. When we accept the consequences of our actions, and do not try to escape from them, we have a right to choose our own course, and do as we will."

The last words scarce reached poor Helen's ear; her heart was far away.

"Tell me, Markham," she said (and she turned her eyes, swimming with tears, full upon him)— "tell me, do not deceive me; you know the world's ways, or something of them. If I go with you, shall I ever see my child again?"

"I shall be all which will be left you then," he answered, slowly. "She is his child, and . . . ."

"And her mother's touch would taint her! Oh,

no, no. Annie, my own darling. I cannot leave
my child. No, Markham, no; all but that. I cannot . . . ." She sunk her head upon his shoulder,
and her breast shook as if her heart would burst its
prison home.

Unhappy lady, wretched Markham, the solving
of their problem was nearer than they dreamed of.
Look your last, poor baby, on that purple sunset.
Turn, gaze out your full on your ill-fated mother. The angels are already cutting their swift
way down the arch of heaven to bear away
your soul. Yon mountain, whose snow-crusted
peaks are melting into the blue of heaven, will
again put on their splendour, and glitter crimson-
flushed in the glories of the morning—but you will
never see them more. One day, and yet another,
and the sun which rises on your eyes will be the
spirit's sun that lights the palaces of heaven when
the blessed are in their everlasting home. Gaze on,
gaze on upon your mother! but a little, and then, it
must be there, if ever, that you will meet her any more.
The pure and innocent are there; you may meet her
there, for she loves you with a pure and holy love,
and love unbroken here is never broken there.

The breeze had fallen with the sunset. The
crimson had melted off the clouds; a few dissolving
specks of gray about the sky were all that was left
of the glorious vision, and through the purple air
the evening star streamed down in its sad, passionate, heart-breaking loveliness. The child had
for a long time lain still, as she had been told. At

last, tired of not being amused, she had crawled out
from under the clothes in which they had wrapped
her against the evening chill, and had begun to
find amusement for herself in looking over the
boat's side, watching the rippling bubbles as they
floated by; and the images hanging in the depths,
as if the water was a window through which she
was looking down.   It was so odd that the bubbles
moved by, and the stars did not at all, but went along
with them always so exactly in the same place.
They were not observing her as they talked.   The
boat moved slower and slower as the surface of the
lake grew still.   The deep hum of the night-beetle
sweeping by sounded strangely on her ear.   The
moon rose up into the sky.   The rays shone cold
into her face, and the little thing shrunk and shivered, and yet she gazed, and gazed.   There it was
so close to her; just under the boat's edge; rolling
and dancing on the wave that washed from off the
bow.   She could almost touch it, so near it was, a
long rolling sheet of gold.   She dipped her fingers
into the water.   It felt warm, deliciously warm,
and, when she held up her hand, the wet skin
glittered in the light.   It was the water then that
was so beautiful; and if she could only reach the
ripple it was all gold there.   She leant over below
the sail, and as she stretched out her hand her
weight brought the boat's side lower and lower
down; just then a faint, a very faint momentary
freshening of the air swept into the sail; the gun-
wale sunk suddenly, and the water rushed up her

arm into her chest. She started back. They saw her then, though they had not seen what had happened to her, and they told her to lie back again where she had been. She was quite wet; but the water seemed so warm and so pleasant, and they might scold her if she told, and she lay back, and did not tell them, and sunk asleep as she was.

———

Two hours had passed, and now they were at home again, and in Mrs. Leonard's room. The child's wet clothes had been taken off her; she was in her little bed, breathing thick and heavily. Markham was standing by her from time to time, laying his finger upon her wrist, and Helen on her knees at the bedside, with her eyes fixed upon his face, and fearing to ask anything lest her ear should be obliged to hear what she already read there too plainly. The fever was gathering every moment. When they took the little thing out of the boat, she could not tell him coherently what had happened to her, she could only moan out that she was very cold, and muttered something about the moon. Since she had been taken home she had not spoken, but every moment her forehead was growing hotter, her poor damp skin parched and dry, and her pulse quicker and more feeble.

Presently she opened her eyes, and stared wildly round her.

" Mamma, mamma," she cried. Helen leant over

her, and kissed her burning cheek, but it did not seem as if Annie was calling her, or knew her, or saw her.

"Mamma, mamma, pretty mamma, take me to you; mamma, why cannot I come to you?"

"I am here, my own darling, my own child," Helen said.

"You are not mamma. Go away, you are not mamma. There is mamma standing there, there, by the bed; beautiful! who is that in white? why do you look at me so? Yes, I wish to go, why can't I go? There, in the pretty moonlight on the water."

"She is wandering," Markham whispered; "she does not see—hush!"

"Where am I, mamma? I was never here before. Where is it? Is this heaven? Where is God? God is in heaven; I don't see him, I only see light and flowers. Ah, it is all gone, dark, dark, dark."

She shut her eyes and rolled her head upon the pillow, moaning painfully.

They had scarcely spoken yet, the other two.

"Markham, tell me," said Helen, with a fearful calmness, "is there any hope?"

"God forbid that I should say there is none, Helen," he answered slowly.

"Well," she said quickly, "tell me all, I can bear it."

"All that man can do is done," he answered; "the fever will be at its height to-morrow; till then I can tell nothing, we must leave her to God." It was all that passed between them. What more

K

at such a time could they say, with this Heaven -
lightning blazing before their eyes?

The night wore on : the shadow of the heavy curtains crept slowly across the room ; the light was painful to them, they had buried it in a shade ; they had
neither of them changed their dress, and, together,
at either side the little bed, they sat out those awful
hours. The room was deathly still ; no sound but
the heavy breathing of the child, and now and then
some strange broken words which her spirit was
speaking far away, and the sinking body was but
faintly echoing. There are some blows which are too
terrible to paralyse us, and, instead of driving consciousness away, only waken every faculty into a
dreadful sensibility. Nature has found a remedy
for the heaviest of ordinary calamities in the torpor
of despair ; but some things are beyond her care,
perhaps beyond her foresight. Perhaps, in laying
down the conditions of humanity, she shrunk from
seeing the full extreme of misery which was possible to it. We will turn in silence from Mrs.
Leonard's heart : would to God she could have
turned from it herself !

Once she raised her eyes to Markham ; the moonlight lay upon his features, and so ghastly pale they
were, that even the spectral light itself could lend
them a warmer colour. While there was anything
left to do, so long his heart had left his mind undis-
turbed to act ; but now reflection woke again, and
the past, the present, and the future shot before him
in terrible review. Let Annie live, or let her die,

he felt God had spoken to him, and he was slowly
moulding in himself his answer. Was it the voice
of warning, or the voice of judgment? To-morrow
would show.

The morrow came; the sun rose and went his way;
so slowly he had not gone the long summer through;
he sank down, and the evening fell upon the earth,
and now the crisis was come. They had never left
the room, they had taken no food, they had scarcely
spoken to each other. From time to time Markham
had turned to the child, had felt her pulse, and
poured cooling medicine between her burning lips,
and still life and death hung uncertain in the trembling balance. Mrs. Leonard had been lying for
an hour, in the greatest exhaustion, on the sofa;
about six o'clock Markham woke her, and said,
firmly, "The crisis is come now; now sit here and
watch her; if at the end of another half hour she
is alive, she will recover." He himself moved
over to the open window. There lay the deep, dark
mountains, and the silver lake, the blue cloudless
sky bending over them in unutterable beauty; the
young swallows were sweeping to and fro far up in
their airy palace; the pale blue butterflies were
sauntering from flower to flower, and every tree was
thrilling in the evening air with the impassioned
melodies of the nightingales. Never, never since
the sad wanderers flung their last lingering look on
the valleys of that fair Eden from which they and
all their race were for ever exiled, had human eyes
yet gazed upon a lovelier earthly scene than that

which now lay out below the window where Markham was standing. Alas, alas! when the heart is indeed breaking, with a grief beyond hope, beyond consoling, how agonizing is the loveliness of nature! It speaks to us of things we cannot reach. It mocks our fevered eyes with Tantalus visions of paradise, which are not for us; floating before us like phantoms in a dream, and gliding from our grasp as we stretch our arm to seize them. It is well, yes, it is well, but it is hard for the bruised heart to feel it so. All, all nature is harmonious, and must and shall be harmony for ever; even we, poor men, with our wild ways and frantic wrongs, and crimes, and follies, to the beings out beyond us and above us, seem, doubtless, moving on our own way under the broad dominion of universal law. The wretched only feel their wretchedness: in the universe all is beautiful. Ay, to those lofty beings, be they who they will, who look down from their starry thrones on the strange figures flitting to and fro over this earth of ours, the wild recklessness of us mortals with each other may well lose its *painful* interest. Why should our misdoings cause more grief to them than those of the lower animals to ourselves? Pain and pleasure are but forms of consciousness; we feel them for ourselves, and for those who are like ourselves. To man alone the doings of man are wrong; the evil which is with us dies out beyond us; we are but a part of nature, and blend with the rest in her persevering beauty.

Poor consolers are such thoughts, for they are but

thoughts, and, alas! our pain we feel. Me they may console, as I think over this farce tragedy of a world, or even over the nearer sorrows of a friend like Markham Sutherland. For Markham himself, in this half hour—they were far enough from his heart.

He was dreaming again of old times, of the old Markham, once simple and pure as that poor dying child, who could once look up with trusting heart to his Father in heaven, and pray to Him to keep him clean from sin; and his sick heart shrunk appalled from the wretched thing which he had become, and the gulf which was yawning under his feet.

A cry from Helen roused him; he collected himself rapidly, and moved across the room to her. Annie's eyes were open, the flush of pain had passed from off her face; she knew them both, and was feebly trying to stretch out her little hands towards her mother. She was dying; her eyes were glittering with a deep unearthly lustre from the visions on which she had been gazing. They had but turned back for a moment, for a last good bye, and earth and all that was dear to her on earth would be lost then, to return no more. One look was enough for Markham; he saw all was over, and he hid his face in his hands. " Good bye, mamma, I am going away; good bye, don't cry, dear mamma, I am very happy." The heavy eyelids drooped, sunk, rose again for one last glance—her mother's image only was all it caught, and the light went out for ever.

That last thought had traced the tiny features into a smile. It was the smile, the same sweet smile Mrs. Leonard knew so well, which night after night she had so often gazed upon, and had stood on tiptoe and held her breath lest she should break the sleeping charm. Ah! she may speak now loud as she will, and have no fear of breaking slumber deep as this. Still lay the little frame, still as the silent harp there before the window, but no cunning hand shall ever sweep those heart-strings to life; their sweet notes shall never, never speak again.

"It is over," Markham said, in a low voice. "She is in peace now. All-righteous God!"

Mrs. Leonard had flung herself upon the bed. The tears burst out, and fell in streams over her dead child's face. She drew it to her breast, where once its baby lips had gathered life and strength. Ah! why may it not be again? Her tears rained down, but they were not tears with which the bruised heart unloads the burden of its sorrow, but the bitter, burning tears of bewildered agony.

Her Annie, her darling; all she had till she knew Markham; she who had first made life delightful to her; who had taught her heart first to love; now dead, gone, torn from her; and, oh! worse, worse; their own doing. How it was she did not know; but their fault it was. Her nature was too weak to bear so complicated a misery, and her mind broke into disorder. Surely, yes, surely, it must have broken, or thoughts like these could never have to come to her now.

She rose steadily, and walked up to Markham, and laid her hand upon his arm.

"Markham," she said, "it is for my sin. Would, oh, would it had been myself, not she, who has been taken! It is for my sin in marrying her father. It was an offence against earth and Heaven, and the earthly trace of it is blotted out, and its memory written in my heart in letters of fire. Now, Markham, if I am not to die too, take me away. I can never see him again."

It would be difficult to conceive words which at the moment could have shocked Markham more fearfully. He, too, had seen Heaven's finger in what had been; but he thought it was a punishment for the sin which he had wished to commit—a stern and fearful interposition to save him from completing it. Strange, too, that even with such thoughts, serious as they really were, it was not duty, it was not Helen, which was predominant with him, it was himself. Not so much that God would prevent a sin as that He would save him. Sceptic, philosopher as he was, this was what he made of it. On her it had come as a punishment for loving him, and for having allowed him to love her.

"What, Helen; with your child dead before you? at such a moment to speak of . . . of . . . what I dare not think of. Oh, Helen, Helen! we must think of duty now. Think of your husband."

"Markham," she said, with dreadful calmness, "these are strange words . . . . from you. Husband I have none. You taught me that I had none." And there, she added, pointing with her finger, "Is not there a witness too?"

"Oh! this is too much," Markham cried; "she is mad; I cannot bear it." He rushed out of the room. His own teaching—with him but words—words in which feelings he now recoiled from, had fashioned themselves into a creed which he had but dreamt that he believed—and now coming back upon him so dreadfully. It is not so easy a business this turning back out of the wrong way. These words and deeds of ours we scatter about us so recklessly find deeper holding ground than in our own memory. It is not enough to say I will turn and go back. What if I must carry back with me all those whom I have taken down; if I have bound up their fate with mine; if, after all, life be something more than these thoughts and feelings, and repentances—not altogether that shadow of a world with which we have been playing. Others, besides unhappy Esau, find no place for repentance, though they seek for it ever so carefully. He hurried to his own room, and, shutting himself in and double-locking the door, he threw himself exhausted upon his bed. He had taken no food all day. Mind and body were worn to the last. He heard her step follow him. He heard her voice imploring him to speak with her; but for a moment if it must be, but still to speak to her. But he would not, he durst not; and, giddy between weakness and excitement, he sunk into unconsciousness. He must have lain many hours as he was, for the day was breaking when he came to himself again. He had lain down in his clothes; he rose

weak and worn, and disordered, but the heavy
sense of wretchedness which entered in with his
returning consciousness left him no strength to
collect or arrange himself. He opened the window,
and looked out. A thick grey fog lay over the
valley, but the air was cool; he thought he would
go out. He stole down the stairs. He paused
opposite her door. Twice he turned to enter. As
often his heart failed him; he feared to see the
state in which she might be. He listened; he
heard her breathing, and then glided noiselessly
to the outer door, which he opened, and went out.
The walk before him led down to the lake; up
that walk he had come the last time with *her*,
and with one who would not pass that way again.
He followed it mechanically now, and wandered
slowly along the shore. The tops of the mountains
were showing out faintly above the mist, so quiet it
was, so still, so peaceful. Ah, it was little to him
how it was with the fever in his own breast; yet
his mind was quick in catching every image which
would add to his agony. Turn where he would,
some dear spot fell upon his eyes round which a
thousand passionate memories were encircled. There
was the little bay where he had first met her. There
was his own old little cottage with the jessamine
twining about the windows, where till that hour,
that fatal hour, he had dreamed of a happy home.
And now —— Yet even the scenes of the love
which he shrunk from were beautiful as he looked
back. No unhallowed light seemed resting on

K 3

them now, and in the shrine of the past they lay sad, and sweet, and innocent. Yes, all was beautiful, except the wretched present and his own most wretched self. What should he do? Go with her. He thought of it; yet he knew that he did not love her—that he had never truly loved her. He had felt remorse and sorrow for it; and it would be as easy to regret a prayer or a saintly action as to be sorry for having truly loved. Why, oh, why has love so many counterfeits, such cunning imitations? No, he would not, even if his eyes had not been opened to the sin—he would not fly with her. What future would there be for them—the world's outcasts—if love was not there to make the bitter cup more tolerable? He could not hope again to weave around him the shadows of feeling to which for the last three months he had surrendered himself. To forsaken truth, to neglected duty, we can return; but tie up again the broken threads of a dream out of which we have been awakened—never.

He walked on along the lonely sands, his uncovered hair moist in the morning air, and the morning breeze playing coldly about his disordered dress. But sense was lost in the dreary wilderness of desolation which lay around his soul; he only felt his misery, and pain would have been a relief to him. What should he do? Go back to Helen? How go back? How bear to look on her again? Never, oh, never. It could not be. He feared to look upon his work. He feared to hear

the voices moaning round the ruin which he had
made—to hear—to hear (was she mad, or was it
his own self that spoke)—to hear his own teaching
echoed back to him; the monster to which he had
given birth, and which now haunted him instinct
with a spectral vitality. To see again that unhappy
lady who, till she knew him, had been happy in a
child whom she loved, in a husband whom she was
ignorant that she did not love; and who, now that
his accursed star had shed its baneful light upon
her, in three little months, ere the leaves which
were then bursting in their young life had turned
to decay, was husbandless, friendless! Oh! and
most of all dreadful, her child too. He could not
leave her that . . . . gone, all gone; and he had
done it. To leave her there, he knew it too well,
was to leave her to die. And yet he must leave
her. Himself, which was all that remained to her,
that too he must tear away. And then, in these
wretched hours, his wasted life came back upon
him; his blighted hopes, his withered energies—a
curse to himself, he had been the grief of his family
—of his friends; of all who should have been most
dear to him. There was a mark upon him; a
miserable spell, a moral pestilence, which made him
his own hell, and tainted whatever he approached.
And now at last, when one had been found who
loved him, loved him with a passion he dared not
think of, this one he had destroyed for ever. What
business had such a thing as he, " crawling between

earth and heaven," with such a trail behind him?
If it was better that the murderer should die, than
remain in the society to which he was a curse; if it
were better for any beings whose presence makes
the misery of their fellow-creatures, that they perish
from off the earth where they never should have
been; then surely it were better far for him. What
future was there to which he could look forward?
As was the past time so would the coming be.
The Ethiopian does not change his skin. The
slimy reptile which has left its track along the
floor will not, for all its own care or others' chiding,
lose its venom, and become pure. He was infected
with the plague. Earth was lost to him. Heaven
was a dreary blank. One by one, as he had wandered in the wilderness of speculation, the beacon
lights of life had gone out, or sunk below the
horizon. He only knew God by this last lightning flash, which had but shown him the abysses
which environed him, and had left his senses more
bewildered than before. Death, as he dwelt upon
it, grew more and more alluring. Years before the
thought of destroying himself had floated before
him as a possibility; and with a kind of strange,
unexplained impulse, by which our deeper nature,
like that of animals, unreflectingly foresees its future
necessities, he had provided himself with a deadly
poison, which he always carried about his person.
As he drew it out and gazed upon it, more and
more clear it seemed to him that here was the goal

to which all was pointing. Round this one light
every shadow seemed to vanish. So he would
expiate his sin So perhaps Helen's life might
be saved. It would be easier for her to bear to
know that he was dead, than to feel either that
he had deceived or forsaken her, or to hope on in a
restless anguish of disquietude. At any rate, as it
was his life which had worked her ill, his life should
be no longer; and so at least she would have a
chance. For her, for all his friends to whom he
had caused so much sorrow — for all those whom
if he lived on he might hereafter meet and injure —
oh! for all, it was far, far the best. For himself,
one of two things he would find in the grave:
either as that bodily framework, out of which such
inharmonious life discords had arisen, became un-
strung and lifeless, the ill music that had poured
from it would die away, and its last echo be forgotten, the soul with the body dissolve for ever
into the elements of which it was composed ——
or else, if what he called his soul, his inward being,
himself was indeed indissoluble, immortal, and in
some sphere or other must live, and live, and live
again, then he would find another existence where
a fairer life might be found possible for him. At
any rate it could not be worse. No, not that dark
sulphurous home of torture, at the name of which
he had once trembled, not hell itself, could be less
endurable than the present . . . . There at least he
would not *do* evil any more, he would only suffer
it; and the keenest external agony which could be

inflicted upon him he would gladly take in change
for the torment which was within him. His mind
grew calmer as it grew more determined. It is
irresolution only, the inability from want of power,
or will, or knowledge, to determine at all, which
leaves us open to suffering: resolution, however
dreadful, determined resolution to do something,
restores us at once to rest and to ourselves . . . .
At first he thought the moment of the determination might as well be the moment of the act.
Himself condemning himself to die, and his own
executioner, with the means ready in his hands, he
need not leave himself an interval of preparation.
Why bear his pain longer when he could at once
leave it?   But the intensity of his determination
he felt presently had itself relieved him.   As it was
to be done judicially, it should be done gravely and
calmly.   He would set his house in order, and
write a last letter to Helen, undoing as far as he
could his own fatal work, and praying for her last
forgiveness.

The sun had long risen; he had walked many
miles, and, as the strain upon his mind grew lighter,
his body began to sink and droop.   At no great distance from where he found himself, he remembered,
was the cottage of a peasant with whom he had
some acquaintance, and to whom, in the last winter, he had been of considerable assistance in
curing him of a dangerous illness.   There he
thought he would go and remain for a few hours,
till he had rested and refreshed himself.   He

dragged himself painfully to the door; it was open, and he went in without knocking. The man was at home, and started at the strange intruder so suddenly presenting himself; scarcely less surprised he was when he discovered who it was that lay under all that disorder.

"Holy Virgin!" he cried; "Signor Sutherland, what has happened to bring you here like this?"

Markham was generally so scrupulous in his dress; and, now he had no hat, his long hair was hanging matted over his face, his cheeks were sunk and hollow, and his eyes bloodshot from long care and watching.

"It is nothing," he said; "only I have been walking long, and am tired. If you will let me have something to eat, and a bed to lie down and rest on for a few hours; and if you, in the meantime, will go yourself into Como for me, I shall thank you."

"To the world's end I will go for you, Signor; but what ——?"

"Do not ask me any questions," Markham said; "but go for me, and do what I shall tell you, and you will be doing me a service."

The man stared, but said nothing more; and, while his wife busied herself to get their strange guest's breakfast, he made ready for his walk.

Markham sat down and wrote three notes; one to his banker with directions for the payment of a few bills left unsettled in the town, and desiring them to make over what remained of his money in their hands to some public charity. The second was to the people of his old lodging. His clothes, and anything else they had of his, they were to keep for themselves; but his books and manuscripts were to be packed together and sent to England to myself. He himself, he said, was going away, and it was uncertain when he might return. The last was to Helen: brief and scrawled with a shaking hand, and blotted with his tears. It was only to say that he was gone: he would write once more, but that she would never see him again. This one was to be left at the gate of the villa, and the man was to hurry on at once, without asking or answering any questions. As soon as the notes were despatched, he took some food and then threw himself on a bed in the inner room, and fell at once into a deep unbroken sleep.

Como was not many miles distant; the messenger soon reached it, and finished his commissions; these were difficulties more easily overcome than his curiosity at the mysterious visit. He was leaving the town again without any acquaintance having fallen in his way to whom he might chatter out the wonder that disturbed him, when he encountered the priest at whose confessional he was occasionally present. He saluted him respectfully, and the father stopped him to ask some trifling question. It encouraged him to relieve himself. His listener knew Markham's name well; he had often heard of his little acts of kindness in the neighbourhood, and had more than once seen him and been struck with his appearance. He knew that he had been living for some months at the Leonards'; and when he heard of his strange appearance in the morning, of the note which he had sent, and of the way in which it was to be given, the father felt that there was some connection between the two things, and that a mystery of some painful kind was hidden under them.

" Ah! father," the man said, " there is something on his mind, I know there is, or his sweet face would never have had that awful look upon it. Perhaps he is mad, and the Devil has hold of him. If you would but come."

" It is no place for me," was the answer. " He is a heretic and an Englishman. I could do nothing."

" Oh, but, father," the peasant said, " it is not an outcast that he can be, so good and so young; and last winter, when the hunger came and the fever, and I was like to die with them, and I prayed to the Virgin to help me, she sent this English signor to me, and he gave me food and money, and he drove the illness away; and it cannot be that she would employ in that way a lost heretic."

The priest thought a little while; suddenly something seemed to strike him. " To-day," he said, " yes, it was to-day, he was to come." He took a letter out of his pocket, and read it rapidly over. " He will pass through Como on the 10th on his way to Rome; we have directed him to St. ——, where you will not fail to see him." It may be so;

yes, he may be here now, and so something might be done. He continued to mutter indistinctly to himself, and, telling his companion to follow him, walked rapidly to the monastery at the upper end of the town.

———

Late in the afternoon Markham awoke; he inquired whether the man was come back from Como, and, on learning that he was not, he sat down again at the table, and, with his purpose steady before him, wrote his last good bye to such of us as cared to receive it. There was one letter to myself, inclosing another to his father, which I was to give him. This last I might read if I pleased; it was very short, but a generous, open-minded, affectionate entreaty to be forgiven all the pain which he had caused him. I, he told me, would receive his manuscripts from Italy. If I thought, he said in his bitter way, that he was one of Bishop Butler's favourites, the end of whose existence was only to be an example to their fellow-creatures, I might make what use I pleased both of them and of what I knew of his life. He had before written to me about Helen, and, giving me a rapid summary of what had passed, added that I should understand the conclusion. It was all over, he thought, as he was writing —— As I read over those last letters now, I could almost wish that his purpose had been fulfilled as he designed it; but I will not anticipate.

The most painful thing was yet to be done: he must

write a few last words to Helen. They never reached their destination; either from inadvertence or from nervousness, he forgot the direction, and this letter was sent with the other to me. The hand was steady at the beginning, as if he had nerved himself for a violent effort; but his heart must have sunk as he went on. Many words were written through the blots of tears, and the end is scarcely legible.

"Helen," he wrote, "you have reason to hate me; yet you will not when you read this, for, by that time, I shall have made my last expiation to Heaven and to you. Yesterday I thought of myself, and I wished I had never seen you. Now I see my own littleness too plainly to care what might have been my fate. But, O Helen! would to God you had never seen me. We have been to blame. If you do not feel it, yet believe it, for me—for my sake; it is all you can do for me now. Believe it, and forgive me. You forgive me; I do not forgive myself till my life has paid for my unworthiness. Forgive me and forget me; I never deserved your love; I do not deserve your remembering. I never really loved you; a heart like mine was too selfish to love anything but itself. I did but fall into a dream, and I tempted you into it waking; the fault was all mine, let my sacrifice suffice. I will not tell you to be happy now—that cannot be after what you have lost. But it is not for nothing that God is visiting you: and if he has taken Annie from you, and taken me from you, it is for your sake, that He may win you for Himself. Turn, then, oh, turn! there *you* will find peace, and pray for yourself and pray for me. And it may be—it may be—O Helen! pray that it may be, that in a little while—but a little—when your body will lie down in the dust by the side of ours, that our spirits may meet again, when I may be better worth your loving, and where love shall be no sin; and the peace we have lost here shall be given us there for ever.

" Farewell! forgive me—farewell!"

Not far from the cottage, on the shores of the lake, was a spot where human hands had piled together a few old massive stones, and a stream of water, perhaps with some assistance, had scooped a basin in the granite. It was said that, many centuries before, a man had made a home there who was haunted by some strange sin; and the worn circle which was traced into the hard surface of the rock was still pointed out as the sign of the victory of penitence. It had been worn by the painful knees of a subdued and broken-hearted man. whose long watches the stars for thirty years had gazed upon, and whose prayers the angels had carried up to heaven; and fast and penance, and the dew and the rain, and the damp winds, had cleansed the spots from off the tainted soul, and God's mercy, before he died, had hung round him the white garments of a saint. It was a holy place; the peasants crossed themselves as they passed by, and stopped, and knelt, and prayed the pardoned sinner's intercession for their sins; and a small rude crucifix, carved, it was said, out of the very wood of Calvary, stood yet over the old stone which had been the altar of the tiny chapel. What strange attraction drew Sutherland's steps there, it would be hard to say; whether it was that, in this forlorn and desolate ruin, this poor wretched remnant of a worn-out creed seemed to find a sympathetic symbol of his own faith-deserted soul—or whether it was some more awful impulse, like that which haunts blood-guilty men, and, compelling them to their own self-betrayal, forces them to hang spell-bound round the scene of their crime, as if the forsaken faith could only fitly there revenge itself on the same spot which once had witnessed its victory—I know not—or perhaps the threads which move our slightest actions are woven of a thousand tissues; and all these and innumerable others drew him there together. He sat down upon the broken wall. The ripple of the lake was curling and crisping on the pebbles at his feet. The old familiar scenes in the distance around him, so quiet and so beautiful—far away a white sail was glittering in the sunlight—happy human hearts were beating where that sail was, bounding along their light life way, with wings of hope and pleasure. Nearer still the island, the fatal island, and the treacherous water, and, last and worst, he could see the trees which hid the house where Helen was now lying—the lost, desolate Helen—alive or dead he

knew not, he hardly cared, when life could be to
her but living death. The scene hung on upon
his senses; but soon it was but floating on their
surface, and his mind turned in upon his memory,
and year by year, scene by scene, his entire life rose
up before him, and rolled mournfully by. His love
had been but a passing delirium; she had never
had all his soul; and now what had the truest hold
on his affections, — old home, and the old church
bells, and his mother's dying blessing, came echoing
sadly back again. And yet the storm was past.
He was calm now, for he was determined. Tears
were flowing fast down his face: but they were not
tears of suffering, but soft tears, in which all his
soul was melting at this last adieu to life, which,
poisoned as it had been for him, he could not choose
but love. He did not regret his purpose; he did
not fear to die. Death must be some time, whatever
death was. But it was the very death which was so
near, which seemed to have taken off the curse from
what he was leaving, as if the dawning light of his
expiation was already breaking over the darkness.
He took the phial from his pocket, with a steady
hand he untied the covering, and poured its contents into a little cup; he put it down upon the
stone. So clear, so innocent, it sparkled there.
"Now for the last, then," he said. Once more he
turned his eyes to the blue heaven, and round over
the landscape, so beautiful, so treacherously beautiful. A thin white cloud was sailing slowly up to-

wards the sun. We often fix our resolution by the
aid of other actions besides our own. The cloud
should give the signal for his going. It would but
veil the sunlight for a moment; but in that moment
a shadow would fall down on his spirit, which would
pass away no more.

" All is over now then," he said, " and to this fair
earth, and sky, and lake, and woods, and smiling
fields, and all the million things which gambol out
their life in them, now good bye, and for ever. You
will live on; and the wind will blow, and men will
laugh and sigh, and the years roll along, with their
great freights of joy and sorrow; but I shall hear
their voices no more. One pang, and I shall be
lying there, among those old stones, as one of them.
Little happiness, at best, there is, with all this fair
seeming. A little—but a little—but I shall not be
here to make that little less. A few friends may be
sorry for me when they hear of this last end; but
their pain will be brief as mine, and the wound will
heal, and time will bear away its memory; and for me
no mortal heart will suffer more. Farewell, Helen!
last witness that earth had no deeper curse than love
of me. Your spirit is broken; but peace may
breathe over its ruins when I am gone. Farewell, farewell! The shadow steals over the earth.
I see it; the dark cloud spot rolling down the hill
so fast, so fast. Oh! may it be a true emblem
—the one dull spot in the great infinity of light!
These stones, this altar. they have echoed to sorrow deep, perhaps, as mine; and faith in this poor

atom, poor carved chip of rotting wood, cheated
the sufferer into a lengthened agony of years. Miserable spell that clings around us! we can but
pass from dream to dream; but change one idol for
another; and place the very Prophet who came to
free us, on the pedestal from which he had thrown
down the image.

Another moment —he raised the poison. " And
Jesus Christ died on this?" he said, as his eyes lingered on the crucifix, " died for our sins . . . . so
I die to lighten others' sorrows, and to end my
own!"

" Die without hope—the worst sinner's worst
death—to bear your sin, and your sin's punishment,
through eternity!"

Was it the rocks that spoke? It was a strange
echo. Markham started. The cup sunk upon the
altar stone. His pulse, which had not shaken before, bounded violently in his heart, as he turned
and looked round him. And the figure he saw, and
the glance he met, was hardly calculated to give
him back his courage. How well he knew it! How
often in old college years he had hung upon those
lips; that voice so keen, so preternaturally sweet,
whose very whisper used to thrill through crowded
churches, when every breath was held to hear; that
calm grey eye; those features, so stern, and yet so
gentle!—was it the spirit of Frederick Mornington
which had been sent there, out of the other world,
to warn him? Was it a dream, a spectre? What
was it? Oh! false, how false, that a man who is

bold to die, is bold for every fear! Markham's knees shook; his hair rose upon his head, and his tongue hung palsied in his throat, as he struggled to speak.

"God sent me here to seek one who might be saved. He did not tell me I should find Markham Sutherland!"

"What are you?" stammered Markham. "How came you here?"

"I have come in time," he answered, cutting every syllable in the air with his clear impassive voice, as if he was chiselling it in marble.

Markham's confused sense began to remember. Mr. Mornington had been for two years in Italy, washing off, in a purer air, the taint of the inheritance of heresy.

"Come with me," he said, with the manner which knows it is obeyed; "you must not stay here;" he crossed himself; "the place is holy!" He took the poison-cup from the stone, and threw it far away, and, with water from the fountain, he sprinkled the place where it had lain, and where Markham had been sitting.

The young man watched him mechanically. This last action did not escape him; he was infected, and what he touched he tainted. He made no effort to resist. He who had but a few moments before philosophised over superstition, was feeble as a child. Again he saw in this the finger of Heaven, which he could not choose but obey.

Mr. Mornington moved out of the consecrated

L

ground, signing to him to follow; and he went without hesitating. Partly it was the reviving of the power with which, in earlier years, this singular person had fascinated him; partly it was his guilt-subdued conscience, which felt that it had forfeited the right to its own self-control. When they were outside the circle that marked the holy ground, his companion turned to him with features which had lost half their sternness, and had softened into an expression of tenderness and feeling.

"And is it indeed you, Markham, you, I find here in this dreadful way? . . . . I spoke sternly to you, I could not speak otherwise there. But, Markham, I do not forget: I can be your friend as a man, if I cannot be more to you. Dear Markham, it was not a chance which sent me here; I was told I should find an Englishman, and an unhappy one. As an English priest my duty brought me here, and I come to find you, Markham, you on the very edge of a precipice so fearful, that it is only now that I have led you from it, that you or I can feel its awfulness; and I feel—yes, and you feel—it was not an accident which ruled it so.

Markham's heart was bursting. "Dear kind Mr. Mornington," he said, "you do not know what you have done. It would have been better if you had left me; you may think so when you hear all that I will tell you."

Mornington's softening face grew softer; he knew the virtue of confession; he knew that only a broken heart would turn to it unconstrained, and how soon the broken heart may become a contrite one. That day Markham told him all, first this long dark story, the last load which lay the heaviest upon him; then, as he began to rise from under the weight, he saw more clearly, or thought he saw, how fault had followed fault, and one link hung upon another; and step by step he went back over his earlier struggles, his scepticisms, his feeble purpose and vacillating creed, all of them outpouring now as sins confessed. His listener's sympathies were so entire, so heartfelt, he seemed himself to have passed through each one of Markham's difficulties so surely he understood them. Nay, often the latter was startled to find himself anticipated in his conclusions, and to hear them rounded off for him in language after which he himself had been only feeling. At last it was all over. The inexpressible relief he felt seemed to cry to him of reconciliation and forgiveness. Mr. Mornington pressed but little upon him; his heart was flowing, the wound had burst for itself, and had no need of urging. When it was finished, he said, "Markham, I have heard you as a friend, I have only to ask you whether your conscience does not tell you that you have found a way at last where you thought that there was none, and whether you are prepared to follow it?"

"Oh, yes,—yes," he said.

"But to follow it now? now while your heart is warm and the quick sense is on you of what you are and of what you were." Again Markham passionately professed his readiness.

Then you will repeat to another what you have confided to me; not as I have heard it, but under the sacred seal of confession; you will undertake the penance which shall be laid upon you; and you will look forward with steady hope to a time when you may be received into the holy church, and may hear your absolution from her lips?

If Markham hesitated it was but for a moment. Mr. Mornington went on . . . . " Your philosophy, as you called it, taught you to doubt whether sin was not a dream; you feel it now; it is no dream, it is a real, a horrible power; and you see whither you have been led in following blindly a guide which is but a child of the spirit of evil.

How true it is that arguments have only power over us while the temper is disposed to listen to them! Not one counterfact had been brought before him, not one intellectual difficulty solved, yet under the warm rain of penitence the old doubts melted like snow from off his soul. He *felt* his guilt, he *felt* that here that dreadful consciousness might be rolled away, and as idle he thought it would be to stand hesitating with frozen limbs with a fire within sight and within reach, till some cunning chymist had taught him why the fire was warm, as to wait now and hang aloof till the power which he felt was explained to him.

Whether all along below his weakness some latent superstition had not lain buried, which now for the first time broke out into activity, or whether he mistook the natural effect of having unloaded his

aching conscience in a kind listener's ear, for a supernatural spiritual strength which was flowing down
upon him from heaven, or whether it was indeed true
that his reason had gone astray; that reason *is* by
some strange cause perverted, and of itself and un-
assisted it can but present a refracted image of the
things of the spirit with every line inclining at a
false angle; and that the strange inexplicable *sense*
which contradicts reason (for we cannot flinch from
the alternative) is the one faithful glimpse and the
only one of the truth of God, enough for our
guidance and enough to warn us against philosophy
—were questions which long after, in his solitary cell,
the unhappy Markham was again and again condemned to ask himself, and to hear no answer, except in the wild rolling storm of eager angry voices
calling this way and that way and each crying down
the other. . . . But there was no such hesitating now.
The overpowering acuteness of his feeling unnerved
what little intellect was left unshaken, and the gentle-
ness and fascination of Mr. Mornington held him like
a magnetic stream. He did all they bid him do; for a
time he felt all they promised that he should feel.
He felt that it was his doubt which had unhinged
him; he had fallen because his moral eye had become
dim.   Deep as his sin had been, Mr. Mornington
told him it was not mortal, because it had been un-
completed; saints had fallen, the man after God's
own heart had fulfilled as deep or a deeper crime. If
he could submit himself utterly and unreservedly to

the holy church, the church in God's stead would accept him and would pronounce his full forgiveness.

He confessed, and after undergoing the prescribed penance, he received the conditional baptism, was absolved, and retired into a monastery. Once and once only his human feeling was strong enough to make him speak again to Mr. Mornington of Helen, and to ask what had become of her. But a cold severe answer that she was cared for, and a peremptory command never to let his thoughts turn upon her again (with a penance for every transgression) until those under whose care he had been placed could give him hopes that his *prayers* might be offered for her unsullied by any impurity — together with the severe rule of discipline under which he had by his own desire been laid—for a time at least drove her out of his mind. His crushed sense became paralysed in the artificial element into which he had thrown himself. His remorse overwhelmed his sympathy with her. . . . . She belonged to the old life which he had flung off, and he endeavoured only to remember her in an agony of shame.

Poor Helen! she was cared for. How that night and those days passed with her was never known. Markham's note was brought her the morning of his disappearance, and she knew that he too was gone when all else was gone—gone!—lost to her for ever! It swept over her lacerated heart like the white squalls over the hot seas of India, with a fury too intense to raise the waves, but laying them all

flat in boiling calm. It appears she collected energy
enough to write to Mr. Leonard, desiring him to
come to her at once. She gave no reason—she did
not even tell him that his child was dead; only he
must come to her, come on the instant. When he
came he found her in a state of almost unconsciousness. Her nerves were for the time killed by what
she had gone through; but when she saw him she
was able to gather herself up. She knew him—she
knew what she had to say to him; and coldly,
calmly, and gravely she told him all. There were
no tears, no passionate penitence, no entreaties for
forgiveness. Her words fell from her almost like a
voice from the shadowy dead sent up out of their
graves on some unearthly mission; and they awed
him as such a voice would awe him. His rude and
simple nature might have broken into passion had
he seen one tinge of shame, or fear, or any feeling
which he would have expected to find. He had
never loved her, though he thought he had. Perhaps he was too shallow to love. But he might
have felt real rage at his own injury, and he might
have persuaded himself, in proper sort, that he felt
all which an affectionate husband ought to feel; but
this unnatural calmness overmastered him entirely.
He was passive in her hands, to do or not to do
whatever she might choose. What could she
choose? Home and kind home-faces there were
none for her. Friends, except Markham, not one;
and him—whatever was become of him—she was
never to see again. He had not even written again

to her as he had promised. Death had not come,
though she had prayed for it. Madness had not
come; she was too single-minded to think of
suicide.

To be alone with the past was all for which she
wished. There was but one gate besides the grave
which she knew was never closed against the broken-
hearted—it was that of the convent. She knew little
and cared little for difference of creeds. It was not
the creed of the Catholic which was the seed out of
which those calm homes of sorrow have risen over the
earth; but deepest human feeling, deepest knowledge of the cravings of the suffering heart. There
at least was kindness, and tenderness, and compassion—there no world voice could break in to trouble
her—there let her go. Her husband made no difficulty. In his heart he was not sorry, as it settled
for him a question which might be embarrassing;
and the few arrangements which money could command were soon made with a relation of one of his
Italian friends, the Abbess of ——. The story
was told her. Such stories were not new in Italy;
though it was new that of her own free will, a lady
who had done what she had done, and had been
bred in the free atmosphere of the world, should
seek out so austere a home. And there went Helen
—and there for two years she drooped, and then
she died. All that woman's care or woman's affection could do to soften off her end was done. The
exhaustion of her suffering left her soul in calm,
and gave her back enough possession of herself to

enable her to entangle into affection for her the
gentle hearts which were round her and watched
over her.   It was a deep, intense affection; deeper,
perhaps, because of the doubt and sorrow which
were blended with it.   For Helen lived and died
unreconciled with the Church.   She loved it—she
loved its austerity, its charity, the wide soul-ab-
sorbing spirit of devotion which penetrated and
purified it, and the silvery loveliness of character
which it had to bestow; and Helen might have
joined it, might have received from its lips on this
side the grave the pardon which may God grant
she has yet found beyond it: only if she could
have made one first indispensable confession that
she had *sinned* in her love for Markham Sutherland—yet, with singular persistency, she declared
to the last that her sin had been in her marriage,
not in her love.   Unlike his, her early training
had been too vague to weigh at all against the
feeling which her love had given her; she had little
knowledge and an unpractised intellect—she had
only her heart, which had refused to condemn her
—she had never examined herself.   The windings,
wheel within wheel, of the untrue spirit's self-de-
ceptions, were all strange to her, for she had always
been too natural to think about herself at all.   Perhaps the heart does not deceive; never does give a
false answer except to those double-minded unhappy ones who do care about themselves, and so
play tricks with it and tamper with it.   At any
rate, whether from deadness of conscience, or from

apathy, or indifference, or because of the unre-
penting tenderness of her love, which never left her
(although they took care to tell her of Markham's
repentance), she still clung to her feeling for him as
the best and most sacred of her life. She acknow-
ledged a sin which they told her was none, for she
felt that she ought never to have promised Leonard
what she had; but Markham she loved, she must
still love. Her love for him could not injure him.
If he was happy in forgetting—in abjuring her,
she was best pleased with what would best heal his
sorrow.

Strange contrast—the ends of these two! She
died happy, forgiven by her husband and going back
to join her lost child, where by and by they might
all meet again, and where Markham need no longer
fly from her; for there, there is " no marrying nor
giving in marriage." It was a hard trial to the
weeping sisters who hung around her departure to
see with what serene tranquillity the unpardoned
sinner, as they deemed her, could pass away to
God.

But Markham's new faith fabric had been reared
upon the clouds of sudden violent feeling, and no
air castle was ever of more unabiding growth;
doubt soon sapped it, and remorse, not for what he
had done, but for what he had not done; and
amidst the wasted ruins of his life, where the bare
bleak soil was strewed with wrecked purposes and
shattered creeds; with no hope to stay him, with
no fear to raise the most dreary phantom beyond

the grave, he sunk down into the barren waste, and the dry sands rolled over him where he lay; and no living being was left behind him upon earth, who would not mourn over the day which brought life to Markham Sutherland.

G. Woodfall and Son, Printers, Angel Court, Skinner Street, London.

SHADOWS OF THE CLOUDS

Bibliographical note:

this facsimile has been made from a copy in the
Beinecke Library of Yale University
(Ip.F939.847)

SHADOWS

OF

THE CLOUDS.

BY ZETA.

LONDON:
JOHN OLLIVIER, 59, PALL MALL.
1847.

LONDON :

C. J. PALMER, PRINTER, SAVOY STREET, STRAND.

Homines se liberos esse opinantur quando quidem suarum volitionum suique appetitûs sunt conscii e de causis a quibus disponuntur ad appetendum et volendum quia earum sunt ignari ne per somnium cogitant.

SPINOZA. *Ethics.*

———————

Wer mit dem Leben spielt
Kömmt nie zurecht,
Wer nicht sich selbst befiehlt
Bleibt immer ein Knecht.

GOETHE.

SHADOW OF THE CLOUDS.

THE SPIRIT'S TRIALS.

MR. HARDINGE was a clergyman; he had a living in the central part of England; but lying as it did exposed unhealthily to the malaria from the marshes of the Ouse, his wife's health had obliged him to be a non-resident, and for many years they had led a wandering life together from curacy to curacy. Mrs. Hardinge's body, like infirm minds tired easily with what was familiar to it, and craved for novelty. They seldom stayed longer at any one place than was enough to enable them to carry away the heart of every

B

creature that had come in contact with them, a
silver sugar-basin, or cream jug, and one more
addition to their family circle.

Mr. Hardinge had been distinguished at college ; but he had married immediately on leaving it, and his nature had rather led him to shed
himself outwards, in acts of kindness to his fellow creatures, than to submit his mind to any
laborious discipline in the study of divines and
philosophers. . . . . The characteristic feature
in him was benevolence—benevolence full,
prompt, active, without a tinge of maudlin in it,
yet so extensive that it could reach to sympathy
even with a broken flower. I have known him
lend his cloak to a beggar in a storm on a wild
moor, and content himself with a mere promise it
should be brought back to him. The repeated
experience of men's unworthiness through twenty
years of life among them as a clergyman, had
not made him distrustful, or even admit the
possibility of the promise being broken. A drive
with Mr. Hardinge was a serious undertaking ;
not a snail or a worm if he saw them (and on
these occasions he was wonderfully sharp-
sighted) might be left in the road for fear that

somebody might hurt them; not a stone of common bigness for fear it might hurt somebody. I remember once his falling in with some boys who were drowning a cat in a pond by the road side. As persuasion produced no effect, he said he would buy it of them, and offered them half-a-crown; the young rascals took the money, and ran off, telling him he might go fetch the creature out of the water for himself. And he did. . . . But an instance of this kind never made him think the worse, or he more suspicious, of people generally. It lumped itself up with the abstract wickedness he preached against on Sundays. He abhorred wickedness, but he seldom or never abhorred people for being wicked, he could not believe any one he came in contact with to be so. . . . . So that it must be pretty plain that of what is called knowledge of the world he had very little. . . . He believed of course that there was badness growing, plenty of it, but he could not suspect any one he knew to have any badness. Men of base minds always estimate others by themselves, and whenever a selfish interested motive can be found for anything any one has done, that motive they are sure must have been the motive, because they have never

acted themselves from any other. Mr. Hardinge
exactly inverted this rule, because he was good,
because he never felt even the most fleeting cloud
of selfishness throw a shadow over his mind, he
thought the best of any action that fell under
his notice, as long as it was possible to entertain
a doubt

This natural tendency was very much height-
ened by a misforfortune which befel him about
his thirty-eighth year, in the termination of a
gradually increasing disorder in almost total
deafness. Thus a physical infirmity coming into
the help of disposition, he was farther than ever
from being able to form correct judgments of
people. Hitherto he had been forced to know
something from what he could not avoid hearing.
Conversation going on about him must have told
him at any rate what other people thought, and
even in their conversation with himself they
could not be for ever on their guard. But it is
different when so much effort is required—you
cannot well be intemperate or selfish or worldly
down a speaking trumpet. . . . . And so it
came to pass that, shut up in himself, and in
his own pure and noble thoughts and feelings,
he loved his fellow-creatures too well to look

at them as anything else than a mirror where he saw all his own goodness reflected and believed it was theirs.

Of the great multitude of the mixed characters of good and ill, neither wholly good nor wholly bad, but for ever oscillating between the two, with a negative and a positive, a selfish and a generous motive for almost all they do; of the difficulties which are thrown in men's way from the artificial structure of society, the conflicting temptations, the fluctuating judgment of public opinion, of all the thousand complicated threads and fibres which draw men up and down, and do really so very seriously affect the character for goodness or badness, of all the actions that are done under them, Mr. Hardinge knew nothing. . . . Right and wrong with him stood each with a rigid outline; there was no shading off of one into the other by imperceptible degrees; if a thing was clearly bad it was bad altogether, and if he was called upon to form a judgment of the person, he was a bad man who did it. He had his own high lofty rule of thought and action, but it was inflexible—that the rule of right and wrong could bend was no article of his creed. Once convince him that any one he knew had done an immoral action, and the avenues of his heart were closed to him for ever. Evil, in its abstract form, was so loathsome to him, and in its concrete so little familiar, that if ever he was obliged to transfer the judgment he had of the general to the particular, it was transferred whole. He could make no allowance, and the abhorrence he would feel after, would be in proportion to the love he had felt before. Mr. Hardinge did not know the infinite variety of natures men received at the hands of Providence, he had never studied the strange laws which govern the moulding of them into characters, he had no idea that the same temptation acts as variously on different men, as the same temperature on metals and gases; that all these things must infinitely modify our judgment on the sinfulness of the individual that falls before them, and as infinitely the degree of moral injury such fall will inflict on his character. . . . . So that it will be seen that however we may admire Mr. Hardinge standing alone; however wonderfully beautiful he might be, as an inhabitant of Paradise, his was not a character to work well among his fellow-creatures; he was likely to bestow his affection

unworthily, to give all when only some was
deserved, to withhold all when some should have
remained ; and as the warmth of his nature
prompted him to immediate and precipitate
action, we shall not be surprised in the sequel of
the story to find one more proof that in so intricate
a world the simple-minded cannot walk innocu-
ously in their simple-mindedness; that benevolence, undirected by knowledge, may do untold
evil, in the unwise pursuit of good. . . . .
The wounds we receive from bad men, deserved
or undeserved, are soon healed again; but when
a good man strikes, and there is no cause, the
wound is poisoned.

CHAPTER II.

AT the time my story begins the Hardinges
were living in Wales; they were fond of mountain
countries.   They had tried all parts of England;
but they were never happy away from the lakes,
and rocks, and hills.   People of strong feeling
and not highly cultivated, generally breathe most
freely where nature is the only artist; and moreover, whoever is fond of mountains at all is fond
of them with a passion, because they are so individual.   Each one of the great giants has his
own form, his own features, and his own name,
and he winds round and round your heart like a
human being with a soul in him, and you love
him as an old friend.   The pine woods, and
cliffs, and waterfalls, become as we grow among
them as it were a part of our mind; they have
done so much to educate us, we reverence them

as our greatest teachers of wisdom; while every
single scene is of so clear and so marked a kind,
and it hardly ever fails to be inseparably twined in
with some bright and sunny recollection.　Besides they are so unchanging.　To a thoughtful
mind like Mr. Hardinge's, which is ever looking
for God, in all God's world around him, fit
emblems they are, in changing scenes, among
changing men, of Him who is the same yesterday,
to-day, and for ever.　Mr. Hardinge used to talk
of the everlasting hills.　It was his nearest approach to irony when he would point to the cloud
on Cadir Idis, and bid us think how just so, the
great giant had curtained himself in his chair, in
the old world before the flood; just so the grim
mountain had frowned in the gathering storm-
cloud of the old deluge, or so smiled between
tears and gladness in the sunshine before the
retiring waters.　There sleeps the enchanted
Arthur, there wrung the mailed heel of Glen-
dower, above the valley where the modern
traveller rolls along his iron road in fire-winged
chariot.　We poor lords of the creation, what a
silly dance he has watched us lead here, down
under him; so loud, so noisy, as it all was, and
sweeping away without an echo.　Yet there sits

he so calm, so serene, so silent; as he smiles on us, so by-and-bye he will smile on our children's children; and there he will be for the last end, when the smoke-clouds of the burning world shall wreathe him in his shroud.

It was within sight of Cadir Mr. Hardinge was living, in a large old house, called Morlands, a few miles below Machrynnleth, at the head of the long salt-water lake at the mouth of the Dovey river. His family had been completed some eight years, and now consisted of four daughters and three sons; besides these were two or three young pupils; in all the brightest, merriest, sunniest party, and, considering Mr. Hardinge's knowing anything about it was totally out of the question, not exceedingly noisy, ... Except indeed, when the porridge bowl came on the table, and then there was a splendid scramble. It was quite beautiful to see them and sit with them at a meal-time; the fathers full, round sweet face, smiling so fondly over them all, with goodness beaming off from it on all he shone upon, like light and heat from off the sun. Of the children, of what they were, and their way of bringing up, I might write much. I must content myself with a little. Born with

all their father's exuberant kindliness, and all
their mother's grace, they had grown up together
in the most natural atmosphere in the world.　It
seemed as if none of them had ever known any
inclination to do wrong, for you never heard a
'You shall not,' or a 'You must not.'　They
said their ten commandments certainly; but
then like healthy children they attached no
meaning at all to them in their negative form,
and understood them only as they are interpreted
into a directer shape in the catechism explanation.　To be sure, they were let to do almost
everything they pleased that was not wrong.
It was no part of the Morlands plan to impose
restraints for their own sake as a discipline of
obedience; it seemed at any rate as if all the
best which people purpose to gain by such means
had been lavished on the young Hardinges by
nature. . . . . There was a school-room, where
they contrived to assimilate a certain quantity
of desultory information; but there was not the
least attempt at strictness of rules. . . . . All
they did, all they got, seemed to flow out of
themselves, as if it could not help it; just as they
grew up they were left to stand: fine young
healthy fruit-trees, that never knew the pruning

hook.   The wonder was they did not degenerate
and grow weeds, but they did not.   The boys
were rather rough certainly, shaggy, like mountain ponies; but well-bred, and clean-limbed,
mind and body—you could see at a glance that
clipped they would show admirably. . . . . This
was as boys—as men who are to take a place in
professions, and in the business of life, it is to
be feared there will be a deficiency, unless they
have talent of a most uncommon kind.   A man
requires a certain quantity of positive acquirements merely to be a fully developed man : and
they will have to be working up the lost ground
at the expense of their professions; but this by
the way ; they were boys at the time I am speaking of. . . . . . Now for the girls. . . . The
eldest was about twenty, the second two years
younger, the other two children. . . . . From
the way these last went on one might form a sort of
conjecture what had been the education of the
elder ones; tossing in the swing, rolling their
hoops along the grass-plat, and wielding rake
and pitchfork in the hay season : at twelve or
thirteen they could row a boat against their
brothers ; and if it had not been for the inconvenient frock they could have played cricket, or

run races up the mountain against either of them.
Luckily they all inherited a liking for drawing
and music, They could spell out a little French,
but it was very troublesome to have to look the
same word out so many times, and altogether it
was little to their taste; but they learnt music
enough to play and sing the wild Welsh airs—
and drawing in a rudish style they succeeded
well with. They loved drawing, for they loved
their lakes and mountains, and it was a way in
which they could appropriate them to themselves.
I paid a visit a short time since to some of the
old cottages in the neighbourhood, and I found
the walls hung round with the Miss Hardinges,
sketches. . . . . Such was their education,
evincing the most shocking deficiency in all its
most essential, even elementary acquirements.
So that by what possible way they justified themselves in being the fascinating creatures they
were I must leave them to tell. . . . . Just at
the time when the girl passed into the woman,
exactly at the right crisis, the change came;
their foot was as light as ever on the mountain-
side; their hand as ready in the hay-field, but
the romping air they had as children passed away
for ever. The laugh was as buoyant, the eye as

bright and sunny, but the gracefulness they had inherited from their mother rounded out the ruder angles of their girlishness into soft flowing lines of beauty, and moulded them into a form as easy and perfect as the most highly-finished art could have done ; the elegance of nature was more perfect in them than in any women I ever saw, and when this is so it has the advantage of all art ; because it does really come, and does not only seem to come, directly from within.

Altogether they were a perplexing family ; one had never met with perfect people ; one did not believe in perfect people—at least not in a perfection that would blow without care or culture like a wild rose in the hedge-row ; and yet one could find nothing at all about them that one could wish to be different. They would do many out of the way things ; many things that with any one else one would have felt doubtful about ; but it was impossible to doubt with them. . . . . With those bright, clear, unconscious eyes of theirs, they might do what they pleased, and in them it would be right. It seemed as if for once Nature had forgot herself ; and the spirit of sin which hangs over the birth throes, and pours itself through every baby's

veins as it breaks into mortality, had shrunk
from its unlovely office, and once again let old
Earth welcome children to her bosom as pure as
those she once wondered at under the palm trees
of Paradise.

CHAPTER III.

It was summer; the beginning of the long vacation. Aberdovey was a favourite place for reading parties from the university. The lake —the sea—the trout in the river—the snipe and duck in the long marshes—the beautiful scenery, and the pleasant, kind, hospitable Welsh gentlemen seldom failed to prove attractive to the numerous class of young students who prefer the society of their friends and their unrestrained amusements (even though accompanied with the presence of a nominal tutor, who has no control over them) to the uninteresting companionship of their sisters and the restraints of home. Courtesy has rendered such parties respectable, by calling them reading parties. But I have myself been attached to several, in both capacities of tutor and pupil,

5

and I cannot say my own experience could justify the name as more than an honorary title. Let the reading part of them, however, be as it may, they are certainly pleasant enough, and profitable enough in other ways; on the whole the pleasantest summers I have to look back upon.

It is a fine hot morning in August, 183—, some hours after post time. Edward Fowler is seen plunging up and down the deep dry sand road in a state denoting a frame of mind anything but harmonizing with the volume of Aristotle under his arm. An open letter is in his hand, into which from time to time he is flinging bewildered glances, and then dashing his foot into the sand, as if he is craving to annihilate somebody, and is not at all particular who.

"Come, Fowler," a voice calls out of the window of one of the lodging-houses, "it is ten o'clock. . . . past. . . . I shall see you this morning at any rate. You promised faithfully, you know, you would be regular this week, when you went up the lake on Friday. Where is the rhetoric?"

" The devil take the rhetoric !"

C

" What! you are not going to cut me again?"
And Sterming's face looked longer out of the
window, and his voice sounded really distressed.

" O Sterming, dear Sterming, you can do me
a thousand times more service if you'll come
and read this, and teach me some rhetoric to
use to my father."

It seemed clear enough to Sterming that
there was occasion now for his services rather
as a man than as a tutor; and as the atmosphere of Aristotle had not yet quite withered
his sympathies, he went.   A kind word was
everything just then to poor Fowler; as soon
as he had found an older friend to listen to
them, he fancied himself almost clear of his difficulties.

The letter which had produced this outbreak
was simple and laconic enough.   Canon Fowler
had heard from some of his own friends in the
neighbourhood, that while he thought Edward
was hard at work over Aristotle and Thucy-
dides, he was spending more than half his time
at Morland with the Hardinges.   Canon Fowler,
with his plain businesslike way of looking at
things, was of all the men I ever met in this
world the very last to sympathize in a boy of

twenty's love affairs.   He told him very briefly
he understood he was making an ass of himself,
and unless he could hear a satisfactory account
of what he was about, he should write to Mr.
Sterming, and desire him to send him home immediately. . . . Nothing could be more reasonable, or more natural, and might, without any
great difficulty, have been believed to have been
dictated by a real desire for Edward's real good.
. . . But a reasonable view of things was the
very last Edward could ever take of anything.
. . . The impulse of the moment was to him
a divine command; and though the impulse of
the next week might be the contradictory of
this, each was alike sacred, and it was sacrilege
to disobey. . . . No, his father had always
grudged him the slightest enjoyment, and now
that the sunlight of the highest happiness was
just beginning to dawn upon him, he was to be
torn from it for ever.   It was always so—it was
his fate.   It was all desperate.   But let Sterming only look at the postscript.

It appeared that Mr. Hardinge's father had
been in confinement, and Canon Fowler had
reason to believe that insanity was hereditary in
their family.   By way of softening the peremp-

c 2

toriness of his letter, he had added this as a
reason why he could not allow Edward to look
forward towards, at any future time, marrying
into it. It was very kindly meant; because it
would at once put an end to the thing, and prevent its being lingered out by hopes to die a
more painful, more protracted death. . . . He
believed he knew his son well enough to be sure
the whole thing was nothing but a freak, which
in the end would die of itself; and it was better
to save the Hardinges from an affair which was
so certain to be distressing. . . . But the effect
produced on Edward was exactly the opposite of
what was intended; he had the strangest knack,
if any body crossed his wishes, of taking the
stick by the burnt end. . . . It happened, un-
luckily, that there was already a degree of un-
comfortableness in the Fowler family from a
precisely similar matter. The eldest brother
wished to marry a lady to whom the Canon
had the same objection; and of course the
younger part of the family were all enlisted
against their father. . . . . " It is always the
same," Edward said. " He cares for none of us.
I believe he would think himself well rid of us
if we were dead." . . . And Sterming's remon-

strances were easily silenced by a "You don't know my father."

The question was, however, what was to be done? Sterming was really a very kind-hearted fellow, and, being younger, could sympathize in the cause of the distress. It was clear it was no joking matter; at least just then joking would do no good, and only irritate. However, he must know more before he could undertake to advise, and he looked up inquiringly. The flood-gates of poor Fowler's heart were gone clean down, and out it all came pouring. He had known the Hardinges before, it seemed, when they had been in Somersetshire. In all he had spent several weeks in their house, and the young ladies had been twice at his father's at Darling. . . . Being such a youth as we have described him, of course he had fallen in love with Emma Hardinge, and he had really good qualities enough, or interesting qualities enough, to gain her affections in return. That the family had settled at Morlands was the principal reason of his having attached himself to Sterming's Aberdovery reading party: and on the expedition up the lake, to which his tutor had somewhat reproachfully alluded, he had said, or

fancied he had said, so much to Emma, that he
could not leave her now without being more
explicit; or at any rate without some explanation.

I cannot take a better opportunity than while
he and Sterming are talking on the sands, of
giving some account of Fowler's earlier history.
. . . He told it me himself long after this, but
it appears to me that with him (perhaps more
or less with every one) if early life is made the
mirror where the after life is shown, the distor-
tion of each will be found to correspond and
correct each other; and so, and so only, can a
real image of him as he was be arrived at. . . .
But if this be not so, Fowler's history is remarkable, and, without doubt, I think, deserves some
attention for itself.

I take it to be a matter of the most certain
experience in dealing with boys of an amiable
infirm disposition, that exactly the treatment
they receive from you they will deserve. In a
general way it is true of all persons of unformed
character who come in contact with you as your
inferiors, although with men it cannot be relied
on with the same certainty, because their feelings are less powerful, and their habit of moving

this way or that way under particular circumstances more determinate. But with the very large class of boys of a yielding nature who have very little self-confidence, are very little governed by a determined will or judgment, but sway up and down under the impulses of the moment, if they are treated generously and trustingly, it may be taken for an axiom that their feelings will be always strong enough to make them ashamed not to deserve it. Treat them as if they deserved suspicion, and as infallibly they soon actually will deserve it. People seem to assume that to be governed by impulse means only 'bad impulse,' and they endeavour to counteract it by trying to work upon the judgment, a faculty which these boys have not got, and so cannot possibly be influenced by it. There never was a weak boy yet that was deterred from doing wrong by ultimate distant consequences, he was to learn from thinking about them. It is idle to attempt to manage him otherwise than by creating and fostering generous impulses to keep in check the baser ones. And the greatest delicacy is required in effecting this. It is not enough to do a substantial good. Substantial good is often dry or repulsive on the surface;

and must be *understood* to be valued; just, again, what boys are unable to do. . . . Strong natures may understand and value the reality. Women, and such children as these, will not be affected by it, unless it shows on the surface what is in the heart. Provided you will do it with a kind, sympathizing manner, you may do what you please with them, otherwise nothing you do will affect them at all. . . . I say it is a fact in human nature that vast numbers of people are so constituted—born so. I am not saying it would not be better if they were otherwise; but they are not. It is idle to be ideal and uto-pian. You must make what you can of things as they are. And yet in this matter of educat-ing, there are no persons more blindly theoretic and ideal than your practical men of under-standing, who bring up every body on what they call their few broad principles of plain com-mon sense.

If fathers could but know, or could but let themselves be taught, how many sleepless nights of anxiety they would save themselves—how many a naturally well-intentioned child they would save from sorrow and suffering and guilt, by but taking the trouble now and then to find

a few kind words to express the real kindness
which in their hearts they feel! You will find
many fathers—substantially kind and good fathers—whose single guide in all they do for
their children is the highest, most imperious
sense of duty. It is far rarer to find one who,
in the little private relations of common life, will
throw them a kind word or a kind smile. Poor
Ned Fowler! I remember him showing me,
with tears in his eyes, the spot in the garden
at Darling, where he had listened to the last
genuine hearty words his father had ever addressed to him. It was the merest trifle, a
flower-bed, where, as a little boy, he was driving
in a stick to bind up a refractory carnation; but
the 'Well done, Ned,' (it was the last time he
had called him Ned,) had rung on the single,
soft sweet note among weary years of discord.

Edward was the youngest of a family of eight.
A talent of itself unhealthily precocious was
most unwisely pushed forward and encouraged
out by everybody, by teachers and schoolmaster,
from the vanity of having a little monster to display as their workmanship, by his father, because

he was anxious for the success of his children in life, and the quicker they got on the better ; they would the sooner assume a position. . . . It had struck no one there might be a mistake about it. No one could have ever cared to see even if it were possible there might, on five minutes' serious talk with the boy, or to have listened to his laugh, would have shown the simplest of them they were but developing a trifling quickness of faculty ; that the power which should have gone for the growth of the entire tree was being directed off into a single branch, which was swelling to disproportioned magnitude, while the stem was quietly decaying. . . . As to the character of the entire boy, his temper, disposition, health of tone in heart and mind, all that was presumed. It made no show at school exhibitions, and at least directly assumed no form of positive importance as regarded after life. So this was all left to itself. Of course, if a boy knew half the Iliad by heart at ten, and had construed the Odyssey through at eleven, all other excellences were a matter of course. . . He was naturally timid, and shrunk from all the amusements and games of other boys. So much the better, he would keep to his books. . .

He was undergrown for his age, infirm, and unhealthy; and a disposition might have been observed in him even then, in all his dealings with
other boys and with his master, to evade difficulties instead of meeting them—a feature which
should have called for the most delicate handling,
and would have far better repaid the time and
attention which were wasted in forcing him beyond his years, in a few poor miserable attain-
ments. . . . The consequence was, that when
sent to a public school he was placed among
boys four or five years his seniors, to live with
them, and do their work, in school and out of
school, with all the rest of him, except his mere
acquirements, undergrown even for his own age.
. . . His nature required treatment the most
delicate, it received the very roughest. Contrary to the advice of several friends (for here
some few did protest) he was pushed upon the
Foundation at Westminster, where for one year
at least to all boys, and to some for every year,
the life was as hard, and the treatment as barbarous, as that of the negroes in Virginia. . . .
What it may be now I do not know. I am
speaking of what it was fifteen years ago. . . .
The juniors in college have, however, in the

midst of their trials, a sympathy with one another which encourages and supports them, and
helps them to bear their miserable life, and
sometimes even draw good from it; years pass
quickly, and each year will find them rising
higher, and by-and-bye they will take their turns
and be masters too.

But such comfort as this was denied to Edward Fowler. The older boys beat him, because
being too young for the work he had to do as
their slave, he could not do it. His own election were jealous of his supposed talents, and
beat and tortured him too. Animal courage he
had none. Moral courage he had never been
trained in; and the consequence was, the poor
boy was crushed. Every one's hand was against
him. He had no open ways of escaping; so
that he soon learnt to find ways that were not
open. You might see him skulking along the
walls and passages, mean, pitiful, and wretched-
looking; right and wrong, truth and falsehood,
honour and dishonour, grown all alike to him.
The one honourable feeling which clung to him
only served to perpetuate his misery. He could
not bring himself to complain to the master of
the way he was treated in college. . . . His life

was so wretched that, lawful or unlawful, anything that would give him momentary ease he
would avail himself of. . . . No one believed
what he said. No one could believe him; he
had quite left off truth speaking. He used to
invent excuses of illness, to escape from the
wretchedness of college to the sanctuary of the
sick-room at the boarding-house. This was
soon found out, and the masters were foolish
enough to treat him as if it was mere school he
wished to shirk, instead of the young tyrants up
the college stairs. They never even suspected
the real cause, and repeated complaints to his
father were the natural consequence.

Any one who has been at a public school
knows how much a very little money adds to a
schoolboy's small stock of comforts. . . . It did
not add to Fowler's,—it made the whole; he
had none else. . . . The scraped mutton bones
and refuse fat would be thrown him for his dinner; if he did not like that he might go without
and crawl off to some back room at the pastry-
cook's. No wonder he had long bills there.
And if by accident money not his own passed
into his hands, it was not sure of coming clear of
them again; at least on one occasion money

belonging to his brother was made away with. His bills at the boarding-house were large, so many days and weeks were spent there in the sick-room. His clothes were always torn and wretched; yet they cost more, and he had more of them, than other boys. His books were taken from him or torn to pieces out of wantonness, and more must be bought. . . . There is one more grave charge I must bring against this school of Westminster. Whether the authorities of the school were aware of the fact I am going to mention I do not know; but whether they were or not it was alike disgraceful to them. . . One of the established duties of a junior in college is to supply the seniors with stationery of every kind, and in the most reckless profusion. Knives, pencils, pens, paper, a daily tale to be daily delivered in. The bricks must be made, make them how they can, and not even stubble to burn them withal. There was no escape except by complaining, and that boys will never do. . . . To high-spirited boys it would never occur as a possibility, and the others will not do it from fear, for they know very well the master cannot, or will not, shelter them from all the consequences they would entail on themselves.

The general way the thing was managed was by a private bill at the stationer's, procured on an order from boys' parents when made acquainted with the circumstance. Ned Fowler, as good for nothing else, was always expected to have the largest supply of these things. He must supply the seniors, and he must supply his brother juniors too. He could not get them in the scramble as other boys could; so that his bill was four times as large as theirs. But he knew how little use it would be for him to apply at home for leave to have such a bill. He was too cowardly to face the beatings which would have ensued on his being unprovided with what was required, so that he represented to the stationers he *had* leave, when he neither had it nor had asked for it. I mention this to show how utterly mean he had become. . . . How he had become so I have partly shown. Whether he was likely to improve under such a system I need hardly inquire. If you beat a dog for every fault, and beat him for your pleasure when there is none, you do not commonly form a very amiable dog; and the evil is that it is so completely the habit of the world to judge a person for what they *are*, without trou-

bling themselves to inquire how they came to
be so, that all people, good and bad, despised
and disliked Fowler, and did not care to hide
from him that they did. . . .

And it was little sympathy or kindness he
could meet with from his friends at home.
How was it possible that he could? with complaint upon complaint being all that reached
them from the masters, and his own wretched
character all they ever saw? . . His father held
threats of removal over him. A threat of removal! As well threaten a prisoner on the rack
with liberty. But then it was to be accompanied
with a degradation which made even Westminster tolerable: he was to be sent off to a cheap
school in Yorkshire, and from thence appren-
ticed to a trade. . . . It was a cruel thing this
threatening, and, under all circumstances, as
useless as it was cruel. Besides which Canon
Fowler never meant it. . . . It was a way he
had, and a most unlucky one, of always over-
saying things, and particularly over-threatening.
He forgot the boy was sure to take him literally
—he forgot that *the fear which is without love*
is the very worst, the very most fatal feeling a
child can be brought to entertain towards his

8

father. The Canon soon forgot, too, the words
he had used, and only remembered his own
meaning, so that a large gulf of misunderstanding was gaping wider and wider between them;
and what but a miracle could ever bridge it
over? Once, and once only, had he complained
of the way he was treated. . . . He wrote to his
brother; but Ned's word experience had taught
him was not good. All but wholly disbelieving
him, he did, however, write to the under-master.
. . . The under-master was a good upright man,
but not a wise one—one who was well satisfied
if all seemed right, and thought it better not to
see many things he might have seen. He argued it was more likely that young Fowler
should be telling lies, than that such things
should be going on and he be unacquainted
with them. William Fowler agreed with him,
and there the matter ended. . . .

Well, Ned struggled on through his three
years and became a senior; but nothing mended
with him. He sneaked and shirked along the
streets, with his head no higher at fifteen than
it had been at twelve,—when he ceased to be
a fag he was beaten for amusement. . . . The
senior boys had places round the fire, and tea,

and many little luxuries; but there were none for Edward Fowler. His worst foes were those of his own election. He would crawl into college after dusk to his corner, and would sit silent in the dark on his bed, happy if each night he was permitted to creep into it unnoticed, or, what was the same thing with him unbeaten. Even when in bed his dangers were not ended. He might be seen sliding into school in the morning with a face all scarred and blistered for weeks and weeks together. The older boys stalking round college at midnight would pause as they passed him; one would hold him down while another would hold a lighted cigar stump against his cheek, till such time as it was clear pain would prevent his eyes from closing again that night at least. About the middle of his senior's year fresh matter of complaint from the head master brough matters to a crisis. His bills were as high as ever; he went home and did not return again. . . He was not sent to a Yorkshire school. . . . What *was* done was perhaps as bad. His father beat him himself, and afterwards kept him at home for two years; at the end of which time, from the way he was treated there, his home was little less loathsome

to him than school had been; and the last frail
fibres that might have wound their hearts together were sundered now for ever. . . . Bill
poured in after bill. The disastrous state of
his wardrobe had to be discovered. The Canon's suspicions led him at once to conclude
things were bought only to be unfairly made
away with; he treated the boy as an accomplished swindler, and told him gravely if he
lived to see him twenty-one he would see him
transported. It had a strange effect on him
this. . . . The one unworthy suspicion which
he knew he did not deserve made him forget the
many that he did; and the sullen, unhappy boy
grew to fear his father and tremble before his
father, almost as he had done before his tyrants
at the school.

This very painful history Fowler told me himself. It will not be thought he has drawn a
picture much to his own advantage, or that if he
has coloured it, it has been with a brush which
can only paint virtues, and throws every fault
into indistinguishable shade. I must be allowed
to add a few remarks upon it of my own. . . .
If I have written it as if I meant to blame the
persons who were concerned in this injudicious

treatment of him, I am very sorry. I mean nothing less. . . . In a scene so crowded as this world is, or as the little world of a public school is, with any existing machinery it is impossible to attend to minute shades of character. There is a sufficient likeness among boys to justify the use of general, very general laws indeed. They are dealt with in the mass. An average treatment is arrived at. If an exception does rise, and it happens to disagree, it is a pity, but it cannot be helped. God forbid, too, I should think of blaming Canon Fowler. He was a busy practical man of the world, far too much employed in being of active service to it to be able to spare time in attending minutely to peculiarities in the disposition of his children; and judging as people generally judge, and dealing with them on the methods usually in repute, after the few first steps all the rest seems to me quite natural, indeed inevitable. "Punish," not "prevent," is the old-fashioned principle. If a boy goes wrong whip him. Teach him to be afraid of going wrong, by the pains and penalties to ensue,—just the principle on which gamekeepers used to try to break dogs. . . But men learnt to use gentler methods soonest with the lower animals. As to the effects of the treatment, results seem to show pretty much alike in both cases; but with the human animal an unhappy notion clung on to it, and still clings, and will perpetuate the principle and its disastrous consequences, that men and boys *deserve* their whipping, as if they could have helped doing what they did in a way dogs cannot. Whipping * is good, but whipping is not the best; there are times when it is the very worst. It would be well if people would so far take example from what they find succeed with their dogs, as to learn there are other ways at least as efficacious, and that the desired conduct is better if produced in *any* other way than in that. . . . Something better might have been made of Fowler. I knew him well in after life, and I am sure that if he had been observed more attentively, many traits would have been seen which would have given a clue to a better management of him. On the whole general rules should have no place in family education. It is just there, and there, perhaps, alone, that there are opportunities of studying

* I employ this word in a general sense, not limiting it to the application of birch.

shades of difference, and it should be the
business of affection to attend to them.   When
affection is really strong it will be an equal
security against indulgence and over-hasty severity.

Do not say what claim had Fowler on affection?   Relationship is a claim, an artificial one
if you like; but it is one of nature's artifices
—to provide supply of love to those who else
might perish for the lack of it.   If any single
person had been found to try and look whether
some other explanation of what his son had
become might not be found, instead of leaving
it as mere unaccountable baseness, Canon
Fowler would have been spared years of anxiety,
and Edward a long catalogue of sins, and a fiery
trial, in which he was purged of them.

The defect in Edward's nature, as I understand it, was that he was constitutionally a
coward.   Constitutionally, I say.   It was not
his own fault.   Nature had ordered him so, just
as she orders others constitutionally brave.   One
may like these the best, but one must be cautious how one praises them for what they have
earned by no merit of their own.   Courage of
this kind—animal courage—is a gift, not an ac-

quirement. . . . Neither animal courage nor
animal cowardice result from any principle,
they are merely passions. . . . So different from
moral courage and moral cowardice, that they
seem to me to have nothing in common except
the name. As far as I can judge from experience, each has about an equal chance of acquiring either. . . . The cowardly boy, if he
is trained, or trains himself, to get his nature
under the control of reason, will hold that passion in equal check with the rest. . . . The bold
boy may give himself the rein, and fall before
every other temptation except that of flinching
from fighting with his fellow-creatures. But I
am wasting words on what is so obvious. What
Fowler had not was animal courage, he was
subject to the passion of timidity, in the same
way as other boys are subject to the passions of
anger, jealousy, cruelty, or gross appetites; and
it ought to have been understood that he was
falling before a constitutional weakness, instead
of being supposed that he had a formed, settled
character of meanness and cowardice. Later in
life, when his nature came into play, he found
out his weaknesses and fought with them and
conquered them. I have seen him in circum-

stances where the boldest of the school prize-
fighters might have turned pale, and his pulse
has not altered, and his voice been as light
and cheerful as ever. . . . Surely a fellow who
had it in him to become this, must have shown
indications of the real stuff there was at bottom
in him. However, we are not at the end, or
nearly at the end, of his errors yet.

Well, he was kept two years at home, crawling about by himself as he best could ; treated
with a uniform cold sternness by his father, and
in consequence avoided as questionable company
by other people. His family took the cue one
from another. Unhappily he had lost his mother when a baby. His brothers thought him a
sawney, despised him, and taught his sisters
to despise him. Amusement he was not allowed to taste. He was ordered to read, but he
had no one to help him ; he was not even al-
owed to look forward to anything ultimately
coming of his reading. Some once in six months
his father would speak to him of his prospects ;
but it was only to tell him that he had none
—that he could not trust him away from home
—that he had thought it his duty to his other
children not to mention his name in his will.

Alas, the madness of supposing he could govern his child so! Edward grew up silent,
proud, and sullen. His talent, such as it was,
had begun to grow again, but now very unlike
what it was before. He had learnt nothing at
school, at least of what was directly taught
there; at home he had no help—no encouragement—no spirit to make him even wish to advance himself. . . . As far as book-learning
went, little prodigy as he had been at seven, at
seventeen he was further back than he was
then. . . . But suffering had made him an
acute observer; not a fault in others escaped his
eye, and he brooded over their failings and
weaknesses, and measured himself against them,
and he never rose from a session which he had
held in council with himself, without deciding
he was the most injured of beings, and pouring
fresh and fresh spleen and venom into his
wounds. . . . So wretchedly things went on. . . .
But Edward was subtle enough not to betray his
feelings. . . . The threatened trade hung over
him, and anything must be borne to escape from
that; and at the end of the two years the Canon
had recovered sufficient confidence in him to
send him to a private tutor, with a view to his

going to the university. . . . He had continued
sullen and unamiable enough, but he had done
nothing, and shown no tendency to positive
evil, and the venture might be made. This
was real kindness; if it had been accompanied
with any kind, hearty words, Edward, even then,
would have thrown himself in tears at his feet,
and his pains and trials would have been at an
end for ever. But unhappily the Canon's plan
was just the opposite. He felt more confidence
than he let Edward see, and the boy was sent
away with the feeling that he was watched and
distrusted; so that consequently the return he
made his father was merely to suspect him too
of unworthy motives, and that vanity and un-
willingness to have a son of his in a station below
his own, was the real moving principle, and no
regard for himself.

The venture seemed, notwithstanding, to succeed—in a way it did succeed. For the first
time since he could recollect he found himself
among people who were truly kind to him, and
his frozen heart began to thaw in the warm atmosphere; nay, more, he, the despised, the
slighted, the trampled on of everybody, now
found himself in a way to be respected. . . .

He was an acute observer and a ready talker,
talents always valued and rewarded in life, and
he passed at once with a bound into a person
whose opinion was to be received, whose advice
was often asked, on serious subjects ; who,
whenever he chose to speak, was sure of
listeners.

What a change ! and it did him both good
and evil.   It did him good in teaching him what
he was, in warming up his faculties into healthy
exercise, and drawing him off from brooding for
ever over the phantom of himself.   His mind
was supplied with objects which strung it again
and tuned it.   But the harm, perhaps, was
greater, for it taught him to contrast the position he held with others with that in which he
stood at home.   The home government continued to harp unwisely on the old strings, and
the discord grew louder and harsher.   It was
with no very enviable feeling that, in the middle
of some serious speculation on which he was
dictating—some question of conduct on which
he was propounding his advice, that he would
find a letter put in his hands from his father or
his brother, reminding him of what he had been,
and what they partly suspected he was still,

and winding up with threatenings that he was
on his last trial, the last time, and so on.   The
two ideas were so opposite he could not recognize himself in each, so that of course he chose
the one which pleased him best, and proceeded
equally to resent the other.   This was rash in
them ; it was scattering sparks over powder
ready strewed for explosion.   The same evil
which had so injured him as a child he was
fast again becoming exposed to.   His talents
were outrunning the rest of him.   There was no
material of character to carry them. . . . What
chance had he ever had of forming any?   Was
there not work *enough* for him, without heaping
more fuel on the fire ?   At eighteen he went to
Oxford.   Once more among young men of his
own age ; but how different a part to play among
them !   The little, weak, diminutive boy had
shot up into a tall, well-made young man—the
cringing, cowardly wretch, that was driven with
blows and curses from the fireside by his brother
schoolboys, into the clever, witty, entertaining
fellow, with apparently every faculty to entitle
him to popularity.   He had not much classical
knowledge.   Poor fellow, that was not his fault ;
but he had managed to assimilate large stores

of information and anecdote on all kinds of subjects. He had a capital knack of talking; he could row, ride, walk—anything with anybody . . . . He was all things to all men; not because he was well principled or unprincipled, but simply because he was without principle; because he was merely an aggregate of talent, and nothing else. As was to be expected, he shot into popularity. Every body liked him; he was welcome everywhere, from the common-room to the vingt'un party. He seemed just what everybody wished, because it was all "*seem*" with him, he *was* nothing. . . . He was quite as honest, quite as much himself, as far as he had a self, at his tutor's tea-table as at a drunken supper party. Frank and open as he always seemed, every one thought they had him as he really was, and disbelieved the stories they heard about him. Kind and open-hearted he really was; enough facts were known of this to entitle him to be loved. But perhaps he was most his real self, most like what he had been, in his behaviour to his father. Who can say how strong, how overpowering is the force of association? At twenty, Edward trembled at the sight of him as he had trembled at twelve.

The old system was still followed steadily; the slightest shadow of a complaint, the slightest cloud that rose above his horizon, and his sun was to set below it, and the warehouse or the tanyard was to be his destiny. . . . An imperious command of confidence with none offered; what on earth could come of that? A journal of each day was required to be sent off weekly. What young man's life at college could bear such a confessional, even without the threat of instant removal? . . . Yet it was not without a pang that Edward stooped to his escape, and left out what would be unsatisfactory.

Another mistake was also made which I think was a great one. Home and college changed places. Home was still the place of discipline and authority; all the amusements were at college. At college there were no " you must" or " you must not;" at home there was nothing else. Till he went to college, (at least since he was quite a child,) Edward had never known the idea which is represented by the word amusement. The Canon had made a point of refusing it to him, and taught him to set an unnatural value upon it, in order to make him feel the more poignantly what it was to be deprived

of it.   Short-sighted enough.   Natural home
ought to be real home, the scene of all our happiness, ease, and *absence of restraint.*   Young
men are sure to have such a place somewhere;
if not at home, it will be where it ought not to
be. . . . Home, away from home, holidays in
term time, and term time in holidays, one set
of friends in the order of Providence and another in the order of affection,—what are these
but the harshest discords of life, chords that
can never vibrate in harmony till art has un-
strung the harp of nature, and retuned it without a heart.

For fear, however, I may be squandering my
words, and the notion of feelings being of so
much importance be thought by some persons
rather ridiculous, I will but mention one practical result which at any rate will deserve their
attention.   To say nothing of the more than
questionable character of the greater part of
college amusements, they cost ten times as much
as ten times the same amount of innocent
amusement at home.   To think young men will
be content to go without amusement, is about
as idle as to expect fire to burn without oxygen;
and when they find no sympathy, no interest, no

7

wish to provide them with such things among those who ought to do so, they are less likely to be scrupulous or to care how much pain or injury they may be inflicting on them, by taking their own way of providing for themselves. I can safely appeal to the experience of every one who knows much of college life, to bear me out in saying, that in nine cases out of ten, when young men go wrong there, they will be found to be such as are kept strictly at home ; and when one goes very wrong indeed it is invariably so. . . . The mass of them are governed by their feelings. It is no use to complain of it—they are so. You must expect it and provide for it. You may try to govern them reasonably by appeals to their understanding,—you will not succeed. You may try severity, and crush the rock with your hammer, and shiver it with your gunpowder, and it will be rock still; but heat it and drop water on it—warm their hearts with kindness and affection, and let a tear of joy or sorrow now and then fall down on them, and they will soften and be pliant as the clay.

I am not surprised that Fowler was idle and extravagant. He had been weighed down so heavily, and at college the weight was so com-

pletely taken off, that he was like a boat without
ballast, and he heaved over at every breath of
inclination.   No wonder that, with so many
temptations, so little natural gift for management, he should have found himself in debt before he was aware of it—no wonder that, with
only threats at home to encourage him to be
communicative on such a subject, he should
have kept it carefully concealed, entangled himself worse and worse in the means necessary to
do so, and passed through two of his three
years, trusting that some lucky accident would
interfere for his deliverance.

CHAPTER IV.

WHAT a load off my mind these last few pages are! I am afraid it will be as dull reading as it has been unpleasant writing. The ink has grown thick while I have been about it. . . . . I have put water with it, and the rest of the beverage, if thinner, will be more palatable.   Nevertheless would not one think it high privilege to have to write a thousand such, if one could save a single soul from such a fate as Fowler's ?

Such was the fellow, however, that we left pouring himself out to Sterming on the sands at Aberdovey; if it be thought surprising that he should have won the hearts of the Hardinges, it must be remembered that in his dealings with every one except with his own family, he was frank, generous, and unselfish. His affections naturally very strong, finding themselves forced out of their proper channel, poured themselves out on any one that happened to attract him. His conversation was so bright, his thought and feelings so delicate and beautiful, his temper (he had inherited that from his mother) so sweet and gentle, that as far as a stranger could see him, he appeared the very perfection of a graceful mind. It was the strongest satire as his relation to his own family, that beyond their circle, and the atmosphere of their influence, he fascinated everybody. And by the way, it added no little to his difficulties with himself, the way, I mean, in which other people treated him. It was too easy for him to persuade himself that the external judgment was the true one, the real fair one, and the other the growth of ignorance, and prejudice, and dislike. And the reverse, alas, so far, far nearer to the truth! If they erred in thinking he had no heart, was not his error as deep, and far more unjustifiable in thinking the same of them? Such as he was, however, the Hardinge family thought him almost faultless, and Emma Hardinge quite so. And if Edward ever knew a genuine, hearty, unselfish feeling, it was his love for her. There is a discovery in modern chemistry that a stream of galvanism passing through a loose heap of powdered metal will convert it to a solid mass. Something very like this was befalling Edward. His loose inconstant nature, which had hitherto refused to retain any form which could be given it, was now receiving a nervous tension and solidity, from the high and noble feeling which was diffusing itself throughout him ; a power was found which would bind all the incoherent crystals into a unit again. Providence has many spare cables, with which she holds her sons at their moorings, when wilfulness, or the waves of circumstances have broke them from their own; and true love of man is accepted in heaven, till the true strength of man, true love of God, be grown again. And so it was with Edward Fowler. . . . . Should this cable part too !

In a general way he contrived to make so much of his position clear to Sterming, that the result was the advice which best harmonized with the suggestion of his own heart, to go off at once to Morlands, have it all out with Emma, and put his father's letter into Mr. Hardinge's hands. . . . . Sterming thought it would all turn on the insanity question. The Canon gave it as a reason, as *the* reason—if it could be removed (and Fowler thought it could) it was not very clear how he could refuse them the little they asked him—to be allowed to look forward at any distance of time to being married ; now and then to write letters, and to walk about with no one to look after them in the woods and by the lake side. . . . . And Sterming was right. The scene was all gone through, explanations made, difficulties suggested and answered. The insanity was not hereditary. It was a single instance, and a special reason could be given for it. So a great letter was written to the Canon, detailing all. . . . . The double current from his brother setting the same way, the difficulty being partially removed in one case, opened a breach in the embankment of objections, and the whole swept away ; and the elder brother married and got rid of his illness, into which anxiety had thrown him, and Edward was to be engaged. It took time though. It was a fortnight before the Canon's answer came to Edward, after the letter had been sent off from Morlands ; he thought it would be better to wait the decision at Aber-

dovey, so he had gone back there immediately.
The fortnight seemed a life to him; day tottered
after day, as if they had caught the palsy, and
were all as much agitated as he was, and could
not go about their functions quietly. . . . The
letter did come at last, however, and it was a
consent. Satirically given enough, but still a
consent. It came in the evening. Edward sat
up to write an answer, the first really hearty
letter he had perhaps ever written to his
father. His heart was almost breaking with
genuine gratefulness, and whoever could have
looked into it then would have seen the noblest
resolutions bravely forming themselves, laying
broad strong roots, and swelling and stretching
in the warmth of so unusual an atmosphere.
If the warm wind will only blow till the resolutions have begun to become acts, what may we
not hope for Edward?

He did not write all he felt, but he did write
a good, upright, sensible, thankful letter. He
told his father he knew, and felt, how much
annoyance he had caused him; he would do so
no more. His character was changed, and he
should find it so. This was more than words.
The words stood all for genuine thoughts and

feelings. At daybreak he posted off over the
hill to Morlands, and the shepherd boys wondered
at the buoyant step of the gentleman stranger,
and the foot on the fell-side lighter and swifter
than their own.

The letter was in his pocket. . . . The letter
. . . . . It was rather too caustic, contained too
many personal reflections, to be altogether pleasant, but it was a consent, a bright and beautiful
consent, a charm which would throw Emma
Hardinge into his arms; and such trifles as
these, perhaps, did but set off the beauty, like
the shadows in a landscape. He was never tired
of reading it. No sooner was it in his pocket
than it was out again, or his hand went in after
it, to be sure it was safe. It is the way to be
sure to lose a thing, this perpetual assuring
ourselves we have it unlost. . . . Edward lost
the letter. . . . Somewhere between Aberdovey
and Morlands he had lost it,—it was gone—into
the bog, or he river, or the lake, or on the
mountain side—somewhere it was gone and not
to be found again. He searched and searched,
but it was no use—he must go on without it. It
was not his fault; but when he came to think
about it, it must be owned he did feel it was a

relief.   He must have shown the letter, but he was not bound to remember all the bitter things. . . . . It is singular how often the accidents which befall people follow the bend of their character, and chance does for them the sort of things they might be suspected of doing themselves.   When real matter of displeasure was afterwards found against Edward, this lost letter was added to it; Mr. Hardinge was led to believe he had purposely made away with it.

At the time, however, no such thing was dreamt of; all was sunshine; all were too happy, to think anything but the best of everybody.   Mrs. Hardinge, the little Hardinges, even Mr. Hardinge himself, welcomed him into the family, as now a permitted member of it, with the kiss of good old-fashioned affection, and Emma with perhaps more than one.   It was a beautiful meeting—as bad men shed their dark influence on all, good and bad alike, that fall in contact with them, and spread round them a halo of suffering and ill; so do the purely good illumine all who come within their sphere, and mixed characters of earth, when absorbed into the higher systems, shine there with a light not their own, reflecting the rays which fall on them.

Edward lost his faults while he was at Morlands; he remembered them only as an old
garment he had outworn, and had now thrown
away for ever. Life was still before him. What
a life would he not make of it? The concluding
two months of the vacation he spent at Morlands; the air and sky seemed to sympathize
with the young lovers. The early part of the
summer had been wet and miserable; but never
did two moons shine through a bluer or serener
heaven than that August and September. And
were not Emma and he happy then? Happy in
each other, living in each other, and requiring
nothing else, and thinking of nothing else; for
they knew that each was all the other valued,
and each had each as fully as they could give
themselves to each other. They climbed the
mountains, and went long scrambling expe-
ditions across the lake. The woods and waterfalls they could never tire of; they were sure of
a kind welcome, and each new time they went
again to an old scene it was richer than before,
for it was rich in the recollection of the last
bright happy visit. Then they would skim
down the river in the little skiff, or at evening
sit watching the boats from the fell-side, as they

passed up and down, and listen to the splash of
the oar, or the distance-sweetened cry of the
far-off boatmen, their arms twined round each
other, and asking no other pleasure. They
did not want to speak, words do but spoil the
charm of such moments, when souls seem to
know a shorter road into each other, and lips
have a dearer use. One evening they went up
the Fell to see the sun set. They were half an
hour too soon; a thick bank of cloud hung
over the sea-horizon; and a veil of mist was
wreathed in heavy folds round the head of
Cadir. They sat down, hoping for a change.
Young lovers never tire of the early history of
their affection ; . . . and, as if in sympathy with
the gloominess of the scene, they were calling up
again the clouds that a few weeks since had hung
so dark over their horizon. . . . . When just
as the lowest rim of the sun's disc touched the
sea, the cloud-banks split right asunder; they
had held close till the pageant was complete, and
now out streamed the sinking monarch, in all
his crimson pomp and splendour. Peak after
peak put on their glory, and begun to gaze,
purple-flushed, on the wonderful vision. . . . .
The black wreath on Cadir turned orange-red,

with a fringe of gold, and began slowly to wind about the summit. . . . . As it moved it grew thinner and more transparent, and the giant chair showed glistening through; a single cloud had settled motionless into it, like the outline of a huge human form enthroned there, and the vapour ring split into fairy-like wavy forms, which swept round and round, trailing their pink, gauzy drapery, and weaving round his temples a coronet of gold. . . . . One might have thought the imprisoned Arthur had woke again on the astonished world, and the fairy queens were paying homage to the undying monarch.

"See, Emma," Edward said; " see how beautiful! How like our fate; our clouds how dark they were! . . . . And now the sun of hope has broken upon us, and the very envious vapour itself is turned to glory inexpressible." Alas, had he but carried on the image it had been too true. . . . . It was the *setting* sun that was so beautiful; almost as he spoke it was gone, and all was dull, and dark, and dreary as before. . . . . But they never thought of that. It is no new thing that Nature is for ever but an echo of our own spirit. Time-server and deceiver as she is, she will but read us the lesson she knows we wish to hear.

CHAPTER V.

TIME whets his scythe to mow our happiest days. . . . . . It is an old story, and we have heaped ill names on him for it, and called him envious. . . . Poor Time! the thin abstraction! The fault, if fault it be, is in ourselves. . . . We live the fastest when the mind is most active, most alive. In perfect life and perfect action, not as we know it, but as it is to be, days and years will cease to stand as reckoning marks, and past and future merge in the never-ending moment of eternity.

And these two months must have been very living—very perfect; all but a moment, and they were gone. October came, and the rain began to fall, and the leaves to heap up grave-mounds over the dying flowers, and the sun sunk behind the hill, and took his last leave of the deep

valley of Morelands, till woods and meadows
were dressed again to receive him ; and Edward
too must bid his farewell, and learn as in this
world,—alas, they are too often disunited to leave
happiness for duty.

And it was for duty. Edward knew now, and
felt now what duty was. As the consciousness
of time wasted, and worse than wasted, rose ac-
cusingly before him, there came with it a strong
conviction of what there was in him, and what
he might still become; a sense of power nerv-
ing and bracing itself, and held steady in one
line by the star on which his eye was now un-
ceasingly gazing. He returned to Oxford, out-
wardly at least so altered a person as to give
cause for the most various speculation among his
many friends. He had done much wrong; he
would do so no more. His expensive companions
were quietly dropped. His place was empty at
the wine party and the gaming table. There
was no affected ostentation of saintliness; no
spasmodic effort, self-exhaustive, and self-
destructive; but a steady, resolute alteration in
all his ways and doings. From being the idlest
man in college, he grew to be known as a hard-
worker, and tutors began to change their views

of him, and look to making more than something of him. The ground that had been lying
so long rotting, was fast covering with luxuri-
ance; and now not Welsh faces only, but higher
faces of the university, came with good reason
to smile on him approvingly.

Alas! how far easier it is to forsake our faults
than to teach them to forsake us! What you sow
will grow, and you must reap it; it is a great iron
law which cannot be broken. Good resolutions
pay no debts. And yet if you cannot pay you
must go on and make more. . . . Resolutions not
to extend existing debts brought those he had
upon him peremptorily. Somehow they must
be met, but how? Experience seems to say
that the difficulty at Oxford is not to get into
debt; that to young men who have had no training in managing, it is next to impossible to avoid
it, and the readiest, and really surest way of pre-
venting their extending would be for fathers to
assume that at least for the first year it will be
so. Encouraging their sons to be communicative, by letting them see they can understand
and excuse it, they will put them right once,
and experience and thankfulness for a help so
timely will keep the boys clear for the future.

10

. . . . But Canon Fowler had not done this; instant removal was to be the consequence of a single debt, and Edward at an early period of his Oxford career, finding himself entangled, he could hardly tell how, had sunk under the temptation, and his ingrained terror of his father had said it was not so. . . . Poor miserable boy, it was wind indeed he had been sowing. . . . . hollow words that were but air, with no truth in them—and now he must reap the whirlwind. . . . He knew too well what would be the result of a discovery. Perhaps if it had been any one else but his father, or if he had had to begin then with his father, even exactly as he was, he would have gone to him notwithstanding, and risked the consequence. But the association of habitual fear was round him to rivet the temptation. It must be kept from him at all hazards. His ultimate prospects were tolerably good. . . . that is, he could be sure of sometime or other being able to meet such an amount of obligation as he must contract to pay his existing debts. He took a sort of counsel with his conscience, and it did not seem to forbid him to try to borrow of one of his friends what would be enough to set him free. At the end of term he

wrote to one of them, who he knew was able and
willing to help him.   He was to spend the vacation at home, and the answer to his letter was
to be directed to him at Darling.   Accident
detained him a day later than he had expected.
His friend's letter arrived before he had arrived
to receive it. . . .   Mistake brought it to the
Canon, and it was opened.

I cannot follow all the reflections that this sort
of chance sends crowding in upon the mind.
But nothing can have a more disheartening
effect upon a young man, meeting him so in the
teeth at the commencement of a return of good
intentions; the more genuine the intention the
worse the effect.   It makes him despair of goodness; distrust Providence, which he assumes
must turn on his side the instant he turns himself; and commonly he will give the matter up,
and fancy himself the sport and victim of a destiny which will have its way, and it is idle to attempt to stem. . .   What is the use of all this
pain to be good, if I am to suffer all the same?
is unhappily always more or less the thought
of all but the very few who have learnt to love
goodness for its own sake. . . .   The Canon
throughout the Christmas vacation was gloomy

and reserved. Except in the common interchange of morning and evening greetings, he never spoke to Edward at all, and even the rest of the family could only conjecture what he intended. What, in fact, he did intend, to this moment I do not know. He reserved the expression of his anger till Edward had returned again to college, and then it began to stream down upon him in letters. Still Edward went on, kept to his resolution, and worked harder and harder, and hoped the Hardinges might not be told. But letter came after letter, each darker than the one before, and at last came one containing an enclosed copy of "what he believed it would be his duty to send to Mr. Hardinge." The increasing darkness of the letters was accounted for by the bills as they came in proving larger (when were bills ever anything else?) than was expected. Edward thought between two and three hundred pounds. They were between three and four hundred. But the question of the immorality of Edward's proceedings did not appear to be affected by that. The real fault, the real important fault, had been the denial two years before. At last, partly from conscience, partly in despair, partly because he

believed if the whole were known at least some
excuse might be found for him, and it was better
to brave the worst, and trust to time to heal the
wound he could not think would be incurable;
he copied out his father's letter himself, and
with a long one of his own, detailing most of his
own history, he sent it off to Mr. Hardinge. . .
It was a thunder-train indeed which he had
fired . . . First there was a frightful silence;
one terror-stricken letter came from poor Emma,
saying her father was dreadfully agitated; and
the next post the hurricane broke upon him in
its brief fury one short stunning letter from
himself, and one more of two lines from Emma,
to say she could never be his wife.

Whether in this proceeding Mr. Hardinge
was acting right or wrong I am not prepared to
say. Such a question to be answered would require a long intricate analysis of the formation
of character, the nature of the obligations, varieties of knowledge, and varieties of disposition
impose on men. That a long, weary course of
suffering and misery, and even worse, resulted
from what he did, and that all this would have
been spared if he had acted differently, is no
proof that he did what he *ought* not. It would

only be so on a supposition of a perfect knowledge of all the past facts, and a thorough understanding of character; mistakes often produce
greater misery than faults—mistakes that seemingly could not have been guarded against. It
is one of the most perplexing parts of the system of this world that it is so. Mr. Hardinge
acted on the vague generalizations which go by
the name of the moral rule of right and wrong,
and the consequence showed that he acted unwisely. But he acted for the best according to
his knowledge. His nature was too zealous and
too religious to calculate, his passions were
all set to his principles . . . . and if the event
showed him wrong, it proves nothing but imperfect knowledge, and the inadequacy of the
existing average maxims of morality. He had
made a multitude of mistakes. He had mistaken Edward from the first; he had assumed
from the surface of him that he was almost perfect, and the shock he received when he heard
of so grievous a failure produced a total and
complete re-action. He had been deceived. . . .
But he forgot he had been deceived by himself,
and he resented it on Edward. The history he
had sent him of himself was all an ingenious

tissue of falsehood; and with the same precipi-
tancy with which he had before assigned him
every good quality, he now refused to believe he
had any. Yet he did what he thought his duty
to his own child. How *could* he trust her happiness in such keeping ? How could he leave
her exposed to such insidious influence? He
forgot that he should have learnt more of Edward before he permited her to entrust herself
so completely to him ; that where she could so
passionately love there must be real good; and
that at least now, if he persisted in his present
feeling, her happiness *must* be made shipwreck
of. . . . What I think his error was, that he
absolutely cut off all hope. Not only he did
not say Edward's future conduct might influence
him : but he distinctly declared, and with the
whole passion and energy of his nature, that it
never should. To Edward's wild, frenzied letters, he only answered (strange mockery) that
he forgave him as a Christian, and would pray
for him.   He guided the pen in his daughter's
hand to write the fatal renunciation of him ;
and exacted a solemn promise from her that she
would never see him again as long as she remained unmarried. Alas ! has not God shown

more long-suffering to greater sinners? Have
not repentance and amendment earned his best
gifts from Him; and if it be said God knows the
heart, and can discern the false from the real,
has not He too been pleased to waive his superhuman power, and like man, and as an example to men, condescended to use visible
amendment as the test of the change?

I am not claiming more for Fowler than his
right. . . . I am far from saying that as yet
he was entirely changed, and that now he was
acting from the best and highest motives. . . .
No; but his conduct was changed, and it was
changed out of love for Emma Hardinge If he
had been left alone, and let go on as he was
going, persisting in right acting, would in time
have changed him really and altogether.

CHAPTER VI.

AND now my two streams, which had flowed together into one channel, and in their combination seemed to promise so fair and beautiful a course, by this fierce lightning stroke are decomposed again, and each sent off to follow alone its weary, melancholy bed, over rock, and stone, and parched sand, and barren wilderness. If earth be a valley of misery, together they might have filled many at least of its pools with water, and garnished its steeps and sides with flowers and pleasant pasturage; now they must wander alone over blasted and blackened plains, and it may be they will never reach the ocean, but sink for ever in the wilderness of sand.

Edward recovered from a violent sickness only to a more complete conviction of his wretchedness. Of all of pure, and bright, and

lovely, and good, which the memory of his past
life held up to him, what was the result?
Heart-breaking misery and despair ! . . It was
all gone. . . . Gone like the pleasant dreams
of his childhood, which had mocked his sleep in
the college at Westminster—gone, 'like a bright
exhalation in the morning,' and had left him
never to hope again. Why should he care any
more for good? What had good cared for him?
What was his life but wretchedness? And if
here and there some few cool oases seemed to
be scattered over it, no sooner had he plunged
into the shade than they sunk away, and the
dreary desert was more dreary than before.
Suicide more than once held out its tempting
promise of release to him. Parhaps he took a
worse course than suicide, for he tried to drown
himself in dissipation ; yet strange enough, evil
as it was, there was an embryo goodness in it ;
it resulted in good of a kind. A brief career
of such madness was soon abruptly terminated.
This time it was his good genius which guided
accident to scourge him from it, and he was
sent away for a time from the university in disgrace. He was not to be led out of his errors,
he was to be flogged out of them. Some people

take more flogging than others. Edward was
obliged to have much. But this last business
was nearly the end. . . In a way it was a relief
to him ; one poison serving as an antidote to
another. Disgraced, and his disgrace published,
wounded pride came in and drew him off his
other sorrows. . . . The smart of self for a time
overpowered his more generous pains, and with
a violent effort he now nerved himself to survey
his position. He could not fall lower,—could
he rise ? To ask the question is to make a beginning. With a haughty stoicism he resolved
to cauterize his wounds or cut them out. If
fate, as he called it, chose to go on persecuting
him, he would rule fate ; and a sternness of purpose, now wholly worldly and irreligious, came
to his help, which enabled him to despise opinion
and once more rise and exert himself ; not to
make people think better of him—he did not
care what they thought ; but because being " in
for life," there was nothing else to be done to
save himself from being for ever trampled on in
the crowd. . . . There was the alternative of
suicide : but the course he chose appeared the
more manly, and at any rate he could have that
always to fall back upon.

Is it strange that this should have succeeded when all else had failed? That a principle of so questionable a character should carry a man right, when what seemed so much better had turned out utterly powerless? Not at all! Anything like a principle, bad or good, so it be a principle which implies consistency, and requiring and compelling consistent action, prevents a man from being blown up and down by impulse, will carry him along on his feet at any rate. . . . To whatever end he comes he is still a man; a match for other men, and more than a match; and sure to rise above all other men, however much purer and better their nature who remain under the dominion of feeling. . . . Directly Edward determined to trust himself and not circumstances, he began to rise. All life, to be worth anything, must be under the control of reason, man's life and boy's life, and even all animal and all organized beings; it is this very conviction that it must be so which makes most education so unreasonable. You see one part of the truth, that your boy must not go wherever any appetite leads him. You appeal to his reason; try to make him govern himself by that, and are angry with him when he fails. You have lost sight of the other half of the truth, that with boys it is simply impossible. Their knowledge is weak and their feelings are strong; they cannot govern them. The secret of true management is to direct the objects which move their feelings by your own reason. Make them

"Most do your bidding following most their own."

They will be obeying your mind while they do not feel they are obeying. By degrees, as their own mind forms the secret will break on them. By-and-by, when the right time is come, the old skin will cast of itself, and leave no wound in the parting. Boys must follow passion; men, if they are to be more than boys, must never follow it. But Edward had none of this done for him. He had to begin all for himself; it was as if the whole moral knowledge the world has been all its long life in gaining he had to earn for himself in his own person. . . . It is with conduct as it is with science. Certain great generalizations are formed easily, which, whether wholly true or not, are partially so, and will do to begin with. Knowledge far outruns practice. . . . While we stand on one step, we look over many more. So that knowledge is driven to shifts and expedients to help

the lagging body after it. . . . Edward tried the
" *vow*" plan. . . . It is a curious feature in our
nature, that one can by a single act of will lay
oneself under a *rule* which shall act like a little
destiny, and save one an infinity of trouble in
overcoming particular temptations. Has one
never got up in the morning by counting ? . . .
He made a few simple vows embracing just so
much of his conduct as it was his object to
control. . . . Of course he did not become all at
once all he ought to be. . . . A form which had
taken years and years to grow is like to take full
as many to metamorphose : but he set himself
earnestly to work to find out his defects, and one
by one to conquer them. He was a remarkable
instance of a character forming entirely *ab extra-
crushing* ; and a painful trimming business it was
with him. Of course there were endless back-
slidings ; but henceforward his face was always
turned one way. In the main it is nothing new that
pride, enlightened selfishness, ambition, or philosophy, of whatever kind, do on the whole prescribe
much the same conduct as religion and real
high principle, and it is lucky for the peace of
the world it is so.

He worked away again at his books. After

such violent interruption, and the short, very
short, beginning he had made before, he did
not expect much to distinguish himself in his
examinations; but he did so partially, and in
some later trials much more. He felt his *line*
was to be a student ; and at the time when most
men's student life is closing, his was but just at
its commencement. He was learning, not for
college honours, but to *know ;* to make himself
a man, and to raise himself above the beings
whose plaything he had been so long. It was
about then I began to know him. I knew
nothing of his history, nothing but one or two
facts which were notorious at the university,
and flung a shadow over him. But I was struck
with a remarkable feature in so young a man,
that though he did not appear to be vain, he was
singularly unable to take other people's opinions
or to be guided in anything by any judgment
but his own. . . . Of course it was not possible
it should be otherwise. He had grown to be a
man with all his work with himself yet to do.
He had perpetual tendencies, from long indulgence, to weaknesses of every kind ; his whole
character was a waste, and he was engaged in
reclaiming it, not with moral or religious but

with logical implements. As he became convinced that this or that thing was not as it should be, he set to work to remodel it his own fashion; but it was impossible for any one to understand or assist him, with his whole method so singularly the reverse of theirs.

I am not going to follow him through the next eight or nine years of his life. From time to time a great deal of the old Edward would appear again, as in a newly reclaimed garden we find year after year some unextirpated weeds and wild flowers shoot again, and call for fresh and fresh care in eradicating them. But though he might temporarily seem to be retrograding, his own resolution or some friendly circumstance in the end always brought him off the conqueror. . . . The winds and currents are on the side of the best sailors, and circumstances, as it always does, was setting with him, and never failed to whip or press him straight.

He had not forgot Emma Hardinge. The third year after he had found his orbit and felt himself moving firmly in it, his mind began to set stronger and stronger back to her. His old visions began to form again, and he could not

10

blame himself, or think it idle in him to hope
that time, which devours everything sweet and
bitter but itself, had consumed the bitter feelings
of the past ; that when Mr. Hardinge heard his
name with honourable mention in the world, his
heart would warm to him again, and that forgiveness more than verbal or religious might reasonably be anticipated.   It was, therefore, not
without a pang, for the time very poignant, that
about three years after he had parted from her
he saw the announcement of her marriage in the
newspaper.   At first, I say, it was most painful.
I had come to know him intimately then, and it
was the occasion which he took to tell me his
history.   But it was only at first that it overset
him.   He had learnt many things in these three
years.   He had learnt to go without his wishes;
he had learnt to know that in a practical as well
as in a religious sense it is the severe high school
in which alone man can grow to be a man. . . .
So that at once he nerved himself to resignation,
and found even a pleasure in seeming to learn
from it that her sufferings could not have been
as great as he had feared, and that he need not
any more so bitterly reproach himself as he had

been lately doing for the sorrow he had brought upon her. . . . How idly we speculate on the internal history of another. !

CHAPTER VII.

Hope, it is said, feeds love; and when hope dies, love preys on itself and dies with it; and it is true, if by love is meant a passion which is to find its "earthly close." Any earthly object which we have not, and is before us as something to be obtained, though it may cost us pains and disappointment, we always give up pursuing it when we know its attainment to be impossible. But Emma's love for Edward was only of the present, and knew no future. Pure unworldly natures like hers always live in the present. It was the very thing the Hardinges had been all trained to from children, not to govern themselves by experience from the past and calculation of the future, but to play out like fountains from within upon every moment as it rolls. So that her mind was not set to think things could ever be other than they were. She had no material to speculate with on changes which were to be brought about by time. She *had* had Edward; not she hoped to have him. And from the moment her father had guided her pen across that miserable sheet of paper, and had drawn the promise from her lips that until she was the property of another man she would never see him more, he was as dead to her. Disappointment was not her feeling; we do not feel disappointment when one dies; a cold, dull, miserable sense that something dreadful had befallen her lay on her breast like lead, and stifled her very breath; the stream of her life, that had flowed on so musically, became choked with snow, and when tears would rise to her relief they hung like ice crystals on her eye-lashes. Day and night, summer and winter, were all alike to her. Her sun had set for ever, at least this side of the grave, and would never rise again; the soul had gone out of her; she moved about like an automaton; except when a spectral life would seem to flit for a moment through her as she was dreaming of the past. She clung to the memory of Edward. His unworthiness had not affected her love for him; it was the disease of which he had died. It was not

G

what he was, for he was not any more : it was what he had been. What lovers see in one another is not the real being, but their own ideal of a perfect being which they attach to one another ; and this is why a second real love is always impossible, that such ideal when once fastened round a person can never be called back again ; it follows and clings to him for ever, and if he changes it goes down with the memory of what he was to a grave from which there is no resurrection. And so poor Emma moved on month by month and year by year, fearing nothing, expecting nothing, hoping for nothing, except perhaps to die. And her sisters grew up beside her beautiful as she had been, and their lovers came and went, and came again, and there was joy about her, and sorrow, and disappointment, and success; but it all flowed by her, not through her. . . . Her own sad, sweet beauty was as fascinating as her brightness had been, and many a fair youth sighed at her feet . . . but they had not the key-note of her heart, and failed to raise in her an emotion even of dislike. . . . At last her brothers went to college, and one vacation brought back one of their friends with them. . . . Henry Allen was one of the class of men who have many considerable talents, but none of the very highest. He could do almost everything well—nothing exceedingly well. Clever he was, very, but without what is properly called genius. With a clear eye for things and people, he seldom failed in anything he undertook, for he knew himself and did not attempt what he was unequal to. Witty, amusing, full of clever stories, and always ready to make one when one was wanted on any subject, he was a delightful companion, and never made a visit without being begged to repeat it. . . . One point at least about him commanded very high respect; his mother was poor, and he contrived to relieve her of the expense of his education by taking pupils while he was an under-graduate. . . . He was not the kind of fellow women would fall violently in love with. He was too sensible, perhaps too good—had too much understanding. To be passionately loved, one must be either a person of the highest genius, or a weak and romantic one, like Edward had been, with a talent for dreaminess, which both with the dreamer himself and with others, is so often a successful pretender to it. . . . Allen had none

of all this. He was essentially unromantic. . . .
He wrote poetry, and good poetry, but it was all
comic. . . . He always was, is, and will be, a
thoroughly excellent and very popular man. If
he can only rid himself of a theological stiffness
which he has assumed no one can tell why, which
does not and cannot become him, and damages
his usefulness, I know few people who will be
able to leave life and point to more genuine good
work done than he will. . . . His only serious
fault at the time he went to the Hardinges was
that he was very poor. What a pity it is that
poverty does not extend to the affections, or if
they must be, that it cannot keep them under
lock and key, with the means of indulging them.
Allen, notwithstanding his sense, and notwithstanding his not being, as I said, a person to
excite a very strong passion, could yet fall in
love himself in his own way; and the mournful
sweetness of Emma Hardinge, perhaps, because,
at least at that time, she was so unlike himself,
made him determine to try if he could not win
her. He knew all the story about Edward,
and he knew Edward himself, and he soon found
he would have an eager listener in Emma if he
talked to her of him. It was strange the way

10

she listened. He talked of Fowler as he had left him a few weeks since, of all he said, and did, and would do. She listened to it all exactly as she would have listened to stories told her of those she had loved in life who had been taken away from the earth; listened as one does when the pain of the first loss is over and one lingers over the sad, solemn melodies of their memory. So entirely had the impossibility of their ever meeting again taken possession of her, that it never even occurred to her, far less took any form of hope; . . . . and she loved to hear Henry speak and to be with Henry, because she found him as it were a revival of Edward. It was not that she did not value him for himself; but it was not in himself that he charmed her; and at last, when he asked her to let him think of her as his future wife, she at once told him he could never be to her what Edward had been. But he knew better than she the almost almighty power of time, and habit, and daily association; he was prepared for the answer; indeed it was involved in the very plan which he had followed. He was too happy to take her promise as she would give it him, on her own terms. . . Love would come after—at least the genuine

esteem and regard which alone deserves to be
called love. The more etherial feeling he
would dispense with; nay, he did not very
much respect. At best he would say it was but
the foam on the champagne, and good for nothing but to intoxicate.

And so another suitor came to Mr. Hardinge
for his daughter's hand, and a qualified consent
was won from him—won not easily, but painfully
and reluctantly. He had no personal objection
to Henry. He liked him very well, and honoured and respected him, as he thought himself obliged to do. . . . But Edward had been
a lesson to him not to be enthusiastic about
young men. . . It was no easy thing for him
to take a lesson, and when it was forced on him
it made a deeper impression than it ought. . . .
From Henry's circumstances many years at
least must elapse before it would be possible for
them to think of marrying; so, though he consented, it was not with a good will, and he was
far too single-minded a person to keep concealed any feeling he might entertain. The
engagement lasted some few months. It gave
no violent pleasure to Emma; she had given
up expecting anything of the kind, but though

it could not give her pleasure, it fevered
and excited her. She could not help seeing
it was a constant wear and tear and anxiety
to her father.   And falling as these things
did upon a mind so harassed and overstrained
as the poor girl's had been before, they brought
about a partial derangement; at least on no
other supposition can I account for the determination she arrived at.   But to explain this I
must go back again

CHAPTER VIII.

IT is not to be supposed that so beautiful, so
fascinating a girl as Emma Hardinge, had lived
twenty years in the world without having seen
many men before Fowler sighing at her feet and
endeavouring to persuade her to marry them
. . . While they were at their last curacy in
Somersetshire, the rector of the parish ad-
joining them, had professed himself very anxious indeed about it. He was an intimate
friend of Mr. Hardinge, and the father did not
at the time conceal the pleasure it would give
him, to see his daughter the wife of so excellent
a man.   Mr. Barnard was indeed a most excellent man.   He was young, about thirty, with a
kind gentle heart, and a clear head, with more
than respectable talent, of good family, well off,

and a face you could not look at without feeling
irresistibly attracted towards it. Why did Emma
find it impossible to think of him as her husband?
Why was Emma not the first girl that had found
it so? Barnard had tried several, and always
with the same result; each lady had felt the
warmest interest in him, and the warmest wish
to see him happy with any one except herself.
. . . The reason was simple. He was only
a Christian, not a man; when duty called him all
the powers and all the temptations in the world
would be but reeds in his path; he would have
bathed his hands in the flames at a martyr-stake,
and smiled on his executioners; but in these
days fortunately the occasions which call out
such extraordinary virtues are uncommon, and he
wanted opportunity to do justice to himself. . . .
In his common duty too in the church or the
school-room, or in conversation on serious subjects, Mr. Barnard showed remarkably well:
so well, it was almost impossible to recognize in
him the shy, hesitating, awkward, irresolute,
nervous being that shrunk from you in ordinary
life. Ordinary life is for the most part made up
of other materials, and in those unhappily he
was wanting. His powers could come little into

play in any relation with women. Theology
makes bad lovers, and his excellence, although
the highest of all, and perhaps the only one
really deserving the name, could not advance
him a step with them. . . . Added to which there
was no earthly passion, not the smallest vestige
of such a thing in him. If St. Anthony had
been made of his material, he would hardly have
been entitled to his saintship; not a breath
would have clouded the enchanted mirror of
the fairy tale when Barnard gazed into it. . . .
Alas! no women, however good, will be contented with a love entirely religious; they could
never believe he was what they understood by
in love with them, and perhaps he himself was
deceived when he thought he was. . . . The
consequence was, however, that such love as
men feel for men, a friend's love, Barnard commanded from all; and from the best men most
of all; the love women bear their husbands,
he could win from none. . . . Mr. Hardinge
would only tell Emma when Barnard spoke to
him, (it was characteristic of Barnard that
he spoke to him, not to her) he knew no one he
would sooner see her husband, but he loved her
far too well to hint or even to feel it would

make him unhappy if she declined. She did decline, and for the time nothing more was thought about the matter.

Well, we left her engaged to Henry Allen. The engagement, as we said, continued only a few months; her own unhappy, unsatisfactory state of mind; the obvious discomfort it gave her father, not once, but many times expressed, a kind of recklessness about the future which she had felt ever since she lost Edward, determined her to give it up. Recklessness is only a working form of superstition: she fancied herself helplessly under the spell of some malicious power which was determined to thwart or blight every prospect however slight a one she proposed to herself of happiness. One black monstrous wave had rolled over the garden of her life; a few frail flowers had begun to show again—again they were destroyed,—what might follow more was almost indifferent to her.

And now in this strangely diseased mind of hers, a purpose began to form itself, which again is of so perplexing a kind that we cannot refuse it our admiration, and yet if once she get it executed, must be fraught with consequences the most disastrous, the most deadly. A sort of

despair of her own goodness, a notion that in all
her life she had never done anything to please
her father, and that it was all her own fault,
took the strangest possession of her.   If she had
done any good, it was not because it was good,
but because it had pleased her herself; she
looked back on her history as a dreary waste of
selfishness.

> Then when in changeful April fields are white,
> With new-fallen snow, if from the sullen north
> Your walk conduct you hither, ere the sun
> Hath gained his noontide height, this churchyard filled
> With mounds transversely lying side by side
> From east to west, before you will appear,
> An unillumined blank and dreary plain,
> With more than wintry cheerlessness and gloom.
> Saddening the heart.

It was the first time, perhaps, poor Emma had
ever reflected on herself.   She looked at her life
like the poet's churchyard visitor from the north,
and a strange business she made of it. . . . Seen
on the south side when the sun shone, how different would the scene have shown !

Something she would do ; some great good
that should be a real sacrifice of self, and give
real happiness to her father. Of all that she

could think of that would most delight him
the greatest would be, to see her married
to Mr. Barnard. She would marry him then.
First it looked like a sacrifice : her thinking it
was so had been what suggested it to her ; but
no sooner had she begun to make np her mind
to it, than it seemed absolutely right ; and she
took it as a fresh proof how selfishly unthink-
ing, how bad she must have been that it
had never seemed so before. Of course her
reason should have guided her, not her inclination ; and equally, of course, her reason should
be guided by her father's reason, who must know
so much better. Her moral eye had lost the
faculty of transmitting any set of rays but one.
Of course the sky was red, red as fire, and the
earth, and the lake, and the mountain, all, all
were burning red, and she had gone on dreaming all her life of blue sky and white light, and
objects painted with every hue of the rainbow.
And so in the unnatural composure which
the resolution she had formed on these convictions wrought in her, she went one day to Mr.
Hardinge and told him she had been thinking
long over the matter, and had seen at last how
wrong she had been in refusing Mr. Barnard.

Her sufferings she looked on in a way as a judgment upon her, experience had taught her what were the real qualities to be looked for and valued in life; that nowhere could she hope to find them in such perfection as in him, and that in case his mind remained the same as it had been, she wished to become his wife.

Her words sounded down her father's trumpet like the whisper of an angel. Little, little could he guess the path she had been travelling. He caught her in his arms and kissed her, and called her his own dear Emma, and he did not see that the love which was beaming in her eyes was not for Barnard, but for him. He flew to his wife, and kissed her, then all his children round that he could catch. He could not stay to tell them why—Emma would do all that. Then he rushed to his writing-desk, could not find the key, though it was in his pocket, and broke the lock to get out ink and paper, though there was an inkstand and full portfolio on the table. The letter written, he ran as fast to the stable; he would ride himself to Machynnlith with it, though it was ten miles over the mountain, and a sleety February. He could not stay for his whip, and lost an hour on the road for want of it; and when at last he came home again it was with his feet uncovered, save by his soaked stockings. He had met a barefoot beggar in the road, and he was far too happy to feel the cold himself.

The post held the letter, the fatal letter. It flew fire-winged, truer than rifle-ball to its mark, through Barnard to Barnard's heart, and he too felt very happy. He had begun to think he was in some way unfitted for women to love, and even Barnard, the pure noble-minded Barnard had found—(oh! how good Barnard must have been, if one is surprised at it,)—he had found it was a mortifying discovery; and now to be so delightfully undeceived; after four years to be remembered and sought for so! What wonder that he wrote and told his friends in higher spirits than were common to him, and that in a few hours he was himself on the way to Morlands.

Oh! if goodness do indeed find favour in the court of heaven, and angels hang about God's servants, to guide them in the mazes of this perplexing world, where, where are those that wait on Barnard and Emma now? The half good, the children of this world, the light and

dark offspring of the sons of God and man's—
daughters, they may be, left to struggle with
what wayward will and untutored nature may
involve them in. . . . But these pure ones, what
have they done? Barnard's eyes are all un-
learned in such studies; he will never read in
Emma's face what is passing in Emma's heart,
though passion scathe her like a thunderstroke.
If Emma's purpose stand the meeting, what hope
is there left for them except in heaven—what
hope for them to escape the vengeance inexorable nature will have for her violated laws !

But the meeting is past and Emma is firm.
Her nature is bound in chains, and the struggle,
if struggle there is, cannot be seen. . . . Days
pass, and the chains hold, but they are tightening now, and Emma's lips are pressed close, and
the clear buoyant voice hisses through them
when she essays to speak, and cold drops hang
upon her forehead. But three weeks to the
wedding day ! Oh save her, save her now, save
her from the mad control of her reason ! What
have such as she to do with reason ? Why, why
will she not trust her heart ? Can she not see
it is conscience which is speaking through it ?
Alas ! if the light within you be darkness, how

great is that darkness! Open your eyes, Barnard.
Fool, fool, can you not see the abyss into which
you are plunging? Rather, fool to call so on
Barnard who has no eyes for sights like these.
Another week is gone, another, and the day
begins to assume its own form, distinct from its
brother days in the same cluster. It is no more
next week, but next Thursday. . . . And Barnard walks with her, and talks to her of his poor-
house, and his school, and his parish, and
theology, and what not, and not one ray of light
has broken or will break on him for all the
bewildered flashes from those blue wildly rolling
eyes. And now the week is come, and Barnard
has written to his father, and his sister, and his
friends—he has sent orders to his housekeeper to
have rooms and fires and tea ready—and the
presents are come, and the dresses are made,
and the ring is bought, and all Emma's friends
except those at home at Morlands, are full of
bright anticipations for the future. . . . Except
those at home I say, not those who are there.
There there is but one heart that is not like to
break with fear, and that is the unconscious
bridegroom's. He alone failed to see. Her
mother and sister, who all knew Barnard, had

H

had misgivings from the first, and had all along
felt an effort in sympathizing with Mr. Hardinge's joy. They suspected, and they watched.
Nor could the father's wishes either keep him
blind. So day passed after day, and the symptoms grew worse and worse, and more unmistake-
able. Her sister spoke at last to her, spoke
earnestly,—and more earnestly, but all seemed in
vain. She had dug a channel for herself, as she
fancied, with her reason, and poured her nature
into it. Her misery was only a sign of the
badness of her heart which she was determined
to conquer, and madness which she took for
principle, goaded her along through all. At last
the day grew terribly near, and more and more
terribly Mr. Hardinge's conviction burned into
his heart. Tuesday came, the wedding was to
be on Thursday. Some symptoms of uneasiness,
which Barnard could not help seeing about him,
he could easily explain; of course they must all
be sorry at so long a parting as was so soon to
be. Emma had not appeared to-day, under plea
of headache. It was after tea. Mr. Hardinge
was moody and silent; some of the girls were
crying; the boys was sitting awkwardly in their
chairs, trying under a look of vacancy to hide

what they were feeling. Barnard was busy writing to say how happy he was, and thinking how nice it would be when all was over. Now and then, in spite of himself, his mind would wander off to the last Tract, and he would make some remark upon it to Mr. Hardinge. Alas! when brought into such collision with such deep throbbing human interests, how small, how trifling, the most religious men feel theology! At last, letters written, thoughts thought, questions settled or not settled, nine o'clock, Mr. Barnard's bed-time, came, and he took his candle and departed. As soon as he was gone, Mr. Hardinge rose solemnly, and desiring his wife and second daughter to follow him, he went up to Emma's room. . . . The room was dimly lighted from the fire which was burning low in the grate. She was lying on her bed in her clothes: she might have been asleep, but for the smothered sobs that rose from it.

"Emma, dear child, you never go to rest without your father's blessing. He could not leave you to-night, when it is nearly the last time. . . . Are you ill, dearest Emma? Speak to me, dear. I can see by your lips what you say."

" It is only a headache, papa; it will be all well to-morrow."

" For days past, dear Emma, you have not been looking well. You have not seemed happy, Emma, as I thought you would."

" Would you like to see me happy, papa, with the thought of leaving you and mamma so very, very soon? "

" And yet, Emma, I do not think your mother loved her family less than you; and yet she never looked as you look. You were crying as I came in. If you are really ill, dear Emma, I must have your marriage put off."

A gleam of pleasure shot across her features at the thought of the cup passing from her even for however short a time. But it passed away again in a moment. It must be now or never; she could never nerve herself to it again, and with the passionate conviction with which it worked upon her, she cried with a wild eagerness,

" Oh, no, no papa, not a day! not for worlds! "

Mr. Hardinge shuddered at the deep agony in her face. He looked steadily at her. Her eyes sunk.

" Emma, Emma, what is this ?" he said, almost sternly,—" there is something here you have not told me."

" Papa !" she answered, and tried feebly to look surprised; but her voice shook, and forgot the note, and the stiffened features refused to lose their blinded look of suffering.

" Emma," he went on more solemnly, " what it is which is on your mind I do not know. . . . But do not think we have not watched you, these many days past. Emma, I adjure you, by your duty to God, by your duty to me, to tell me whether you love Mr. Barnard? It is a dreadful question for me to ask of child of mine on the eve of her wedding-day. Speak, Emma, I can see what you say."

Emma was silent.

" Emma, you know how I love Barnard ; you know how I admire, how I revere him. What happiness it has been to me to think of you as his wife. . . . But Emma, here I tell you, and I call God to witness what I am saying, if child of mine is to give her hand to any man because she honours and admires him, or for any other reason, when she cannot give him her heart, may He of his mercy take me away from off

the earth, before I witness so dreadful a violation of his laws."

Emma looked up bewildered. What! this
heroic self-sacrifice then to which she had so
desperately nerved herself; this, which was to
be the one good act to atone for a life of selfishness; this, this called a violation of the laws of
God, called so by that very father for whom she
was to make it? What did it mean? What
was it all?

" Think, Emma, think of the high and holy
nature of love. Think what love is; for what
God's gracious providence in His wisdom ordained it, and remember the oath you will have
to swear. Emma, will you dare to trifle with
God? Will you stand before his altar with a
lie upon your lips?"

A lie! It went like a lightning stroke through
the poor girl's brain. She had never thought
of that—still she could not speak.

" Emma, Emma! by your love of the most
High God; by your love for me, for your
mother — on my knees, I pray you speak;
speak to her if you will not to me."

Emma raised her eyes. Half blinded as
they were with tears, she could still see that

most fearful sight, a father on his knee before his child. Great tears were streaming down the old man's cheeks. She threw herself into his arms, and lay there sobbing as if her poor heart would break. Her mother raised her gently, and laid her again upon the bed; and at last, when she recovered herself enough to speak, she threw off the burden from her weary-laden heart, and told them all. What followed then is too pure and holy for me to travel over; the pen cannot whisper, nor hush its voice to speak with reverence such words and thoughts as that small chamber witnessed then. Let me draw back and close my ears to what I have no share in. Let the veil hang before the Holy of Holies. God would be alone with the pure when they are offering their hearts to Him.

CHAPTER VIII.

THE morning came clear, bright, and frosty. The water-birds were skimming up and down the lake to warm themselves. The sun shone into the breakfast-room through mimic shrubs, and trees, and flowers; the ice crystals splitting the rays in pieces, and glittering with a thousand hues. You might think each window-pane was a camera, and you were looking into the real garden. It was such a morning as Barnard had foreseen when the clear calm moon had shone in upon him the night before, the few moments he lay awake after his candle was extinguished. Barnard could read the heavens and discern the signs of them; he had no skill to read the signs of the workings of the human heart, and the moral morning was not as he had foreseen it. He studied man with his theology, and could see nothing except what it could shine upon. And alas, in these days of ours, if theology be at all a science of things Divine, it is not as they walk on earth, but far away as they exist in the pure ether of abstraction. Briskly he drest himself; briskly he ran down stairs; and when he found the breakfast-parlour empty, ran out upon the crisp gravel and crunching grass; and he rubbed his hands, and composed a brisk reproof for Emma, when she should appear, upon her laziness, and as near an approach to a joke as his nature would permit him, in a sly allusion to the morrow. And he walked up and down till the soles of his feet, and his fingers' ends, and the tips of his ears tingled in the frost; and each time as he passed he looked in at the breakfast-room window, and it was empty still. Strange the prayer-bell did not ring. The breakfast things came in; the urn came in and hissed and sputtered away to be taken notice of, and at last cooled down into sulky disgust that he should have been put into such a state of excitement and no tea come of it; and on went Barnard up and down, and rubbed his hands, and wiped his eyes, and wondered pleasantly,

and thought of the many pleasant things he
would say ; and behind the window-blinds more
than one pair of child's eyes were peeping at
him, and shame to say, they were laughing.
At last, in a voice half sunk, half trembling
from fear it should be wrong, he called up to
Emma's window ; and, poor fellow, he may call
and call on, but unless his voice can reach to
Aberystwith, she has poor chance of hearing.
If his sleep had not been so very sound, the
noise of wheels leaving the house very early
that morning might have let some light in upon
him before the sun rose.   There was no Emma
for him.   But there was a letter from Emma,
and it was lying then on the breakfast-room
table, and he has not seen it ; they know he
has not seen it by his air, and his voice, and the
tone he is calling in, and they cannot make
up their mind to go down to him till the unpleasant news is broken and in part realized.
The elder ones in the family are very serious ;
the younger ones have a rather vivid feeling of
the ridiculous.   But it is characteristic of them,
that not one in the whole family had an idea
that he had been used ill, or even that he could
possibly think he had.   If there had been the

slightest notion that it was possible, Mr. and
Mrs. Hardinge would of course have communicated what had passed to him themselves ;
but it was out of pure tenderness of him that
they chose the other way. Deep and sincere
pity is what they are feeling for him, and that
is all. Anything wrong in what has been done
now there cannot be. Have not all their proceedings obeyed natural impulse ? even Emma's,
was not that an effort of misguided heroism,
which, now that it has been so happily interrupted, it is impossible not in a way to admire.
Even that he has made a great mistake, does
not come before Mr. Hardinge in that form.
He does not look at it all as something which
he has brought about and might have pre-
vented, but as an event in Providence ; and he
regards Barnard, and feels for and sympathises
with him as with a person suffering some heavy
undeserved affliction.

Each hour as it passes steeps us in its incidents, and rolls away and leaves us to the
next ; and the moment in which the Fates
held the disclosure suspended, brought it in
due time to Barnard : bear it in such sort as he
may, he had no resource but to bear it. He

must go away from Morlands, return to his place as he came out; and those who know him will feel the high respect and love they bear him will not allow them to smile at so untoward an issue of his hopes. They will sympathise with him as really as, and with, perhaps more real right than, the Hardinges; and, till they *know* all, and till the entire Hardinges are brought before them, they will feel an indignation for him which he does not feel himself. He retires; his trial is over; he has been tempted out from his quiet haven upon a sea where vessels of his build commonly find a worse fate than his. Let him go home then once more, and thank God upon his knees, that foul weather was sent not too late for him to escape; that the treacherous sun had not shone on and tempted him to his destruction. If Emma had married him, within a year Emma would have been insane. The Hardinges do not escape so. Most vessels founder the day after the storm, when the waves are still rolling, and there is no wind to steady the ship under their blows. So long as the marriage had been before her a real prospect, self-imposed by her own voluntary choice, her mind was held fixed upon it at however fearful a strain; it was fascinated as people are by breakers at sea under their bow, or the intention of suicide. It was not madness; but an awfully reasonable composure, reasonably, firmly, and resolutely following as a decision of madness. And now, with one sudden sweep, all this was gone. One has heard of men going apparently quite calmly to the scaffold, who being met there by an unexpected reprieve, have gone raving mad.

Emma did not become mad, but she became something so like it, that with the tendency in her family to which I have alluded, the most painful alarm was felt. She was in the house of one of their friends at Aberystwith. The day after she got there, an express had to be sent off for her mother; and in one day more it was thought necessary to write to the family physician, who was then at Edinburgh, desiring him to come to them post-haste. On his arrival, which was as rapid as possible, he was put in possession of all the facts of her case, as far as any but herself were acquainted with them; and supposing, as he did, from what they all believed and told him, that the secret of her suffering was the secret affection she was che-

rishing for Henry Allen, he told her father he
believed the only thing to save her mind was to
get her married to him as quickly as possible.
Mr. Hardinge, always precipitate, wrote immediately off to him,

> An exact command,
> That on the supervision, no leisure bated,
> No not to stay the—

" packing of his portmanteau," he should come
off and be married to his daughter.

Poor Henry! it was a strange order to come
upon him by the very post which he expected
was to bring him the news that she was lost to
him for ever. . . . He, like a sensible man, had
subdued his mortification, and was busy im-
pregnating himself with Aristotle for his degree
examination, then about a month distant; and
it is not to be denied, that he thought the
proceeding unphilosophical exceedingly.   He
pleaded hard for that but one month, and
sheltered himself under want of money even for
the common purposes of travelling; but the
mind to which he addressed his entreaties was
deafer than the ear.   Answer came—never did
post bring a swifter—that it was to be then or
never.   Five pounds were in the envelope, and

the next coach which left Oxford for Birmingham was to bear him on its roof. Mr. Hardinge was inexorable, and so it came to pass that within a fortnight of the morning on which Barnard received his dismissal, (one is almost out of breath as one writes it,) the advertisement, announcing the marriage was in the paper. Barnard read it, and condescended to a common-place, on the no faith to be placed in women. Fowler read it, and knowing nothing of all this story, and feeling what I told you above he felt, he took the occasion to tell me his history.

Was Emma happy? Perhaps. It seemed her fate, and she surrendered herself to it, if not readily yet without reluctance.

CHAPTER IX.

In the beginning of February 1846, (the last page ends in 1840,) I found a letter on my table one morning in Fowler's handwriting, with the post-mark of Torquay. My mind misgave me when I saw from where it came. Life was indeed changed with him since we left him. He was alone in the world—one by one his family had gone down before that luxurious feeder on youth and beauty, consumption. His father had been dead about a year; Edward himself had shown symptoms enough of delicacy to make us all uneasy, but he was sanguine himself, and we had begun to hope he might get over it. I tore the letter hastily open, and found my worst fears confirmed.

"MY DEAR ARTHUR,—You know how I was crowing about myself when my cough went last spring; I thought I had cleared the point at last where my brothers and sisters had gone down, and was well out at sea for a life voyage; and now I have got to sing my last Paliodia as my last chance to propitiate the deities I have affronted by my confidence. Unless the wind changes, and that speedily, before this spring is out, my vessel will be stranded, and the soul of it will be with the elements. I was going on very well till the autumn, and so much was clearing up about me, and my mental horizon at any rate losing so many of its clouds, when all at once, no leave asked or notice given, down came this vile cough upon me again; the wind is blowing dead upon the rocks, and I feel myself daily and hourly drifting perceptibly to leeward. I tried to work out at Ventnor, but it was no use, and I ran off here—but I am doing no better. I have tried my vessel on all tacks and at all points, in doors and out of doors—cold water and hot, cod's liver and homœopathy, riding and walking, but each time I take my bearings, there is no mistake about it, I am nearer and nearer in . . . And so now I have pretty well made up

I

my mind to the worst, and can look calmly at it.
How thankful I must be it has pleased God to
bring me down with a disorder which promises to
leave me my mind to the last unimpaired, so
that I can meet what is to come with composure.   It is not that I think much of dying.   I
am in God's presence now ; I cannot be nearer
to or further from Him ; and what else is there
for a serious person to hope for or to fear ?   I
have not found the taste of life this side of the
grave so very sweet that I should be unwilling
to exchange it even for the charms of what I
may find beyond.   But what is really distressing, is to feel I have to go with no work done
to follow me, without one single point to look
back upon, in which I have made the earth better or happier by my presence on it, and so
much, alas ! that I have done so different !   It
had been my hope in such time as this, to have
been able to say, my ' *Vixi*,' to have tried the
sword I have tempered myself, in one battle at
least, for truth against dreams, and then I could
go, O how gladly !   But I shall have nothing to
hand in, except intentions,—what they say the
road to the wrong place is paved with.   Plans
and designs, not one of which has begun to

grow even upon paper.   Are such accepted?
And I have had all my work to do with myself
so late, the work of a life patched up in a few
years ; built downwards too, the foundation last
and hardly finished ! What a weary, weary business these last few years have been to me!
and now that the work seemed done, that I
had begun to feel I might go out and labour to
help my fellow-creatures, as I laboured with
myself—the time is up, the accounts have come,
and I am called to send in the books. . . . . .
How far I have done will for myself remain to
be seen then.   As I understand it, the question
will be rather.   What are you? What have you
made of yourself?—then one by one what are
the specific things you have done?   By a subtle
enough, but exact enough power, each thing
you do leaves its indelible scar upon you, and
remain recorded, like two stones in a piece of
masonry, not separate but in a collective result.
But the great question of right and wrong seems
far too complicated to let me think each act can
have a specific value, with an equivalent of pain
or pleasure weighed over against it in a scale.
I cannot believe we are any more answerable
for the mistakes of our early life than a young

student of painting for his bungling first attempts.   The analogy, I think, holds good further than people will commonly allow it. They
have all gone wrong some time, but they think
to make up for it by the strictness of their
creed; and the least charitable people are
always those whose life gives them the least
right to condemn.   We are started only with
faculties and materials ; we have to become acquainted with the nature of both, and equally
require time and practice to get skill in their
use.   Certainly what we know of man in fact,
proves, as far as induction can prove anything,
that the experimental skill of another, is as little tranferable in morals as in art.   You may
say this or that thing is to be done, and the
other is to be let alone, and what can be
easier ?   Just as the artist will make such and
such strokes which will be easy enough to him,
and till you try, seem so to you ; but which, when
you do try, you do not find you can imitate
Both artist and moralist will wonder at your
perseverance, and one will call you stupid, and
the other vicious, when there is neither stupidity nor vice in the case, and you are only
going over the same ground as they themselves

once went over and have forgotten. Of course, teaching does much, and bringing up more. Perhaps when the science of the thing is thoroughly understood, they may do everything; but at present there are many mistakes which science has failed to understand, and one is obliged to make them to know they are mistaken; one must fall to know what it is to stand; and one is unwilling to believe this must be so always. Why, for instance, is it so hard to get men to believe they must often cross their inclinations, when the inclination is innocent? We find it so written in books; tutors teach it or dwell upon it, lecture upon it in their way, and off we go from their presence, and make haste to find a gratification for every evil; and we go on so, till experience scourges us into conviction. I am not speaking of such of our teachers as tell us one thing, and set us the example of another—take God's covenant in their mouths, and never take the trouble to reform themselves, but almost of the best we have. One great reason, I think, why they so little affect us, is the pedantic rigidity with which they bring their doctrines before us. We believe nothing of what they tell us, because we know half of it to be false. . . . Say they have gone wrong and been led right; they shrink from dwelling upon their aberrations in a way that would enable them to analyze them, but throw all that away as not only wrong, but absolutely and entirely sinful and depraved. They call it bad names, corrupt, unregenerate, state of servitude to evil spirits, and what not ; and when they see us going wrong, they speak to us in the same strain—whereas, in fact, it certainly is not so. Let them say what they will, human nature never can take pleasure in evil. Its worst alternatives are bewildered seekings after what is considered good. Nothing is liked or can be liked for being evil. The worst men account for themselves to themselves in their own way, varnish their doings with their idea of good ; and some element of real good there is sure to be in every man's notion of good. You may as well tell me I would drink poison knowing it to be so, as that I would do one act which I knew to be not only generally, but in that particular case bad.

" I beg your pardon for troubling you with these speculations of mine, but it is a solemn time this for me, and I am chiefly busy in sum-

ming up and scrutinizing my own past. . . . It
is a melancholy business with a retrospect so
dreary. To have been obliged so many times to
be taught and taught the same thing over and
over; each time forgetting the meaning of the
word, and having to look it out again in the
dictionary of suffering. . . . . One seems to
wonder at the little use other men's experience
is to us, when one thinks how very often one's
own has to be repeated. Pray forgive me—my
pen runs off with me. Do not think I am looking for excuses for what I find in myself so
unsatisfactory.   I have had teaching enough
and practice enough if ever any man had, and
it is shame enough to me to be only what I am.
I am not letting metaphysics run away with me,
and prevent me from calling good good, and
bad as bad can be. Only I wish to discriminate.
I fancy there is as much, perhaps more harm in
this wholesale way of blaming them than there
is in none at all . . . it is a very untrue, and it
pretends to be so true.

" I assure you I want all my philosophy in
this place to keep me up; I am, I believe you
know, the last of my name; I have no brother,
no sister, not a friend, (at least with me,) to

look after me, and talk to me, and keep my spirits up with telling me how much better I look. One by one I saw them lowered down into the grave, where, unless I am far wrong, I shall very soon follow; and my soul will be with theirs . . . . Alas! will it?   Philosophy says it is so unlikely we shall ever meet where we shall know each other as we have been ; and yet it may be weakness, but I must let my heart mould my creed for me. The parting cup would be bitterly mixed if I could not hope I should again see my father, where there can be no misunderstanding more, and hear him tell me he has forgiven me for all I made him suffer.

"The doctor has just been here; he has looked me over, felt my lungs, and persists in telling me I shall get well again. I do not mean to let myself believe him; I measure myself by other people; I march about in this city of consumption. . . . One sees them at first pretty strong about everywhere, and at all times; then they subside to the middle of the day walk and the respirator. . . . From that to the carriage is a short step, and a shorter then to the easier chair. Then we meet their wives

and daughters about alone, and in a few weeks
there is a notice to let in the house-windows, or
black gowns and bonnets in the place of the
blue ones. . . . 'So runs the round of life'—
rather of death—here at Torquay. I am at the
respirator stage, where I am sticking longer than
most of them do, and this makes Doctor ———
sanguine about me.   But there is no mistaking
the face that stares at me out of the looking-
glass. There they are every feature the same
as it was in those I watched down. . . . I wish
you could contrive to come down to me.   It is
selfish to ask I know, but when one is ill, one is
entitled to be selfish.   It is really lonely for me,
almost dismal at times.   I am not allowed to
work—even this letter has fatigued me. Perhaps
when Easter vacation comes, you will . . . . .
if . . . . if . . . . I still want you.

" Your affectionate,
" ED. FOWLER."

What a letter! with such a story to tell, and
so calm and quiet with it all.   Something too,
as it seemed to me, so thoroughly unsatisfactory
in its tone and feeling.   Such speculations, at
such a time ! What one should write to him one

could not tell in the least. I would have gone down at once had it been possible, but for six weeks there was not a chance of my getting away, and in the mean time what might not happen! I knew Fowler too well to doubt the painful reality of all he said; if it was not real it was too shocking. . . . No; he felt what he said; he would go quietly on to his end, and except what disease might do, his pulse would never alter. I wrote what I could, commonplace enough, as consolation always is. His views I could only half understand, and not at all sympathise in. For three weeks I heard nothing more from him! After such a letter as the first, what might one not fear? For the down-hill of consumption is the side of a sphere. At first the decline is scarcely perceptible, but it becomes fast steeper and then steeper, and at last it is the side of a precipice. . . . . But at the end of the month came another letter.

" Feb. 27.

" Since I last wrote to you, one of those curious things has befallen me which baffle all conjecture to account for them, and tie up the broken threads of our life when we had lost the

clue; one of those things which befall most people once in a life, and seems sent on purpose to
silence incredulity, forcing us to believe there
are other powers at work upon this web of life
than are seen at the loom.

"It has shaken me very much, perhaps made
my time shorter,—at any rate it has settled the
question for me if there was any doubt remaining that I am to go. In my own private history
it has served to furnish all that was wanting, and
now it is completed.

"I was walking one fine morning up and down
the end of the quay; there was no wind, the
warm sun was pouring down a heat which almost
makes February into July here. My cough had
been growing easier, and now and then
a thought had been stealing into me, that the
doctor might be right, and there was a chance
for me after all. . . . The boats were passing
in and out, a large vessel was lying outside
which had been waiting for the tide, and now at
high water was to be towed in. You know
there is a double pier at Torquay, and a pair
of hawsers had been run out from the vessel's
bows to each; she was to be brought up the
opposite side of the harbour to where I was, so

that all the people were collected there, and
I, with a nurse-maid and little boy, who was
watching the proceedings with the intensest interest, were the only occupants of mine.   The
line from the vessel to my pier was run round a
capstan at the point of it, so that it could be
slipped from on board the ship when it was of no
further service. . . You know how I love the sea
and all to do with it. It is almost the only thing I
feel a passion for.   I was leaning against the
parapet, half-watching, half-dreaming of the
many bright beautiful voyages I had had, and
the many more I had once hoped to have, when
I was startled by a scream from the nurse, and
on running forward, I saw the little boy in the
water.   He had ventured too near the edge in
trying to get as close to the ship as possible,
when the hawser was suddenly slipped, and the
bight of the rope as it ran round, had caught
his leg and he was thrown over.   There were
boats enough about, and sailors would have
been in the spot almost instantly, but, like a fool
as I was, nothing would satisfy me but I must
forget all about my cough, and jump in after
him.   It was near enough to the steps.   The
water, when I was well, was as much my home

as the firm ground; so we were soon out again, neither of us at the time feeling any harm from it, except the drenching. I was not very anxious to form any acquaintance at Torquay, still less under circumstances which might be exciting. Whoever the child's friends were, they could not know how little they really owed to me, and would most likely bother me with their gratitude.

"You know how I always hated scenes, so I splashed off home with all speed, without telling the nurse, who, poor thing, was almost out of her wits for fear, who I was. I went directly to bed, as the best thing I thought I could do. The next day I could not leave that . . . nor the day after could be more than removed out to my sofa. . . . If any one called, I had given orders, of course, to be invisible, as I had misgivings that I might be found out. I was just beginning to recover strength to think what a goose I had been, when a card was brought up to me, with a name and a few words in pencil. . . . The name was the Rev. Henry Allen; . . the words were, 'For God's sake let me see you.' . . Yes; it was Allen, and the boy was their child—their only child. . . . I

can hardly tell you what I felt; irritation I believe principally . . . Why must they track me
down to my grave, and make the end as bitter
as they had made the middle ? . . . I had sent
down to name another hour when he might
come, and then I set to work to think what it
might all mean. . . . It was they certainly.
Allen had been obliged, unexpectedly, to vacate
his curacy in the north of England, and being
unemployed, he had availed himself of an offer
of a chapel at Torquay. He had been here
but a few days when the accident happened. . .
I got over my annoyance as well as I could. . .
My worser nature tempted me to complain, to
wish with all my heart it had not happened. . .
But I cannot think it is a mere coincidence, so I
try to endure and wait the issue in faith. . . .
Allen came at the time I said; I had met *him*
more than once since his marriage, which softened off the angels of the scene. But it was
very, very awkward. A more awkward hour I
never passed. He took my hand as he came
in, with a few real, frank, manly words; but I
was too weak to do more than tell him how
little he owed to me, and intreat him not to
think what I had done had in any way altered

my chances for the future.   The superstitious
feelings I had about it he was not a person to
understand, so I let them alone.   But what I
did tell him was quite true. . . . My case was
desperate before, and it would be far more
likely to shorten my few weeks, or whatever might be before me, I said, to know that
they were distressing and disturbing themselves
so needlessly. . . . But there we paused.   Each
of us wished to speak of Emma, and neither of
us seemed able to be the first.   When we had
met before, of course we had never mentioned
her.   At last Allen got out that she wished to
see me. . . . I felt it must be, yet I shrunk
from it.   Long, long ago every trace of my old
feeling for her disappeared. . . . There was
that strange story some one told me about Barnard, and the way she had behaved to him.
How much to believe of such things one does
not know, but there was something rather strange
about it certainly.   And then her having been,
as they say, so passionately attached to Allen,
and so soon having been able to forget me:
one felt so disappointed in her, that one could
not go on even regretting very long that one
had lost her.   As far as my own feelings go, I

could meet her calmly enough. But she is painfully excitable; and if there are to be any spasms and outbreakings, I am selfish enough to wish her well at the other end of Yorkshire again. . . . However, I see it is laid upon me; it is no use to resist, and I bow my head to the breath of destiny. She is coming to-morrow. Nine years ago. I wonder if she is changed. Some one told me I should not know her again."

" March 10.

" I have seen her again. . . . Nine years;—it is strange, very strange! Yes, I have seen her again; again I have held her in my arms; once more I have felt her warm breath upon my cheek, and her lips upon mine. I had lived for this. This was the secret of this strange meeting, and now I suppose I may die. She came: Allen brought her. I was startled to see how like she was to what she had been. I saw no change, except in the sweet sad expression in that once so bright and sunny face. And even it seemed to link on closer to the moment when we parted. She had looked just so then. I had felt the meeting, the first meeting at least, would be so painful to me, that I nerved myself for an effort, and, as well as my strength would let me, I talked away of a thousand quite indifferent things, to give her time to recover herself. . . . But it would not do. It is ill talking of such matters to a heart that is full to bursting. Emma's eyes were swimming in tears. Allen, noble-minded fellow as he is, felt his presence a restraint upon her; since he knew what then I had never guessed at; he knew what she had felt so long, what she still felt for me, and which this unlucky accident had now made break out again in a form almost agonizing, and he rose and left us. . . . Coward as I am, I would gladly enough even then have escaped from what was to follow, and I half wished she had gone too. But it was to be. She at least would be miserable if she could not speak; and I, too, how could I tell whether there was not something I was bound to hear? or if not, why should I care for myself? What right had I? So Allen went, and then down went the floodbank, and out rushed the full torrent of her soul. Out it came—such a history, and for me to hear! She told me of that bitter farewell letter. She

K

had never written it, her father's hand had governed hers; and then a fatal promise he had wrung from her, that though she loved me still, and never could cease to love me, she would never see me more till she was the wife of another. . . . This to me! God forgive me the unworthy thought that my unworthy soul gave birth to. Could the hope of meeting me again, then, have found some corner of your heart to hide in when you married? But the clear blue eyes met me so steadily, and yet with such bitter melancholy, that mine sunk abashed. . . . There was not a thought in her mind her husband might not have shared in; perhaps not one he had not. I never knew till that moment how much a purely virtuous person could dare. And then I had to hear about Allen how he had long wooed and sought her; how she had warned him what she felt, what she always must feel for me, though she knew that I was lost to her for ever. . . . Then all her struggles, her father's anxiety and displeasure, the true story of the Barnard business, (the brave heart in her! It is a true piece of heroism; I will tell it you when you come to me,) which foolish people have made such mockery of, and

treated as a comedy. . . . Then how she came
to be married at last; and Allen how good, and
kind, and generous he was: but for years, she
said, it had been her one great wish to see me
again, and tell me all. . . . And now to meet
me so; I had saved her child, Allen's child,
and I must die. . . . O no, no, not die! and
she threw herself on her knees beside the sofa,
and flung her arms around me, and laid her
face upon mine: and tears were hanging on my
eyelashes, which had not flowed from me. All
this passed so rapidly, it was so strange, so
utterly unlike what I had looked for, that I
knew not what to think. . . . Again I looked
wonderingly at her for a trace of such feeling
as in any other woman on earth, at such a
moment, would have been the all-absorbing one.
But there was none. If ever spotless conscience lay in human soul, it was behind those
features, and again I had to feel ashamed of my
suspicions. To the pure, all things are indeed
pure. My heart, if I ever had one, turned long
ago to Greenland ice; but if it had not been
so, and a sentence had passed my lips which
betrayed an unlawful thought, even an unlawful
regret, she would have turned away, and left

K 2

me for ever, and perhaps broken her heart in grief for me. But to blood like mine there was no danger; if my pulses beat as strong, and life was as full and bounding in me as when last I saw you, I could have passed through the same scene as calmly as I have now. But she perplexes me strangely. I cannot but wonder at and admire her. . . . If it is right or not, I cannot tell. As a phenomenon, she seems to come under no class which moralists have pronounced their opinion upon. I hope I do not sin against her, when at times I think it fortunate I am going to die. The real difficulty with me about her is, however, that she ever married Allen at all. She will be happier with him when it is all over with me, now that she has seen me, and in a way delivered her diseased memory of me. . . . But I cannot say I see why she did not wait, and hope and hope. What can love do, if it cannot make one hope when there is no reasonable ground for hope, or, if you like, none at all? . . . I am afraid, from what she said, her mind was unsettled. But perhaps it is better as it is. At any rate it soon will be so. I hardly know what to say about myself, how soon it may be.

It may be weeks, it may be months. I may weather out another summer still. The Allens are with me every day. Emma almost lives here, and my little Jemmy has installed me into the dignity of an uncle. . . . Children don't seem to be equal to the idea of a friend who is not a relation. Allen comes himself when he can, but he is busy. . . . You will soon be free. . . . And you will come to see me, will you not?"

The first day I was free, I hurried down from Oxford. It was the beginning of April, bright clear, cloudless weather; the hedges smothered in primroses and blue violet, the fields yellow with daffodils. There had been a draught of wind from the east all March; but it blew so lightly, that except at night one could almost fancy it was summer. It was evening when the coach set me down at the inn at Torquay, about an hour before sunset; one of those yellow evenings we never see except in Devonshire in spring. Fowler was living in one of the large new houses in the Rock walk. He had chosen the place himself, in spite of its being so ex-

7

posed, for the sky and the sea had been his earliest friends, and they were all now that he loved with an enthusiasm. I was expected. The servant opened the door before I had had time to knock; he had seen me coming, and took my bag without more question than to pronounce my name. He just told me, as we went up stairs, I should find his master worse. Poor fellow, he had hardly strength to say so. For Edward was so kind and thoughtful of every one about him, that though he loved none of them, they all adored him. He opened the drawing-room door. It was a long double room, divided with folding-doors, one of which was half-open, and I could see, without being seen, into the further end of it. There was a deep oriel window projecting outwards over the sea, deep enough for a person lying in it, with his back towards the room, to command the entire bay through the centre and side windows; and there lay, on a slanting spring couch, my old friend,—I could not doubt it was him,—drinking in the beautiful evening, and lingering out the last lagging moments of his life over that happy sea where he had known so many happy, happy hours. . . . A lady was sitting by him, with a work-table, and various books and papers lying scattered about. It seemed she had been reading aloud to him. There was a sweeter voice than his in the room as I entered, and I saw her turn a book down upon its face as the servant opened the door. I thought it was my coming in which had disturbed her, . . . but it was not; a side door I could not see had opened at the same moment in the room where they were, and a little boy came in, holding the corner of his apron in both hands. I motioned to the servant not to move, and stood for a few moments watching.

"There, uncle Ned, see here what I have got!" and he showered out his little treasure of cowslips and white violets into his lap, and lifted himself up on tip-toe and kissed him. He seemed ashamed of what he had done, and half really, half pretending to be afraid, he turned down and hid his face in his mother's lap.

"You told me uncle was going away, mammy, so I thought I'd go and see if I couldn't get something pretty for him to make him stay with us. You won't go now, will you?" and he ventured up again, and parted Edward's damp hair from off his pale forehead, and stroked his cheeks with his little pink fingers.

" Not directly, dear Jemmy, I hope; not quite directly: but I believe I must go some-time, soon, . . . I should like very well to stay with you, Jemmy; but we can't always do as we like, you know."

" Not you, uncle? Can't you? so old and so big as you are? But, uncle, papa goes away sometimes, and comes back again to us after a little bit; and then he goes again, and he always comes back. And you will, uncle, won't you? You'll come back and stay with us, and never go away any more. Where are you going, uncle?"

" Where will these pretty violets here go next week, Jemmy?"

The child looked up puzzled.

" Will the violets come back from where they are going, uncle?"

" Yes, next spring, Jemmy."

" But these violets, uncle? These very same ones? Shall I go out again with Nanan and find them again just where they were, these same ones, and bring them in to you, uncle ? Uncle, will you come again next spring ?"

" Yes, my next spring, Jemmy."

And Edward's voice passed lightly over the second word, and the child's face grew bright again.

I beckoned to the servant to go in and say I was come; I waited a moment more, for the lady, I saw, made a movement as if to go. " O stay, Emma dear; don't go; stay and see Arthur. He is no stranger to you. What I know he knows. He knows all." . . . But this only seemed to quicken her movements, as she and Jemmy were out of sight in a moment.

I could barely catch a glimpse of her face. But the glimpse was quite enough to tell me how far short even the passionate description I had heard of her fell of her singular beauty. Edward half rose as I came forward. " This is indeed kind of you," he said. " These sick rooms, they are a dreary piece of business at the best. At least to others."

Nothing you may have been told can really prepare you for the changes you are to find in

a person you left in full health. The strongest
imagination is too weak to unfix the last
image your senses gave you; and do what you
will, it is with that you will make your comparison. Edward had talked of a chance of
another summer; another summer! no, he
would never see another May! I looked at
him, I suppose, with so very woebegone an expression, that he began to laugh. "Don't
make such dreadful faces at me," he said. "You
look almost as hideous as my own image of
myself in my looking-glass. Why, Arthur, you
know no more of me now than I told you. . . .
I thought you were above mere nervousness.
Come, come, it's bad enough to have to die,
without one's friends making it worse for one,
instead of better. You must get yourself together, or I shall be packing you off again. That
pretty boy's violets! Will you put them, please,
into the water there? Jemmy Allen brought
them to me just before you came in."

"I saw him."

"And you heard him, poor little fellow! I
hope I am not swelling my sins with the many
tricks and cheats I have to play him. He comes

to me day after day, always with some strange question I cannot answer."

" And the lady was his mother?"

" Yes, that was Emma. She was shy of you, and would run away; but you will see her again by-and-bye. . . . I believe I didn't tell you of it. They are here altogether now. I talked it over with them. She was making herself restless and wretched, at the notion of my being here alone in this way, and they were kind enough to say they would all move up and take up their abode here for a time ; in fact till, I suppose, there is no more occasion for them here. . . . I let Emma alone. I do not think there is another woman in the world who might go on as she is doing ; . . . but it is a case, I think, upon which a woman should judge for herself, and to advise her would be to insult her. Allen and I both know her so well, and how purely single-minded she is. She thinks no evil, and so can do none. Suggest to her any earthly interpretations people might give to her conduct, she would not understand it. She would look as strangely at you as poor Jemmy did just now at me, when I talked to him about the violets."

" But suppose you should recover."

There is little fear of it," Edward said, with a faint smile. " But if I were to do so, I do not see that there would be any danger to her. . . . And as I see more of her, I almost think it might be better for her. It is easier to continue sentimental over a memory of a person who has loved you, than over a living one who does not. The common intercourse of ordinary life, with all its humdrum features, would very soon exorcise her, if it really is an evil spirit in her, and she wants exorcising; and if it is not, why not let her continue as she is. I do not think it is an evil spirit myself. You do not doubt *me*, I suppose. . . . Even if I were all I once was, or all I might have been, were I ever so disposed to take unprincipled advantage of her affection for me, I feel quite easy that the most cunningly suggested thought of what is wrong would fall on her like fire sparks into a heap of snow."

" The metaphor would seem better to apply to you," I said, " from what I can see. However, you may be right, and if you are, it staggers one's philosophy, and makes one's fancied knowledge of human nature look rather discre-

ditable. . . . But how can you be so sure she
is so different from other women? What right
have you to be so confident of yourself? to be
so certain, as you seem to be, that if you were
well and strong again, you could hold yourself
so immaculate, and go on letting her entertain
the feelings she does to you without being
tempted? Why is it so impossible that, allowing herself to think, as you acknowledge she
does, that she would have been happier with
you for her husband, some day some unlawful
wish may not raise its hideous head in her?
some unlawful regret that she ever married
Allen? . . . God forbid I should think it possible such wishes should ever be realized; but
the shadow of a passing thought would dese-
crate a mind so beautiful as hers, and if there
would be danger then, she ought not to be with
you now."

Why, Arthur, you are so eager, I shall begin
to think you suspect me of intending really to
get well and run away with her. They are
neither of them very likely. Were I to recover,
and Emma by accident to be free again, I could
never think of her as a wife. All hopes of
such kind of happiness I saw into their graves

years ago. If I were to live as many years as I am likely to do days, I would not raise them out of it. They say that beyond the grave they never live again under the best circumstances, and I have given up letting myself take interest in any thing that dies.

<hr />

Whatever uneasiness I might feel, I was soon set at rest about it. It was as he had said; at least as far as he was concerned.' I had interpreted him by myself; I was afraid that, knowing he was so near his end, his weakness might unnerve him ; and he might sink to sentimentalize with the lady in a way that, end how it would, might drop poison into her peace of mind, and canker her life with the thought of him. But it was not so. I had been alarmed at something in the tone of one of his letters; but if he had warmed at all at the first meeting with her, it was but with the warmth the living lend the dead by their embrace, and now he was cold again as ice. I fell easily into my place among them. She shrunk from me for the first day or two, but she soon became used to

my presence, as she would to a new piece of
furniture, and took no more notice of me. . . .
Edward spoke little to her, and his conversation
never took a tone which would excite any
tinge of morbid feeling. If he spoke to me of
her, it was only with a kind of intellectual
interest, as of any other phenomenon which
struck him as curious. It was a *case* of disease
to be *treated,* and he went on treating it as
he had made up his mind it would best be got
rid of, that is, letting it alone; taking the same
kind of notice of her that he did of me; but
almost always addressing himself to me as
likely to make more out of his thoughts. . . .
His mind seemed absorbed in contemplating
what was coming upon him. He could still
talk easily. His cough had left him, and his
disorder now was a general wasting of the whole
system, without specially affecting any particular action. He liked speaking, and to me,
(jarring as his entire method of looking at
things was against all I had been taught to
think myself,) what he would say had a strange
fascination. When a man is at the end of life,
and can really cast his eyes round him and
before him calmly, let his creed be what it will,

his senses have an unnatural clearness; the body falls away from around his mind when the earth for which it is made is fading away, and there is no more interest in self deception. And certainly, a faith which could go so resignedly and so hopefully to meet its end, had, must have had, something real in it. What Fowler's faith exactly was, I did not know; nor could I tell what his grounds of hope were; but that he was most earnestly and intensely looking for something which was to come, I was as sure as that I was myself. I had heard him say once that his belief in a future state was the only thing which had saved him from suicide; indeed he could hardly think any one who thought at all, who had trained himself to correct the impression of his senses, to weigh the future against the present, and could calculate the balance of suffering and enjoyment in this world, would be brought to remain in it, except from such conviction, with the means of escape everywhere ready at his hand. . . . One day I pressed him to tell me how he had contrived to fortify himself against a fear which most men found so insupportable.

"My only difficulty," he said, "is to know

what there is to be afraid of. . . . The only
passion with which it affects me is curiosity;
but I try to subdue it, because I think it is
irreverent. . . . But why should I be afraid to
die? Why should any man who believes in
God? I believe that God has all goodness and
all power. Therefore he will do with me what
is best; and how can any serious person be
afraid of what is best for him? Few men's
lives can be more unsatisfactory to look back
upon than mine—I know it. It is a point
which now I cannot affect one way or the other.
If it be good for me to suffer for it, I shall; and
I shall accept with thankfulness whatever suffering is laid upon me; as I should accept it now
if I knew where to find it in the best way. If
we are to pass, as we are taught, more immediately into God's hands than we are here, what
can there be for which we should be more
grateful? into the hands of an all-wise Being.
who knows all we require, and will save us
from the infirmity of our own wills in *inflicting*
upon us what we should flinch from inflicting
upon ourselves? . . . You may say I shall have
to suffer hereafter as a penalty, and not for my
own benefit. . . I cannot see however how this

can be.   If what is inflicted as a penalty is
what I deserve, it must be for my own benefit,
because it is always better for every one to have
what he deserves. . . . The real evil is to have
what one does not deserve, good or bad.   And
if it be hard for you to be convinced of it in
your own person, you must at least acknowledge it must be in some sense or other *good*,
and a manly person therefore would of course
choose it. . . Pain is in itself an evil.   It cannot be that God, who, as we know, is perfectly
good, can choose us to suffer pain, unless either
we are ourselves to receive from it an antidote
to what is evil in ourselves, or else as such pain
is a necessary part in the scheme of the universe, which as a *whole* is good.   In either case
I can take it thankfully. . . . But in the eternity of punishment, as you commonly hear it
explained, I simply do not believe. . . . It
cannot profit the *sufferer* if he is never to
change.   He cannot deserve it; because his
sins have been in time, and between the finite
and the infinite there is no comparison, and so
no proportion. . . . If you take too, as I believe
the history of even the worst man that ever
defiled God's earth with his filthy presence,

and know it from first to last, in all its bearings, as the Almighty knows it, you would not say it deserved any very terrible retaliation; if, that is, it did really take its beginning here on earth—and what we are in this life is not, as some people think, a consequence of what we were even in some other state which we are not permitted to remember. . . . Eternal punishment cannot benefit by example; for all trials are supposed to be over when time is swallowed up in eternity. It may be that time ceases to all of us at our death; our clock has been wound up to go a certain period, and when it is run down, it remains for ever pointing at the same index; and then what we are at that moment will be for ever our reward or our punishment. . . I do not believe this, but it may be so; but badness, as I understand it, is negative not positive; the absence of good rather than the presence of evil; and its punishment therefore will be a privation of just so much happiness as corresponds to the good which is wanting. . . . That there is in man a principle of evil warring against good in him, and with a power and tendency to become positive and to absorb or annihilate such good as is left remaining in a

L 2

man at his death, it is blasphemy against God even to dream it. . . Evil for evil's sake man cannot love ; by the law of his nature he is ever seeking for good, and the difference between men is only in degree corresponding to the degree of their knowledge. If men continue for ever as they die, what of positive good there is in them will find its answering state, and that is all."

" And we may meet again ?" Emma said quickly.

Edward smiled. " If it is better—surely yes. . But we are in God's hands. There may be better things—though we cannot think of any."

The most painful feature about him was that he appeared to feel no regret at leaving earth, or any one upon earth. He had disentangled his affections so completely from persons and fixed them upon things, that he had resigned his mind entirely to the ideas of the better, and he felt only for that. I said something to him about this. . . " But why should I regret them ?" he said. " I should not be taken away without it was ordered so. . . . Whatever creed we hold, if we believe that God is, and that he cares for His creatures, one cannot doubt that.

And it would not have been ordered so without it was better either for ourselves, or for some other persons, or some things. To feel sorrow is a kind of murmuring against God's will, which is worse than unbelief."

" But think of the grief of those you leave."

" They should not allow themselves to feel it. It is a symptom of an unformed mind. What pain they experience they should learn to take as a discipline, ἐν πάθει μαθεῖν ; to submit themselves to be taught to see and love the world, and the things and people in the world, not as they are in themselves, but as they are in God."

What had I to say against this? But my heart shivered—but indeed I never thought of arguing with him. . Not for fear of exciting him, for he was so easy and quiet about all he thought, that nothing ever could excite him. But belief like his lies deeper than argument, and it was no use. . . . His belief was the result of his life, and of the cold stern method in which he had trained himself. . . . The little bit about his father, in one of his letters, was the one only symptom of a human heart I could find in him. Had mature life been given him, he might have come to think differently. I cannot tell. He might; but I do not think so. Passions once entombed do not grow again, and Edward's faith was peculiarly, and almost necessarily, what a mind arrives at which has neither passion nor prejudices.

———

The month passed on, the weather continued beautiful, every day gaining in warmth, and length, and beauty. The sun rose up each morning out of the sea, and drove his coursers through the cloudless sky to linger longer ere he went down to his repose. . . . He was ever waxing as Edward waned, and the strong fire fed upon the heart of the expiring feeble one. . Each day we saw too clearly he was going and going. The oil of his life-lamp was wasted, and his feeble frame was now but the poor desolately wasted wick just languidly smoulder-ing in its socket. . . . At one moment but the spectre of a flame glimmering on the edge of night, then with a fresh effort flashing up again, and then sinking once more, each new burst weaker and ever weaker. . . . Flicker unsteadily as did the body's light however, his mind, like his eye, grew ever brighter, and the steady flame burnt more intensely tranquil. Emma and I hardly

ever left him. Yet sitting by her as I did, day
after day, I never grew to know her any better.
Quietly she sat on there, happy to be there,
and seemingly wanting nothing more. If he spoke
she seemed, whether she understood it or not,
to drink each word as if it was a revelation; but
she seldom said anything herself. What passed
if I was away I cannot tell. . . . I sometimes
caught the low murmuring of her voice as I
came into the room; but what she might have
to say to him, she might well shrink from
betraying to a stranger's ear. . . . To me she
said but little, and that little almost mechanically. Every faculty was absorbed in Edward,
and I thought it best to let her alone. One
knows so little of the workings of a mind like
hers, that one speaks at random when one tries
to interest, and words the most kindly intended
may be daggers. . . . She read to him if I was
away, but never before me; for Fowler liked
listening, and I suppose I could get through it
more intelligibly. But at times he would want
rest, and sink back upon his pillows, gazing out
on the bright, the beautiful sea; and then I
have seen her work drop upon her knees, and
her clear blue eyes full *set* upon him with an

expression so strange and unearthly, that I felt
awed, and shrunk into myself; thoughts unworthy alike of her and me, would at times
intrude, and I have tried to drive my eyes into
her heart and read what was written there; but
always I had to feel the same as Edward had
described on his first interview with her, and
hang my head ashamed. My nature to sit in
judgment upon hers!!

But at all times both she and Edward affected
me unpleasantly. I could so little understand
her, that she fairly frightened me as a creature
of another world would. And Edward, beautiful
as it all seemed, was in a state of mind so unlike
what I had always considered Christian, that,
little as even to myself I could find to answer
to what he would say, I fancied his composure
unnatural, and as if he had no right to it. So
that there were times when I felt driven into
myself, and scared and chilled by them, and it
has been like waking from a night-mare, when
little Jemmy would come running in with his
little sweet beauty of naturalness.

One touch of nature makes the whole world kin;

then I should see Emma look like a true

earthly mother, and a tear glistening in Edward's eye which I knew sprung from the same human fountain as my own.

He brought us flowers every day. One morning he came flying in out of breath with hurry and exultation, with a wild dogrose, and a slip of briar, a sheltered nook in Anstis cove had warmed and nursed into prematurely blooming.

"Here uncle, I have got it; we've watched it every day, and it came out so slowly, and Nan said I should never be able to give it you, because you'd be gone away first. Ah, uncle, you are not going," he said with a sly look, "just yet; you can't go for a long time; you can't go till you get well. I remember when I had a cold, when I tumbled into the water. I was in bed, I couldn't go out, O, not, not, for I don't know how long; and you can't, uncle. Oh! I'm so glad you're ill!

"But, uncle, for shame, you told a fib the other day; you said you were coming back next spring, and Nan says you are never coming back at all; and if I am ever to see you again, I must go where you are going. Uncle, take me with you now? Why can't I go now?"

" No, Jemmy, you will come, I hope, bye and

bye, but not now.   What would mamma say if I took you away with me now ?"

" Oh ! but mammy 'll come too, won't you, dear mammy? you'd always be happy with uncle Ned; and Nan too, we'll all go, Nan says it's such a beautiful place."

" Yes, Jemmy, it is a beautiful place. But you cannot come there just yet ; you must stay here, and grow to be a man first, a great big man, and mammy 'll stay and take care of you, and make you a good man too."

" But, uncle, Nan says people do go, when they are no bigger than me; and directly we get there we are made into beautiful angels, with bright beautiful wings, like the birds.   Oh, do let us go, and then we'll fly about up in the air; in the blue air, uncle Ned, up, up, up, and never come near this dark nasty room any more.

" Uncle Ned, do the little angels grow to be big angels up there?"

"Yes, Jemmy, when they grow wise they grow big."

Oh ! I see, yes,—you told me the other day I must grow wise, when I grow big. But, uncle Ned, how can getting wise make them grow ?"

" Wisdom is what they feed upon, Jemmy."

" What do they eat wisdom ? What, is it like ? Is it in books ?"

" No, Jemmy, they don't have books up there. It is in God. The angels live with God, you know, in heaven."

" But they don't eat God ?"

" Why, not exactly. That privilege is reserved," he said, turning to me, " for the children of earth." But the child's questions were getting perplexing.

" The angels, you know, Jemmy, are a sort of ghosts, and their eating is not regular eating, but a sort of ghost of eating."

Of all things in the world, it is the most difficult to know how to answer children. Their small minds, when they wake seem to see the unanswerable question first, just as the first thing their eyes see is the sky. One cannot say one does not know, for they cannot understand what not knowing means. One may not dare to tell them what is false, yet when our own idea is so small, how to convey even a part of that, without it being tied to any positive falsehood, is a problem that puzzles our wisest. Generally, however, the best loophole is some monstrous nonsense like this of Edward's. Jemmy was just satisfied with his ghostly idea.

I dreaded, and yet I wished to have some more direct conversation on his religious belief with Fowler; to hear him say one word which would assure me, and save me from my painful misgivings. Allen and I talked it over: we could give each other little comfort, as Edward uniformly avoided any specific reference to the subject with him; we agreed that taking occasion of the coming Passion-week, we would give the conversation a definite direction, and leave it to him to speak if he would.

An opportunity soon came. Newman's name was mentioned; one of us had seen a snarling piece of sarcasm in a newspaper about him.

" Yes," Edward said, "let them hoot on; they have driven out their Coriolanus, and these are their triumph shrieks. Let them see to it he does not come again in power; and no Virginia and Volumnia to beg him back again."

"It is an apt comparison," I answered. "Power has been his aim, and himself has been his God, from the first to the last."

" May my tongue be blistered then for giving it you," he said. " Oh Arthur, if you had known him as I knew him!" Fowler's face was flushed, and his voice shook as he spoke. It was years since I had seen him so affected. . . " You know my story," he went on, " but I never told you in my dark hour I went to Newman. I was with him some hours, laying bare the secrets of my soul to him, and he left me with a feeling for him I never had for man. He pressed my hand in his, and dropped tears upon it,—yes, tears. Yes Arthur, your idolater of self, he told me my sins, and he wept for me. Throw away your cant about him; he was the truest and best friend the Church of England held at the hands of Providence, and she has spurned him from her, and set the seal on her own hollowness."

" Fowler, this from you? Do you believe him right?"

" Right, yes. He would have been right all, if you had not been all mad. . . . Any man who believes in God with all his heart, and does his duty to man with all his might, has right,—and right in a quite other sense than you seem to dream of. He may express his faith in what form he will, I revere him as a man —The Church of England indeed, to dare anathematize him for want of orthodoxy. . . . To be sure she is lenient enough on the other side. All her members have to guard against is, believing too

much. They may believe as little as they
please.

" But, Fowler, there are certain things we are
taught are necessary."

" Yes," he interrupted, " I know what you
would say. These certain things, I nnderstand to
be belief in God, and belief in duty. Whoever has
this faith in him clearly is in no danger, I
believe, of exclusion from heaven ; at least in the
present time, and in the existing state of knowledge. Whatever is beyond this, is unessential
either way. The test of orthodoxy is how it
affects our conduct. Experience shows uniformly, or so uniformly that it may be taken for
a law, that whoever denies the being of a God,
and the difference between right and wrong,
leads a life disgraceful to him as a human
being. I cannot find that the number of articles
you introduce after these produce any corresponding effect upon character, or that the
Socinian leads a less virtuous life than the
Anglo-Catholic. I do not say that to surrender
any point of faith one has been brought up in,
plenary inspiration of the Bible for instance—is
not *primâ facie* an objection against a man of
an unhealthy state of mind, in him, and that

it is not found very often accompanied by a
vicious life. But the vicious life is not the consequence of the wrong belief, it is more likely the
cause of it. When unbelief and vice go together,
it is not a partial, but a total unbelief; it may be
only partially expressed, but the attack upon the
Bible would really be only meant as a means
not of getting truth, but getting rid of all obligation of all kinds. Our entire system of moral
and religious belief, is so popularly bound up
together, that men think if they can make a
breach in a single point, the entire fabric falls.
To rid themselves of the inspiration of the
Bible, is to rid themselves of God and duty.
That is what they really disbelieve, and what
really injures them. . . . If you can show the
same or nearly the same amount of evidence,
that when a man believes this article in addition
to the other two, he is in virtue of this a better
man than the equally serious person who cannot
extend his faith beyond these, and your point is
proved, at least to me. But you cannot; and
till you can, I must be allowed to extend my
charity, and love, and honour, and learn of
Newman, as I love, and honour, and learn of
Carlyle."

" You are certainly an admirer that Newman would be very proud of, Edward; with his creed he is likely to approve of yours, do you not think so ?"

" I cannot help, and he cannot help his exclusiveness. It is part of the Catholic idea. I may love him without expecting him to return it. . . . But there are some fires which will burn out if they are let alone, and are only kept in blaze by blowing at them. What was the use of shrieking at him as you all did ?"

" Would you have had us let him be then, and look tamely on while half the University, and half England were going blindfold, into what it cost Europe five million lives to free herself of? Surely we should be very basely betraying our high trust if we had not."

" I think you hardly know exactly yet what it has been these five million lives have freed Europe from. But if you suppose it lies with any one man, or with all the frenzied efforts of the whole race of man to put back the great clock of time, and to undo the work of centuries, I pity your faith. Catholicism stood for one idea then; but its teeth are drawn, and it is something quite other than what it was. It cannot

7

burn, and rack, and imprison any more,—you may thank the common sense of the world for it. Let it alone. . . . Let it say out what it has to say. What is true in it will live, and blend with the eternal laws of the developement of mankind, and the lie will as surely perish. . . . Do you not see that you are feeding the fire by your outcries, and exalting what would have passed away as the eccentricity of genius into a real enemy in martyrdom for truth: genius always has its eccentricities; and for a system which cannot work without ostracising such men as Arnold or Newman, the sooner we are rid of it the better. . . . Wieland says, Luther delayed the birth of the real religion which will be the faith of the manhood of the human race for centuries, by introducing popular clamour to influence what should have been left to the thinkers. And this wretched enemy of all that is bright, and noble, and chivalrous; this water bucket, this miserable negative Anglican-Protestantism is playing the same foolish part over again with none of old Martin's heroic daring to qualify it. . . But it is weighed in the balance, and found wanting. Its kingdom is divided, and thank God its days are numbered."

M

" Forgive me, Arthur, if I have pained you,"
he said ; " I did not seek this. . .It is better left
to be written, and be read in books, when no
bitterness and ill-feeling can rise from it to
poison truth, and poison friendship; we have
none of us outgrown attaching blame to opinions,
and thinking worse of one another when we
cannot agree. . . . Few people can argue without being excited, and irritation, not conviction,
is its only fruit. . . . Let us leave this, it is
very painful."

———

It was a late Easter.   Passion-week had gone
by, and for the last few days, as if he had felt the
spell of the awful season, the sun had veiled his
face behind a heavy mass of cloud.   A chilly
east wind had folded up the opening flowers,
and sent the young leaves shrinking back into
the bud, and the dull yellow waves broke
wearily and wearily along the shore. . . . The
streets were hushed into an ascetic solemnity.
The warmest face had forgot to smile ; the wind
bore death upon its wings, and many a poor sufferer who had lingered through the sunshine of

the spring, was cut adrift in this week of mourning.

Twice I passed the churchyard, and twice the same sad death pageant was waiting there to meet me; a hearse and a single mourning coach, with the same pale attendants standing shivering by, half forgetting, from the cold air and colder custom, the chilly home to which they had borne one they perhaps had known and dreamt they loved in life, and where bye-and-bye, they would have to be borne along like him. It was Saturday evening; Dr. ———— had been with us, and had taken leave of Edward with more emotion than was usual with him. As he went out of the door, he called me after him, to tell me we had better watch that night by him, as perhaps he might never see another morning. . . . He had not told Edward himself, but I felt I ought, and I did. He bore to hear it far better than I to speak it. A light pressure of my hand, and a thank God was all the emotion he showed, and he lay back and folded his fingers together on his breast, as if he meant to lay there to wait his end. But it was only to think over what he had to do. " My last sacrament—I hoped it should have been Easter

morning! No, better now, better now. . . .
That should be for the saints, not for one like me,"
he muttered to himself. Then he turned to me.
" Go tell Allen to come; Allen must give me the
sacrament." . . I went to look for him: he was
out. It was half an hour before I came back
with him. As we entered the room, something I
saw had been passing between him and Emma.
What it was I never heard. If she ever spoke of
it, it was to her husband. She was kneeling by
his-bed side, and clasping Edward's long thin
hand, which was wet with her tears. I heard
him say, "Emma, remember. It was wrong, it was
really, it might have been a fearful peril. . . .
Ah! they are come now for the last." Allen had
been surprised at Edward's wish. He thought,
we both thought, perhaps we ought to ask him
why, in what sense he wished it. But there was
no time to ask questions such as that. Why ask,
when perhaps he had no strength to answer? and
when let his answer be what it would, we could
not dream of refusing him. Why press our
poor misgivings on a soul so far above ours, so
intensely peaceful? He had asked, was not that
enough? Emma did not rise, but she turned
her face to her husband, and her features spoke

more softly and sweetly to him than I had ever
seen before. She took his hand; he knelt
between her and Edward. We had prepared
everything that was wanted before we came in,
and he began the service. I fell back behind
them.   Edward spoke once, and only once,
through it all. At the words, " Ye that do truly
and earnestly repent," I heard him whisper,
"Yes, I repent. To repent is to leave living to
oneself, and to try to live to God. Yes, I repent." And then he folded his hands together
again on his breast, and Allen's fingers gave the
bread into his mouth, and held the cup against
his bloodless lips. . . . He neither spoke nor
moved again till Allen's blessing fell upon him,
and then he broke into an Amen, so sad, so
earnest, so musically sweet, I could have thought
it had been the voice of an angel sealing the
words of the priest.

" And now let me go to my God with one good
act to offer at his knees.   Emma—Allen—give
me your hands." He laid them together, and
clasped them in his own. " Emma," he said,
" if your heart has ever lingered upon me with
a thought which should have been his—if my
form has ever lain as a shadow between you

two, and remembrance of me has shed one tear of bitterness into the cup of happiness you two should drink through life together, take this last scene away with you as all the place hereafter I shall hold in your memory, and my blessing and my prayers, to dash out this dark drop for ever ; may the true love your hearts henceforth shall pour into each other, plead between me and my many sins before the throne of the Almighty. Love him, Emma, love him with as warm or warmer love than ever you felt for me. He deserves it far better than I. Good-bye, God bless you. The mercy which chose me to restore to you your child, twine the thought of me into a cord to bind you more close together. May you see your children's children, and peace upon your house !"

His voice grew firmer as he ended. He had drawn our strength from us into himself —we were all in tears . . . . Emma fell into her husband's arms, and as Allen hung over her and kissed her, Edward smiled with a look of happiness so intense, that if such thought as was in him then might abide within him for ever, he would be blessed indeed. . . . . " Yes, it is accepted," he said, " it is ac-

cepted—my work is done. O God, I thank
thee thou hast preserved me for this !

"Now, Arthur, I have something to say you.
Take these keys, they belong to my writing-
desk ; you will find there a number of papers
and essays which contain the main of what I
have thought in the last few years of my life.
They are almost all on the subject of which
we have spoken together, and about which what
I had to say seemed so much to disturb you.
They are what they are, but I believe they
express, however badly, much which the course
of the world is tending towards, and if it lives
long enough, will by-and-bye confess. Whether
they have truth in them, God knows. He
knows how I have laboured for truth, that
I have earnestly and single-mindedly sought
and struggled for that only ; but our thoughts
are so much governed by our history, that
opinions blow on character as necessarily and
as variously as the various flowers on their
stems. Take them and read them ; my thoughts
are such as belong to me as a man. You know
from first to last what I have been ; you will be
able to know something of the character for
good and evil of what you will find in them, with

my life a commentary. For those two, they are at peace. I have done one good thing in life at least. Bring me the desk, please."

I brought it and opened it. It was full of papers lying all in confusion. I was taking them out. . . . "Never mind these now," he said; "there is one at the bottom by itself, give me that." . . . I looked, and found a few sheets of paper, written out with more care than Edward commonly bestowed on his compositions. They were tied together with a strip of black ribbon, and a title on them. "Jean Paul's peace in death." . . . "Do you know Jean Paul, Arthur? He wrote it for a time like this, and I translated it some time back for myself. Read it to me, will you? I am very happy now—happier than I thought I might be, for God has let me go without blinding me with suffering. But read it. . . . . I cannot talk to you any more. I have no more to do. It will keep the heart up in all of us."

I took it and read:

"And now the warm fountains of healing were bathing the languid earth, and streaming down from the trees upon the grass; the storm was fast passing, the thunder had rolled away to the far off mountains, and the flashes came no longer like hot fierce gleams of wrath, but glanced mildly across the sky, like the light streaks in tears of joy. The sick man pointed upwards with his finger, 'Behold,' he said, ' the goodness of God. Now, my son, my soul is fainting, feed me—bring it food—bring it spirit food. But do not speak to me of repentings now . . . . I stand before my God in righteousness . . . . Speak as you spoke in your spring sermon : tell me of the Almighty and His works, and the richness of His love.' The young man's eye swam in tears. ' His Recollections !' He had designed them for his own dying, and he must bring them to his father's. . . . He told him what they were. ' Make haste, my son, make haste !' was the only answer. With shaking voice Godfrey began to speak, and burning tears streamed down the cheek of the betrothed maiden ; she must have been thinking of two death-beds, the father's and the son's.

" Remember, in the hour of darkness, that the splendours of the universe once swelled in thy breast, and thou hast known the grandeur of thy being. In the star-sown heaven at night, thou hast beheld one-half of the Infinite, and by day the other. Think away this phantom of room and roof, and the earth binding and crushing thee, and over thee as over their central point the universes are bending; worlds above thee, and around thee, and beneath thee, rolling on upon their course, and all the suns floating about their common centre, whose shadow is on thee—away along the eternities, through the all seen! Here in this void dreary place, thou knowest not what thou art. The void is only between the worlds, not round the world.

"Remember in the hour of darkness, of the burning time when thou hast prayed to God, and thy soul has throbbed with the highest thought permitted to the finite, the thought of Him who is the Infinite.

"The old man clasped his hands in prayer. Godfrey went on.

"Hast thou not known, hast thou not *felt* that Being whose infinity standeth not alone in power, and wisdom, and eternity; but in love and in righteousness? Canst thou forget the day when the blue heaven of day and the blue heaven of night raised their eyelids before thee, and thou knowest them from the blue orbs out of which God was softly looking upon thee?

" Hast thou not felt the love of the Infinite One, when it has shed itself down upon its mirror, in loving hearts of men; ay too, and in hearts of beasts, as the sun pours its bright day beams, not on the moon alone to light our night, but on the stars of morning and of evening, and on every wandering orb, the farthest distant from the earth. Remember in the hour of darkness, how, in the spring days of thy life, the grave hillocks seemed to thee as the distant mountain peaks of another world,—how when life was in its fulness thou couldst know the greatness, the worthiness of death. The snow-capped hillocks of the grave warm into new life the frozen prisoners of age and decay. As the sailor knows no long transition-time from cold to warm, but passes at once from a cold, ice-bound ocean, to lands all beaming with the warm pure life of spring, so do we land—or Christ remained a corpse for ever, and only His earth-dust was immortal,—so do we land, our ship strikes once, and the voyage is over, out of winter into everlasting spring. Canst thou look fearfully on thy parting, when so many poor short-lived mortals fling themselves, whole nations of them, in heaps, into the grave of war,

and sweep like night moths into the flame;
when heroic champions of the Fatherland can bear
young hearts and tender eyes, and fair un-
wrinkled brows, in the path of the hissing ball,
and the sharp steel. Think of the desolation
of war in thy own death, which is but one, and
follow manfully the long march of great nations,
and great heroes to the hallowed grave.

("'It was for myself I meant this, father,'
Godfrey broke in,) but the old man quietly
shook his head, and said, 'Go on.'

"In the hour of darkness rejoice," he continued, "that thy life has its dwelling in the great
life of the Infinite. The earth-dust of the globe
is inspired by the breath of the great God.
The world is brimming with life; every leaf on
every tree is a land of spirits and the All is in-
haling and exhaling. Each little life would
freeze and perish were it not warmed and sustained, by a life round wrapping and enveloping
it. The sea of time glistens like the sea of
waters with unnumbered beings of light; and
death, and resurrection, are but the flaming
valleys and flaming mountains of the ever rolling ocean. There are no lifeless skeletons,
what seems such are but other bodies. Yet,

but for the universal Being, what were all, but
one broad endless death ? We hang like moss
upon the Alps of nature, and inhale our being
among the clouds that wreathe around their
summit. Man is as the butterfly fluttering on
Chimborazo, and high above the butterfly soars
the condor in his pride; but small and great
alike, the giant and the child walk free in one
garden ; and the insect of the summer day can
trace the long long line of his forefathers through
storm and foe to the bright pair that once
played in the evening sun on the rivers of Paradise. Never, O never forget this thought which
is now so clear and bright before thee, that in
the fiercest pains spirits ever know, the ' I '
holds on, as unscathed as in their warmest pleasures, yea, then grows clearest and most trium-
phant, when the body is breaking asunder in its
agonies. The soul of man, like the wandering
light of the moon, plays brightest in the wildest
storms.

"Canst thou forget, in the hour of darkness,
the great ones that have gone before thee ; and
that thou art but following in their steps ? Stay
thyself on that glorious band of spirits who
built themselves mountains on which to stand,

and beheld the storms of life not above them, but rolling far beneath. Call back to thy soul the majestic company of wise men, and inspired poets, who brought light and life to nation after nation.

" ' Speak of our Redeemer,' the father said. The son went on.

" In the hours of darkness think of Jesus Christ, for He too knew them. Think on the soft moon of the Son of God beaming down on the night of humanity; let life and death be alike holy to thee; for He has hallowed both in sharing them with thee. His mild and lofty eye is now beholding thee, in this thy last cloud, and He will bring thee to His Father and thine."

" A slight peal of thunder rolled along the clouds; for a moment they parted open, and the evening sun slowly filled the room with fire.

" Think, in the last hour, how the heart of man can love ; think of the holy time when thou hast offered up thy tears, eyes, heart, when thou wouldst have thought it gain to surrender all, thyself, thy happiness, to one beloved being. Remember—remember those blessed hours in which one heart was more to thee than a million, and thy soul, a whole life long could find in other soul its food, and light, and life; the oak of a hundred years, rooted fast in the same old place, and gathering new strength and beauty along a hundred springs.

" ' Do you mean me—me ?' said the father.

" ' I was thinking of my mother,' Godfrey said. Justa burst into tears, her lover's highest happiness, in his last hour, would be in the remembrance of her. The father thought of his lost one, and muttered slowly under his breath, ' Meet again—meet again.'

" Remember, in thy last hour," Godfrey continued, " Remember the days of thy youth, when life was before thee in its beauty and grandeur, when thou couldst weep at the birth of spring, for very joy,—when thou couldst soar to heaven on the wings of prayer, and see God upon His throne, the first and the last, the everlasting heart of love. . . . Remember, remember this, and close thy eyes in peace.

" At that instant, the storm cloud broke asunder in two huge mountains of vapour, and between them, as down a valley, the deep sun was gazing in beauty, beaming once more upon the earth with a mother's eye.

" ' What a flash !' muttered the dying man.

" ' It is only the evening sun, father.'

" ' Yes, yes,' he continued ; ' I shall see her again . . . . again . . . . and to-day.'—His thoughts were with her who had gone before him to her rest.

" Godfrey remembered what he had been that day composing in anticipating the joy of an earthly meeting; but his feelings choked him, and he could not go on. He might have drawn a beautiful scene ; he could have told how when those who love meet again, after a long parting, the best feelings they have ever known are born again in a higher sphere, and as early friendships float in a life that is to come, so glancing backward into what is gone from among the flowers of the future, wreathes them into one garland with the fruits of the past. But how could Godfrey speak of the blessedness of meetings upon earth to one who was already gazing into the glories of the unearthly?

" There was a pause ; a sudden motion in the bed ; Godfrey started.

" I remember in the hour of darkness—I remember,—yes, this—and this,—and this—and death is beautiful, and my parting is in Christ.'

" The old man caught his son's hand as he spoke, but he did not press it, it was but the unconscious spasm of the last struggle. He fancied Godfrey was speaking still, and said once more in clear and burning tones, 'O thou my all merciful God!' For the mock suns of life were gone out within him for ever, and God, the only true sun, stood alone before his soul. Once more he raised himself in his bed, and stretched out his arms, and cried, 'There, there, see the bright rainbow over the sunset, I must follow the sun ; after . . . . with it.'

" He fell back and all was over. The sun's disc hung on the horizon—lower— lower it was gone, and the last rays slanting upwards spanned the eastern sky with a giant rainbow.

" 'He is gone,' Godfrey said ; his voice shook, ' He is gone from us to his God, in pure and tranquil joy. Do not cry, Justa.' But the tears he had only held back with strong effort burst in streams from his own eyes ; he pressed his dead father's hands against his burning cheeks. It grew dark, and the rain fell softly over the darkening earth.

" The two lovers left the silent form, and went to weep their sun which they had lost—their

N

father who had passed away from the storm-cloud of life in a gleam of splendour, to the daybreak of another morning."

I ended. I turned to look at Edward. These beautiful words were his passing bell. His eyes hung wide, and fixed, and glassy, and his features were stiffening into repose.

"Yes, yes," he said, " I too shall—I shall see them again. . . yes; my father. Death—birth. Yes, it is morning—bright beautiful morning; . . . . open . . . . let me see . . . it is day— . . . . come to see me go. Push the curtain . . . . let me see the sea once more—the beautiful, beautiful sea." The lamp was paling under the rays of morning, which were streaming between the shutters. I threw them back, and there lay the sweet bay before me, half clear, half veiling its glossy surface in wreaths of amber-tinted vapour. The east wind had passed away, and left Nature in serene tranquillity, that heaven and earth might meet together in joy for the glorious Easter festival. The mist hung out over the horizon in folds of dazzling beauty, painted pink by the raybrush of morning. It seemed lying there as apparel for the sun to array himself in splendour as he rose.

" He comes !—he comes !—away I must go . .
Open, open the windows . . all, all! God's blessing is in the breath of the Easter morning."
His eyes were straining on the east. . . . . .
" See, see ! he is come !" . . . . The mist
opened suddenly, and the great orb was hanging in crimson majesty on the water, which was
glowing like melted gold.   Far along along the
surface, a thousand thousand wavelets flashed
triumph lit under the eye of their Lord.   The
Easter bells broke up out of the town with their
glad welcoming peal, and every tree was joining
in unison as the choral birds chaunted in with
their unconscious melodies.   For one moment
four human hearts were thrilling under the
spell of that entrancing scene—the next, and
one of them had ceased to beat for ever. . . . .
Yes, Edward was gone.   The long clouded
night of his earthly sojourn had past out into
undying light, and his soul was gone in the
sunrise to the day which shall never end.   A
smile still lingered on his lips; they were parted
as if to speak, but the last words had melted
into a sigh which had winged the spirit to its
fulfilling, and the shell was left silent in beautiful
desolation.

The hearse and the mourning coach stood once more at the gate of the churchyard; again a few solitary mourners watched by a grave-side, while the earth fell sadly on a brother's last dwelling-place, and his memory began to fade out of life as his body to resolve into the dust. Another week, and we were all gone. Allen's voice was heard no more in the chapel, and Jemmy was never seen again on the pier or on the downs. They could not stay in a place which were crowded with such recollections; they sought and found in a distant part of England a true home and a second day-spring of life; and if the hearts of those above are warmed by the happiness of those they love on earth, then surely Edward is not losing his reward for the last good deed which was given him before his end.

Mine was a more melancholy occupation, to fulfil his last command to study through the history of an unhappy mind, which started out of nothing, and found its way through philosophy to faith,—found its way to a faith, a faith he could die in as he died; but it were idle for me to try to deceive myself into thinking it was the faith popular at the present day. A profound belief

in God and in God's providence, lay at the very
core of his soul; but all beyond it seemed but
shifting cloud, at a distance forming into temples
and mountains, and skyey palaces, but seen
close and examined, all fog and choking vapour.
He appeared to believe and disbelieve alike
every religion which had ever worked among
any number of mankind from the beginning.
Religions were all myths.   In the region of the
supernatural, you were far away from fact, and
the religious histories were the symbolic growths
of an idea, marking a step in the progress of mankind. How exactly he would apply his theories,
how far he would extend them. how he could
face the history of the world with such a clue to
its interpretation, is not for me to say. . . . He
has left his ideas but in germ, and elsewhere they
are growing into form which may be seen.   Till
such time, let them rest.   I had thought of publishing some few of the more finished essays, if
I could find any to which any degree of the
word finished could be attached; but after turning and turning them over, I found it hopeless,
and I thought it best to sow them where, if there
be power of growth in them, they may come to
fruit in after time; where let them all for the

present hide themselves, except these two fragments. . . . . . The first seems part of an un-
sent letter to some one who had remonstrated
with him for writing *in* the "Lives of the
Saints."

" June 1843.

" I thought you knew me too well to be surprised at my taking to the "Lives of the Saints,"
taking to anything that offered itself. You
know I affect to be a philosopher who does not
believe that truth ever shows herself completely
in either of the rival armies that claim so
loudly to be her champions. She seems to me to
lie like the tongue of the balance only kept in
the centre by the equipoise of contending
forces, or rather, if I may use a better illustration, like a boat in a canal, drawn forward by
a rope from both sides, which appear as if they
would negative each other, and yet produce
only a uniform straightforward motion. I throw
myself on this side or on that as I please, without fear of injuring her. The thought of the
great world sweeps on its own great road, but it
is its own road ; quite an independent one . . .
not in the least resembling that which Catholic
or Protestant, Roundhead or Cavalier, have

carved out for it. All you have to care for is, that you make an acute angle, not an obtuse one, with the line of its course. . . . Fancy the French Revolution and modern Germany, the lawfully begotten children on the bodies of Martin Luther and the Alva persecutions. Fancy Sir Robert Peel round the neck of England, as tight as the old man of the sea round Synbad, within ten years of the Reform Bill. . . . I am not such an ass as to claim any superior wisdom for thinking in this way. Only a very weak person indeed thinks all the goodness and talent on his side, and all the wickedness and stupidity on every other. I suppose my mind is set to its way of looking at things as others are set to Catholicising, and others to Protesting. Of course I feel myself infinitely below the great men, (even in these days when great men are so little,) who represent the exclusive claims of the opposites. It is the water which is pent up into a narrow bed that has the force in it, not what spreads itself out in platitudes. The genius of the rival powers is nearer to mankind and walks more grandly among them than the great arbitrator who stands so high up in the middle above their heads; and if I am born

under his star, I must be content to be a looker
on in the world's drama, not an actor. . . . But
for these lives I certainly do wonder Newman
should have asked me to help him with them.
Newman, with his profound knowledge of
human nature, and who had so lately given me
a proof how well he knew me . . . .
Within two months of this, I might naturally be
surprised to be asked by him to write Lives of
Saints. . . . It was impossible I could really
feel towards them as he did, or believe the
stories I was to have the relation of. Yet simply to sympathize with his view, and with an
effort for a particular purpose, to throw myself
into his way of looking at things, though it might
not interfere with what I was to produce as a
composition, he at least would think the most
dangerous trifling, and the result of a complete
moral disorganization. Of course I do not
think so, but he would. . . . Perhaps he fancied it was an employment which would do me
good. . . . But he must have known that in my
state of mind, even if I did in theory believe that
that kind of sanctity was the real thing one was
to live to arrive at, I could not heartily sympathize with them as yet, and it was a most dan-

gerous piece of proceeding to start with, to assume and to pretend so much of it.

" You will say this holds equally of all our young clergymen, or at least of far the greater part of them. I know it does, and few things sicken me more than to hear fellows spiritualizing away in the pulpit, and prating of heaven and hell and every holy mystery, whose single preparation has been a course of port wine and fornication."

The other is very different; it has the appearance of having been written off hastily, under the feeling of the moment directly after what it relates.

" February, 1844.

" I have had a fearful nightmare this afternoon in Magdalen Chapel. I went to the evening service. I was too late to be taken into the choir, and I had to remain in the ante-chapel. . . . At the best times one is little more than a spectator there : it is very hard to join in the service. But this evening—it was not a dream, for I was broad awake,—it was not a thought, for I tried to shake it off and I could not. . . .

I was under a spell. Out of the dark ante-
chapel I was gazing up into the brilliantly
lighted choir, up long rows of white choristers
and surpliced priests, past fantastic forms carved
quaintly out of the old black oak. . . . By the
light of two giant tapers which hung before it, I
could see in the far back-ground the beautiful
white altar, and dim above it, as behind a veil,
looking down, the awful features of the Saviour
stooping under His Cross. The organ swelled
up the chapel and echoed down again upon me.
The sweet voices of the choristers answered
each other along the walls, and down along the
fretted roof. Inside all was so beautiful; all
seemed an outpouring from the divinest depths
of purest devotion ; all there were God's own
chosen ones. . . . Outside, where I was, all was
dull, and dark, and dreary. The west window
frowned above me with the awful judgment day
stained in upon its surface. The moon was
setting behind it. I could see the outline of
the dreadful figures sweeping off with their
writhing victims into a huge abyss, which was
yawning for them, down the jaws of a monstrous
serpent fiend. On the pavement, ranged round
the walls, or lounging up and down, were those

who, like me, were spectators of a scene they
did not wish for a nearer share in; loose, idle
dilettante worshippers of the beautiful, drawn
there by love of sweet sounds, and women with
that upon their forehead which seems to say a
love less pure than that had brought them to a
scene so holy. . . . I leant against a pillar; the
scene hung before me like a living picture;
but where I was passed away from me, and I
fancied I was in the other world. Inside the
chapel was Heaven, where the angels were
hymning their praises before the throne of God,
and I, alas, was not among them. . I had come
too late, and all that was given to me was to be
a gazer upon the splendour of a scene from which
I was to be an outcast for ever. My dwelling
was under the scowl of judgment, and my everlasting companions the scorner, the voluptuous,
and the fool. Alas for me, they were happier
than I. They could taste no higher pleasure;
they could listen to the eternal melodies of the
angels' harps, and their base souls could yet
find their pleasure from the far-off sounds and
visions of the serene beauty of Heaven. They
had sought no more, and what they sought they

had found. . . I alas had come to seek the
best, but had come too late. I was doubly
curst. I felt I might fall back and be as they,
but that I would not do. . . . I longed still for
the better and still could see it ; I loathed the
outcasts I was thrown among, but my portion
was with them—the portion I had earned for
myself ; and the crystal gate of Paradise was
barred against me for ever.

"I heard a voice say, such is the penalty of
those who seek Heaven their own way, and not
by the way of the sanctuary ; they shall see the
glories they crave, but they shall be taken
with their pride, and their eternal inheritance
is with the evil. I thought I bowed my head
and answered: 'Thy will, O Lord, be done!
I must dwell with them, but I will not be of
them. I will turn still to Thee, and desire
Thee, if I may not find Thee.' The vision
past. I heard the priest's last blessing thrill
around the heads of the favoured ones ; a brief
pause, and the organ broke into a long sweet
voluntary, and underneath the music, two and
two, the white worshippers past slowly out
among the profane. But when they came

among us they became of us. They mingled in the crowd, and became like the crowd. Close by me one surpliced figure whispered under a deep overhanging bonnet. I caught the words— they were an assignation.".

THE LIEUTENANT'S DAUGHTER.

ἄνω ποταμῶν ἱερῶν
χωροῦσι παγαί.

MEDEA.

THE LIEUTENANT'S DAUGHTER.

CHAPTER I.

I HAD often been haunted by Hooker's defini-
tion of time, as " the measure of the motion of
the heavens." If time depends on the movements of the great bodies in space, as they go
time goes, at a rate parallel to theirs, or rather
at the same rate; as the hand of a clock would
go which was set to mark exactly the swings of
the pendulum; so that it would seem, that if
from the interposition of some unknown cause,
the planets were to double their velocity, the
earth fulfilled its orbit twice as rapidly as it does
now, and every other body equally accelerated

its speed ; time must also, following their
bidding, go twice as fast too. . . . If they went
slower, time must go slower, if they stood still,
time would draw rein and wait also till they
moved again.   If a general bouleversement of
the system of the universe were to take place,
and they moved the other way, time would roll
backwards along with them, and unfold the coil
of all the incidents it has brought with it.

Then I came to remember that as we measured time, and indeed all things, not according
to the real order of nature as it is in itself, for
of that we know nothing, but according to the
order in which phenomena present themselves
to our senses ; so if it were possible in such a
way to dispose things on our planet, as that the
visible system should only *seem* to reverse its
movement, the sun to rise in the west and set in
the east, and evening and morning exchange
their order and position, time and all it had
brought with it would ebb like a tide.

Let a railroad be run round the earth's girdle,
(there is nothing absurd in such a supposition,
a single line would be sufficient, and the equi-
noctial is ready made to the hand,) and set
a carriage running on it in the same direction

with that of the earth's motion and with double
the velocity, exactly the reverse order of the
phenomena would in fact be brought about. . . .
From to-day we should pass into yesterday, from
yesterday into the day before; month before
month, and year before year, the earth would
uncoil its life, and with it all the lives of all her
children with all their doings, fates, and fortunes.

It appeared to me so certain it would be so,
that I used to make it a matter of serious speculation, and try and see what would be the effect
produced on the mind by looking at death at the
wrong end, and the prospect of passing out into
eternity through the gate of infancy instead of
old age. . . . If " that we are" implies, that we
shall be, it implies of course equally that we
have been. It is only the change of names,
the past becomes the future, and the future the
past. Eternities lie each side of life, and we
are equally ignorant of both. Forward and
backward are but modes in which we express
our relation to ourselves and things, and there is
nothing more unlikely in such a change in fact
taking place, or more unnatural in the character
of it, than in the tide of a great river turning to

ebb again when we have seen it for half a day
flowing continuously one way. . . . I say there
is nothing *a priori* impossible, or even improbable in such a change some time or other taking
place in the order of nature; philosophically,
perhaps it is the readiest way in which we can
conceive the ultimate passing away of the universe; still less is there anything unlikely in
some of its effects being brought about artifici-
ally in the way I have suggested.

I have mentioned the fact of this speculation
of mine, because it may help to account for the
incident I am going to tell. . . . I call it incident, because it was a thing which befell me; I
do not mean to say it befell me externally, but
it befell me internally—a phenomenon of mind
which may or may not admit of natural explanation.

Perhaps my speculations had so disposed the
particles of my body, that of themselves, when
the control of my volition was taken off, they
presented it to me in the form of a picture. If
so, it is valuable as a fact of science, for it was
methodical, and so would prove that the particles of body have a power of harmonious production. . . . But this is a point I leave to

the psychologist.   All I know about the matter
is, that a series of incidents were presented to my
notice; not in a dream, because I was awake,—
not produced by an act of will, because if so, I
could have controlled them, which I fonnd
I could not.   Not forced upon my mind because
I could turn away from them, and several times
did so by a very simple process; not shutting
my eyes, but opening them, and pouring in
another set of objects on my mind, just as an
ordinary window pane, if you look directly at it,
transmits the objects to you, which are beyond
it; but you may so dispose yourself that it shall
serve as a mirror, and show you yourself, and
the room which is behind it.

———— and I were travelling on the west
coast of Ireland; we were about a good deal
among the people, and I either from carelessness or bad fortune found myself one day con-
fined to my bed with all the symptoms of
incipient small-pox.   At the end of a week I
was in high fever; sleep, heartless friend that it
is, forsaking us at our greatest difficulties, had
taken leave of me from the commencement of
my illness, and seven long weary nights and
days I had lain sulkily tossing, and as long as I

was strong enough grumbling grandly.   In vain
I counted thousands upon thousands, solemnly
humming above my breath, and courting silence
by monotony of sound ; it was all to no purpose.
The eighth night, as the long July evening
closed in at last, I thought myself particularly ill used.   I had been twice bled in the
day, and my body was weak and exhausted.
The control on the nerves was taken off, and
my imagination began to revel in its emancipation, and dazzle me with a thousand brilliant
images. . . . If I could only go to sleep, what
dreams might I not have ? for once in my life,
real poet's dreams, and to be so disgustingly
cheated of them !   My feeling of disappointment however did not last very long.   I found
that although I could not go to sleep, imagination was for once disposed to be polite, and was
going to stay up with me and entertain me. . . .
I suppose it was a kind of delirium, but it was
only half delirium, for the whole night I was
conscious: I could at any time collect myself,
open my eyes, look about at the objects in the
room, and reflect on what I had been seeing. . .
On the other hand, I had no power at all (or I
did not feel that I had) over the images that

presented themselves to me. It was all as really
and truly external, and independent of my power
of willing, as the ordinary incidents of orderly
daylight life.

In the early part of the night I found I had
a sort of Aladdin's lamp, and was waited on by
troops of the most charmingly obedient genii.
In the wretched place in which I was, I had
been able to get nothing in the way of food
which did not nauseate me. Visions of fruits had
been tantalizing me; had I had a birthright,
I should have been as profane as Esau, and sold
it for a bunch of grapes. Now with my genii,
how I would indulge myself! no sooner had
I wished, than the markets of Covent Garden
had poured their treasures at my bed-side. I
was in the act of stretching out my hand to seize
an exquisite peach that lay blushing like a young
bride for the touch of my lips, when a light blue
flame began to play and flicker round it, and
made me start like Faust at the witches' draught;
but my genii allayed my alarm, with telling me
their fire never hurt any one who was not to
belong to them. . . . That was pleasant, and
emboldened me to take liberties. I had long
been troubled with various lurking scepticisms;

there was certainly no danger, and now was the time to get them satisfied.

Our books, I said to one of them, inform us that you gentlemen are not an independent fraternity; you have, they say, a certain superior to whom you all owe allegiance, and if all accounts be true, a person of no small power and capability, and playing a considerable figure under the rose in the history of this world of ours. . . . Now I want to know first, whether there is such a person?

" Oh, certainly !"

" Might I see him ?"

" He will have the greatest pleasure in waiting upon you."

And he came. A great curtain was stretched across the room, and on the surface of it, like a figure in a phantasmagoria, was hung the image I had summoned. What it was I cannot tell; it has passed away like the dream of Nebuchadnezzar, and I remember nothing but my disappointment. It was a meagre anatomy; I could have made a far braver one myself. I begged for more light I remember, for a clearer vision of him; but this fact was the remarkable one about him, that the more I had the light multiplied the feebler became the shadow, and at last, as I went on increasing and increasing, it seemed to melt away from off the canvass, and the white rays fell off unstained and unbroken.

But whatever the master was, my genii were splendid. Nothing seemed too great for them, all power was in their hands, and for the time they were slaves to me. What should I do next? All the world before me, and nothing but to take my pleasure in it, and find employment for them.

The great dead heroes came up out of their graves for me to look at; stately cities, temples, palaces rose at my bidding, and the splendours of infernal art were lavished on their decoration; and still my genii were at my elbow crying for work, work. Like a boy with a holiday I was trying to make the most of my time, and wasting it in thinking how best I should use it, and the spirits were impatient only of idleness, and left me no rest with their crying. Unless I could make an effort, I felt it would turn into a vulgar nightmare, and I was thinking in despair of Merlin's remedy and the ropes of sand, when my old speculation flashed across me. I was unwilling to be driven to Merlin's plan; it was such utter waste, and besides it was not original, so I turned with a proud voice to them, proud of my own cleverness; and I said, '' Go, reverse the order of the universe, and make time flow backwards. . . . In a moment they were gone! The next, and I found myself among my friends in the common life of common days; there it was all the same, yet all so altered, for all was going back. There I saw my own family, my father, mother, brothers, sisters; there was my second " *me*," there we all were, altogether as usual, and all living upside down. Yesterday, with all yesterday had brought, came up one thing before another, and then the night, and then the day before; and the wonderful part about it was, that to the people themselves, and to the other " *me*" I saw among them, there seemed to be nothing out of the way in it all, it was a perfect matter of course. The scene where I first found myself, was my own house, a short time before my illness; but I soon discovered I was outside, and independent of it all. I could transport myself at will, up and down, backwards and forwards, along the time river, and see any one I pleased at any period of his progress or retrogression, with whatever he was, what he was doing, and what he was thinking. To be sure, how strange it was; and it seemed to them as if it had been always so. They went upwards from hunger, through repletion to their meals, and down from them with a spring to hunger. The aged heavy-laden patriarch gathered up his children into his loins again, and laid off his burden of experience year by year, and walked lighter and gayer, and more foolishly for it. Nature followed the same inverted rule. You saw the tea coiling up like a water-spout, out of the tea-cup into the mouth of the pot, and no one looked surprised. Great ships came up out of the sea, and joined their seamy planks, and drowned sailors gathered up their lives again, and back, sternforemost, they went to port. Effects and causes had changed places. Final became efficient, and efficient final; and the odd people had got their systems of philosophy that accounted, as they called it, for the order of the phenomena of nature, and they fancied they understood the principles of things. Some were contented with observations of facts, and generalized experimental laws for themselves; others were more hardy, and proved their theories form the constitution of the soul, and the necessities of the Divine Nature. . . . But what struck me most, was the very comical idea they all had, that they were quite at liberty to do or not do, that they were perfectly free agents with uncontrolled volition, when they were not only going along a course so rigidly determined, uncoiling, and uncoiling everything, so exactly as it had been; but it was their very own footsteps they were treading back along, and they could not see it. At first it perplexed me to make out why they did not recollect; but I remembered how hard it is to repeat the most familiar sentence backwards, and how utterly unlike itself it looks, and sounds if spoken so, or written so. Only now and then a sound will strike which seems familiar; why, or how, one cannot tell, and so it was with them in their lives. Now and then a flash of conviction, that a word or an action or a scene was familiar to them, gleamed into their minds; but strange things followed close, and effaced the momentary image; the clue was but glimpsed to be lost again, and the wiser of them put away such trifles as beneath the notice of the serious mind.

When the first perplexity was over, and I had got my nature set to watch them systematically, (how long it took I cannot tell, for time, as may be supposed, was in strange disorder with me,) I employed myself in watching my own self, and other persons I knew, into earlier periods of their lives, and comparing, and contrasting, and trying to make out in what idea their character had crystallized. . . . Then I would try people I did not know. I would watch something they had done, and form an opinion from it of what they were, and test my judgment on the order of circumstances along which they had passed, and which had determined them. My judgment of character I might be right in, my estimate of action was invariably wrong.

Scherazade, in a thousand and one nights, could hardly tell all I must have seen in those few hours. Out of all of them I select a single one, not in itself, perhaps, nearly the most remarkable; but it has the merit of being the most complete, because one of the genii arranged it for me, and obliged me to see it through, and through the close of it himself attended me, not letting me, as my own taste generally suggested, fly off from an unfinished experiment, to the fresher fragrance of novelty. It was the last, and I remember it the best, and it has the further advantage of being the easiest to tell from the way in which he showed it me.. I suppose he wished it to make an impression, for although he did not interfere with the backward order of the scenes, he reinverted each separately for me, and I read them straight off in natural order, just as in the translation of a Hebrew book, when the European version stands on the opposite page to the original, the Semitic order and arrangement of pages is preserved, and the beginning is at the end, while the words and lines and verses are reversed, and we read down each page our way without difficulty.

CHAPTER II.

WHEN the first scene opened, I was in a churchyard; it was night with a still clear air, and a sky serenely brilliant. The moon in silver splendour high up as the summer sun at noon, and the stars dressed out as if they were keeping festivals in heaven. The dew-drops glittered over all the graves with a white lustre, which made the glow-worms pale; they had crawled into the black shadows, where they could still shine without a rival, for fear the insects of the grave should forget the homage which they owed them, and turn idolaters of the images of the sky they saw mirrored there in those crystal globes. The leaves of the great yew-tree, and the ivy that, vampire like, clung round it and fed upon its life's juices, were turned to frosted silver, and rustled crisply as the owls flew in and out. The tall arched windows were lit with spectral light, as if from spectral tapers; one might have thought the spirits of the old dead monks were busy there fulfilling the night services and night worship the unworthy living had forgotten. I stood below the great tower, where high up hung the deep-voiced symbol and chronicler of time; slowly, surely, steadily crept on the spectral finger its allotted path, pointing as it went to the numbers on the dial-plate, like the hand on the wall of the Royal Feasters' Banquet Hall. Ever as each half hour rolled off into eternity, out rung its awful death knell; and far above glistened the warning cock the remembrancer of prayer; so far, far up it seemed from earth, as if inlaid into the sky.

The great ocean lay stretching away where no eye could follow, from under the hill, still as I had never seen it. The moon and all the stars lay then each with its single image clear and unbroken, as if on a polished sheet of steel. I could have fancied I was on the edge of the world, and looking down into another sky. So awfully still it was, there was not a voice, there was not a sound, save when an old owl was scornfully wooing his mistress with his sad serenadings, and one far-off nightingale whispering its sweet good night. So still it was, that although I knew well there was something to be enacted there, which I was brought to witness, the noise of a footfall made my cheek as pale as the pale earth; it seemed to splash into the stillness like a stone into glassy water. It came on and on over the path towards the church yard stile; heavily, yet quickly, as the steps of a tired traveller within sight of his journey's end, and mustering his expiring energies for all the effort he wanted more. It came on, it came in, and under the shadow of the black yew-tree a woman passed up among the graves. For a few moments she stood still as if uncertain which way to turn: perhaps she was fainting, for she clutched a tombstone convulsively, and only so just saved herself from sinking to the ground. Presently she collected herself again, and staggered past me into a corner of the churchyard, where two graves lay apart from the rest close side by side; and then it seemed she had reached her end, for she flung herself down upon the grave and lay there motionless.

P

I followed her, for I felt I was charmed against sight or hearing, and sate down too on the far end of the mound opposite her. Her tattered shoes had not served to cover her feet, which were wounded and bleeding; her dress was torn and soiled, and her long dark hair, which flowed out unconfined from under her bonnet, was all the shading which hid her neck from the moon. The haggard profile lying up in the light on that mournful pillow, showed deep fierce lines of famine, and the twenty summers she might have numbered must have served her to drain out the dregs of the cup of bitterness of life. So thin she was, the grass seemed scarcely to bend under her weight. I could almost fancy I saw it through her.

Between the two graves, crossing at their head and joining them, was a single stone, the humble monument of those who slept below it. A *Hic jacet,* with the names Lieutenant Gray and his wife Ellen, was the unpretending inscription, with one verse below out of the Bible :

" Now they sleep in the dust: Thou shalt seek them in the morning and they shall not be."

The husband had been dead eight years; the wife had gone to prepare his place twelve years before him.

And the woman that lay there, what was she? The living monument of those two! the poor forlorn one come *there* to *them* for shelter! Was this all that was left to her of home? She had fainted where she lay. Oh! would that she had never woke again! But she did wake. A short, short space of life remained for her for one more miserable deed before she sank again into the trance out of which is no waking. She turned slowly, and with languid pain raised her head. What hideous tale was written on those ghastly features !

"Oh God," she said, "and I am alive still. And there is no other way."

She caught the gravestone in her long thin fingers, and strained her eyes upon the words that lay written there, as if to be sure that it was indeed real, and was not all a frightful dream. . . . And there lay the two names all cold and passionless, and froze her gaze till it was stony as themselves.

"Oh mother, mother, father ! are you here ? here ? And will you not speak to me ? Tell

me, tell me I may come to you. . . . Do you
hate me? Speak! Oh, they will drive me
from them too. I am a degraded outcast, and
I may not lay beside them in their grave. Oh,
no, they do not hear! They sleep in the dust.
I shall seek them and they shall not be. . . .
No, no; they can, they can. They hear me,
they do hear me, and they hate me."

She put her hand to her head.

"I am mad," she said. "Oh, no, not mad,
would I were! It is all true; there it is, yes,
there is old home." I followed her eyes—across
a little valley towards the sea stood a white
cottage in a small group of trees, glittering in
the moon, and beyond a tall mast with a yard
and cordage, marking the station of the coast-
guard. . . . "Old home—all there; all, all the
same. Why is it the same? or why am I not
the same? . . . There is the old porch and the
old room, and there is my little window. There
is a candle burning there on the ledge where I
used to put it when I said my prayers before I
went to bed. . . . Who put it there now? Is
she saying her prayers?"

Her eyes hung glazed upon the house; suddenly she drew herself up and strained herself
upon her knees.

" Oh, Father Almighty, hear me. Father of those who have none else. In misery and wretchedness I cry to Thee to let me die. Punish me, if it must be,—and I am not punished?—but not here. Why am I to drag about with me this loathsome life; to be scorned and hated, and trod upon, and to hate myself worst of all? There is no hell worse than this; for here it is all hate. But God is just, and they told me once God was merciful. Is there no place in all the universe where He can hide me? There no mercy here. . . . God is not here; I will go to God. Oh, Father, if the prayers of one like me can reach to Thee; if there is any mercy in heaven for a wretched castaway, oh, kill me, or give me a sign that I may come."

A shooting star flashed across the horizon, streaking the dark sky-vault with a trail of fire, and a startled sea-bird's scream was heard dying away over the water. At the same moment the church clock pealed midnight, marking the death of the day, and the candle in the cottage window was extinguished.

" He hears me, He hears me !" she cried. " I may go." . . . I saw the fatal phial in her hand, and sprung forward to snatch it from her; but my grasp was lighter than the lightest breath of summer air. Another moment and it was gone. . . " Father, mother, I come,—He says I may come, He says it! You will take your child to you."

She fell across the graves. Her head sunk pillowed above her sleeping father without a struggle. The right arm drooped heavily round the end of the mound, and the slackened limbs stretched down along the hollow between the graves. It was all over, and the moon shone on as clear and calm, and no star veiled its light. The warm body grew stiff and cold as the blood thickened in the veins, and the bold owls flitted round it as it lay and hooted on in solemn mockery.

CHAPTER III.

THEY were busy next evening at the printing
house at Exeter. . . The types were setting
for the weekly paper, click clicking into the iron
frames, off which were to roll the great electric
conductors of modern enlightenment. The thick
flat reams of paper were lying damp to the
hand of the journeyman. The columns were
all full, all but one staring blank which had
been left open for an advertisement, which had
not yet arrived. The patience of the superintendent ebbed with the minutes. Our own
intelligencer must draw again upon his magazine for some laughter-moving or harrowing
incident. But our own intelligencer, alas! responds but dully to the call. He had overstrained his inventive faculties already that day
in the creating of facts, and he had turned them

out prematurely to refresh themselves over rum and water; so that now, when put into harness again, he could no more move than a tired horse put away for the night led out unexpectedly to a heavy carriage, and a mountain road.

It was hoped that, with pen and paper, his hand might move mechanically to its work, but it was found capable only of an Irish outrage; and on that bank the newspaper had already overdrawn its account. The superintendent was hanging doubtingly between the last Pickwick and the least threadbare of his devotional sentiments, when a young clerk who was lounging smoking in the compositors' room, and had volunteered his services in blowing snuff up the intelligencer's nostrils, now offered to supply his place for him. He cocked his hat on one side, dropped upon the stool, and dipped his pen into the ink. Now, what shall it be? some young lord pitching into the police, eh! or a spice of scandal? The Reverend —— , whose name we forbear to mention, out of respect to his sacred office. . . . Or what d'ye say to something touching and romantic? I was down at Exmouth to-day at the Royal. They were sitting up-stairs on a girl they'd found in the churchyard in the morning. Poison, so they say; took it herself, little fool. You and I, Jack, would have taught her better, if she'd come to us."

" Aye, that'll do, Ned; anything so you're quick about it,—trim up."

" Well then, here goes."

Touching and romantic.—" No, hang it, that won't do either; we mustn't make it interesting." Vice and suicide.—" Aye, that's right. Vice and suicide.—This morning an inquest was held at the Royal Arms, Exmouth, on the body of a young woman —"

" Female, Ned, female; woman don't sound respectable."

" Well, on the body of a young female, who was recognised by several of the inhabitants as Catherine Gray, and from her appearance must have been lately given to abandoned habits. (That's moral, eh, Jack?)　She left Exmouth, it will be remembered, a year since with a gentleman, (whose name, out of deference to his honoured and respected relatives, we think it best to conceal,) under circumstances betraying peculiar ingratitude; and it was for some time

a subject of great alarm to the friends of the
gentleman, that she might have been privately
married to him.   From this fear, however, they
were happily soon relieved, as he was recovered
from his abandoned companion, and she had not
since been heard of.   A person answering the
description of deceased had been seen the day
before in the neighbourhood in a state of extreme destitution, and this morning she was
found in the churchyard quite dead.   It appears
the unhappy creature must have retained some
spark of better feeling, as the spot where she
was found lying was the burial-place of her
father.   Dr. Wilson examined the body, and gave
it as his opinion that death had been occasioned
by poison.   A bottle containing remains of such
deleterious substance was found at her side, and
it was too plain she had met her end by her
own hands.   There being no evidence to the
contrary, and from the general appearance of
the deceased, the jury returned a verdict almost
immediately of temporary insanity.   A slight
difficulty was raised by one of the jurors, on the
ground that the spot she had chosen argued the
presence of reason ; but as it could not amount
to certainty, he withdrew his objection.   Our

excellent coroner, whose taste and feeling is so
well known, complimented the jury highly on
the discernment they had shown in their verdict: and after giving it as his opinion that no
person in proper possession of their faculties
could be guilty of the daring and desperate act
of the unhappy person before them, concluded
by an eloquent address on the miserable effects
of the indulgence of unlawful passions, and
trusted that all young persons in the neighbourhood would take warning from the dreadful
example before them, how they listened to " the
soft whisper of deceiving love," when offered
them in any but honourable fashion.

" There, I think I have been and done it;
give us another cigar, Jack."

" Who was the fellow, Ned ? "

" Why that cursed scamp young Carpenter.
I hope the poor girl's ghost won't plague me
for laying it off on her so."

" I am doubting about that bit at the end,
Ned—the other part's capital; but I'm afraid
the lines about the deceiving love won't do for
us, Sir John won't like it. . . Of course the
fellow is a scoundrel, and the uncle not much

better for that matter; but it don't do to say so.   However, perhaps it may go as it is."

———

And so ended the earthly sufferings of a human soul.   Unheeded by any mortal man more.   Unwept by any eye save, perhaps, God's angels.   And that wretched record is all the world ever knew of a tale so mournful that if a poet had been found to mould it into music generation after generation would have wept unnumbered tears to wash out their sister's wrongs from the records of the earth.

CHAPTER IV.

BACK rolled the great wheels of time; whizzing by me so fast, the objects all melted into haze. Glimpses I saw of lamplit streets and glittering rooms, and men and women, and I caught shrieks of frantic revelry. Once there seemed to be a pause, and before me was a gaudy saloon, in the middle of which a young woman was clinging passionately to the knees of a man; the man was rudely trying to spurn her from him, while another woman in paint and feathers, and rustling in splendid silks, had her hand twisted into the hair of the first, and was tearing her away from the man; and I thought I saw in that unhappy one some traces of the figure and the features of her I had seen the end of in the churchyard. But the scene swept away again, and the saloon faded away, and incident after incident whirled by me like a train at full speed when you meet it, till I found myself on the platform of the Railway Station at Paddington.

An elderly well-dressed woman alighted from a carriage followed by one whom I knew now for Catherine, my Catherine, the same Catherine; but oh, how different! The same full melting eye, the same long raven hair, but health sat smiling on her cheek; her rounded elegant form moved lightly on the bounding step, and though then too a line of sad thought there was across her forehead, yet there was light buoyant hope there also, and her eye was gleaming with some eager expectation.

" Now, where will you go, my dear ? " I heard the elder lady say to her; " I have a carriage waiting here and I can take you where you please."

" Oh, take me to him," Catherine said; " my husband, of course. .. You say you know him—you know where I shall find him ? "

Her companion smiled. " You hardly know how young men live in London," she said. " You say he is not expecting you ? You may not find him."

"Let me go—let me try," she answered
eagerly.

"Oh, certainly, dear; you can go if you like.
I do not think it wise; but his chambers lie in
my way, and I will drop you there."

The rapid crowd edged them into the lady's
vehicle, and they were gone.

"How can I ever thank you, madam?"
Catherine said. "So kind—so very kind, and
to an entire stranger."

"Henry Carpenter's wife is no stranger to
me, my dear. I am only too glad I fell in with
you. I shall give it him properly when I see
him, to leave such a pretty creature about in
this way. What on earth could have become of
you, turned out in such a place as this by
yourself?"

The carriage to which they were consigned
rattled on and on, street after street; at last it
stopped at a door in a handsome street, where
the lady said Mr. Carpenter's chambers were.
They knocked; the door was opened. It
seemed the servant must have met before the
older lady, as glances of some kind of understanding certainly passed between them.

"Is Mr. Carpenter at home?"

7

" No, madam ; out of town,—returns to-morrow."

" My dear, I think your best plan would be to come with me. I can never leave you here alone. You will meet no one but my sister, and I will take care of you till he comes back. Indeed," she said playfully, " he doesn't deserve that I should let him have you at all after treating you in this way."

Why should Catherine not go? so good, and so kind a person, and Henry's friend too. Would not he be better pleased, was he not sure to be better pleased, to find her in such good hands ? And yet there was something, a something she would not, perhaps could not explain to herself, that made her wish to stay where she was, and wait her husband's coming in her husband's chambers.

What can the elder lady know of the arrangements in a lodging-house ? What control has she over them that the servant's eyes wander to her face to learn what to answer ?

Mr. Carpenter's rooms are locked, he has the key with him. There are no other rooms in the house disengaged, he replied at last.

" You see there is no help for it, Mrs. Carpenter," her companion began, again laughing. " Come with me, you must, the fates say so. Nay, if you talk in that way," (Catherine was still hesitating at the open carriage door, and muttering faint apologies about inconveniences and intrusion,) " I shall be quite angry with you."

With a show of unaccountable misgiving for which she bitterly reproached herself as so ungrateful, she resumed her seat in the carriage, and in a few minutes they stopped before a large showy-looking house in the corner of Soho Square. On a brass-plate on the door glittered the names of the Misses Arthur.

The rap rap of the coachman was answered by a slovenly bold-looking servant girl. . . And the two ladies passed into the hall. . . . The girl's air and look was so unpromising, that the lady made a sort of apology.

" Our establishment is not large, you see, Mrs. Carpenter. The house is far beyond our two or three servants, and it is impossible for them to keep themselves very tidy. Open the drawing-room door, Harriet, and let my sister know we are come. We ! what was Catherine expected then ?

The two ladies turned into the room. No one in the house but the Miss Arthurs' two servants? Surely there is laughter, and many voices too—What is it? Only a door slamming, and the wind upon the staircase? It did not sound like that.

The room too was an unpleasant room. It was one of those rooms that are kept for occasions; and being so seldom lived in, looked coldly on the occasional intruder. The walls were hung round with pictures; but if beauties, they were the beauties of an Eastern harem. You could not tell what they were like for the veil of yellow they were buried behind. There was fine furniture certainly but it did not lie about easily. The place seemed conscious of its finery, like a shop-boy on a Sunday in his young master's clothes. The dirty housemaid threw the blinds up and got a fire into the grate, and departed to search of the lady's sister. As she turned at the door, she darted one glance on the unconscious girl; a glance so cold and devilish, it might have been caught from the faces of the fiends that sat watching Eve under the tree.

Miss Arthur joined them in a few moments;

in person large, bony, and resolute looking, far less attractive in appearance than her sister, several years older, and a flush upon her cheek, which might have passed for joy at the return of her sister, and the introduction of her friend's wife under her roof, if it had not stayed too long and been so uniform. . . . Miss Caroline Arthur introduced Catherine, and explained briefly the circumstances under which she had met her. The usual questions were asked and answered, and Catherine was presently let escape to her room. The elder lady had eyed her, she thought, rather impertinently, but she had played the part of a plain spoken, honest woman, whose vulgarity might be only old-fashioned bluntness; and as soon as the poor girl could breathe freely, and think over freely the whole of the circumstances, she repented of her foolish misgivings, and congratulated herself on having fallen into kind and hospitable hands.

But we must not leave the sisters in the drawing room.

"She'll do, Car., this one," said the old lady; "but who the deuce is she—Carpenter's wife?"

" She says so."

" What, our young fellow ?"

" Yes, but she's not married to him for all that; there is no ring on her finger, and Carpenter's wife wouldn't be left to travel up to London by herself in that way, looking for him."

The old lady whistled. " So sly and so innocent looking: we must watch her; she'll be playing her own game, if we don't look out."

" No, you're wrong there. No fear, she is soft enough. She's not married, but she knows she ought to be, and she has no idea yet, the pretty darling, she is not going to be."

" Ah ! I see—weak, weak . . . and you think she will not like the exchange we'll provide for her. Ha! ha! that's all the better. Your whiners and whimperers for my money. One's used to that, and knows how to manage it. . . . But your sharp ones, curse 'em, that know how much one and one make, they leave us old ones in the lurch. I curse 'em, but I like 'em too, the dears; they're like what you and I were, Car. I should like to have seen the old woman that could have made her game out of us. Well, talent is talent, and there's the end of it."

"And Lord William offers two hundred pounds you said, if it's quite fresh. That'll do. Is he coming here to night?"

"No, to-morrow."

"I think I'll go then and see Carpenter in the morning, and find out if he'll bid, or if he means to do anything. We sha'n't keep her in very well through to-morrow, without making her suspect, unless I can speak to him. She wanted to go straight to him. I told her I would show her where he lived, and we stopped, as we came along, at the Branch. . . . The fool at the door said he would be there to-morrow, instead of swearing he didn't know when. He missed my sign, so she will be off there in the morning, and we sha'n't keep her from finding out. . . . I'll go to him; I think I know him pretty well. He has left her, and he won't take to her again. I will make him write her a bit of a note that shall settle the matter. She'll go wild and do what we please . . . Get the women out of the way ; you had better go with them yourself, I think. She heard their cursed laughing as she came in, and she won't believe it's the wind if she hears it again."

"They are off, Car., by now. I sent 'em off

before I came down.   Pretty dears, bless them !
. . . I love them like my own daughters.   Yes,
I'll go with them, and will drink our new young
friend's health, and speedy arrival among us."

CHAPTER V.

Mr. Henry Carpenter was sitting in his Temple chambers breakfasting next morning, in his arm-chair and dressing-gown. He was languidly sipping his chocolate, and dawdling over the pages of Paul de Kock, when his servant opened his door, and persuming on a general order to admit all women at all hours, ushered in Miss Caroline Arthur.

" Well, mother damnable, what do you want ? got anything new ?"

" So good a friend as Mr. Carpenter has always the earliest notice of our arrivals. We have."

" The more shame for you, you old witch. Poor thing ! she must be in high favour with the devil, whoever she is, to have been put into your hands."

Mr. Carpenter was very moral in his estimate of other people. It was his saving clause
that he was to get to heaven by.

"Well, I don't know, Mr. Carpenter; you
gentlemen are so kind as to patronize us,—our
trade would not be good for much else. We do
the thing respectably enough, and it's the demand that makes the trade. Nothing low ever
comes to our house, and if we didn't do it, somebody else would. We are very kind to our young
ladies, and if it does not last very long, it is
merry enough while it does."

"Yes, kind, precious kind, as the butcher to
the calf he fats for the shambles, only it is the
living bodies you trade upon, not the dead
meat. Where do they go when their year is
out?"

The old woman shrugged her shoulders.
"Way of the world, sir. Good example again.
Nobody is much better. You keep your people
to work for you as long as they are any use to
you, and when they can do no more you turn
them off, don't you? Every body does. Make
what we can out of one another, that's the way
with everything. . . . Eat one another if you
like it, like the beasts do. I don't see much

difference; some ways of eating are thought respectable, and others are not, but it is only a question of names. You law gentlemen, for instance, you get fat on the sins, as they are called, of your fellow creatures; the more they sin, the merrier it is with you. And I don't see either, that we are any worse than your rich gentlemen from the country, that spunge the poor creatures under them, till they can spunge no more, and then come and spend it up here in their carriages, and horses, and fine houses, leaving just enough at home to keep the work going, as you put just coal enough on the fire to make the kettle boil.

" If our girls are sharp, they can do very well. Coronets have been made out of our house. If they ain't, why they take their chance. We put them in the way, if they can't go along it, it's their fault, not ours. . . . However, most times we are only the friends of the friendless. You good gentlemen pick the flowers, and when you have had as much of the sweet as you want, you fling them away in the road: we only pick them up and put them in water."

Mr. Carpenter did not seem quite easy, for

he swore at the woman, and told her to go. He did not want anything.

"This time, for instance, there is no harm done,"—she went on without shewing any intention of moving—"work all ready cut out. Came up from Clifton yesterday,—met her in the train."

From Clifton? The name seemed to startle him. He looked up, and caught Miss Caroline's eye glaring at him with devilish intelligence.

"Come, Mr. Carpenter, old friends like you and I shouldn't be falling out, we may want each other again, more than once. You began to be so moral, I stretched you a bit to punish you,—but it is as well to have it out. I fell in with your girl you left at Clifton yesterday. She was on her way up here, poor little thing, to see after her husband. I found she had no idea where to look for you, so I took compassion on her, and we have got her at home."

The law student turned pale, red, and pale again. His hand shook. He writhed in his chair. His eyes fell ashamed before the woman he had but a moment ago been reviling for her wickedness.

" Come, come sir ! it is no use to make a fuss
about it now; the thing is done,—you did it.
There is nothing so ridiculous as doing a thing,
and then being ashamed of it. You did what
you had quite a right to do, if you could of
course. What, you a man, and fooled by old wives'
fables ! . . . The girl was pretty, and you were
in luck. Leave the thing to me. I will save
you all trouble, only you must tell me a thing or
two first. Who is she ?"

The old woman's mocking tone strung his
pride up. If one frail fibre of pure feeling did
vibrate for a few moments through him, he could
not show such weakness before her.

Why, she was a sort of nursery governess, he
said, at my uncle's, down at Exmouth. " My
aunt treated her worse than the housemaid, and
the poor thing was so pretty, I thought I could
not do better than make up for the sins of my
family by being kind to her. It ended as such
things often do end. There were faults on both
sides, I was too forward, she was too yielding. .
. . I went off to stay at Clifton, and, like a fool,
left her my direction. My aunt found out what
had happened, and of course turned her out of
doors. She came up to me, and I had not the

heart to say no to her, when she begged to be taken in; so she stayed with me for a month, till I began to get rather tired of the thing. I was doubting what I had best do, when one morning came a letter from my uncle. Curious, I have it here in my desk—listen!"

"MY DEAR HENRY,—Lady Carpenter and I have learnt, with extreme sorrow, that the unworthy creature whom we found it necessary to dismiss from Belmont, has found an asylum under your roof. Indeed we have been told that you are privately married to her. We will not believe until we are forced that any member of our family can have disgraced the name he bears by such an act as this; but there is no doubt that she is with you, and if my wishes have any influence, and if you yourself have a wish to continue to be regarded as my heir, you will let me know, by return of post, that your connexion with her is at an end, for ever."

"Your affectionate uncle,

JOHN CARPENTER."

"What could I do, you see? I couldn't afford to turn my back on ten thousand a year.

It is not creditable either, living with a mistress, and marriage was out of the question; it was ridiculous enough in her to follow me at all. Why the deuce couldn't she have got a place at a milliner's in Exeter? A thousand things she might have done. Well, I paid the lodgings as for three weeks, and left her with what money I had, and came up here. Something I thought would be sure to turn up for her—things always do, or nearly always. What possessed her to follow me here?"

" And is this all?" said the old woman steadily.

" Yes, pretty well all," he answered.

" She said something about a marriage. But you are not married?"

" I should hope not," he said.

" Was there a pretended marriage?"

" How dare you suspect me of dishonour?"

" Then there was a promise?"

Carpenter blushed. He tried to force out one indignant denial; but his tongue hung fire, and he was silent.

" Oh! It is nothing, you know," the old woman said in a tone of encouragement; "a matter of course merely ; one always does say so under the circumstances. It means nothing, every body knows that; only one likes to know exactly what the facts were."

" Well, yes then," he answered, " there was something of the kind I dare say. But how could she be such a fool as to believe it?"

" Now I know it all, then," she said. " Well, then, here is what I came to say to you. I will undertake to save you all further trouble about the girl. She shall be in good hands, and well provided for. In return for which you must be so good as to write a note which I will dictate to you."

" You dictate to me ? How dare you ?"

" Oh ! I only mean it for your own good. If you do not like it, I will go home, and let her have your direction."

For a moment he seemed to hesitate. What, is there one feeling of remorse or mercy lingering in that ice-walled heart? " I will write myself," he said; " I cannot see her, but I can advise her, and I can help her."

" That will hardly answer my purpose," she replied. " You will pardon me. I have had

longer experience in these matters than you.   I
am professional, you are only an amateur—you
must take what I say."

"I *must* !"

"If I am to help you, you *must*."

A pause again.

"What will you do ?" the woman said.   "If I
go back without your note, I must tell her where
you are, and she will come to you. If you receive
her, or provide for her, what becomes of Belmont
and your ten thousand a year ? Sir John will hear
of it.   I may choose to let him know myself."

"You ! I think I may venture that.   He is
likely to take notice of information from you. . .
You !"

"Yes, I.   Venture it if you will, and see.
He will find it worth inquiring into, if he does
owe it to me.   I want this girl for my own purposes, and I must have her.   If you see her or
do anything for her, I shall write to Exmouth.
If you do not, she has not a relation in the
world, you allow that, and she goes out upon the
streets.   Now, where will she be best off ?
There or with me ?"

Once more the same baseness which made
him leave poor Catherine at Clifton won the

victory. " Give me the pen," he said. " Now what am I to write?"

" MY DEAREST CATHERINE,—I regret exceedingly you should have taken a step so unadvised in following me. If you had remained at Clifton, a few days would have brought you a letter, which would have saved you the expense and danger, and would have suggested to you some line of conduct, which might in the end lead to your good. I am sorry I must tell you, I can never see you again. I have received a positive command from my uncle, who is my guardian and second father, not to do so, and I need not tell you how sacred are the commands of a parent. What is past cannot now be helped, but it may be repented of. Let me entreat you, dear Catherine, to follow my example, and let our future good conduct atone as far as it may for our sins. I grieve too, that my uncle's orders forbid me to assist you further than by my advice. But it is my greatest comfort to know that you are in the hands of my truly excellent friends, the Miss Arthurs. They, Catherine, are truly good ; they will think for you, and decide for you. I have explained to

Miss Caroline Arthur the history of your connection with me, and she has promised to take
care of you, and see you well provided for.   Her
feelings as a woman prevent her from taking the
same view of my duty as I do myself, and I fear
I suffer in her esteem, but my conscience assures
me I am right, and I am happy in believing the
regard she once felt for me is transferred to
one whom I have unhappily been a means of
injuring.   Let me beseech you to place implicit
confidence in her; and believe me ever, dear
Catherine,

" Your affectionate friend,

" HENRY CARPENTER."

" And you dare to think I am going to write
that?"

" Oh !" the lady answered, " it is merely professional.   If you do not like me for a counsel,
you had better send for some other advice.

" And I am to call you my truly excellent
friends?"

"I think on this occasion," she said, " we have
the honour of showing ourselves so.   I have
come to you to relieve you of a very embarrass-

R

ing piece of business, and all I ask you in return is a few lines on a sheet of paper."

" Which, my truly disinterested devil, is a piece of as infernal villany as ever was enacted on God's earth."

" Nay, nay, Mr. Carpenter, don't take God's name in vain. . . . We shouldn't be too hard upon ourselves; we are neither of us very immaculate, you know; and I really don't see what there is in the letter you need so much object to. A grain or two extra in the scale, when it is already so many pounds overweighted, is no such great matter. Only look at it in this way. Here is this girl that you have brought,— *you*, I say, have brought into a difficult position. She is there; the thing is done, it is not to do. It is too late to be moral about it; you should have thought of that before. . . . The question is, what is to be done now? You are not such a fool, I suppose, as to think of marrying the girl, or keeping her yourself, after your uncle's letter which you read me."

Mr. Carpenter bit his lip.

" You cannot be such a fool. . . There are men in the world (pray do not be offended) as

attractive as Mr. Carpenter. We need not
believe a girl who admitted him prematurely to
her favour, is likely to confine herself to him ;
he would be scarcely wise to incur a certain
loss at such a risk. Nay, now, I see I must be
peremptory. I can have no shilly-shallying.
Listen to what I say. If you do anything for
the girl of any kind whatever, I shall let Sir
John know of it,—mind that. It is as well to have
it a clear point. I tell her where you are she
will come to you, and I will suppose after what
I have said you will not receive her. So then she
will wander about the streets ; she falls into what
hands she may, the last and most likely into that
of the police. She is taken to the office. The story
comes out, and Mr. Carpenter's name is likely to
hold a prominent and not very creditable place in
the papers. . . You read me your uncle's letter :
I may think it desirable to furnish her with a
copy of it. I believe I recollect it. One of
those precious documents it is not easy not to
recollect. This I think—(she repeated part of
it.) In fact, it strikes me I may go myself to
the police court. It would not be undesirable
to establish myself in a respectable character
before the world, and I may fight her cause for

her. In that case I shall certainly advance this letter you have been weak enough to read to me. It will appear in the papers; it will be commented upon. Your uncle will recognise it for his own, and your chance of Belmont will be nearly equal with mine."

"I wish you and Belmont, and the whole thing, were at the devil together," he said.

"All in good time," answered Miss Caroline. "On the other hand, write my letter. I will guarantee that the girl shall be well taken care of; in good hands; in a good position; one, in fact, where if she pleases, with her face and steady conduct, she may raise herself to any-thing ——"

"Good hands. Yes, raise herself; aye, by-and-bye, to such high honour as yours is, I suppose. Curse you. To be led step and step down your hell's ladder, and leave her own soul in the devil's treasure house, while a legion of fiends bring up her body again to set his traps in, and do his work for him. . . . Oh, fool, miserable fool that I am!" he cried. . . "It is not enough that I must have the recollection of what I have done already to this unhappy woman clinging to me like a nightmare, but I am to be

10

made the slave and tool of this infernal hag, to
snare her down to deeper perdition."

"I can wait till you have done," said Miss
Caroline.

"Wait, no, d—n you—you sha'n't wait here
for fear the roof fall on our heads. Give me
the pen, since—it must be done."

"Oh! I am glad you are getting reasonable,"
she said. "Write the letter and give it to me,
and I will relieve you of my presence immediately."

He wrote off the concluding sentence and
signed it. "There," he said as he gave it her ;
"if I am damned for this, I shall have the pleasure of seeing you in flames ten times hotter.

Miss Caroline took it, folded it up deliber-
ately, and put it in her pocket.

"I may say *auf evoir* then, *there*. Should
any thing of the kind occur again, you'll know
where to come. Good morning."

"I do not know that I do want the girl so
much after all," she said to herself as she walked
down stairs ; "but I like to make these young
gentlemen stoop to me ; it is entertaining. The
mean, dirty, cowardly rascal. . . . She doesn't
deserve as good as she'll have for being taken in
by such a fellow."

And what were the feelings of the "such a fellow," to whom she was so politely alluding? He had begun to rave about his chance of damnation at the end of the scene, but he had no real idea that there was any danger of his getting it. God never would venture to damn a baronet with ten thousand a year, or even the heir of a baronet. It was only a way of speaking. . . Fortunately for him his pride was so hurt at the way he had been tricked, that it diverted his attention from his conscience; and as Catherine was in a way indirectly the cause of it, he was not in a placable mood towards her.

"Confound her," he muttered, "why the deuce hadn't she strength of mind enough to keep me off? and of all people in the world the one she must choose to fall in with is this damned old woman. Really one doesn't know what one ought to do. . . A man can't marry a woman he has seduced. If they are weak and foolish enough to let you persuade them, why, as the old hag said, they are sure to let some one else by-and-bye. And if I was to do anything for her, why she must—she'd be sure to come to that in the end any how, and I should be losing my chance for nothing. It is best as it is, perhaps. . . But the old brute, to dictate to me,"—and Mr. Carpenter returned again and again to the first bleeding wound in his self-love, and found it far harder to reconcile himself to that, than to the fate into which he had assisted Catherine.

Still it is not to be said he was quite easy. Awake he was conscious there was something not quite satisfactory; and in his sleep he was disturbed by visions not the most delightful. Indeed, I believe a whole week had passed before he began to regard himself again in his looking-glass with perfect self-contentedness, and pursue his easy meditations on the discovery of truth, (for Carpenter went out as a philosopher,) and his theories of universal philanthropy, and the new reformation.

———

On Catherine the letter worked as Miss Caroline had anticipated. Her honour lost, her lover false, of course it was a terrible shock to her; but the taunting insolence of the letter had scattered every feeling in her heart, and

even her pride—little pride as then was in her
—came to her help, and in a way assisted her to
bear it. Miss Caroline's sympathy was most
judiciously administered; neither making too
much nor *too little* of her fault, and of course
execrating the heartless cruelty of her friend. . .
Had she known he had dared to insult her by
calling her his friend, she would have torn the
letter to atoms and thrown it in his face. The
future was not alluded to. A fortnight was let
to pass, and she was asked to see nobody; even
the elder sister had been banished to preside at
the Branch, and they had the house to themselves.

At the end of the fortnight, a visit of a day
or two was announced from *my nephew*, Mr.
John Arthur, a young man rising in business at
a country town. This was Lord William. His
terms rose when he saw Catherine. Nothing
within the compass of his fortune was to be
thought too great; he was put in possession of
her history; but the rose was sweet enough still
to make him forgive the taint upon its perfume.
He put himself under the control of Miss
Caroline, and consented to be guided by her
advice . . . He continued under his feigned

name; paid repeated visits, and prosecuted his suit diligently, as if for honourable marriage. He was not at all listened to at first, and but coldly listened to afterwards. . . Catherine had been too severely wounded to be able to think of any more affection; and she felt too degraded even to allow herself to think of it. . . The truly kind explanation, however, of Miss Caroline, so ingeniously contrived as to undermine her own natural principles in conveying her nephew's feelings, induced her at last to listen. Gratitude might warm into affection; and an honest man who could love her in spite of what had past, was at least entitled to her regard. . . This was all they were waiting for. Drugs did the rest, and the unhappy girl awoke one morning to find herself a second time betrayed.

Lord William, of course, swore unalterable affection, disclosed his rank, accounted for all from his passionate love of her. Miss Caroline let fall a corner of her veil, and advised a continuance of the *liaison*; and Catherine, at first overpowered with horror, and then, as the whole thing began to disclose itself, bewildered at the hideous devil-web in which she found herself entangled so hopelessly, yielded in desperate

miserable acquiescence to Lord William's entreaties ; and believed, or persuaded herself
she believed, his oaths of unalterable attach-
ment.

For her share of the transaction, Miss Caroline received 500 guineas. . . . In three weeks
the jewel had lost its novelty, and the pretty
plaything must find the fate of all pleasures,
that are only pleasures till they are obtained. . .
I cannot go on with the nauseous history of
the downward progress. One cannot tell how
powerful to make persons recklessly degraded
is the believing that they have already become
so. . . . She surrendered herself in despair to
what appeared to be her destiny ; there was no
escape for her except suicide, and for suicide
she was not yet ready, her cup was not full.
She was pitched along from hand to hand, the
period of each new friend's constancy growing
shorter and shorter at each transfer, for Catherine was too miserable to please ; till at last her
haggard painted face was seen nightly in the
theatre or the saloon, and the wretched victim
was only saved from madness by the self-forget-
fulness of unbroken intoxication.

One night — it was the scene which had

seemed to pause before me for a moment in the shifting of the slides—at one of the rooms in which the unhappy beings meet together like the hack horses of the livery stables, for the accommodation of the public, they met again, face to face, the destroyer and the destroyed. . . She flew to him, such as she was ; she could not resist it. She flew to him and clung around his knees ; so changed as she was, so degraded as she felt she was, she forgot the history of her wrongs in the sight of him again ; she forgot it was he who had disgraced, betrayed, and insulted her, and she hid her face and sunk ashamed before him on the ground. She was ashamed even to raise her eyes to him. . . . He pushed her from him with a brutal jest ; but she clung to him still. His companion, jealous of another claimant intruding upon her right, tore her rudely away by the hair, and she had sunk fainting on the floor ; in which state she was carried out into the street, and laid down on the nearest doorstep to recover as she could. . . . This was the last ; from that doorway she had crawled away to Exmouth to die.

CHAPTER VI.

AGAIN the scene shifts,—I am now I know not where. A lamp is beside me, and a bundle of letters in my hand. They are tied together in a paper band, and carry written on them, Henry C—— to E. Hardaway; but the seals are broken, and it seems I am to read them.

"Belmont, Aug. 16.

"You have a good right to grumble at me, my dear Hardaway; a fortnight is passed since the day I promised to be with you, and I am still here, and I have not written. But you see I have taken a large sheet now, and I am going to fill it; and so I shall quit all scores with you for the reason I shall give you for my non-appearance will make a long and amusing epistle. You say true, that my uncle's house can have

no great charm for me; my aunt's vulgarity and
his emptiness and conceit, are so intolerable
that, night after night as I go up into my room,
I grind the heel of my boot through the carpet
for very spite that I am forced to bear their
name. And then the nauseous way in which
they patronize me,—introduced at parties as,
' My nephew Henry;' as if I, I were to be
indebted for the consideration of society to my
kinsmanship with such a family. . . The house
is always full of people, but I cannot enjoy
anything. Few of them are well-bred enough
to hide their contempt for my uncle (I can
pardon them for feeling it). They know very
well they are conferring infinite honour upon
him; with Lord this, and Sir John that, it is
all plain sailing. He has more money than they
have. They being little suns in their little
neighbourhood, throw a kind of reflected lustre
on whoever they choose to smile upon ; he pays
their election expenses, and this service they
are content to accept as the price at which they
will sell themselves like wax candles to shine at
his parties.

" You remember our Ethics Lecture at Oriel,
how old ——— used to hammer into us that

doing went before knowing, and you acted on a
principle ages before you understood it; well,
my good aunt and uncle are just cases in point.
They act on this principle of buying and selling,
and yet they have never confessed it to themselves ; nay it has never once occurred to them.
Their plebeian instinct teaches them what they
must do, but vanity has hold of their under-
standings, and they flatter themselves they are
adored for their own sakes. . . My uncle means
to found a family; and he has not obscurely
hinted to me that his daughters are to have
good fortunes, but that I am to be his heir.
Ten thousand a year is not to be sneezed at,
yet I often doubt whether it is worth the price
I have to pay for it. Verily it is enough to
make one despair of this world, or at any rate
of the thing we have made of it, when a man
like my uncle is the sort that its system smiles
upon, and that rises from nothing to an earl's
fortune. What if the money should exert a
formative influence upon one, and model whoever owns it after the idea' it was acquired
upon ! Experience luckily does not confirm
this theory, and one comforts oneself with remembering Vespasian. Well, you may fancy I

should have found an excuse before this to be
off if there were no other attraction; but there
is, and the history of this is the part of my
letter which is to excuse and compensate for my
absence. . . . I had several times seen a very
pretty girl about with my young she cousin on
the beach and in the garden; but as nobody
ever mentioned her name in the house, and my
aunt, if she ever said anything to her, always
spoke in the same overbearing impertinent tone
in which she did to the rest of the servants, I
concluded she was merely a nursery-maid; and
as in these matters I make a point of following
Lord Chesterfield's advice, and eschew all low
intrigues, I contented myself with admiring her
beauty at a distance, and exercising the whole-
some discipline of self restraint.   Well, about
three weeks ago, a few days before I was to
have made a start of it for you, I was strolling
about the grounds just after sunset, and happened to turn into one of the little vulgar brass
cupola'd summer-houses. I sate down to wonder
at the row of coloured Vauxhall lamps standing as sentinels round the melancholy pond,
(they have shut out the view of the sea).   The
seats are all pink cushioned, so that a very

trifling uneasiness I felt in arranging myself, made me alter my position to ascertain the cause of it. I found I had sate down upon a book, and I experienced the same kind of emotion as Robinson Crusoe at the foot print in the sand. A book at Belmont! My uncle had sent the dimensions of his library to his bookseller, and since the thousand volumes had taken their places upon the shelves, not a soul of them had had his repose invaded. . . One I had once tremblingly taken down, but the dust met me with such a look of beseeching reproachfulness, that I put him gently back without waking him. . . . And now here! out of doors in a summer-house, the very epicureanism of studiousness. What are you? I asked, hardly daring to touch him. I made an effort, gathered courage, and took it up. . . . The Revolt of Islam!—a second thunderstroke. What garden fairy; but imagine a fairy in a summer-house with pink cushions, and the sea shut out by clipped box-trees and coloured lamps. . . It was a fairy though, and at that very moment she came in upon me to claim her forgotten property. It was the girl I had seen with the children. . . She started, and seemed uneasy

when she saw me; she recovered herself however immediately, and then she had an advantage of me. She had seen me every day, knowing who I was, so that I was less strange to her
than she to me.   For me, not Anchises could
have been more astounded when the goddess
disclosed her majesty to him. This graceful
elegant creature I had taken for a maid; this . .
But I know you hate rhapsodies, and I shall
be keeping her waiting if I describe; which was
just what she did not do, for her embarrassment
was gone in a moment. She apologised very
quietly for disturbing me, she believed she had
left a book there, if I would be so good as to
allow her to look for it. . . . But at that moment
she caught sight of it in my hands; she coloured
and hesitated; I felt my advantage instantly.
I might keep her with the help of the book,
just long enough to get something said, which
should serve for the beginning of an acquaintance. You know I manage these things very
gracefully; I had time for several very choice
sentences before her face resumed its natural
colour, and then I gave her the book directly;
she would have resented it had I kept it longer;
as it was, she took it with a faint smile of thanks

S

and vanished. I returned to the house, determined not ungratefully to neglect so promising
an opening, and to make some inquiries which
should enable me the next time we met to
know better what to make of so unaccountable a
phenomenon. On inquiring, I found, as I was
sure I should, that she was a lady; a lady be it
known, of better family, by a great many steps,
than we *libertino patre nati.* She is the daughter of an old lieutenant who died here a few
years back; who, because he served his king
like a gentleman, and never troubled himself to
bow down and worship the golden image of
Cheapside and the Stock Exchange, had fallen
under the displeasure of that Divinity, and been
summoned out of life, leaving his daughter to
the tender mercies of the world. My aunt, good
charitable soul, with a heart overflowing with
pity, and a mind, with true Cheapside meanness
in little things, keenly alive to the advantage
of securing a governess for her children, without
having anything to pay for her, took her to
live here at Belmont. Truly a sweet life, to
live with the servants, and to teach the children
to be ladies, to be reminded three times a day by
my aunt, of the infinite debt of gratitude she

owes to her, to be hated alike by the whole household, because she is graceful, beautiful, and refined, and they are all alike odious, vulgar, and detestable, and because her persevering sweetness will continue to pour the fire drops of patience and kindness on them in spite of their ill treatment; really the Carpenters have run up so very long an account the wrong side of the book, that I, as the future representative of the family, think I can do no better than pay it all off by anticipation, and throw myself, and all that I have or shall have, at her feet. It is no great sacrifice. I believe, if the truth is known, the balance will be found her side of the score still, for what am I, or what have I, that I can have a right to hope for so exquisite a creature? I have not spoken to her since, but I am wildly in love with her. I see her continually with my cousins, but she has never given me an opportunity of exchanging a word with her, and scarcely even of catching her eye; but evening after evening I stray about the garden and the summer-house, and fortune by-and-bye will smile on truth and patience. I will write again in a few days.

"Yours affectionately,

"H. C."

Three weeks later—a fragment extatic.

" Catherine loves me,—yes, she loves me,— she has told me so. Our lips have touched each other; how long they hung there, God knows, I know not. It was but one long thrilling moment of extacy. Time was not for us, for those are no earthborn enjoyments, but true children of heaven; and we hung entranced in a flash of the everliving now of eternity. What is life to me now? O Hardaway! Hardaway! how does the burning truth shoot over me now of the inspired words of the old prophets, who teach us that love was the creator of the universe; and curses on the freezing systems of our misera- ble heartless teaching, which scatters 'snow flakes on those words of fire, and pieces them out into the wiredrawn articles of our con- temptible theology! That religion! That divi- nity! O the profanation of the holy name! What can they know, the drivelling dotards of the pulpit and the lecture-room, of the full flood tide of spirit that rolls in with the great wave of love into the free heart of man, and recreates for him the splendour of God's uni- verse, as it was when the open secret first glittered in unveiled magnificence before the hierarchy of heaven? I do not know myself again,—I cannot find myself again. I am God's freedman, and now for the first time I know what it is to be a man. Wisdom, truth, beauty. God, duty,—I know them all now! Verily am I now reborn of the Spirit, the child of love, whose new life now beginning shall be lovely as the lives of angels are. O! when I think what I have been. But now that is past, gone. The old Adam, the old nature. Ah! now I am free again, once again baptized in fire the heir of heaven! And Catherine . . . you, you are the means of grace, the mighty channel through which God pours this blessed gift on me. . . . Truly these messengers of heaven take forms among us, in which we children of earth are slow to find them; the God was among the herdsmen of Admetus, and they knew it not. And Catherine was here in the form of a servant; and I—I dared to think I should be bringing new life to her."

It appears our young friend had been getting up Germanesque philosophy, and conceived he had found a northwest passage into heaven. From the next letter it would seem he had been teaching his young lady, and that her own studies had in a way manured the ground to receive it.

"Catherine is a true child of passion, she has no idea of duty when she does not love, and no sacrifice is too great for her when she does; she has known her fellow creatures only to despise them, because she has only found heartlessness, when there was the greatest pretence of respectability; and it is easy to teach her that the forms of society, which men make so much fuss about, are but modes of legalized selfishness, built together upon the theory that all mankind are trying to overreach each other; serving at best but as protection against injuries, which a pure-hearted child of nature would either be ashamed to consider injuries, or which, if they are real, can receive no compensation for. Love knows no law, because it fulfils all law; love can work no ill, and can believe none; the laws of the heart are the only laws which it is virtue to observe, and sacrilege to break. Laws written and systematized may be for the impure and the base, but they shall never hinder her from obeying what her heart tells her she may do, because they can never redress what she would

consider an injury. She has no half feeling,
she cannot doubt me, because she loves me;
and so long as she has my love, she cares for
nothing else.

" To a heart which has for a long time been
thrown in upon itself, and been forced by the
hardness or unkindliness of the element into
which it has been cast to live and feel for itself
only, to a mind which since it has learnt to
think has never known a friend, the first word
of sympathy from without, is like the kiss which
awoke the enchanted sleeper. It has but been
in a dream before—it only becomes conscious of
itself, when it sees its own reflection in the mind
of another. This is why books can do so little;
they only tell you what others have thought
and suffered; nothing of what you are thinking
and suffering; only here and there you fall
across some feature you recognize as your own,
but you find it linked on to others that are as
strange to you, and so it merely perplexes you
the more. Catherine only sees herself in me,
neither thought nor feeling can go alone yet.
Her spirit's baby children prattle along holding
by my hand; now and then I have to carry
them in my arms, when they are tired, and

sometimes take the mother's office too, and nurse them at my heart, as by-and-bye, please God, she will do for my bodily children ; but that is to be, and the time is not yet ripe.   In the mean time, she loves me, and must love me, because she only exists through me, and it is my highest pleasure to be her guide and teacher ; and all her visions, which till now have only been flitting before her, I have been able to call out into an expressed faith of the most beautiful kind.

"What are all these laws and restrictions by which the simplest and most innocent actions are fenced in and restrained, but a school which teaches us to sin by destroying the loving confidence which, if we were left to ourselves, would of itself compel us to all that is best and loveliest ?   Who would ever have thought of killing his brother, except the law had suggested it to him, by insisting that he should not ?   Because these miserable negatives are so bedrilled into us, we learn to believe that there is a necessity for it, and men become wicked in fact, because they are taught they have a tendency to become so ; we distrust our neighbours, and our neighbours distrust us ; but destroy suspicion, and you destroy the cause of it; assume that there is no sin and can be no such thing, and the spectre will vanish out of the world with the belief in it. This is the style of our conversation, and this is Catherine's morality, pure and noble-minded as she is, she can live by it, and she shall live by it; and if it be a dream it is too beautiful for me to spoil with my matter-of-fact detail of the depravity of mankind. After all, it is, you know, true ideally. It should be so; noble minds can even now live and die by it, and Catherine's purity shall new inspire mine. To her, as she is, I at least feel I can never be untrue. I know myself, and I can trust myself; married or unmarried, she knows no difference. The form that a priest can read would not tinge her cheek with one hue of happier brightness, because it could add nothing to her security. She supposes I must wish it, because I have to live in the world, and the childish prejudices of our fellow-mortals might be in the way of our doing all the good we are by-and-bye to do together. But for herself she would not marry me at all if she felt even the shadow of a wish for it as a protection; and so we sail on, as yet I know not whither. The cloud that hangs over the future makes it even more intensely alluring, and I leave to time to develope in its own way what it is beyond my skill to unravel, and what it is most likely I should only spoil by intefering with. We are the sport of destiny; you and I, and all of us. To-day has had its own incidents, to-morrow has a fresh store to come. Dragged through them we must be, as we have been; and the day after them too will belong to the past. It is only our own ignorance of it, that make the future seem uncertain. . . . When I shall leave this, I know not; what I shall do, I know not, and do not care to know. I crave, and yet I hang back; why, I cannot tell. I cannot, O no, I do not doubt myself."

And so rises the cloud castle, which when the wind changes, will tremble into ruins. He, wretched fool, deceiving and deceived; knowing at his heart his own emptiness, yet dreaming too that he believes what he is saying; she, simple and untaught, having lost at the hour of need the hand which should have led her the

way that she should go, falling across this mock
sun, and dazzled by its wordy brightness, listens
to all this, and because she loves him, dreams
she understands. Love holds her heart, and
his tongue has bewildered her uneducated conscience. She cannot choose but believe him,
as he sweeps her on to perdition ; she has never
known a teacher ; she has wandered at her own
wild will in the garden of the poets. She has
never seen a flower fade, and dreams that it is
spring for ever. . . .

"And what," I said, turning to my genius as
the papers I seemed to hold passed out of form
and melted into cloud; "what is this wretched
girl's own early history, what miserable sin has
she, or what have her fathers committed, that
she was plunged so into this inevitable destruction?"

"Neither had she sinned, nor her parents,"
answered the genius; "unless indeed it be a
sin to bring children into the world at all—as
perhaps it is."

"What!" I said, "are there not enough of

the worthless and the wicked in the world, if God will afflict it, to bear his judgments, without dragging out this poor innocent child, and plunging her in a net of circumstances, into an ocean of guilt!"

"When circumstances compel, there is no guilt," replied the genius. "But it is not the least idle of the dreams of you mortals that you prescribe to Providence the way that it shall go, and murmur if it does not obey you. You make such a prating in your sermons and philosophies, about God's way in punishing vice and rewarding virtue, and you forget altogether that it is you men that do it and not He. He does not strike the tyrant with his thunderbolts; the conspirator assassinates him. You punish what on the whole interferes with your enjoyment, and reward what furthers it; to make your system respectable you call it divine; and then when anything falls out you find it hard to reconcile with your theories, you are like to turn infidels. . . Listen, however, to her history.

"The father of Catherine Gray was one of Nelson's old lieutenants. He had no interest, and only common merit. He always did his duty, that is, he always did whatever he was told to do. Had he ever been thrown into circumstances which called for anything more, he might have shown himself equal to them; but as he never was, he continued to serve in ship after ship plain Lieutenant Grey. A man who did his every-day duties in an every-day way, was never mentioned in dispatches; and at the peace was considered sufficiently rewarded by his country with a coast-guard lieutenancy at Exmouth. Here, with fifty years and an old uniform upon his shoulders, his pay, and his pockets tolerably lined with prize-money from a lucky last cruize, he considered his quarters and his daily allowance large enough for one more besides himself; and forgetting that in such cases one and one might not make a simple sum of addition, he married the daughter of an old brother officer, with a pretty face and true sailor-daughter's heart for her only recommendation. Old Gray was as young on his wedding-day as he was the first time he was ever cut down in his middy's hammock; and the light-hearted maxim of his life was, Look out for to-day, and to-morrow will look out for itself. . . They spent their prize-money in a

honey-moon, which this time was kind enough
to take longer than usual on its sky journey,
giving them six weeks of itself instead of four ;
and at the end of it they came back to live in
their little whitewashed cottage, with its door
and two windows down stairs, and three windows
in a row up stairs ; and the lieutenant's ten
shillings a day to keep two backs covered from the
rays of the sun and the eyes of their fellow mortals,
and three stomachs (for they had ventured, impru-
dent people, on an old woman for the kitchen
department), with three breakfasts, three dinners, and three teas daily ; and the backs were
always covered, and the various meals came
regularly on the table; and where could you
find a couple over whom the wheels of life ran
lighter or more smoothly, as he would sit in his
porch on a summer evening before the door
and smoke his long Dutch pipe, and weave his
little wife long stories of the mad exploits of
himself and her father, when they first sailed
together in the little Firefly. And she would
sit opposite and knit her old husband his worsted
overalls against the long rough nights of winter ;
or if a lucky seizure had enabled her to indulge
in so pardonable a vanity, bind a few smart
slips of ribbon into her Sunday bonnet.

" There were times indeed when he was out upon his watch, and his eyes as they fell upon the sea marked the shadows of the clouds staining with their inky spots the deep bright green, that a shade would pass too across the old man's mind, as he thought of the small handful of sand that most likely remained for him in his life-glass, and his poor wife left alone in the wide world, with none to love or to take care of her. . . And the clouds came oftener, and the smile in the morning at breakfast played less freely on his lips, after she had whispered to him one night, half happy and half frightened, that another little soul, before spring came again, might perhaps be sent down into their family. . . And then in the dark hour, the old man would go wipe his spectacles, and take down the big old Bible and open it at random, and the first text he lit upon would be sure to be a messenger of peace to him. . . . He had always feared God and done his duty, and the seed of the righteous, he would find, were never left to beg their bread. And so he smoked his pipe and took comfort, and trusted that if it pleased the Allmerciful to call him away out of life, He would find some means of showing pity on those he left behind him. . . And the winter came, and the spring was coming, and God did provide for his poor wife, though not exactly in the way the lieutenant had wished and hoped for. . . . No worthy relative died and left them money; no Admiralty news of his own promotion came to lighten his troubles and lay another epaulette upon his shoulders; but a few hours after she had left a little lady upon the bed to bear her name and fill her place on earth, God took her away and gave her promotion into heaven. . . Poor fellow! he had loved his little Catherine with his old boy heart, with a true boy's love; and no young wooer ever mourned a lost mistress with a deeper or truer sorrow. . He felt as a man might who had toiled through a long weary voyage all alone in a little boat. Towards an evening he had reached what seemed safe harbourage, the high land round him and between him and the broad sea; but in the morning, wakes to find his high land was but cloud-bank, and his harbourage a coral reef, and the wide weary infinite of ocean all around him still.

"The lieutenant had seen death in many awful forms; he had faced him in the thunder of the battle and the war of the tempest; he had been at the storming of great cities, and seen young wives dragged off the bodies of their murdered husbands, and done to death at their sides in a way too horrible to speak of. . . He had heard from his berth—well for him it was not his watch—he had heard the shriek from the deck of a returning Indiaman, mixed with crash of timber and falling spars, as his own proud tyrant ship had struck her, and she went down under the keel of the destroyer; yet it seemed as if he had never known what death was, till he saw life and death so fearfully contrasted on that little bed; the tiny infant stretching its little hands towards the mother's breasts, which were not yet cold; one might have thought the soul had not left the earth, but, chrysalis-like, the old shell had broken when the new body was ready to receive its life, and the soul of the mother was living still in the person of the child. . . So came the little Catherine into the world: the child of sorrow. The angel of death who was sent on an errand so unlovely, wrecked his anger on the innocent

T

cause of his coming. As he passed away with the mother's soul he turned to frown upon the child; and if those say true who tell us that the forecast of its destiny is written on the features of the new-born infants, the father might have read a strange tale of misery in the painful glances of those new-awakened baby eyes.

" Howbeit no such misgivings occurred to the lieutenant; he was too much absorbed in the thought of what he had lost to pay much attention to what had been left him in her place; and when the first gush of sorrow was over, and he could ask to have his child brought for him to see, the cloud had passed away, and the tiny creature looked into his face and smiled. . And March and April rolled past, and the spring came up upon the earth in all its beauty, and the sea was clear and the sky was blue; the choral birds morning and evening chanted their thanksgivings to the goddess of the May, and once more the sun shone in upon the old man's heart, and he too could thank God for what God had given, and bow his head in resignation for what had been taken away. . .

" Fourteen years sped away fast as your own

first fourteen years seem to have sped as you look back on them,—fourteen years of calm unclouded sky; while the beauties of autumn and of spring grew together in the little cottage, the silver cord of the lieutenant's life slackening slowly as he melted off towards the winter of the grave; and young Catherine's rosebuds swelling year by year into fuller and fresher beauty. Some part of his little income the father sank year by year in the insurance office for his child's use after he was gone; and as the future seemed in that way provided for, what more time God might please to let him continue upon earth, he could spend carelessly in the fulfilment of his then easy duty; and in tranquil expectation of the hour when he should have earned his discharge, and be let go with a retiring pension into heaven. . . . The motherless Catherine nature adopted for her child, and nature seemed the only schoolmistress she had the patience to learn from. There was a day-school at Exmouth, which for several years she used to attend, and very rapidly she contrived to pick up a smattering of the common things which were taught there; a little French and English, and music enough to enable her to

T 2

sing, in her own wild way, the old romantic ballads she had gathered out of such books as were not school-books, which she could come across. But she liked best to chase the goats over the cliffs and the butterflies in the cowslip meadows, or to sit under the flag-staff with her father's men and hear them tell their wild stories of savage life in the glorious islands of the southern seas. . . . And they would teach her their high soul-stirring war songs of the ocean, which she would go pour into the delighted ears of her happy father, as night after night in the fine weather he would sit and smoke his pipe in the old jessamine porch, and she would now fill it for him as her mother used to do.

"Time speeds swiftly when the road is smooth, and only limps and stumbles over the rocks and stones ; and sailors seldom see their three-score years and ten, for the rough seas shake the sand in their life-glass, and it runs quicker than that of other men. . . . The lieutenant's sixty-fourth birthday past and he was never to see another. He might, perhaps, have lingered out the fine-drawn thread one more, perhaps another, had not the frown of Catherine's evil angel whetted the scissons of the fates, and misfortune abruptly severed it.   The insurance office, where his forty pounds a year was to have secured a provision for his daughter, suddenly stopped payment.   The dishonesty of one of the partners, and the carelessness of the rest, had exposed the whole capital to the chance of a dangerous speculation ; and it was lost utterly and irredeemably.   The fibres that bound together the old man's soul and body were too feeble to bear the strain of anxiety and distress which fell upon him. . . They parted suddenly, and Catherine was left an orphan."

CHAPTER VI.

You very nearly have her history; little remains to be told. . . . Sir John and Lady Carpenter had lately come to live at Exmouth. Sir John was a retired tradesman of Cheapside. With a knighthood and three hundred thousand pounds, he existed at Exmouth, it would seem, for the sole purpose of giving his lady a title, entertaining her friends, and paying her ladyship's bills. . . In London he had been of some importance, for he was a good steady man of business, knew the interests of trade, and followed them out in the part he took in politics. In Devonshire his object was to metamorphose himself and come out as a gentleman, to endeavour, by the best dinners and the best claret, to blot out the stains of his extraction. No plumes waved higher than her ladyship's in the well-curtained and cushioned pew on a Sunday. The gold on her Bible and Prayer-book would have given a new set of clothes to the whole Charity-school; and three scarlet footmen, with gold canes, formed her body-guard as she passed up the aisle. . . Sir John, true to the interests of his new order, paid the expenses of the election of the Conservative member, and never lost an opportunity of crying up the Corn Laws and railing at Free-trade, as the party cry of a few selfish designing money-makers. Nay, on one occasion he was so self-devoted as to sacrifice his old Cheapside self to make the present self glitter brighter by the comparison. " No one," he said, " had a better right to know what they were than he had, for he had himself once been one of them, and no motive but love of money had ever influenced him." . . . In fact, the Carpenters were the family of Exmouth; no balls were better attended; the officers of the Exeter garrison never failed; their distinguished and select parties went the round of the county papers: in short, for selfishness, uselessness, vulgarity, and ostentation, it would have been difficult, if not impossible, to have provided them with rivals. . . . Two children, both girls, filled up their social circle ; the eldest eight, the second two years younger. . . . But the Carpenters, with all their magnificence, had not thrown off their trading habits ; and extravagantly profuse as they were in large matters when there was eclât to be got for it, they were as extravagantly mean in trifling ones ; a feature in their character which involved them in many petty difficulties, as they particularly wished to be considered charitable,—the very father and mother of benevolence. True, there was not a subscription list in the county where their names did not appear. Yet people often observed the sums were rather insignificant. This, however, they contrived in a way to obviate, by dividing their donations ; and, instead of Sir John's name appearing with the whole, his lady's stood elsewhere in the list at full length besides, contriving so to double the display without adding to the expense.

It was under this good lady's eye that our Catherine had the fortune to fall. . . . The orphan's friend was a delightful title; what honour would she not get on earth by it, and what an angel would she not be by-and-bye in heaven ! What if she was to take her to live with her little girls? Catherine was very pretty, quite clever enough, and had learned enough for them at any rate to begin upon. . . Understanding whispered it would save the expense of a governess. The very thing. She talked the matter over with her lady's-maid in the morning; with Sir John at the twelve-o'clock breakfast; and in the evening Catherine, who was still too much stunned, stupefied by her father's loss, to know or care what was done with her, was in the hands of her ladyship's housekeeper. . . .

"And that is all," said the genius to me. "Think it over now and link on the beginning to the end; and see if you can tell when sin came in, and she began to deserve what fell upon her. Is not rather the idea of "deserving" but a dream? and does not one thing follow another as it cannot choose but follow, as the grass grows when the rain falls, and withers and parches under drought? Nay, you must judge and think for yourself; do not bring your ideas to me," he said, as I was going to interrupt him. "I show you what I have to show you; it is for you to leave it or to profit by it.

" I have another scene for you before we part."

And again we were in the old Exmouth churchyard. It was daylight now, and all the birds were singing; and the sun was shining, and the bells were pealing, and a thousand bright eyes were flashing from the tiny waves as they danced in the light before the summer breeze.

A pyramid of gaudy streamers were floating up the flag-staff; and the king's cutter, which lay under the hill, was trailing her broad banner over her stern. The church door was open, some service was just over, for the bells only began to ring as we settled down there, and a troop of people were coming filing out of the porch. They seemed most of them to be the coastguard men, by their round jackets and anchor buttons, and trousers white as swan-down. Their wives and children were all with them, all in holiday costume; and the men had roses in their button-holes, and the women and children nosegays in their hands, and many shouts of laughter came ringing out of the group of bright and sunny faces. A nurse with a baby in her arms, swathed carefully in at least

a hundred shawls and wrappers, though it was
burning July, made her way through an opening in the crowd, amidst a shower of wishes of
good luck, accounting in a way for the collection there, and walked rapidly with her charge
across the fields, to the white cottage at the
station. A clergyman shortly followed out of
the church, and close after him, a gentleman in
a naval officer's uniform; and could I believe
my senses? a lady they seemed to tell me was
the same Catherine, with a little boy some two
years old, holding on by her glove.

The clergyman shook the officer warmly by
the hand.

" May you know many such happy days, my
dear captain," he said; " and may I live to offer
many children of yours to God in this church."

" Ah, there is the cutter with her flags out,
and the station too; what a pleasure it must be
to you, to see yourself so beloved, your happiness so shared in by all these people."

"Thank you, Doctor; I believe, though, I
may thank my little wife for it," answered the
captain; "she is the men's darling. She has
grown up among them, and lived among them,
and the old sailors love her as their own child.

I am pretty well, but I am not what her father was to them; I fancy I owe most of their favours to my having had him for my father-in law."

" And this is your little boy, the Doctor said, pinching the rosy cheek between his fore and middle finger." " Bless me how he grows, a sailor every inch of him; true sailor lad, he has the quarter-deck walk already. Let me see, how old is he? dear dear, yes indeed, two years last month. Yes, he was born the week before his grandfather died. How time flies! Are we to have you long with us, captain?"

" That is as it pleases our good Lords of the Admiralty," he replied. " It is five years now since I came; you know I was put on when the force was increased, as a sort of extra superintending officer, and I have heard nothing of my being superseded; you may be sure I shall not seek it. It would break Catherine's heart to go away, and I can be well enough contented to live and die at the place which first gave her to me. To be sure, what a providence it was I was ever sent here at all. It happened just when they wanted an officer here, that my friends had applied for something to be given me to do, and as there was not any ship in the way, I was posted off here; what a chance these things turn upon!

"It was much against my will, I can tell you, Catherine; I was sulky enough about it, till I had to come here and take up my quarters with your father; and then you know you managed to reconcile me to my fate. . . . Dear old man, what a brave heart there was in him, and how he bore up against his many troubles! That business with the insurance office, Catherine; he told me many times, his anxieties for you then were like to have made an end of him, and it was only God's mercy that they didn't ; and so it was God's mercy, dear Catherine, for if he had not lived, I should never have known you, and some other lucky fellow might have worn my jewel."

"See, madam," the Doctor said, "the very dead are smiling to-day; those pretty children have dressed your father's grave in flowers. How does death lose his terrors, and change into the sweetness of sleep, when it is made beautiful so by children's hands."

The grave mounds were fenced in by a little row of wooden crosses; fresh gathered roses and lilies hung from one to the other in long festoons; and down between them were sleeping these two in sweet and blessed peace; they had suffered in life, they had borne some pain together upon earth, and they had borne the sharper pain of separation; but now they lay there together never more to part, and on their crosses hung no longer crowns of thorns, but wreathes of sweetest flowers.

" Follow them," the genius whispered, as the three moved slowly across the churchyard towards the spot.

" The inscription," he said again, as I hung behind the pensive group . . . " read it."

I did so; it was the same, word and word the same, but with this one difference. The old man had outlived the date I had first read five summers; and sixty-nine, not sixty-four, marked the number of the year of his pilgrimage."

O God! and that was all; five links hung on upon the chain, and the shadow of the father's life had held aloof the blistering footsteps of sorrow and of sin, and the child's path lay along through a garden of roses, into a life of virtue, and an end of peace.

" And which is true ?" I asked.

"Come with me to the light, and I will show you," he replied.   I staggered after him, behind drawn curtains to the open light of day, the cool sea breeze played upon my face, and woke me to life and reason.   I had crawled to the open window of my bed-room, and my eyes were on the wide sheet of the Atlantic, and the peaks of Achill were purpling in the rising sun.

THE END.

LONDON:

PRINTED BY G. J. PALMER, SAVOY STREET, STRAND.

BOOKS BY RANDALL JARRELL

POETRY

The Rage for the Lost Penny (in *Five Young American Poets*)	*1940*
Blood for a Stranger	*1942*
Little Friend, Little Friend	*1945*
Losses	*1948*
The Seven-League Crutches	*1951*
The Woman at the Washington Zoo	*1960*
The Lost World	*1965*
The Complete Poems	*1968*

ESSAYS

Poetry and the Age	*1953*
A Sad Heart at the Supermarket	*1962*
The Third Book of Criticism	in preparation

FICTION

Pictures from an Institution	*1954*

CHILDREN'S BOOKS

The Gingerbread Rabbit	*1964*
The Bat-Poet	*1964*
The Animal Family	*1965*
Fly by Night	in preparation

TRANSLATIONS

The Golden Bird and Other Fairy Tales of the Brothers Grimm	*1962*
The Rabbit Catcher and Other Fairy Tales of Ludwig Bechstein	*1962*
Faust, Part I	in preparation

ANTHOLOGIES

The Anchor Book of Stories	*1958*
The Best Short Stories of Rudyard Kipling	*1961*
The English in England (Kipling Stories)	*1963*
In the Vernacular: The English in India (Kipling Stories)	*1963*
Six Russian Short Novels	*1963*
Modern Poetry: An Anthology	in preparation

THE THREE SISTERS

ANTON CHEKHOV
The Three Sisters

English Translation and Notes by

RANDALL JARRELL

The Macmillan Company

Collier-Macmillan Limited / London

Library of Congress Catalog Card Number: 69-10784

First Printing

Acknowledgments are made to Little, Brown & Co. for quotations from Chekhov's letters from *Chekhov* by Ernest J. Simmons; also to Grove Press for quotations from David Magarshack's *Chekhov: A Life*.

The Macmillan Company
Collier-Macmillan Canada Ltd., Toronto, Ontario

Printed in the United States of America

Grateful acknowledgment

is made to MR. PAUL SCHMIDT *for his excellent*

literal translation provided for the

final revisions of the script and to

MR. PETER KUDRIC *for many helpful*

conversations on the work

THE THREE SISTERS

CONTENTS

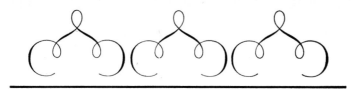

T H E
T H R E E
S I S T E R S

Cast of Characters

Prozorov, Andrei Sergeevich

Natalya [Natasha] Ivanovna, *his fiancée, then his wife*

Olga

Masha } *his sisters*

Irina

Kulygin, Fyodor Ilich, *a high school teacher, husband of*
  Masha

Vershinin, Alexander Ignatyevich, *Lieutenant Colonel,*
  Battery Commander

Tuzenbach, Nikolai Lvovich, *Baron, Lieutenant*

Solyony, Vasili Vasilevich, *Staff Captain*

Chebutykin, Ivan Romanovich, *Military Doctor*

Fedotik, Alexei Petrovich, *Second Lieutenant*

Rode, Vladimir Karlovich, *Second Lieutenant*

Ferapont, *janitor from the county board, an old man*

Anfisa, *nurse, an old woman of eighty*

The action takes place in a provincial city.

The Actors Studio Production in 1964
Photograph by MARTHA HOLMES

PREMIERE PERFORMANCE JUNE 22, 1964

THE
MOROSCO THEATRE

The Actors Studio, Inc.

presents

THE ACTORS STUDIO THEATRE

production of

THE THREE SISTERS

A Play by
ANTON CHEKHOV

New English Translation by
RANDALL JARRELL

THE COMPANY

Luther Adler	Barbara Baxley	Tamara Daykarhanova	John Harkins
Gerald Hiken	Shirley Knight	Robert Loggia	Salem Ludwig
Janice Mars	Kevin McCarthy	Brooks Morton	James Olson
Geraldine Page	Albert Paulsen	David Paulsen	Kim Stanley

Scenery Designed by
WILL STEVEN ARMSTRONG

Costumes Designed by
THEONI V. ALDREDGE and RAY DIFFEN

Lighting by
FEDER

Directed by
LEE STRASBERG

ACT I

THE LIVING ROOM IN THE HOUSE OF THE PROZOROVS
—*a row of columns separates it from a large dining
room at the back. Midday; outside it is sunny and bright.
In the dining room the table is being set for lunch.*
OLGA, *in the dark blue uniform of a teacher in a girls'
high school, is correcting papers, standing or walking
to and fro.* MASHA, *in a black dress, her hat on her knees,
is sitting reading a book.* IRINA, *in a white dress, stands
lost in thought.*

OLGA   Just a year ago, a year ago on this very day, Father
died—on your birthday, Irina, on the fifth of May. It was
very cold, the snow was falling. I thought I'd never live
through it; you had fainted, and lay there as if you were
dead. But now a year's gone by and we can remember it
calmly; you're already wearing white, your face is
radiant. . . .

   [*The clock strikes twelve*]

And the clock struck just the same way then. (*A pause*)
I remember that as they took Father there the band was
playing, they fired a volley over his grave. He was a
general, he was in command of a whole brigade, and yet
there weren't many people. Of course, it was raining.

Raining hard—rain and snow.

IRINA   Why think about it?

[*Behind the columns, in the dining room,* BARON
TUZENBACH, CHEBUTYKIN, *and* SOLYONY *appear*]

OLGA   It's warm today, we can have the windows wide
open—and yet there still aren't any leaves on the birches.
They gave Father his brigade, we left Moscow with him,
eleven years ago, and I remember distinctly that in Moscow
at this time, at the start of May, everything is already
in bloom; it's warm, everything is bathed in sunshine.
That was eleven years ago, and yet I remember it all as if
we'd left it yesterday. Oh, God! When I woke up this
morning I saw that everything was light, that it was
spring, and I thought my heart would burst with joy. I
longed so passionately to go home.

CHEBUTYKIN   The devil it is!

TUZENBACH   Of course, it's all nonsense. (MASHA,
brooding over her book, softly whistles a tune)

OLGA   Don't *whistle*, Masha! How can you? (*A pause*)
Being at school every day and then giving lessons all
afternoon—it makes my head ache all the time, the thoughts
I have are an old woman's thoughts already. Really and
truly, these four years I've been at the high school I've
felt the strength and the youth being squeezed out of me
day by day, drop by drop. And just one dream grows
stronger and stronger.

IRINA   To go back to Moscow! To sell the house, finish
up everything here, and—off to Moscow!

OLGA   Yes! As soon as we possibly can, to Moscow!
(CHEBUTYKIN *and* TUZENBACH *laugh*)

IRINA   Brother will probably be a professor, he won't be

living here anyway. The only thing wrong is poor Masha.

OLGA Masha's going to come and spend the whole summer in Moscow every summer. (MASHA *softly begins to whistle a tune*)

IRINA Please God, it will all come out right! (SHE *looks out of the window*) It's such a beautiful day, I don't know why I feel so happy. This morning I remembered it's my birthday, and all at once I felt joyful and remembered my childhood, when Mother was still alive. And what marvelous thrilling thoughts I had—what thoughts!

OLGA You're radiant today—I've never seen you lovelier. And Masha looks lovely, too. And Andrei would be good-looking, only he's got so fat; it isn't a bit becoming. And I've got older and so much thinner—I suppose it's because I get so cross at the girls at school. Today now, I'm free, I'm at home, my head doesn't ache, I feel so much younger to myself than I did yesterday. I'm only twenty-eight. . . . It's all good, it's all as God means it to be, but it seems to me that if I were married and stayed home all day it would be better. (*A pause*) I'd love my husband.

TUZENBACH You talk such nonsense I'm sick of listening to you. (*Coming into the living room*) I forgot to tell you. Today you are to be visited by our new battery commander. His name's Vershinin.

OLGA Really? I'm delighted.

IRINA Is he old?

TUZENBACH No, not very. Forty or so—forty-five at the most. He seems quite nice—and he's certainly no fool. Only he talks a lot.

IRINA Is he interesting?

TUZENBACH Yes, interesting enough—only there's a wife, a mother-in-law, and two little girls. What's more, she's his second wife. He goes around calling on people and telling them he has a wife and two little girls. He'll tell you that. His wife isn't exactly all there: she has long braids like a girl's, talks only of lofty things, philosophizes, and regularly tries to commit suicide—to annoy her husband, evidently. If I were Vershinin I'd have left such a woman long ago, but he puts up with it and just complains.

SOLYONY (*Entering the living room with* CHEBUTYKIN) With one hand I can only lift sixty pounds, but with two hands I can lift a hundred and eighty-two—two hundred, even. From that I deduce that two men aren't twice as strong, they're three times as strong as one man . . . or even stronger. . . .

CHEBUTYKIN (*Reading a newspaper as* HE *comes in*) For falling hair: Two ounces of naphtha in half a pint of alcohol . . . dissolve and apply daily. (HE *writes it down in his notebook*) Let's make a note of it! (*To* SOLYONY) So remember what I told you, you want to cork the bottle tight and push a glass tube down through the cork. Then you take a pinch of alum, plain ordinary alum—

IRINA   Ivan Romanich, dear Ivan Romanich!

CHEBUTYKIN   What is it, my child, my treasure?

IRINA   Tell me, why is it I'm so happy today? As if I were sailing along with the wide blue sky over me and great white birds floating across it. Why is that? Why?

CHEBUTYKIN (*Kissing both her hands tenderly*)   My white bird . . .

IRINA   When I woke up this morning and got up and bathed, all at once I felt as if everything in the world were clear to me, and I understood the way one ought to live. Dear Ivan Romanich, I understand everything. A man must work, must make his bread by the sweat of his brow,

Andrei and Natasha
Photograph by FRIEDMAN-ABELES

it doesn't matter who he is—and it is in this alone that
he can find the purpose and meaning of his life, his happiness, his ecstasies. Oh, how good it is to be a workman
who gets up at dawn and breaks stones in the street, or a
shepherd, or a schoolteacher who teaches children, or a
locomotive engineer! My God, it's better to be an ox, it's
better to be a plain horse, and *work*, than to be a girl who
wakes up at twelve o'clock, has coffee in bed, and then
takes two hours to get dressed. . . . Oh, how awful that
is! Sometimes I—I *thirst* for work the way on a hot day
you thirst for water. And if I don't get up early and
work, give me up forever, Ivan Romanich!

CHEBUTYKIN (*Tenderly*) I will, I will.

OLGA Father trained us to get up at seven. Now Irina
wakes up at seven and lies there till nine at least, and
thinks about something. And she does look so serious!
(*Laughing*)

IRINA You're so used to considering me a child that you're
surprised I should ever be serious. I am twenty!

TUZENBACH That thirst for work—good God, how well
I understand it! I've never worked a day in my life. I
was born in Petersburg, cold, lazy Petersburg—born into
a family that never knew what work or worry meant. I
remember that when I'd get home from cadet school a
footman would pull my boots off for me, and I'd do
something idiotic and my mother would look at me in awe,
and then be surprised when everybody else didn't. I've
been sheltered from work. But they've hardly succeeded
in sheltering me forever—hardly! The time has come: a
thundercloud is hanging over us all, a great healthy storm
is gathering; it's coming, it's already almost upon us,
and is going to sweep out of our society the laziness, the

indifference, the contempt for work, the rotten boredom. I'll work—and in another twenty-five or thirty years everybody will work. Everybody!

CHEBUTYKIN *I'm* not going to work.

TUZENBACH You don't count.

SOLYONY In another twenty-five years, thank God, you won't be here on this earth. In two or three years either you'll get apoplexy or I'll lose control of myself and put a bullet through your head, my angel. (HE *takes a little bottle of perfume from his pocket and sprinkles it over his chest and hands*)

CHEBUTYKIN I really never have done a thing. Since I left the university I haven't lifted a finger, I haven't opened a book—I just read the newspapers. (HE *takes another newspaper out of his pocket*) Here we are. I know from the papers that there was, say, somebody named Dobrolyubov, but what he wrote I don't know. God only knows. (*A knock is heard from the floor below*) Listen. They want me downstairs, somebody's come to see me. . . . I'm coming right away. Wait a minute. . . . (HE *goes out hurriedly, combing his beard*)

IRINA He's up to something.

TUZENBACH Yes. He went out looking solemn—plainly, he's about to bring you a present.

IRINA What a nuisance!

OLGA Yes, it's awful. He's always doing something silly.

MASHA By the curved seastrand a green oak stands, / A chain of gold upon it . . . (SHE *gets up and hums softly*)

OLGA You're not very cheerful today, Masha. (MASHA, *humming, puts on her hat*) Where are you going?

MASHA Home.

IRINA. That's strange.

TUZENBACH To walk out on a birthday party!

MASHA What's the difference? I'll be back this evening.
Good-bye, my darling. . . . (SHE *kisses* IRINA) I'll wish
all over again: may you always be well and happy! In the
old days, when Father was alive, there'd always be thirty
or forty officers here on our birthdays, there was lots
of noise, and today there's a man and a half and it's as
silent as the tomb. . . . I'm going. I'm depressed today, I
feel miserable—don't you listen to me. (SHE *smiles
through her tears*) We'll talk afterwards—good-bye till
then, dearest, I'm going.

IRINA (*Discontentedly*) Oh, how can you be so . . .

OLGA (*In tears*) I understand you, Masha.

SOLYONY If a man philosophizes, you get philosophy or,
anyway, something that looks like philosophy; but if a
woman philosophizes, or two do, you might just as well
suck your thumb.

MASHA And what is that supposed to mean, you terribly
dreadful man?

SOLYONY Nothing. Before he'd time to get his breath /
The bear was hugging him to death. (*A pause*)

MASHA (*To* OLGA, *angrily*) Don't sit there sniveling!

[*Enter* ANFISA *and* FERAPONT *with a cake*]

ANFISA In here, uncle. Come on in, your feet are clean.
(*To* IRINA) From the county board, from Mikhail Ivanich
Protopopov—a cake.

IRINA Thank you. And thank him for me, please.

FERAPONT How's that?

IRINA (*Louder*) Thank him!

ANFISA Come on, Ferapont Spiridonich. Come on. . . .

[SHE *goes out with* FERAPONT]

MASHA   I don't like that Protopopov, that Mikhail Potapich or Ivanich or whatever it is. He ought not to be invited.
IRINA   I didn't invite him.
MASHA   That's fine!

[CHEBUTYKIN *enters, behind him an orderly with a silver samovar; there is a hum of amazement and displeasure*]

OLGA (*Covering her face with her hands*)   A samovar! This is awful!

[SHE *goes to the table in the dining room*]

IRINA   Darling Ivan Romanich, what can have possessed you?
TUZENBACH (*Laughing*)   I told you so.
MASHA   Ivan Romanich, you're simply shameless.
CHEBUTYKIN   My darlings, my blessed girls, you are all that I have left, to me you are the most precious treasures that there are upon this earth. Soon I'll be sixty years old: I'm an old man, a lonely worthless old man. The only good that there is in me is my love for you—if it weren't for you I should have left this world long ago. (*To* IRINA) My darling, my own little girl, I've known you since the day you were born. . . . I carried you in these arms. . . . I loved your sainted mother. . . .
IRINA   But why such expensive presents?
CHEBUTYKIN (*Through his tears, angrily*)   Expensive presents! Oh, get out! (*To the* ORDERLY) Carry the samovar over there. (*Mimicking*) Expensive presents!

[*The* ORDERLY *carries the samovar into the dining room*]

ANFISA (*Walking through the living room*) My dears,
there's a strange colonel. He's already taken off his overcoat, children, he's coming in here. Irina darling, now
you be a nice polite little girl. (*As* SHE *goes out*) And
it was time for lunch hours ago. . . . The Lord have
mercy!
TUZENBACH   It must be Vershinin.

[VERSHININ *enters*]

TUZENBACH   Lieutenant Colonel Vershinin!
VERSHININ   I have the honor of introducing myself:
Vershinin. I'm so glad, so very glad to be here in your house
at last. But how you've grown! My, my!
IRINA   Do sit down. We're delighted.
VERSHININ   How glad I am! How glad I am! But surely
there are three of you sisters. I remember—three little girls.
I can't remember your faces any longer, but your father,
Colonel Prozorov, had three little girls—that I remember
distinctly; I saw them with my own eyes. How time does
fly! My, my, how time does fly!
TUZENBACH   Alexander Ignatyevich is from Moscow.
IRINA   From Moscow? You're from Moscow?
VERSHININ   Yes, from Moscow. Your father, God bless
him, was a battery commander there, and I was an officer
in the same brigade. (*To* MASHA) Now that I—it seems
to me I do remember your face a little.
MASHA   Yours—I—no!
IRINA   Olga! Olga! (SHE *calls into the dining room*) Olga!
Come here!

[OLGA *comes in from the dining room*]

IRINA It seems Colonel Vershinin's from Moscow.

VERSHININ You must be Olga Sergeevna, the eldest. . . . And you're Marya. . . . And you're Irina, the youngest.

OLGA You're from Moscow?

VERSHININ Yes, I went to school in Moscow and went into the service in Moscow, I was stationed there for many years, and finally they gave me a battery here and I've moved here, as you see. I don't exactly remember you, I just remember that there were you three sisters. But I remember your father so well: if I shut my eyes I can see him standing there as plain as life. I used to come to see you in Moscow. . . .

OLGA It seemed to me I remembered everybody, and now all at once. . . .

VERSHININ My name is Alexander Ignatyevich.

IRINA Alexander Ignatyevich, so you're from Moscow! What a surprise!

OLGA We're about to move there, you know.

IRINA We'll be there by this fall, we expect. It's our home town, we were born there. . . . On Old Basmanny Street. (THEY *both laugh with delight*)

MASHA We've met someone from home—and so unexpectedly! (*Animatedly*) Now I remember! Remember, Olga, they used to talk to us about "the love-sick major." You were a lieutenant then, and in love with somebody, and for some reason they'd all call you major to tease you.

VERSHININ (*Laughing*) That's it! That's it! The love-sick major. That was it!

MASHA You just had a moustache then. But how old you've got! (*Tearfully*) How old you've got!

VERSHININ Yes, when they used to call me the love-sick major I was young, I was in love. It's different now.

OLGA But you still haven't a single gray hair. You've got older, but you're still not old.

VERSHININ Just the same, I'm forty-two. Has it been long since you left Moscow?

IRINA Eleven years. Oh, Masha, what are you crying for, you crazy thing? (*Through her tears*) You've made me cry, too.

MASHA I'm all right. What street did you live on?

VERSHININ On Old Basmanny.

OLGA We did, too.

VERSHININ For a while I lived on Nyemetski Street. From there I used to go back and forth to the Red Barracks. On the way there's a gloomy-looking bridge, you can hear the water under it. A lonely man gets melancholy there. (*A pause*) But here you've such a broad, such a splendid river! A wonderful river!

OLGA Yes . . . only it's so cold. It's so cold here, and there're mosquitoes.

VERSHININ How can you say that? You have such a splendid, healthy, Russian climate here. The forest, the river . . . and there're birches here, too. Dear, modest birches—of all the trees I love birches best. It's good to live here. The only queer thing, the railroad station is ten miles away. . . . And nobody knows why.

SOLYONY I know why. (EVERYONE *looks at him*) Because if the station were here it wouldn't be way off there; and if it's way off there, then of course it can't be here. (*An awkward silence*)

TUZENBACH He's a joker, Vasili Vasilich.

OLGA Now I've remembered you. I remember.

VERSHININ I knew your mother.

CHEBUTYKIN She was a lovely woman, bless her soul.

IRINA   Mother is buried in Moscow.

OLGA   In the Novo Devichy. . . .

MASHA   Imagine, I'm already beginning to forget her face. And the same way, they won't remember us. They'll forget us.

VERSHININ   Yes. They'll forget us. That is our fate, there is nothing we can do about it. Everything that seems to us serious, significant, profoundly important—the time will come when it will be forgotten or will seem unimportant. . . . (*A pause*) And what's so interesting is that there's no way for us to know what it is that's going to seem great and important, and what it is that's going to seem pitiful and ridiculous. Take Copernicus or Columbus, for instance—didn't their discoveries seem useless or ridiculous at first, and some fool's empty nonsense seem the truth? And it may be that the life we lead now, the life we reconcile ourselves to so easily, will seem strange some day, uncomfortable, unintelligent, not clean enough—perhaps, even, wrong.

TUZENBACH   Who knows? Or perhaps our life will be called great and be remembered with respect. We don't torture people any more, we've no more executions and invasions—but just the same, how much suffering there is still!

SOLYONY (*In a high-pitched voice*)   He-ere, chicky, chicky, chicky! Don't feed the baron chicken feed, just let him philosophize.

TUZENBACH   Vasili Vasilich, leave me alone, please. (HE *sits down in another place*) After all, this sort of thing gets to be boring.

SOLYONY (*In a high-pitched voice*)   He-ere, chicky, chicky, chicky!

TUZENBACH   The suffering we see now—there's still so
much of it—itself is a sign that our society has reached a
certain level of moral development. . . .
VERSHININ   Yes, yes, of course.
CHEBUTYKIN   You said just now, Baron, that they'll call
our life great: just the same, people are very small.
(HE *stands up*) Look how small I am. If anybody were
to say that my life is something great, something that
makes sense, he'd just be saying it to make me feel good.

[*Behind the scene someone is playing the violin*]

MASHA   That's Andrei playing, our brother.
IRINA   He's the scholar of the family. We expect he'll
be a professor someday. Father was a military man, but his
son has chosen an academic career.
MASHA   Father wanted him to.
OLGA   We've been teasing him all morning. It looks as
if he's a little bit in love.
IRINA   With one of the local girls. She'll probably be here
before long.
MASHA   The way she does dress! It's not that her clothes
are ugly or old-fashioned, somehow they're just pathetic.
Some sort of queer gaudy yellowish skirt with a cheap
fringe on it—and a red blouse. And her cheeks scrubbed
till they shine! Andrei isn't in love with her—I refuse
to admit it, he does have some taste—he's just making fun
of us, playing some sort of joke on us. I heard yesterday
that she's going to marry Protopopov, the chairman of
the county board. That would be perfect. (*Through the
side door*) Andrei, come in here! Just for a minute, darling!

[ANDREI *enters*]

OLGA   This is my brother, Andrei Sergeeich.

VERSHININ   Vershinin.

ANDREI   Prozorov. (HE *wipes the sweat off his face*)
You're our new battery commander?

OLGA   Just imagine, Alexander Ignatich is from Moscow.

ANDREI   You are? Well then, I congratulate you—my
sisters won't give you a moment's peace.

VERSHININ   I've already succeeded in boring your sisters.

IRINA   Look at the frame Andrei gave me today!
(*Showing the frame*) He made it himself.

VERSHININ (*Looking at the frame and not knowing what
to say*)   Yes. It's . . . it's a thing . . .

   [ANDREI *waves his hand in disgust and walks away*]

OLGA   He's our scholar, and he plays the violin, and
he can make *anything* with his fretsaw. In fact, he's a kind
of universal expert. Don't go away, Andrei! That's the
way he is, always going off by himself. Come back here!

   [MASHA *and* IRINA *take him by the arms and, laughing,
   lead him back*]

MASHA   Come along! Come along!

ANDREI   Please let me alone.

MASHA   Isn't he absurd! They used to call Alexander
Ignatevich the love-sick major, and he never got angry,
not even once.

VERSHININ   Not even once!

MASHA   I think we ought to call you the love-sick violinist!

IRINA   Or the love-sick professor!

OLGA   He's in love! Our little Andrei's in love!

IRINA (*Applauding*)   Bravo! Bravo! Encore! Our little
Andrei's in love!

CHEBUTYKIN (*Coming up behind* ANDREI *and putting both hands around his waist*)   Male and female created He them! (HE *laughs.* HE *still has the newspaper.*)

ANDREI   Well, that's enough, that's enough. . . . (HE *wipes his face*) I couldn't sleep all night and this morning I'm not quite myself, as the phrase goes. I read till four o'clock and then went to bed, but it wasn't any use. I'd think of something, and then think of something else— and it gets light so early here: the sunlight simply pours into my bedroom. This summer while I'm here there's this English book I want to translate . . .

VERSHININ   You read English?

ANDREI   Yes. Father, God bless him, absolutely loaded us down with education. It's absurd, it's idiotic, but just the same I've got to admit that after his death I began to gain weight—in a year I've got fat like this, just as if my body had taken the chance to break loose from him. Thanks to Father my sisters and I know French, German, and English, and Irina even knows Italian. But what's the use of that?

MASHA   In this town knowing three languages is a useless luxury. Not even a luxury but a sort of useless appendage, like a sixth finger. We know a lot that isn't any use.

VERSHININ   Really now! (HE *laughs*) You know a lot that isn't any use! I don't think that there is a town, that there can be a town, so boring and so dismal that it doesn't need intelligent, cultivated people. Suppose that among the hundred thousand inhabitants of this town— this obviously crude, obviously backward place—suppose that there're only three people like you. It's plain that you won't be able to get the better of the darkness and ignorance around you; as you go on living, little by little

you'll have to give up, you'll be lost in this crowd of a
hundred thousand human beings, their life will choke
you out. But you'll have been here, you'll not disappear
without a trace: later on others like you will come, perhaps
only six at first, then twenty, and so on, until at last people
like you will be in the majority. In two or three hundred
years life on earth will be unimaginably beautiful, unimaginably wonderful. Mankind needs such a life—and
if it isn't here yet then we must look forward to it, wait,
dream of it, prepare for it; and to do that we must see
and know more than our fathers and grandfathers saw
and knew. (He *laughs*) And you say you know a lot
that isn't any use!

MASHA (*Taking off her hat*)   I'm staying to lunch.

IRINA (*Sighing*)   Really, all that ought to be written down.

[ANDREI *is not there;* HE *has gone out unnoticed*]

TUZENBACH   After many years, you say, life on earth
will be beautiful, wonderful. That is true. But to have a
share in it now, even from a distance, we must get ready
for it, we must work.

VERSHININ   Yes. (He *gets up*) But what a lot of flowers
you have! (He *looks around*) And this beautiful house.
I envy you! My whole life has been spent in little apart-
ments with two chairs, a sofa, and a stove that keeps
smoking all the time. It's just such flowers as these that
have been missing in my life. (He *rubs his hands together*)
Well, there's nothing to be done about it now. . . .

TUZENBACH   Yes, we must work. Probably you're
thinking: the German is getting sentimental. But I give
you my word of honor, I'm Russian, I can't even speak
German. My father's Orthodox. . . (*A pause*)

VERSHININ   I often think, suppose it were possible for us to begin life over again—and consciously, this time. If only the first life, the one we've lived through already, were a rough draft, so to speak, and the other the final copy! I believe that each of us would try above all not to repeat himself—or at least would create a different set of circumstances for his life, would manage to live in a house like this, with flowers, with plenty of light. . . . I have a wife and two little girls, and not only that, my wife's an invalid, and so forth and so on—well, if I were to begin life over again, I'd never get married. . . . Never, never!

[KULYGIN *enters, in a schoolteacher's uniform*]

KULYGIN (*Going up to* IRINA)   Dear sister, allow me to congratulate you on the day of your birth—and to wish for you, sincerely and from the bottom of my heart, health and everything else that's appropriate for a girl of your age. And to offer you as a gift this little book. (HE *hands her a book*) An insignificant little book, written only because I had nothing else to do, but just the same, read it. Good morning, gentlemen! (*To* VERSHININ) Kulygin, teacher in the local high school, court councillor. (*To* IRINA) In this book you will find a list of everyone who has graduated from our high school in the last fifty years. *Feci, quod potui, faciant meliora potentes.* (HE *kisses* MASHA)

IRINA   But you gave me one Easter!

KULYGIN (HE *laughs*)   Impossible! Well, in that case give it back—or better still, give it to the colonel. Take it, Colonel. Some day when you're bored, read it.

VERSHININ Thank you. (HE *is about to leave*) I'm
extremely glad to have made your acquaintance—
OLGA You're leaving? No, no!
IRINA Surely you'll stay and have lunch with us. Please.
OLGA I beg you.
VERSHININ I can see I've happened in on a party for
your birthday. Forgive me, I didn't know—I haven't
congratulated you.

[HE *goes into the dining room with* OLGA]

KULYGIN Today, gentlemen, is a Sunday, a day of rest,
so let us rest, let us rejoice, each in accordance with his
age and position. The rugs must be taken up for the
summer and put away till winter . . . with moth balls or
naphthalene. . . . The Romans were healthy because
they knew both how to work and how to rest, they had
mens sana in corpore sano. Their lives were organized
into a definite routine. Our principal is fond of saying
that the most important thing in any life is its routine.
. . . That which loses its routine loses its very existence—
and it is exactly the same in our everyday life. (HE *takes*
MASHA *by the waist, laughing*) Masha loves me. My wife
loves me. And the curtains too, along with the carpets.
. . . I am gay today, in the very best of spirits. Masha,
at four o'clock today we are due at the principal's. An
outing has been arranged for the teachers and their
families.
MASHA I'm not going.
KULYGIN (*Aggrieved*) But dear Masha, why?
MASHA We'll talk about it later. . . . (*Angrily*) Oh, all
right, I'll go, only please leave me alone. . . .

[SHE *walks away*]

KULYGIN   And afterwards we're to spend the evening at the principal's. In spite of the precarious condition of his health, that man tries above all else to be sociable. A stimulating, an outstanding personality! Yesterday after the faculty meeting he said to me: "I am tired, Fyodor Ilich! I am tired!" (HE *looks at the clock on the wall, then at his watch*) Your clock is seven minutes fast. "Yes," he said, "I am tired!"

[*Behind the scene a violin is playing*]

OLGA   Ladies and gentlemen, please come to lunch. There's a meat pie.

KULYGIN   Ah, Olga, my dear Olga! Yesterday I worked from early morning till eleven o'clock at night, and I was tired, literally exhausted—and today I am happy. (HE *goes into the dining room by the table*) Ah, my dear . . .

CHEBUTYKIN (*Putting the newspaper into his pocket and combing his beard*)   A meat pie? Splendid!

MASHA (*To Chebutykin, sternly*)   Only—listen to me!— nothing to drink today. Do you hear? It's bad for you.

CHEBUTYKIN   Oh, come on, that's ancient history. I haven't been drunk for two years. (*Impatiently*) And, my dear girl, what's the difference anyway?

MASHA   Difference or no difference, don't you dare drink! Don't you dare! (*Angrily, but so that her husband doesn't hear*) Oh, damnation, damnation! for another whole evening to sit and be bored to death at that principal's!

TUZENBACH   If I were you I just wouldn't go. It's perfectly simple.

CHEBUTYKIN   Don't you go, my darling!

MASHA   Yes, don't you go! . . . A damnable life! an insufferable life!

[SHE *goes into the dining room*]

CHEBUTYKIN (*Going after her*)   Now, now!
SOLYONY (*Going into the dining room*)   He-ere, chicky, chicky, chicky!
TUZENBACH   That's enough, Vasili Vasilich. Stop it!
SOLYONY   He-ere, chicky, chicky, chicky!
KULYGIN (*Cheerfully*)   Your health, Colonel! I am a pedagogue, you know, and here in this house I'm one of the family, Masha's husband. . . . She is kind—so kind. . . .
VERSHININ   I'll have some of this dark vodka here. (*Drinking*) Your health! (*To* OLGA) I feel so good here at your house! . . .

[*Only* IRINA *and* TUZENBACH *are left in the living room*]

IRINA   Masha's not in a very good humor today. She was married when she was eighteen, and he seemed to her the most intelligent of men. It's different now. He's the kindest of men, but not the most intelligent.
OLGA (*Impatiently*)   Andrei, *please* come on. After all! . . .
ANDREI (*Offstage*)   This minute.

[HE *comes in and goes over to the table*]

TUZENBACH   What are you thinking about?
IRINA   This: I don't like that Solyony of yours, I'm afraid of him. Everything he says is so stupid. . . .
TUZENBACH   He's a strange man. I'm sorry for him and irritated at him too, but mostly I'm sorry for him. It seems to me he's shy. . . . When he's alone with you he's quite intelligent and pleasant, but when there're other

people around he's rude, a sort of bully. Don't go, let's
let them sit down without us. Let me be near you a little.
What are you thinking about? (*A pause*) You're twenty,
I'm not thirty yet. How many years we still have left—
so many days, row on row of them, all full of my love
for you. . . .

IRINA   Nikolai Lvovich, don't talk to me about love.

TUZENBACH (*Not listening*)   I long so passionately to live,
to struggle, to work—and because I love you, Irina, the
longing's stronger than ever: it's as if you were meant
to be so beautiful, and life seems to me just as beautiful.
What are you thinking about?

IRINA   You say life is beautiful. Yes, but suppose it only
seems that way! For us three sisters life hasn't been
beautiful, it's—it's choked us out, the way weeds choke
out grass. I'm crying. . . . (SHE *quickly wipes her eyes
and smiles*) I mustn't cry. We must work, work. We're so
unhappy, we take such a gloomy view of life, because
we don't work. We come from people who despised work.

[NATALYA (NATASHA) IVANOVNA *enters*; SHE *has on a
pink dress and a bright green belt*]

NATASHA   They've already sat down to the table. . . .
I'm late. . . . (*As* SHE *goes by it* SHE *looks into the mirror
and tidies herself*) My hair seems to be all right. . . .
(*Seeing* IRINA) Many happy returns of the day, dear Irina
Sergeevna! (SHE *gives her a vigorous and prolonged kiss*)
You've got such a lot of visitors, I really do feel em-
barrassed. . . . How do you do, Baron!

OLGA (*Entering the living room*)   Why, here's Natalya
Ivanovna! How are you, dear?

[THEY *kiss*]

NATASHA   Many happy returns! You've got so much company I really do feel terribly embarrassed.
OLGA   You mustn't, it's only the family. (*In an undertone, alarmed*) You have on a green belt! Dear, that's too bad—
NATASHA   What's wrong, is it bad luck?
OLGA   No, it's just that it doesn't go with . . . somehow it looks a little strange.
NATASHA (*In a tearful voice*)   It—it does? But it isn't really green, it's more a sort of a neutral shade.

> [SHE *follows* OLGA *into the dining room.*
> *In the dining room* THEY *sit down to lunch; there is no one left in the living room.*]

KULYGIN   I wish you, Irina, a good fiancé! It's time you were getting married.
CHEBUTYKIN   Natalya Ivanovna, I wish you a fiancé too.
KULYGIN   Natalya Ivanovna already has a fiancé.
MASHA   I'll have a little drink! What the—life's a bed of roses! Come on, take a chance!
KULYGIN   For that you get a C-minus in deportment.
VERSHININ   This liqueur's good—what's it made of?
SOLYONY   Cockroaches.
IRINA   Ugh! How disgusting!
OLGA   For dinner we're having roast turkey and apple pie. Thank the Lord, I'll be home all day today and home all evening. Everybody must come this evening.
VERSHININ   Let me come this evening, too.
OLGA   Please do.
NATASHA   They certainly don't wait to be asked twice around here.

CHEBUTYKIN   Male and female created He them! (HE *laughs*)

ANDREI (*Angrily*)   Oh, stop it, everybody! Don't you ever get tired of it?

[FEDOTIK *and* RODE *enter with a big basket of flowers*]

FEDOTIK   Look, they're already having lunch. . . .

RODE (*Loudly and affectedly*)   Already having lunch? That's right, they're already having lunch.

FEDOTIK   Hold still a minute! (HE *takes a photograph*) One! Wait, just one more! (HE *takes another photograph*) Two! Now it's all right.

[THEY *pick up the basket and go on into the dining room, where* THEY *are greeted noisily*]

RODE (*Loudly*)   Many happy returns! I wish you everything, everything! It's wonderful out today, absolutely magnificent. I've been out all morning with the high school boys, on a hike. I teach the gym class at the high school, you know.

FEDOTIK   You can move, Irina Sergeevna, you can move now. (HE *takes a photograph*) You look simply beautiful today. (HE *takes a top out of his pocket*) By the way, here's a little top. . . . It makes the most wonderful sound. . . .

IRINA   How *nice*!

MASHA   By the curved sea-strand a green oak stands, A chain of gold upon it . . .
A chain of gold upon it . . . (*Tearfully*) What am I saying that for? It's been going through my head all day. . . .

KULYGIN   Thirteen at table!

RODE (*Loudly*)   But surely, ladies and gentlemen, you

do not actually take such superstitions as these seriously? (*Laughter*)

KULYGIN   If there're thirteen at table it means that one of them's in love. It's not you by any chance, Ivan Romanovich? (*Laughter*)

CHEBUTYKIN   I'm an old reprobate, but why Natalya Ivanovna is so embarrassed I simply can't imagine.

[*Loud laughter.* NATALYA *runs out of the dining room into the living room;* ANDREI *follows her.*]

ANDREI   Please don't pay any attention to them! Wait. . . . Don't go, please don't. . . .

NATASHA   I'm ashamed. . . . I don't know what's the matter with me, and they're all making fun of me. I know it's bad manners for me to leave the table like this, but I just can't help it. . . . I just can't. . . .

(SHE *covers her face with her hands*)

ANDREI   Dear, I beg you, I implore you, don't let them upset you. Honestly, they're only joking, they mean well. They have such kind hearts—my darling, my dearest, they're all such good, kindhearted people, they love both of us. Come over here by the window, they can't see us here. . . . (HE *looks around*)

NATASHA   I'm just not used to being in society!

ANDREI   Ah, youth, marvelous, beautiful youth! My darling, my dearest, please don't be upset! Believe me, believe me. . . . I'm so happy, so in love—I'm so blissfully happy. . . . Oh, they can't see us! They can't see us at all! Why I first fell in love with you, when I first fell in love with you—I don't know . . . My dearest, my darling, my innocent one, be my wife! I love you, love you as nobody ever—

[THEY *kiss.*
TWO OFFICERS *come in and seeing the two kissing, stop in amazement.*]

CURTAIN

ACT II

THE SCENE IS THAT OF THE FIRST ACT. IT IS EIGHT
*o'clock at night. The faint sound of an accordion comes
up from the street. The room is dark.* NATALYA
IVANOVNA *enters in a dressing gown, with a candle;*
SHE *walks over and stops at the door of* ANDREI'S *room.*

NATASHA   Andrei . . . dear, what are you doing? Reading? Nothing, I just . . . (SHE *goes to another door, opens
it, looks inside, and then shuts it*) No, there isn't one. . . .
ANDREI (*Entering with a book in his hand*) What,
Natasha?
NATASHA   I was looking to see whether there's a light.
. . . Now it's carnival week the servants are simply
impossible, you have to be on the lookout every minute
to make sure nothing goes wrong. Last night at midnight
I went through the dining room, and there on the table
was a lighted candle! Now, who lit it? I still haven't been
able to get a straight answer. (SHE *puts down her candle*)
What time is it?
ANDREI (*Looking at his watch*) Quarter after eight.
NATASHA   And Olga and Irina not in yet. They aren't
in yet. Still hard at work, poor things! Olga at the teachers'
council and Irina at the telegraph office. . . . (SHE *sighs*)
I was saying to your sister just this morning, "Irina

darling," I said, "you simply must take better care of yourself." But she just won't listen. . . . Quarter after eight, you said? I'm worried, I'm afraid our Bobik just isn't well. Why is he so cold? Yesterday he had a temperature and today he's cold all over. . . . I am so worried!

ANDREI   It's all right, Natasha. The boy's all right.

NATASHA   Just the same, I think we'd better put him on a diet. I *am* worried. And tonight at almost ten o'clock those carnival people are going to be here, they said— it would be better if they didn't come, Andrei dear.

ANDREI   I don't know. They *have* been asked, you know.

NATASHA   This morning the little thing woke up and looked at me, and all of a sudden he gave a big smile: he knew me! "Good morning, Bobik!" I said. "Good morning, sweetheart!" And he laughed. . . . Babies understand, they understand perfectly. So Andrei dear, I'm going to tell them they mustn't let those carnival people in.

ANDREI (*Indecisively*)   But that's up to my sisters, you know. This is their house.

NATASHA   Yes, theirs too. I'll speak to them. They're so kind. . . . (SHE *starts to leave*) I've ordered cottage cheese for your supper. The doctor says you mustn't eat any- thing but cottage cheese or you won't ever get any thinner. (SHE *stops*) Bobik is *cold*. I'm afraid he must be cold in that room of his. At least till it's warm weather, we ought to put him in a different room. For instance, Irina's room is a perfect room for a child, it's dry and the sun simply pours in all day long. I must speak to her about it. She could stay in Olga's room with her, for the time being. . . . It won't make any difference to her, she's never at home in the daytime anyway, she only

Masha and Vershinin
Photograph by FRIEDMAN-ABELES

spends the night there. . . . (*A pause*) Andrei-Wandrei, why don't you say something?

ANDREI   I was just thinking. . . . Anyway, there isn't anything to say. . . .

NATASHA   Uh-huh. . . . There was something I meant to tell you about. . . . Now I remember: Ferapont's here from the county board, he wants to see you.

ANDREI (*Yawning*)   Send him on in.

[NATASHA *goes out.* ANDREI, *stooping over the candle.* SHE *has left, reads his book.* FERAPONT *comes in;* HE *is in a worn-out old overcoat, the collar turned up, a scarf over his ears.*]

ANDREI   How are you, Ferapont, old man? What have you got to tell me?

FERAPONT   The chairman's sent you a little book and some kind of paper. Here . . . (HE *gives a book and an envelope to* ANDREI)

ANDREI   Thanks. That's fine. But what did you come so late for? It's already past eight, you know.

FERAPONT   How's that?

ANDREI (*Louder*)   I said you're late, it's past eight.

FERAPONT   That's right. I got here when it was still light but they wouldn't let me in. The master's busy, they said. Well, if you're busy you're busy, I'm not in any hurry. (*Thinking that* ANDREI *has said something*) How's that?

ANDREI   Nothing. (HE *examines the book*) Tomorrow's Friday, we don't have any meeting, but I'll come any-way. . . . I'll do something. It's boring at home. (*A pause*) Ferapont, old man, it's funny how life changes, how it fools you. Today out of pure boredom, just because I

hadn't anything else to do, I picked up this book here,
some old university lectures, and I couldn't help laughing. . . . Good God! I'm the secretary of the county
board, the board Protopopov's the head of; I'm the
secretary, and the very most I can ever hope for is—to
be a member of the board! I a member of a county
board—I who dream every night that I'm a professor at
the University of Moscow, a famous scholar of whom all
Russia is proud!

FERAPONT   I couldn't rightly say . . . I'm a little hard
of hearing. . . .

ANDREI   If you could hear as you ought I might not be
talking to you like this. I've got to talk to somebody and
my wife doesn't understand me, I'm afraid of my sisters,
somehow—I'm afraid they'll make fun of me, make me
feel ashamed. . . . You know, I don't drink, I don't like
cafés, but . . . good old Ferapont, what I'd give to be
sitting in Moscow right now, at Testov's or the Great
Muscovite!

FERAPONT   In Moscow, there was a contractor at the
board the other day that said so, there were some merchants
eating pancakes, and it seems as how one of them ate
forty pancakes and he died. It was either forty or fifty.
I don't remember.

ANDREI   In Moscow you sit in the main room at a
restaurant, you don't know anybody and nobody knows
you, but just the same you don't feel like a stranger. And
here you know everybody and everybody knows you,
and you're a stranger, a stranger . . . a stranger and
lonely.

FERAPONT   How's that? (*A pause*) And the contractor

said—maybe he was lying, though—that there's a rope
stretched all the way across Moscow.

ANDREI   What for?

FERAPONT   I couldn't rightly say. The contractor said so.

ANDREI   That's nonsense. (HE *reads*) Have you ever
been to Moscow?

FERAPONT (*After a pause*)   I never have. It wasn't God's
will I should. (*A pause*) Shall I go now?

ANDREI   You can go. Good-bye. (FERAPONT *goes out*)
Good-bye. (*Reading*) In the morning come back and
get these papers. . . . You can go. . . . (*A pause*) He's
gone. (*The bell rings*) Yes, it's a nuisance. . . .

> [HE *stretches and walks slowly into his room.
> Behind the scene the* NURSE *is singing, rocking the
> baby.* MASHA *and* VERSHININ *enter. While* THEY *talk,
> a* MAID *is lighting the lamp and candles.*]

MASHA   I don't know. (*A pause*) I don't know. Of course,
a lot of it is just habit. For instance, after Father's death
it took us a long time to get used to not having orderlies
in the house. But even if you disregard habit, it's only fair
to say that—maybe it's not so in other places—that in
our town the nicest people, the decentest people, the
best-mannered people, really are the ones in the army.

VERSHININ   I'm thirsty. I'd certainly like some tea.

MASHA   It'll be here before long. They married me when
I was eighteen, and I was afraid of my husband because
he was a teacher and I was barely out of school. He
seemed terribly learned to me then, intelligent, and important. It's different now, unfortunately.

VERSHININ   I see . . . yes.

MASHA I'm not talking about my husband, I'm used to
him, but among civilians in general there're so many coarse,
unpleasant, ill-bred people. Coarseness upsets me—insults
me; when I see that a man isn't polite enough, isn't refined
or delicate enough, I suffer. When I'm with the teachers,
my husband's colleagues, I'm simply miserable.

VERSHININ Yes. . . . But it seems to me it doesn't make
any difference—whether they're army men or civilians,
they're equally uninteresting . . . in this town, at any rate.
It makes no difference! If you listen to one of the local
intellectuals, civilian or military, all you ever hear is that
he's sick and tired of his wife, sick and tired of his house,
sick and tired of his estate, sick and tired of his horses.
. . . When it comes to lofty ideas, thinking on an exalted
plane, a Russian is extraordinary, but will you tell me
why it is he aims so low in life? Why?

MASHA Why?

VERSHININ Why is a Russian always sick and tired of his
children, sick and tired of his wife? And why are his
wife and children always sick and tired of him?

MASHA You're a little depressed today.

VERSHININ Perhaps. I didn't have any dinner—I've had
nothing to eat since breakfast. One of my daughters isn't
exactly well, and when my little girls are ill I get anxious
about them, my conscience torments me for having
given them such a mother. If you could have seen her
today! What a miserable creature! We began quarreling
at seven in the morning, and at nine I slammed the door
and walked away. . . . (*A pause*) I never mention it to
anybody—it's strange, it's only to you that I complain.
(HE *kisses her hand*) Don't be angry with me. If it
weren't for you I'd have no one—no one. (*A pause*)

MASHA   Listen to the chimney! Just before Father died there was a howling in the chimney—there, just like that!

VERSHININ   You're superstitious?

MASHA   Yes.

VERSHININ   That's strange. (HE *kisses her hand*) You're a splendid woman, a wonderful woman. Splendid, wonderful! It's dark in here, but I can see how your eyes sparkle.

MASHA   (*Moving to another chair*)   The light's better over here.

VERSHININ   I love, love, love . . . love your eyes, the way you move, I see them in my dreams. . . . Splendid, wonderful woman!

MASHA   (*Laughing softly*)   When you talk to me like that, somehow, I don't know why, I laugh, even when it frightens me. But don't do it again, please don't. . . . (*In a low voice*) No, you can, though—it doesn't make any difference to me. . . . (SHE *covers her face with her hands*) It doesn't make any difference to me. Someone's coming. Talk about something else.

[IRINA *and* TUZENBACH *come in through the dining room*]

TUZENBACH   I've got three last names, my name is BARON Tuzenbach-Krone-Altschauer, and yet I'm Russian and Orthodox, just like you. There's hardly anything German left in me—nothing, maybe, except the patience and obstinacy with which I keep boring you. Every single night I see you home.

IRINA   I'm so tired!

TUZENBACH   And every single day for ten years, for twenty years, I'll come to the telegraph office and see you home, as long as you don't drive me away. . . . (*Seeing* Masha *and* Vershinin, *delightedly*) Oh, it's you! How are you!

Irina　Here I am, home at last! (*To* Masha) Just before I left a lady came in—she was wiring her brother in Saratov that her son had died today, and she couldn't manage to remember the address. So she sent it without any address, just to Saratov. She was crying. And for no reason whatsoever, I was rude to her. I said, "I simply haven't the time." It was so stupid! Are the carnival people coming tonight?

Masha　Yes.

Irina　(*Sitting down in an armchair*)　I'll rest. I'm so tired.

Tuzenbach　(*Smiling*)　When you come home from work you seem so young and so unhappy. . . . (*A pause*)

Irina　I'm tired. No, I don't like working there, I don't like it.

Masha　You've got thinner . . . (She *begins to whistle*) And younger, and your face looks like a little boy's.

Tuzenbach　That's the way she does her hair.

Irina　I must try to find some other job, this one's not right for me. What I longed for so, what I dreamed about, is exactly what's missing. It's work without poetry, without sense, even . . . (*A knock on the floor*) The Doctor's knocking. . . . (*To* Tuzenbach) You knock, dear. . . . I can't . . . I'm so tired. (Tuzenbach *knocks on the floor*) He'll be right up. Some way or other we've got to do something about it. Yesterday he and Andrei were at the club, and they lost again. They say Andrei lost two hundred rubles.

Masha　(*Indifferently*)　Well, there's nothing we can do about it now.

IRINA   Two weeks ago he lost, in December he lost. If only he'd hurry up and lose everything, maybe then we'd get out of this town. My God, every night I dream of Moscow, it's as if I were possessed. (SHE *laughs*) We're moving there in June, from now to June leaves—February, March, April, May . . . almost half a year!

MASHA   The only thing is, Natasha mustn't hear anything about what he's lost.

IRINA   I don't think it makes any difference to her.

[CHEBUTYKIN, *just out of bed*—HE *has taken a nap after dinner*—*enters the dining room combing his beard, then sits down at the table and takes a newspaper from his pocket*]

MASHA   So, he arrives. . . . Has he paid anything on his apartment?

IRINA (*Laughing*)   No. For eight months, not a kopeck. Evidently he's forgotten.

MASHA (*Laughing*)   How grandly he sits there! (EVERY-BODY *laughs. A pause.*)

IRINA   Why are you so silent, Alexander Ignatich?

VERSHININ   I don't know. I'd like some tea. I'd sell my soul for a glass of tea! I've had nothing to eat since breakfast. . . .

CHEBUTYKIN   Irina Sergeevna!

IRINA   What is it?

CHEBUTYKIN   Please come here. *Venez ici*! (IRINA *goes and sits down at the table*) I simply cannot do without you.

VERSHININ   Well, if they won't give us any tea, at least let's philosophize.

TUZENBACH   Yes, let's. What about?

VERSHININ   What about? Let's dream . . . for instance,

about the life that will come after us, in two or three hundred years.

TUZENBACH   Well, after us they'll fly in balloons, their clothes will be different, they'll discover a sixth sense, maybe and then develop it; but life will stay the same, a difficult life, full of mysteries, and happy. And in a thousand years people will be sighing, the same as now: "Ah, life is hard!"—and along with that, exactly the same as now, they'll be frightened of death and not want to die.

VERSHININ (*After a moment's thought*)   How shall I put it? It seems to me that everything on earth must change, little by little, and that it is already changing before our eyes. In two or three hundred, in a thousand years—the length of time doesn't matter—a new and happy life will come. We can have no share in it, of course, but we are living for it, working for it, yes, suffering for it: we are creating it—and in that and in that alone is the aim of our existence and, if you wish, our happiness. (MASHA *laughs softly*)

TUZENBACH   What's the matter with you?

MASHA   I don't know. All day today, ever since morning, I've been laughing.

VERSHININ   I finished school there where you did, I didn't go on to the Academy; I read a lot, but I don't know how to choose the books, and what I read, maybe, isn't exactly what I need to read. But the longer I live the more I want to know. My hair's getting gray, I'm an old man, almost, and yet I know so little, oh, so little! Still, though, it seems to me that what matters most, what's absolutely essential—that I do know, and know very well. If only I could make you see that there *is* no happiness, that there should not be, and that there will not be, for us. . . . We must only work and work, and happiness— that is the lot of our remote descendants. (*A pause*) Not mine but, at least, that of the descendants of my descendants.

> [FEDOTIK *and* RODE *appear in the dining room;* THEY *sit down and softly begin to sing, one of them playing on the guitar*]

TUZENBACH According to you, we ought not even to dream of happiness! But suppose I *am* happy?
VERSHININ No.
TUZENBACH (*Throwing up his hands and laughing*) Obviously we don't understand each other. Well, how am I going to convince you? (MASHA *laughs softly*)
TUZENBACH (*Showing her his finger*) Laugh! (*To* VERSHININ) Not just in two or three hundred but in a million years, even, life will be the same: it doesn't change, it goes on the same as ever, obeying laws of its own— laws that are none of our business or, anyhow, that we'll never be able to discover. Migratory birds, cranes for instance, fly and fly, and no matter what thoughts, great or small, wander into their heads, they'll still keep on flying, they don't know where, they don't know why. They fly and will fly, no matter what philosophers appear among them; and they can philosophize as much as they please, just so long as they still fly.
MASHA But still, it means something?
TUZENBACH Means something. . . . Look, it's snowing. What does that mean? (*A pause*)

MASHA   It seems to me a man must believe or search for
some belief, or else his life is empty, empty. . . . To live
and not know why the cranes fly, why children are born,
why there are stars in the sky. . . . Either you know what
you're living for or else it's all nonsense, hocus-pocus.
VERSHININ   Still, it's a pity one's youth is over.
MASHA   Gogol says: Life on this earth is a dull proposition,
gentlemen! I give up.
CHEBUTYKIN (*Reading a newspaper*)   Balzac was married
in Berdichev. (IRINA *softly begins to sing*) I really ought
to write that down in my book. (HE *writes it down*)
Balzac was married in Berdichev. (HE *reads his newspaper*)
IRINA (*Pensively, as* SHE *lays out the cards for solitaire*)
Balzac was married in Berdichev.
TUZENBACH   The die is cast. You know, I've handed in
my resignation, Marya Sergeevna.
MASHA   So I hear. But I don't see anything good about
that. I don't like civilians.
TUZENBACH   What's the difference? . . . (HE *gets up*)
I'm not handsome, what sort of soldier am I? Well,
anyway, what's the difference? . . . I'm going to work. If
only for one day in my life, work so that I come home
at night, fall in bed exhausted, and go right to sleep. (HE
goes into the dining room) Surely workmen must sleep
soundly!
FEDOTIK   I got these crayons for you—on Moscow
Street, at Pyzikov's. . . . And this little penknife. . . .
IRINA   You keep on treating me as if I were a little girl,
but I'm grown up now, you know. . . . (*Taking the
crayons and the knife, joyfully*) How lovely!
FEDOTIK   And I bought myself a knife. . . . Look. . . . One

blade, two, three, this is to clean your ears with, a pair of scissors, this is to clean your nails with. . . .

RODE (*Loudly*) Doctor, how old are you?

CHEBUTYKIN I? Thirty-two. (*Laughter*)

FEDOTIK I will now show you a new kind of solitaire. . . .

[HE lays out the cards.

THEY *bring in the samovar;* ANFISA *stands by it; a little later* NATASHA *comes in and begins to straighten things on the table;* SOLYONY *enters, is greeted, and sits down at the table.*]

VERSHININ What a wind!

MASHA Yes. I'm bored with winter. I've forgotten what summer's like.

IRINA I'm going to go out, I can see it. We're going to get to Moscow!

FEDOTIK No it's not—see, that eight's on the deuce of spades. (HE *laughs*) So you're not going to get to Moscow.

CHEBUTYKIN (*Reading the newspaper*) Tsitsikar. Small-pox is raging here.

ANFISA (*Going up to* MASHA) Masha, have some tea, darling. (*To* VERSHININ) Please, your honor. . . . Excuse me, sir, I've forgotten your name. . . .

MASHA Bring it over here, nurse. I'm not going there.

IRINA Nurse!

ANFISA Coming-g!

NATASHA (*To* SOLYONY) Babies, little babies still at the breast—they understand perfectly. "Good morning, Bobik!" I say. "Good morning, sweetheart!" Then he looks up at me in a very special way. You think I'm just saying

that because I'm a mother, but that isn't so, no indeed
it isn't so! He really is the most amazing child.
Solyony   If that child were mine I'd fry him in a frying
pan and then eat him.

[He *picks up his glass, goes into the living room, and
sits down in a corner*]

Natasha (*Covering her face with her hands*)   Rude,
common man!
Masha   If you're happy you don't notice whether it's
summer or winter. It seems to me that if I were in Moscow
I wouldn't care what the weather was like.
Vershinin   The other day I was reading the diary of
some French cabinet minister—he's been sent to prison
because of that Panama affair. With what rapture, with
what delight he describes the birds he sees from the window
of his cell . . . birds he'd never noticed in the days when
he was a minister. Now that they've let him out again,
of course, it's the same as it used to be: he doesn't notice
the birds. Just as when you live in Moscow again, you
won't notice it. We aren't happy, we never will be, we
only long to be.
Tuzenbach (*Picking up a box from the table*)   What's
become of the candy?
Irina   Solyony ate it.
Tuzenbach   All of it?
Anfisa (*Serving tea*)   A letter for you, sir.
Vershinin   For me? (He *takes the letter*) From my
daughter. (He *reads*) Yes, of course. . . . Forgive me,
Marya Sergeevna, I'll slip out quietly. No tea for me.
(He *gets up, disturbed*) The same old story. . . .
Masha   What is it? It's not a secret?

VERSHININ (*In a low voice*) My wife's poisoned herself again. I must go. I'll slip out so no one will notice. All this is horribly unpleasant. (HE *kisses* MASHA'S *hand*) My good, darling, wonderful woman. . . . I'll just slip out quietly. . . .

ANFISA Where on earth's he going now? After I've poured him out his tea. . . . If he isn't a . . .

MASHA (*Losing her temper*) Stop it! Bothering every-body to death, you never give us a moment's peace. . . . (SHE *goes over to the table with her cup*) I'm bored with you, old woman!

ANFISA What are you so mad about? Darling girl!

ANDREI'S VOICE (*Offstage*) Anfisa!

ANFISA (*Mimicking him*) Anfisa! There he sits . . .

[SHE *goes out*]

MASHA (*By the table in the dining room, angrily*) Let me sit down! (SHE *mixes up the cards on the table*) Sprawling all over the place with your cards. Drink your tea!

IRINA Masha, you're just mean.

MASHA Well if I'm mean don't talk to me. Don't bother me!

CHEBUTYKIN (*Laughing*) Don't bother her, don't bother her. . . .

MASHA You're sixty years old and yet you behave like a spoiled child, always jabbering the devil knows what. . . .

NATASHA (SHE *sighs*) Dear Masha, why *must* you use such expressions in conversation? With your looks you'd be simply fascinating in society if only it weren't for these—I'm going to be frank with you—for these expres-sions of yours. Excuse me for mentioning it, Masha, but your manners *are* a little coarse.

TUZENBACH (*Trying to keep from laughing*)   Give
me . . . Give me . . . It seems to me there's some cognac
somewhere. . . .

NATASHA   It looks like my little Bobik isn't asleep any
more, he's waked up. He isn't well today. I must go to
him, excuse me. . . .

[SHE *goes out*]

IRINA   And where's Alexander Ignatich gone?

MASHA   Home. Something about his wife again—something odd.

TUZENBACH (*Going over to* SOLYONY *with a decanter of
cognac*)   You always sit by yourself thinking about
something, and there's no telling what it is. Come on, let's
make peace. Let's have some cognac. (THEY *drink*) I'll
have to play the piano all night tonight, I expect—all sorts
of trash. . . . Well, come what may!

SOLYONY   Why make peace? I'm not mad at you.

TUZENBACH   You always give me the feeling that something's gone wrong between us. You're a strange character, you've got to admit it.

SOLYONY (*Declaiming*)   I am strange, and yet, who is not
strange? Ah, be not wroth, Aleko!

TUZENBACH   You see! How'd that Aleko get in? (*A pause*)

SOLYONY   When I'm alone with anybody I'm all right,
I'm just like everybody else, but when there are people
around I get depressed and shy and . . . just talk nonsense.
But just the same, I'm more honest and sincere than lots
of people—lots and lots of people. And I can prove it.

TUZENBACH   I'm always getting angry at you, you keep
bothering me so when there're other people around,

but I like you just the same . . . why I don't know. . . .
Come what may, I'm going to get drunk tonight. Let's
have another!

SOLYONY   Yes, let's! (HE *drinks*) I never have had anything against you, Baron. But I have a disposition like
Lermontov's. . . . (*In a low voice*) I even look a little like
Lermontov . . . so I'm told. . . . (HE *takes a bottle of
perfume from his pocket and sprinkles some over his hands*)

TUZENBACH   I've sent in my resignation. Finished! For
five years I've been thinking about it and at last I've made
up my mind. I'm going to work.

SOLYONY (*Declaiming*)   Ah, be not wroth, Aleko. . . .
Forget, forget thy dreams. . . .

[*While* THEY *are talking* ANDREI *comes in quietly, a
book in his hand, and sits down by a candle*]

TUZENBACH   I'm going to work.

CHEBUTYKIN (*Coming into the living room with* IRINA)
And besides that, they had real Caucasian food for me—
onion soup, and for the meat course *chekhartma.*

SOLYONY   *Cheremsha* isn't meat at all, it's a vegetable
like an onion.

CHEBUTYKIN   No indeed, my angel. . . . *Chekhartma*
isn't onion, it's roast lamb.

SOLYONY   And I tell you, *cheremsha's* onion.

CHEBUTYKIN   And I tell you, *chekhartma's* lamb.

SOLYONY   And I tell you, *cheremsha's* onion.

CHEBUTYKIN   What's the use of arguing with you! You
never were in the Caucasus, you never ate any *chekhartma.*

SOLYONY   I never ate it because I hate it. *Cheremsha*
smells—it smells like garlic.

ANDREI (*Imploringly*)   That's enough, gentlemen! I beg
you.

TUZENBACH   When are the carnival people coming?

IRINA   They promised about nine—and that means any
minute.

TUZENBACH (*Embracing* ANDREI *and singing*)   "O my
porch, O my porch, O my new porch . . ."

ANDREI (*Dancing and singing*)   "My new porch, my
maple porch . . ."

CHEBUTYKIN (*Dancing*)   "Porch with my new trellis!"
(*Laughter*)

TUZENBACH (*Embracing* ANDREI)   Ah, the devil take it,
let's have a drink! Old Andrei, let's drink to our eternal
friendship! And Andrei, I'm going right along to Moscow
with you, to the University.

SOLYONY   To which university? There's two universities
in Moscow.

ANDREI   There's one university in Moscow.

SOLYONY   And I tell you, there're two.

ANDREI   There can be three for all I care. The more the
better.

SOLYONY   There're two universities in Moscow! (*Murmurs
of protest; people say,* "*Ssh!*") There're two universities
in Moscow, the old one and the new one. And if you
don't want to listen to me, if my words annoy you, then
I don't have to talk. I can even go in the other room. . . .

[HE *goes out through one of the doors*]

TUZENBACH   Bravo, bravo! (HE *laughs*) Get ready,
ladies and gentlemen, I'm about to sit down at the piano!
That Solyony, he's a funny one!

[HE *sits down at the piano and plays a waltz*]

MASHA (*Waltzing by herself*) The Ba-ron's drunk, the
Ba-ron's drunk, the Ba-a-ron is dru-unk! (NATASHA
comes in)
NATASHA (*To* CHEBUTYKIN) Ivan Romanich!

[SHE *speaks about something with* CHEBUTYKIN, *then
quietly goes out.* CHEBUTYKIN *touches* TUZENBACH *on
the shoulder and whispers to him.*]

IRINA What's the matter?
CHEBUTYKIN It's time we were going. Good-bye.
TUZENBACH Good night. Time we were going.
IRINA But—but what do you mean? What about the
carnival people?
ANDREI (*Embarrassed*) There aren't going to be any
carnival people. You see, my dear, Natasha says that Bobik
doesn't feel very good, and so . . . To tell the truth, I
don't know anything about it, it doesn't make any difference to me.
IRINA (*Shrugging her shoulders*) Bobik doesn't feel good!
MASHA Oh, what's the difference! If they run us out,
then we've got to go. (*To* IRINA) There's nothing wrong
with Bobik, there's something wrong with her. . . . Here!
(SHE *taps her forehead*) Common little creature!

[ANDREI *goes into his room;* CHEBUTYKIN *follows him;
in the dining room* THEY *are saying good-bye*]

FEDOTIK What a shame! I was counting on spending
the evening, but if the little baby's sick then of course . . .
Tomorrow I'll bring him a little toy. . . .

RODE (*Loudly*)   I took a long nap this afternoon on purpose, just because I thought I was going to get to dance all night. Why, it's only nine o'clock!

MASHA   Let's go on out and talk things over there. We'll decide about everything.

> [*Sounds of* "*Good night!*" "*Good-bye!*" TUZENBACH *is heard laughing gaily.* EVERYONE *goes out.* ANFISA *and a* MAID *clear the table and put out the lights. The* NURSE *is heard singing.* ANDREI, *in a hat and overcoat, and* CHEBUTYKIN *come in.*]

CHEBUTYKIN   I never did manage to get married, because life's gone by me like lightning, and because I was crazy about your mother and she was married. . . .

ANDREI   People shouldn't get married. They shouldn't because it's boring.

CHEBUTYKIN   Maybe so, maybe so, but the loneliness! You can philosophize as much as you please, but loneliness is a terrible thing, Andrei boy. . . . Though on the other hand, really . . . of course, it doesn't make any difference one way or the other!

ANDREI   Let's hurry.

CHEBUTYKIN   What's the hurry? We'll make it.

ANDREI   I'm afraid my wife might stop me.

CHEBUTYKIN   Oh!

ANDREI   Tonight I won't play any myself, I'll just sit and watch. I don't feel very good. . . . Sometimes I feel as if I had asthma—what should I do for it, Ivan Romanich?

CHEBUTYKIN   Why ask me? *I* don't remember, Andrei boy. I don't know. . . .

ANDREI   Let's go out through the kitchen.

[THEY *go out. A ring, then another ring; voices and laughter.* IRINA *enters.*]

IRINA   What's that?

ANFISA (*Whispering*)   The carnival people! (*Another ring*)

IRINA   Nurse dear, tell them there isn't anyone at home. They'll have to excuse us.

[ANFISA *goes out.* IRINA *walks back and forth, lost in thought;* SHE *seems disturbed.* SOLYONY *comes in.*]

SOLYONY (*Perplexed*)   Nobody here. . . . Where is everybody?

IRINA   Gone home.

SOLYONY   That's funny. You're alone here?

IRINA   Alone. (*A pause*) Good-bye.

SOLYONY   A little while ago I lost control of myself, I wasn't tactful. But you are different from the rest of them, you are exalted, pure, you see the truth. . . . You are the only one there is that can understand me. I love you so, I'll love you to the end of—

IRINA   Good-bye. Go away.

SOLYONY   I can't live without you. (*Following her*) Oh, my ideal! (*Through his tears*) Oh, bliss! Those marvelous, glorious, incredible eyes—eyes like no other woman's I've ever seen. . . .

IRINA (*Coldly*)   Stop it, Vasili Vasilich!

SOLYONY   For the first time I'm speaking to you of love, and it's as if I were no longer on this earth, but on another planet. (HE *runs his hand across his forehead*) Well, it doesn't make any difference. I can't make you love me,

of course. . . . But rivals, happy rivals—I can't stand
those . . . can't stand them. I swear to you by all that is
holy, I shall kill any rival. . . . Oh, wonderful one!

[NATASHA *comes in, a candle in her hand.* SHE *looks
into one room, then into another, but walks by her*
HUSBAND's *door without stopping.*]

NATASHA There Andrei is. Let him read! Excuse me,
Vasili Vasilich, I hadn't any idea you were in here. I'm not
dressed.
SOLYONY It doesn't make any difference to me. Good-
bye!

[HE *goes out*]

NATASHA And you're tired, dear—my poor little girl!
(SHE *kisses* IRINA) If only you would go to bed a little
earlier!
IRINA Is Bobik asleep?
NATASHA Asleep. But not sound asleep. By the way, dear,
I keep meaning to speak to you about it, but either
you're not home or else I haven't the time. . . . It seems
to me that it's so cold and damp for Bobik in the nursery
he has now. And your room is simply ideal for a child.
My darling, my precious, do move in with Olga for a while!
IRINA (*Not understanding*) Where?

[*A troika with bells is heard driving up to the house*]

NATASHA You and Olga will be in one room, for the
time being, and your room will be for Bobik. He's such a
little dear, this morning I said to him, "Bobik, you're
mine! Mine!" And he looked up at me with those darling

little eyes of his. (*A ring*) That must be Olga. How late she is!

[A MAID *comes in and whispers in* NATASHA'S *ear*]

NATASHA   Protopopov! What a funny man! Protopov's here and wants me to go for a ride in his troika with him. (SHE *laughs*) Men are so funny! (*A ring*) Someone else's come. I suppose I might go, just for a few minutes. (*To the* MAID) Tell him just a minute. . . . (*A ring*) There's that doorbell again, it must be Olga.

[SHE *goes out*]

[*The* MAID *runs out;* IRINA *sits thinking;* KULYGIN *and* OLGA *enter,* VERSHININ *just behind*]

KULYGIN   Well, this is a fine state of affairs! And they said they were going to have a party!

VERSHININ   Strange. I left a little while ago, a half hour ago, and they were expecting the carnival people.

IRINA   They've all gone.

KULYGIN   And Masha's gone too? Where's she gone? And why's Protopopov waiting down there in his troika? Who's he waiting for?

IRINA   Don't ask questions. . . . I'm tired.

KULYGIN   Little crosspatch!

OLGA   The meeting lasted till just this minute. I'm exhausted. Our headmistress is ill and I've had to take her place. My head, how my head aches, my head . . . (SHE *sits down*) Andrei lost two hundred rubles yesterday, playing cards. Everybody in town is talking about it. . . .

KULYGIN   Yes, and I got tired at the meeting, too.

VERSHININ   My wife decided to give me a scare just

now, she almost poisoned herself. Everything's turned out all right, and I certainly am glad—I can relax now. . . . Then of course, we ought to leave? Well then, let me wish you good-bye. Fyodor Ilich, come somewhere with me! I can't go home tonight, I absolutely can't. . . . Come on!

KULYGIN   I am tired. I'm not going. (HE *gets up*) I am tired. Has my wife gone home?

IRINA   I suppose so.

KULYGIN (*Kissing* IRINA's *hand*)   Good-bye. Tomorrow and the day after tomorrow I'm going to rest all day long. Good-bye! (HE *goes*) I surely would like some tea. I'd been counting on spending the evening in congenial company and—O, *fallacem hominum spem!* Accusative of exclamation. . . .

VERSHININ   It means I go by myself.

[HE *goes out with* KULYGIN, *whistling*]

OLGA   My head aches, my head . . . Andrei's lost—everybody in town's talking about it. . . . I'll go lie down. (SHE *starts to go*) Tomorrow I'm free. . . . O my God, what a relief that is! Tomorrow I'm free, the day after tomorrow I'm free. . . . My head aches, my head . . .

[SHE *goes out*]

IRINA (*Alone*)   They've all gone. There's no one left.

[*An accordion is heard in the street, the* NURSE *is singing in the next room*]

NATASHA (*Crossing the dining room in a fur coat and cap, followed by a* MAID)   I'll be back in half an hour. I'll only go for a short drive.

[SHE *goes out*]

IRINA (*Alone; yearningly*)   To Moscow! To Moscow!
To Moscow!

CURTAIN

ACT III

Olga's and irina's room. to the left and right *are beds, with screens around them. It is past two o'clock in the morning. Offstage a fire bell is being rung, for a fire that began a long time ago. No one in the house has gone to bed yet.* Masha *is lying on the sofa, dressed as usual in a black dress.* Olga *and* Anfisa *come in.*

Anfisa They're down there now, just sitting by the stairs. I said, "Come upstairs. Please," I said, "you can't just sit here like this!"—they were crying. "Papa," they said, "we don't know where he is—" they said, "Maybe he's burned to death." What a thing to think of! And there're some people in the yard—they're not dressed either. . . .

Olga (*Taking dresses from a wardrobe*) Here, this gray one, take it . . . and this one here . . . the blouse, too. . . . And this skirt—take it, nurse dear. . . . My God, what a thing to happen—all Kirsanov Street's burned down, evidently. . . . Take this. . . . Take this. . . . (She *piles the clothes in* Anfisa's *arms*) The Vershinins, poor things, certainly did get a fright. . . . Their house nearly burned down. They must spend the night here with us. . . . We can't send them home. . . . Poor Fedotik's had everything he owns burnt, there isn't a thing left. . . .

ANFISA   You'll have to call Ferapont, Olga darling, or
else I can't carry it. . . .
OLGA (*Ringing*)   Nobody answers. (SHE *calls through
the door*) Come here, whoever's down there. (*A window,
red with the glow of the fire, can be seen through the
open door; the fire department is heard going past the
house*) How terrible it all is! And how sick of it I am!

[FERAPONT *comes in*]

OLGA   Here, take these downstairs. . . . The Kelotilin
girls are down there by the staircase—give them to them.
Give them this, too. . . .
FERAPONT   Yes'm. In the year '12 Moscow burned too.
Good God Almighty! The Frenchmen were flabbergasted.
OLGA   Go on, get along. . . .
FERAPONT   Yes'm.

[HE *goes out*]

OLGA   Nurse darling, give it all away. We don't need
anything, give it all away, nurse. . . . I'm so tired I can
hardly stand on my feet. . . . We *can't* allow the Vershinins
to go home. The little girls can sleep in the living room,
and put Alexander Ignatich downstairs at the Baron's . . .
Fedotik at the Baron's, too, or else in our dining room.
. . . The Doctor's drunk, terribly drunk, just as if he'd
done it on purpose—we can't put anyone in with him.
And put Vershinin's wife in the living room too.
ANFISA (*Wearily*)   Olga darling, don't drive me away!
Don't drive me away!
OLGA   You're talking nonsense, nurse. Nobody's driving
you away.

Irina and Tuzenbach
Photograph by FRIEDMAN-ABELES

ANFISA (*Laying her head on* OLGA's *breast*) My own, treasure, I do the best I can, I do work. . . . I'm getting weak, they'll all say, "Get out!" And where is there for me to go? Where? Eighty years old . . . my eighty-second year. . . .

OLGA You sit down, nurse darling. . . . You're tired, poor thing. . . . (SHE *gets her to sit down*) Rest, my darling. How pale you look!

[NATASHA *enters*]

NATASHA They're saying we ought to organize a committee right away to aid the victims of the fire. Well, why not? It's a fine idea. After all, we ought to help the poor, that's the duty of the rich. Bobik and Baby Sophie are both sound asleep—sleeping as if nothing had happened! . . . There're people here everywhere, wherever you go the house is full of them. And there's all this flu in town now, I'm so afraid the children may catch it.

OLGA (*Not listening to her*) From this room you can't see the fire, it's peaceful here. . . .

NATASHA Uh-huh. . . . I must be a sight. (*In front of the mirror*) They keep saying I've gained. . . . And it's not so! It's not a bit so! And Masha's fast asleep—dead tired, poor thing. . . . (*To* ANFISA, *coldly*) Don't you dare sit down in my presence! Get up! Get out of here! (ANFISA *goes out. A pause*) What you keep that old woman for I simply do not understand!

OLGA (*Taken aback*) I beg your pardon, I don't understand either. . . .

NATASHA She's around here for no reason whatsoever. She's a peasant, she ought to be in the country where she

belongs. . . . It's simply spoiling them! I like for everything in the house to have its proper place! There ought
not to be these useless people cluttering up the house.
(She *strokes* Olga's *cheek*) Poor girl, you're tired. Our
headmistress is tired. When my little Sophie gets to be
a big girl and goes to the high school, I'm going to be
so afraid of you.
Olga   I'm not going to be headmistress.
Natasha   You're sure to be, Olga. It's already settled.
Olga   I won't accept. I can't . . . I'm not strong enough.
. . . (She *drinks some water*) You were so rude to nurse
just now. Forgive me, I just haven't the strength to bear
it. . . . It's getting all black before my eyes. . . .
Natasha (*Agitated*)   Forgive me, Olga, forgive me. . . .
I didn't mean to upset you.

[Masha *gets up, takes her pillow, and goes out
angrily*]

Olga   Try to understand, dear . . . perhaps we've been
brought up in an unusual way, but I can't bear this. This
sort of thing depresses me so, I get sick. . . . I just despair!
Natasha   Forgive me, forgive me. (She *kisses her*)
Olga   The least rudeness, even, an impolite word—it
upsets me. . . .
Natasha   Sometimes I do say more than I should, that's
so, but you must admit, my dear, she *could* live in the
country.
Olga   She's been with us thirty years already.
Natasha   But now she just can't do anything, you know
that! Either I don't understand you or you don't want to
understand me. She's not fit for any work, she just
sleeps or sits.

OLGA   Well, let her sit.

NATASHA (*Surprised*)   What do you mean, let her sit? Why, she's a servant. (*Tearfully*) I simply cannot understand you, Olga. I've got a nurse, a wet nurse, we've got a maid, we've got a cook. . . . What do we have to have that old woman for too? What *for*?

[*Behind the scene a fire alarm rings*]

OLGA   Tonight I have aged ten years.

NATASHA   We've got to settle things, Olga. You're at the high school, I'm at home; you have the teaching, and I have the housekeeping. And if I say something about the servants, I know what I'm talking about: *I—know —what—I'm—talking—about* . . . and tomorrow morning that old thief, that old wretch (SHE *stamps her foot*), that witch is going to be out of this house! Don't you dare irritate me! Don't you dare! (*Collecting herself*) Honestly, if you don't move downstairs we'll be quarreling like this for the rest of our lives. This is awful!

[KULYGIN *comes in*]

KULYGIN   Where's Masha? It's time to go home. They say the fire's dying down. (HE *stretches*) In spite of all the wind, only one block's burned—at first it looked as if the whole town would burn. (HE *sits down*) I am exhausted, Olga my dear. . . . I often think if it hadn't been Masha I'd have married you, Olga dear. You have such a generous nature. . . . I am exhausted. (HE *listens for something*)

OLGA   What is it?

KULYGIN   As if he'd done it on purpose, the Doctor's got drunk, he's terribly drunk. As if he'd done it on purpose!

(HE *gets up*) I do believe he's coming up here. . . .
Hear him? Yes, up here. . . . (HE *laughs*) If he isn't the
. . . I'll hide. (HE *goes to the wardrobe and stands between
it and the wall*) What a rascal!
OLGA   For two years he doesn't drink, and now all of
a sudden he goes and gets drunk. . . .

[SHE *follows* NATASHA *to the back of the room.*

CHEBUTYKIN *enters; without staggering, like a sober
person,* HE *crosses the room, stops, looks around, then
goes to the washbasin and begins to wash his hands.*]

CHEBUTYKIN (*Gloomily*)   The devil take every one of
them . . . every one of them. . . . They think I'm a
doctor, know how to treat anything there is, and I don't
know a thing, I've forgotten everything I ever did know,
I remember nothing, absolutely nothing.

[OLGA *and* NATASHA *leave the room without his
noticing*]

CHEBUTYKIN   The devil take them. Last Wednesday I
treated a woman at Zasyp—dead, and it's my fault she's
dead. Yes. . . . Twenty-five years ago I used to know a
little something, but now I don't remember a thing. One
single thing. Maybe I'm not a man at all, but just look
like one—maybe it just looks like I've got arms and legs
and a head. Maybe I don't even exist, and it only looks like
I walk and eat and sleep. (HE *cries*) Oh, if only I didn't
exist! (HE *stops crying; gloomily*) The devil only knows.
. . . Day before yesterday they were talking at the club;
they talked about Shakespeare, Voltaire. . . . I haven't
read them, I never have read them at all, but I looked
like I'd read them. And the others did too, the same as me.

So cheap! So low! And that woman I killed Wednesday—
she came back to me, and it all came back to me, and
everything inside me felt all twisted, all vile, all nauseating.
. . . I went and got drunk. . . .

[IRINA, VERSHININ, *and* TUZENBACH *come in;* TUZEN-
BACH *is wearing new and stylish civilian clothes*]

IRINA   Let's sit in here. Nobody will be coming in here.
VERSHININ   If it hadn't been for the soldiers the whole
town would have burnt up. Brave men, those! (HE *rubs
his hands with pleasure*) The salt of the earth! Ah,
those are first-rate men!
KULYGIN (*Going up to them*)   What's the time, gentle-
men?
TUZENBACH   Going on four. It's getting light.
IRINA   They're all sitting there in the dining room, nobody
thinks of leaving, and that Solyony of yours sits there.
. . . (*To* CHEBUTYKIN) Oughtn't you to go to bed,
Doctor?
CHEBUTYKIN   Doesn't matter. . . . Thank you. . . . (HE
combs his beard)
KULYGIN (*Laughing*)   You're tight, Ivan Romanich!
(HE *slaps him on the back*) Bravo! *In vino veritas,* as
the ancients used to say.
TUZENBACH   Everybody keeps asking me to get up a
concert to help the people whose houses burned.
IRINA   Yes, but who's there to . . . ?
TUZENBACH   We could arrange one if we wanted to.
Marya Sergeevna, in my opinion, is a wonderful pianist.
KULYGIN   Yes indeed, wonderful.
IRINA   She's forgotten how, by now. She hasn't played
for three years—four.

TUZENBACH   Here in this town there is not a soul who understands music, not a single soul; but I, I do understand it, and I give you my word of honor that Marya Sergeevna plays magnificently, almost with genius.

KULYGIN   You're right, Baron. I love her very much, Masha. She's wonderful.

TUZENBACH   To be able to play so beautifully and all the time to know that no one, no one, understands you!

KULYGIN   (*Sighing*)   Yes. . . . But would it be proper for her to appear in a public concert? (*A pause*) Really, gentlemen, I know nothing about it. Perhaps it would be quite all right. You have to admit that our principal is a fine man, in fact a very fine man, very intelligent, too; but his views *are* a little . . . Of course, it isn't any of his affair, but just the same, if you think I ought to, I'll speak to him about it.

[CHEBUTYKIN *picks up a porcelain clock and examines it*]

VERSHININ   I got all covered with dirt at the fire—I look pretty disreputable. (*A pause*) Yesterday just by accident I heard someone say that they may be sending our brigade a long way off—some of them said to Poland, some of them said to Siberia, to Chita.

TUZENBACH   I heard that too. Well, what is there you can do? The town will be completely empty.

IRINA   And we'll leave too!

CHEBUTYKIN   (*Drops the clock, smashing it*)   To smithereens!

[*A pause; everyone looks embarrassed and upset*]

KULYGIN   (*Picking up the pieces*)   To break such an expensive thing—oh, Ivan Romanich, Ivan Romanich! You get a zero-minus in deportment!

IRINA   That's Mother's clock.
CHEBUTYKIN   Maybe. . . . If it's Mother's, then it's
Mother's. Maybe I didn't break it but it only looks like
I broke it. Maybe it only looks like we exist, and really we
don't. I don't know anything, nobody knows anything.
(*At the door*) What are you staring at? Natasha's having
an affair with Protopopov, and you don't see that.
You sit there and see nothing, and Natasha's having an
affair with Protopopov. . . . (*Singing*) "Tell me how
you like this little present!"

[HE *goes out*]

VERSHININ   Yes. . . . (HE *laughs*) How strange all this
is, in reality! When the fire started I rushed home; I got
there, looked around . . . the house was safe and sound,
not in any danger at all, but there my two little girls
were, standing in the doorway in just their underwear, their
mother gone, people rushing around, horses running by,
dogs, and my little girls' faces were so anxious and
terrified and beseeching and—I don't know what; it wrung
my heart to look at those faces. My God, I thought,
what these girls still have to go through in the rest of their
lives, in all the years to come! I picked them up and ran,
and I kept thinking one thing: what they still have to
live through in this world! (*Fire alarm; a pause*) I got here
and here was their mother—she was shouting, she got
angry.

[MASHA *comes in with the pillow and sits down on the
sofa*]

VERSHININ   And while my little girls were standing in
the doorway in just their underwear, and the street

was red with the fire, the noise was terrible, I started thinking that it's almost what happened long ago, when the enemy attacked unexpectedly, looting and burning. ... And yet, in reality, what a difference there is between what things are now and what they were then! And when a little more time has passed, two or three hundred years, people will look in horror and mockery at this life we live now, and everything we do now will seem to them clumsy, and difficult, and terribly uncomfortable and strange. Oh, what life will be like then! What life will be like then! (HE *laughs*) Sorry, I've started philosophizing again. But do let me go on, ladies and gentlemen. I feel terribly like philosophizing, I'm in just the right frame of mind. (*A pause*) Looks like they're all asleep. So I say: What life will be like then! Can you imagine! Here in this town there are only three of your kind now, but in the generations to come there will be more and more and more; the time will come when everything will get to be the way you want it to be, everybody will live like you, and then after a while you yourselves will be out-of-date, there'll be people born who'll be better than you. . . . (HE *laughs*) I'm in a most peculiar frame of mind tonight. I want like the devil to live. (HE *sings*) "Unto love all ages bow, its pangs are blest . . ."

MASHA   Da-da-dum . . .

VERSHININ   Da-dum . . .

MASHA   Da-da-da?

VERSHININ   Da-da-da! (HE *laughs*)

[FEDOTIK *comes in*]

FEDOTIK (*Dancing*)   Burnt to ashes! Burnt to ashes! Everything I had in this world! (*Laughter*)

IRINA   What kind of joke is that? Is it really all burnt?
FEDOTIK (*Laughing*)   Every single last thing! There's
not one thing left! The guitar's burnt, and the camera
burnt, and all my letters are burnt. . . . And I meant to
give you a little notebook, and it's burnt too. . . .
   [SOLYONY *enters*]
IRINA   No, please go away, Vasili Vasilich. You can't
come in here.
SOLYONY   But why is it the Baron can and I can't?
VERSHININ   We ought to be going, really. How's the
fire?
SOLYONY   They say it's dying down. No, it's a very
strange thing to me, why is it the Baron can and I can't?
(HE *takes out a bottle of perfume and sprinkles it on
himself*)
VERSHININ   Da-da-dum?
MASHA   Da-dum!
VERSHININ (*Laughing, to* SOLYONY)   Let's go on in the
dining room.
SOLYONY   All right, but there'll be a note made of this.
"This moral could be made more clear. But 'twould
annoy the geese, I fear." (HE looks at TUZENBACH)
He-ere, chicky, chicky, chicky!

   [HE *goes out with* VERSHININ *and* FEDOTIK]

IRINA   That Solyony! There's smoke all over everything. . . . (*In surprise*) The Baron's asleep! Baron! Baron!
TUZENBACH (*Waking up*)   I'm tired, only I . . . the
brickyard . . . I'm not delirious, I really am going to
start work there soon. . . . I've already talked it over with
them. (*To* IRINA, *tenderly*) You're so pale and beautiful
and enchanting. . . . It seems to me your paleness brightens

the dark air like light . . . You're sad, you're dissatisfied
with life. . . . Oh, come away with me, let's go and work
together!

MASHA Nikolai Lvovich, go away from here!

TUZENBACH (*Laughing*) You're here? I didn't see you.
(HE *kisses* IRINA's *hand*) Good-bye, I'm going. I look
at you now, and it reminds me of how long ago on your
birthday you were so happy and cheerful, and talked
about the joy of work. . . . And what a happy life I saw
before me then! Where is it? (HE *kisses her hand*) You
have tears in your eyes. Go to bed, it's already getting
light. . . . It's beginning to be morning. . . . If only I
might give my life for you!

MASHA Nikolai Lvovich, go away! Why, really, what . . .

TUZENBACH I'm going.

[HE *goes out*]

MASHA (*Lying down*) Are you asleep, Fyodor?

KULYGIN What?

MASHA You should go home.

KULYGIN My darling Masha, my precious Masha . . .

IRINA She's worn out. . . . Let her rest, Fyodor dear.

KULYGIN I'll go in just a minute. My good, wonderful
wife . . . I love you, my only one. . . .

MASHA (*Angrily*) *Amo, amas, amat, amamus, amatis,
amant.*

KULYGIN (*Laughing*) No, really, she's amazing. I've
been married to you for seven years, and it seems as if we
were married only yesterday. Word of honor! No, really,
you're an amazing woman. I am satisfied, I am satisfied,
I am satisfied!

MASHA   Bored, bored, bored! ... (SHE *sits up*) I can't
get it out of my head. It's simply revolting. It sticks in
my head like a nail, I can't keep quiet about it any longer.
I mean about Andrei . . . he's mortgaged this house at
the bank and his wife's got hold of all the money. But
the house doesn't belong just to him, it belongs to the four
of us! He ought to know that if he's a decent man.
KULYGIN   Must you, MASHA? What's it to you? Poor
Andrei's in debt to everybody—well, God help him!
MASHA   Just the same, it's revolting. (SHE *lies down*)
KULYGIN   You and I aren't poor. I work, I go to the
high school, I give lessons afterwards. . . . I'm an honest
man . . . a simple man. . . . *Omnia mea mecum porto*,
as the saying goes.
MASHA   I don't need anything, but the injustice of it
nauseates me. (*A pause*) Go on, Fyodor.
KULYGIN (*Kissing her*)   You're tired, rest for half an hour,
and I'll sit there and wait. . . . Sleep. . . . (HE *starts to
leave*) I am satisfied, I am satisfied, I am satisfied.

[HE *goes out*]

IRINA   No, really, how petty our Andrei's become, how
lifeless and old he's got, at the side of that woman! Once
he was preparing to be a professor, a scholar, and yesterday
he was boasting that he's finally managed to get made
a member of the county board. He a member, Protopopov
chairman. . . . Everybody in town is talking about it,
laughing at it, and he's the only one that knows nothing,
that sees nothing. . . . And now everybody's run off to
the fire, and he sits there in his room and doesn't pay
any attention to anything, he just plays the violin.

(*Nervously*) Oh, it's awful, awful, awful! (SHE *cries*)
I can't stand any more, I can't stand it! . . . I can't, I
can't. . . .

[OLGA *comes in and begins to straighten her dressing
table*]

IRINA (*Sobbing loudly*) Throw me out, throw me out,
I can't stand any more!
OLGA (*Alarmed*) What is it, what is it? Darling!
IRINA (*Sobbing*) Where? Where's it all gone? Where
is it? Oh, my God, my God! I've forgotten everything,
forgotten . . . it's all mixed up in my head, I don't remember what *window* is in Italian, or—or *ceiling.* . . . I'm
forgetting everything, every day I forget, and life goes
by and won't ever come back, won't ever, we'll never
go to Moscow, we won't ever . . . now I see that we
won't ever . . .
OLGA Darling, darling . . .
IRINA (*Trying to control herself*) Oh, I'm miserable . . .
I can't work, I'm not ever going to work. That's enough,
that's enough! First I worked at the telegraph office,
now I work at the county board, and I hate and despise
every last thing they have me do. . . . I'm already almost
twenty-four, I've been working for years and years
already, my brain is drying up, I'm getting thin, getting
ugly, getting old, and there's nothing, nothing—there isn't
the least satisfaction of any kind—and the years are
going by, and every day, over and over, everything's
getting farther away from any real life, beautiful life,
everything's going farther and farther into some abyss. . . .
I am in despair, I can't understand how I'm alive, how
I haven't killed myself long ago. . . .

OLGA Don't cry, my own little girl, don't cry. . . .
I suffer, too.

IRINA I'm not crying, I'm not crying. . . . That's enough.
. . . See, now I'm not crying any more. . . . That's
enough, that's enough!

OLGA Darling, I tell you as your sister, as your friend:
If you want my advice, marry the Baron!

[IRINA *weeps silently*]

OLGA You know you respect him, you think so much
of him. . . . He's ugly, it's true, but he's such an honest
man, such a good man. . . . You know, people don't marry
for love, but for duty. At least, I think so, and I would
marry without being in love. If someone proposed to
me, no matter who it was, I'd marry him, as long as he
was a decent man. I'd marry an old man, even. . . .

IRINA I was always waiting till we moved to Moscow,
I'd meet the real one there—I used to dream about him,
love him. . . . But it's all turned out nonsense, all nonsense!

OLGA (*Embracing her* SISTER) My dear, beautiful sister,
I understand it all: When Baron Nikolai Lvovich left
the army and came to see us in his civilian clothes, he
looked so homely to me I absolutely started to cry. . . . He
said, "Why are you crying?" How could I tell him!
But if it were God's will he should marry you, I'd be happy.
That would be different, you know, completely different.

[NATASHA, *with a candle, comes out of the door on
the right, crosses the stage, and goes out through the
door on the left, without speaking*]

MASHA (*Sitting up*) She walks like the one that started
the fire.

OLGA Masha, you're silly. The silliest one in the whole family—that's you. Please forgive me. (*A pause*)

MASHA I want to confess, dear sisters. Inside I—I can't keep on this way any longer. I'll confess to you and then never again to anybody, never again. . . . In a minute I'll say it. (*In a low voice*) It's my secret, but you ought to know it. . . . I can't keep quiet any longer. . . . (*A pause*) I love, love . . . I love that man. . . . The one you just saw. . . . Oh, why not say it? In one word, I love Vershinin.

OLGA (*Going behind her screen*) Stop it. Anyway, I don't hear you.

MASHA What is there I can do? (SHE *holds her head in her hands*) At first he seemed strange to me, then I felt sorry for him . . . then I fell in love with him, fell in love with his voice, his words, his misfortunes, his two little girls. . . .

OLGA (*Behind the screen*) Anyway, I don't hear you. Whatever silly things you're saying, anyway, I don't hear you.

MASHA Oh, you're so silly, Olga. I love him—it means, it's my fate. It means, it's my lot. . . . And he loves me. . . . It's all so strange. Yes? It isn't good? (SHE *takes* IRINA *by the hand and draws her close to her*) Oh my darling, how are we going to live our lives, what is going to become of us? When you read some novel then it all seems so old and so easy to understand, but when you're in love yourself you see that no one knows anything, and everyone has to decide for himself. . . . My darlings, my sisters, I've confessed to you, now I'll be silent. . . . From now on I'll be like Gogol's madman . . . silence . . . silence . . .

[ANDREI *comes in, followed by* FERAPONT]

ANDREI (*Angrily*) What is it you want? I don't understand.

FERAPONT (*Standing in the doorway, impatiently*) Andrei Sergeevich, I've told you ten times already.

ANDREI In the first place, to you I am not Andrei Sergeevich, but your honor!

FERAPONT The firemen, your honor, want to know if you'll please let them go to the river through your garden. Because the way it is they have to go around and around, they're getting all worn out.

ANDREI All right. Tell them all right.

[FERAPONT *leaves*]

ANDREI What a bore! . . . Where's Olga? (OLGA *comes out from behind the screen*) I've come to get the key to the cupboard from you, I've lost mine. You've got one of those little keys. . . . [OLGA *hands him the key, without speaking.* IRINA *goes behind her screen. A pause.*) What a tremendous fire! It's started to die down now. . . . The devil, that Ferapont made me lose my temper— that was stupid to say that. . . . Your honor. . . . (*A pause*) Why don't you say something, Olga? (*A pause*) It's about time you stopped this silliness . . . pouting like this without rhyme or reason. . . . Masha, you're here, Irina's here, well, that's just fine—let's get things settled once and for all. What is it you've got against me? What is it?

OLGA Let it go now, Andrei dear. We'll straighten things out tomorrow. (*In an agitated voice*) What a dreadful night!

ANDREI (*In great confusion and embarrassment*) Don't

get all upset. I'm asking you perfectly calmly: What is
it you've got against me? Come right out with it.
VERSHININ'S VOICE (*Offstage*) Da-da-dum!
MASHA (*In a loud voice, getting up*) Da-da-dah! (*To*
OLGA) Good-bye Olga, God bless you! (SHE *goes behind*
the screen and kisses IRINA) Have a good sleep. . . .
Good-bye, Andrei. Leave them alone now, they're worn
out. . . . Tomorrow we can straighten things out.

[SHE *goes out*]

OLGA That's right, Andrei dear, let's put it off until
tomorrow. . . . (SHE *goes behind the screen on her side*
of the room) It's time to go to sleep.
ANDREI I'll only say this much and go. Right away. . . .
In the first place, you've got something against Natasha,
my wife, and I've seen that from the very first day we
were married. Natasha is a splendid, honest person, straightforward and sincere—that is my opinion. I love and
respect my wife—respect her, you understand, and I
demand that others respect her too. I repeat, she's an honest,
sincere person, and anything you've got against her, if I
may say so, is just your imagination. . . . (*A pause*) In
the second place, you seem to be angry with me because
I'm not a professor, don't in some way advance knowledge.
But I am in the service of the government, I am a member
of the county board, and this service of mine is to me just
as sacred and lofty as the service of knowledge. I am a
member of the county board and I am proud of it, if
you want to know. . . . (*A pause*) In the third place. . . .
I have something else to say. . . . I've mortgaged the house
without your permission. . . . For that I am to blame,
I admit it, and I beg you to forgive me. My debts forced

me to. . . . Thirty-five thousand. . . . I no longer play cards, gave them up long ago, but the main thing I can say to justify myself is this, that you—that you're girls, you get a pension, I, though, didn't get . . . earnings, so to speak. . . . (*A pause*)

KULYGIN (*At the door*)   Isn't Masha here? (*Anxiously*) But where is she? This is strange. . . .

[HE *goes out*]

ANDREI   They won't listen. Natasha's a splendid, honest person. (HE *walks up and down silently, then stops*) When I got married I thought we'd be happy . . . all of us happy . . . but my God! . . . (HE *cries*) My dearest sisters, darling sisters, don't believe me, don't believe . . .

[HE *goes out*]

KULYGIN (*at the door anxiously*)   Where's Masha? Isn't Masha here? What an extraordinary thing!

[HE *goes out*]

[*Fire alarm; the stage is empty*]

IRINA (*Behind the screen*)   Olga! Who's that knocking on the floor?

OLGA   It's the Doctor, it's Ivan Romanich. He's drunk.

IRINA   What a miserable night! (*A pause*) Olga! (SHE *looks out from behind the screen*) Did you hear? They're taking the brigade away from us, sending it way off somewhere.

OLGA   It's only a rumor.

IRINA   Then we'll be left all alone. . . . Olga!

OLGA   Well?

IRINA   Dearest sister, darling sister, I respect the Baron,

I admire the Baron, he's a marvelous person, I'll marry him, I agree, only let's go to Moscow! Let's go, oh please let's go! There's nothing in this world better than Moscow! Let's go, Olga! Let's go!

CURTAIN

ACT IV

THE OLD GARDEN OF THE PROZOROVS' HOUSE. AT THE *end of a long avenue of fir trees there is the river. On the other bank of the river is a forest. To the right of the house there is a terrace. Here on a table there are bottles and glasses; it is evident that they have just been drinking champagne. Occasionally people from the street cut through the garden to get to the river; five or six soldiers go through, walking fast. CHEBUTYKIN, in a genial mood which does not leave him during the act, is sitting in an easy chair in the garden; HE wears his uniform cap and is holding a walking stick. IRINA, KULYGIN with a decoration around his neck and with no moustache, and TUZENBACH are standing on the terrace saying good-bye to FEDOTIK and RODE, who are coming down the steps; both officers are in parade uniform.*

TUZENBACH (*Embracing* FEDOTIK) You're a fine man, we got along so well together. (HE *embraces* RODE) One more time. . . . Good-bye, old man. . . .
IRINA *Au revoir!*
FEDOTIK It isn't *au revoir*, it's good-bye; we'll never see each other again!
KULYGIN Who knows? (HE *wipes his eyes and smiles*)

Here I've started crying.

IRINA   Some day or other we'll meet again.

FEDOTIK   In ten years—fifteen? By then we'll hardly recognize each other, we'll say "How do you do" coldly. . . . (HE *takes a photograph*) Stand still. . . . One more time, it's the last time.

RODE (*Embracing* TUZENBACH)   We'll never see each other again. . . . (HE *kisses* IRINA's *hand*) Thank you for everything, for everything!

FEDOTIK (*Annoyed*)   Oh, stand still!

TUZENBACH   Please God, we'll see each other again. Write us now. Be sure to write us.

RODE (*Looking around the garden*)   Good-bye, trees! (HE *shouts*) Yoo-hoo! (*A pause*) Good-bye, echo!

KULYGIN   With any luck you'll get married there in Poland. . . . Your Polish wife will hug you and call you *kochany*! (HE *laughs*)

FEDOTIK (*Looking at his watch*)   We've less than an hour left. Solyony's the only one from our battery that's going on the barge, the rest of us are going with the enlisted men. Three batteries are leaving today, three more to-morrow—and then peace and quiet will descend on the town.

TUZENBACH   And awful boredom.

RODE   But where's Marya Sergeevna?

KULYGIN   Masha's in the garden.

FEDOTIK   We must say good-bye to her.

RODE   Good-bye. We must go, otherwise I'll start crying. (HE *hurriedly embraces* TUZENBACH *and* KULYGIN, *and kisses* IRINA's *hand*) It was so nice living here.

FEDOTIK (*To* KULYGIN)   This is for you to remember

us by . . . a notebook with a pencil. . . . We'll go on down to the river this way. . . .

[THEY *go off, both looking back*]

RODE (*Shouting*)   Yoo-hoo!
FEDOTIK (*Shouting*)   Good-bye!

[*At the back of the stage* FEDOTIK *and* RODE *meet* MASHA *and say good-bye to her;* SHE *goes off with them*]

IRINA   They're gone. . . .

[SHE *sits down on the bottom step of the terrace*]

CHEBUTYKIN   And forgot to say good-bye to me.
IRINA   And what about you?
CHEBUTYKIN   Well, I forgot, somehow. Anyway, I'll be seeing them again soon, I'm leaving tomorrow. Yes. . . . Only one more day. In a year more they'll retire me, I'll come back again and live out the rest of my days near you. . . . Only one more year and I get my pension. . . . (HE *puts a newspaper in his pocket, takes a newspaper out of his pocket*) I'll come back here to you and lead a completely new life. I'll get to be such a sober, Gu-Gu-God-fearing, respectable man.
IRINA   Yes, you really ought to, my dove. Somehow or other you ought.
CHEBUTYKIN   Yes. I feel so. (HE *begins to sing softly*) Ta-ra-ra-boom-de-aye . . . / Sit on a log I may . . .
KULYGIN   You're incorrigible, Ivan Romanich! You're incorrigible!
CHEBUTYKIN   Yes, if only I had *you* for a teacher! Then I'd reform.

IRINA   Fyodor's shaved off his moustache. I can't bear to look at him.

KULYGIN   And what of it?

CHEBUTYKIN   I could say what that face of yours looks like now—but I don't dare.

KULYGIN   Well, what of it? It's the accepted thing, it's the *modus vivendi*. . . . Our principal's shaved off his moustache, so when they made me the assistant principal I shaved mine off too. Nobody likes it, but it doesn't make any difference to me. I am satisfied. With a moustache or without a moustache, I am satisfied. . . .

[HE *sits down.*

ANDREI *walks across the back of the stage, wheeling a baby carriage with the baby asleep in it.*]

IRINA   Ivan Romanich, my dove, my darling, I'm terribly worried. You were on the boulevard yesterday, tell me, what happened there?

CHEBUTYKIN   What happened? Nothing. Piffle! (HE *reads the newspaper*) What's the difference!

KULYGIN   What they say is that Solyony and the Baron met each other yesterday on the boulevard, up by the theater—

TUZENBACH   Stop it! Why, really, what . . .

[HE *waves his hand and goes into the house*]

KULYGIN   Up by the theater . . . Solyony started bothering the Baron, and the Baron wouldn't stand for it, he said something insulting . . .

CHEBUTYKIN   I don't know. It's all nonsense.

KULYGIN   There was a teacher in some seminary that wrote *Nonsense!* on a theme, and the pupil thought it

was *Nonesuch!*—thought it was Latin. (HE *laughs*)
Amazingly funny! They say it looks like Solyony's in love
with Irina, and he hates the Baron. . . . That's understandable. Irina is a very nice girl. She's quite like Masha,
even—always thinking about something. Only you have
a milder disposition, Irina. Though as a matter of fact
Masha has a fine disposition too. I love her, Masha.

[*At the rear of the garden, behind the stage, someone
shouts: "Yoo-hoo!"*]

IRINA (*Shivering*)   Somehow everything frightens me
today. (*A pause*) I've got everything packed already,
I'm sending my things off right after dinner. The Baron
and I are getting married tomorrow, tomorrow we leave
for the brickyard, and day after tomorrow I'll already be
at school, the new life will have begun. Somehow God
will help me! When I passed my teacher's examination
I wept for joy . . . so grateful . . . (*A pause*) In a little
the horse and the cart will be here for my things. . . .
KULYGIN   That's all right, only somehow it isn't
serious. It's all just ideas, and hardly anything really
serious. Still, though, I wish you luck from the bottom
of my heart.
CHEBUTYKIN (*With emotion*)   My dearest, my treasure.
. . . My wonderful girl. . . . You have gone on far ahead,
I'll never catch up with you. I'm left behind like a bird
that's grown old, too old to fly. Fly on, my dears, fly on
and God be with you! (*A pause*) It's a shame you shaved
off your moustache, Fyodor Ilich.
KULYGIN   That's enough from you! (*HE sighs*) Well,
the soldiers leave today, and then everything will be the
way it used to be. No matter what they say, Masha is a

good, honest woman, I love her very much, and I'm thankful for my fate. . . . People have such different fates. . . . There's a man named Kozyrev that works in the tax department here. He went to school with me, but they expelled him from high school because he just couldn't manage to understand *ut consecutivum.* Now he's terribly poor, sick, and when we meet each other I say to him, "Hello, *ut consecutivum!*" Yes, he says, that's it, *consecutivum,* and he coughs. . . . And I've been lucky all my life, I've even got the Order of Stanislav Second Class, I myself am teaching others, now, that *ut consecutivum.* Of course, I'm an intelligent man, more intelligent than lots of people, but happiness doesn't consist in that. . . .

[*Inside the house someone plays "The Maiden's Prayer" on the piano*]

IRINA   Tomorrow evening I won't be hearing that "Maiden's Prayer" any more, I won't be meeting that Protopopov. . . . (*A pause*) And Protopopov's sitting there in the living room—he's come today too. . . .
KULYGIN   The headmistress still hasn't arrived?
IRINA   No. They've sent for her. If only you knew how hard it is for me to live here alone, without Olga. . . . She lives at the high school; she's the headmistress, all day she's busy with her job, and I'm alone, I'm bored, there's nothing to do, I hate the very room I live in. . . . So I just made up my mind: If it's fated for me not to live in Moscow, then that's that. It means, it's fate. There's nothing to be done about it. . . . It's all in God's hands, that's the truth. Nikolai Lvovich proposed to me. . . . Well? I thought it over and made up my mind. He's a good man, it really is extraordinary how good . . .

and all at once it was as if my soul had wings, I was happy, I felt all relieved, I wanted to work all over again, to work! . . . Only something happened yesterday, there's something mysterious hanging over me. . . .

CHEBUTYKIN   Nonesuch. Nonsense.

NATASHA (*At the window*)   The headmistress!

KULYGIN   The headmistress has arrived. Let's go on in.

[HE *and* IRINA *go into the house*]

CHEBUTYKIN (*Reading the newspaper and singing softly to himself*)   Ta-ra-ra-boom-de-aye . . . / Sit on a log I may . . .

[MASHA *comes up;* ANDREI *passes across the back of the stage wheeling the baby carriage*]

MASHA   He sits there. There he sits. . . .

CHEBUTYKIN   So what?

MASHA (*Sitting down*)   Nothing. . . . (*A pause*) Did you love my mother?

CHEBUTYKIN   Very much.

MASHA   And she loved you?

CHEBUTYKIN (*After a pause*)   I don't remember any more.

MASHA   Is my man here? That's the way our cook Marfa used to talk about her policeman—my man. Is my man here?

CHEBUTYKIN   Not yet.

MASHA   When you get happiness in snatches, in shreds, and then lose it the way I'm losing it, little by little you get coarse, you get furious. (SHE *points to her breast*) In here I'm boiling. . . . (SHE *looks at* ANDREI, *who again crosses the stage with the baby carriage*) There's that little brother of ours, our Andrei. . . . All our hopes vanished. Once upon a time there was a great bell, thousands

of people were raising it, ever so much work and money
had gone into it, and all of a sudden it fell and broke.
All of a sudden, for no reason at all. And that's Andrei. . . .

ANDREI   Aren't they ever going to quiet down in the
house? What a hubbub!

CHEBUTYKIN   In a little. (HE *looks at his watch*) I've
got an old-fashioned watch, it strikes. . . . (HE *winds
the watch, it strikes*) The first and the second and the fifth
batteries leave at one o'clock sharp. (*A pause*) And I
leave tomorrow.

MASHA   For good?

CHEBUTYKIN   I don't know. Maybe I'll be back in a
year. Except . . . the devil knows. . . . What's the difference! . . .

[*Somewhere in the distance a harp and violin are
playing*]

ANDREI   The town will be deserted. It will be as if they'd
put all the lights out. (*A pause*) Something happened
yesterday up by the theater—everybody's talking about
it, but I haven't any idea.

CHEBUTYKIN   Nothing. Just nonsense. Solyony started
bothering the Baron, and he got mad and insulted him, and
finally Solyony had to challenge him to a duel. (HE
looks at his watch) It's already about time. . . . At half
past twelve, in the state forest over there, the one you can
see across the river. . . . Piff-Paff! (HE *laughs*) Solyony's
got the idea he's Lermontov, and even writes little poems.
A joke is a joke, but this is his third duel already.

MASHA   Whose?

CHEBUTYKIN   Solyony's.

MASHA   And the Baron?

CHEBUTYKIN   What about the Baron? (*A pause*)
MASHA   It's all mixed up in my head. . . . Just the same, I say it isn't right to allow them to. He might wound the Baron or even kill him.
CHEBUTYKIN   The Baron's a good man, but one baron more, one baron less—what's the difference?

[*Someone shouts from beyond the garden: "Yoo-hoo!"*]

You wait. That's Skvortsov shouting, one of the seconds. He's in the boat. (*A pause*)
ANDREI   In my opinion, to take part in a duel, to be present at one even in the capacity of a doctor, is simply immoral.
CHEBUTYKIN   It only looks that way. . . . We're not here, there's nothing in this world, we don't exist, it looks like we exist. . . . And what's the difference anyway!
MASHA   That's how it is—the whole day long they talk, talk. . . . (SHE *walks away*) To live in a climate where you have to expect it to snow every minute—and then on top of it, that's the way they talk. (SHE *stops*) I won't go into that house, I can't bear it. . . . Tell me when Vershinin comes. . . . (SHE *goes off along the avenue of trees*) And the birds are flying south already. . . . Swans or geese. . . . (SHE *looks up*) My beautiful ones, my happy ones. . . .

[SHE *goes out*]

ANDREI   Our house will be deserted. The officers are leaving, you're leaving, my sister's getting married, and I'll be the only one left.
CHEBUTYKIN   And your wife?

[FERAPONT *comes in with some papers*]

ANDREI A wife's a wife. She's honest, sincere—well, kind, but at the same time there's something in her that makes her a kind of blind, petty, hairy animal. In any case, she's not a human being. I'm saying this to you as my friend, the only one I can really talk to. I love Natasha, that's so, but sometimes she seems to me astonishingly vulgar, and then I just despair, I can't understand why I love her as much as I do—or anyway, did. . . .

CHEBUTYKIN (*Getting up*) Brother, I'm going away tomorrow, we may never see each other again, so here's my advice to you. Put on your hat, take your walking stick in your hand, and get out . . . get out, keep going, don't ever look back. And the farther you go the better.

[SOLYONY *walks across the back of the stage, along with two* OFFICERS; *seeing* CHEBUTYKIN, HE *turns toward him—the other* OFFICERS *walk on*]

SOLYONY Doctor, it's time! It's already half past twelve. (HE *shakes hands with* ANDREI)

CHEBUTYKIN In a minute. I'm sick of all of you. (To ANDREI) If anybody wants me, Andrei boy, tell them I'll be back in a minute. . . . (HE *sighs*) Oh—oh—oh!

SOLYONY Before he'd time to get his breath /
The bear was hugging him to death. (HE *goes with him*) What are you groaning about, old man?

CHEBUTYKIN Well . . .

SOLYONY How're you feeling?

CHEBUTYKIN (*Angrily*) As snug as a bug in a rug!

SOLYONY The old man's unduly excited. I'm only going to indulge myself a little, I'll just shoot him like a snipe. (HE *takes out a bottle of perfume and sprinkles it on his hands*) I've used up the whole bottle today, and they still smell. They smell like a corpse. (*A pause*) So. . . . Remember the poem? "But he, the rebel, seeks the storm / As if in tempests there were peace . . ."

CHEBUTYKIN Uh-huh. "Before he'd time to get his breath The bear was hugging him to death."

[HE *and* SOLYONY *go out.*

PEOPLE *shout,* "*Yoo-hoo! Yoo-hoo!*" ANDREI *and* FERAPONT *come in.*]

FERAPONT Papers to sign. . . .

ANDREI (*Nervously*) Leave me alone! Leave me alone! *I beg you!*

[HE *goes off with the carriage*]

FERAPONT But that's what papers are for, you know, to sign.

[HE *goes to the back of the stage.*

IRINA *and* TUZENBACH *come in;* HE *is wearing a straw hat.* KULYGIN *crosses the stage, calling:* "*Yoo-hoo, Masha! Yoo-hoo!*"]

TUZENBACH I believe he's the only person in town that's glad the soldiers are leaving.

IRINA That's understandable. (*A pause*) The town's getting all empty.

TUZENBACH (*After looking at his watch*) Dear, I'll be back in a minute.

IRINA Where are you going?

TUZENBACH I have to go in to town, to—to say good-bye to my friends.

IRINA That's not so. . . . Nikolai, why are you so upset today? (*A pause*) What happened yesterday, by the theater?

TUZENBACH (*With a movement of impatience*)   In an
hour I'll come back and be with you again. (HE *kisses her
hands*) My beloved . . . (HE *looks into her face*) For
five years now I've been in love with you, and still I can't
get used to it, and you seem more beautiful to me all the
time. What marvelous, wonderful hair! What eyes!
Tomorrow I'll take you away, we'll work, we'll be rich,
my dreams will come true. You'll be happy. Only there's
one thing wrong, just one thing wrong: you don't love
me!

IRINA   It isn't in my power! I'll be your wife, I'll be
faithful and obedient, but it's not love, oh, what is there
I can do? (SHE *cries*) I never have been in love in my life,
not even once. Oh, I've dreamed so about love, dreamed
about love so long now, day and night, but my soul is
like some expensive piano that's locked and the key lost.
(*A pause*) You look so worried.

TUZENBACH   I didn't sleep all night. There isn't anything
in my life terrible enough to frighten me, only that lost
key tortures me, it won't let me sleep. Say something
to me. (*A pause*) Say something to me. . . .

IRINA   What? What is there to say? What?

TUZENBACH   Something.

IRINA   That's enough, that's enough! . . . (*A pause*)

TUZENBACH   What senseless things, what idiotic little
things suddenly, for no reason, start to matter in your life!
You laugh at them the way you did before, you know
they're senseless, and yet you go on and on and haven't
the strength to stop. Oh, let's not talk about it! I'm happy.
It's as if I were seeing for the first time in my life these
firs and maples and birches, and they are all looking at me

curiously and waiting. What beautiful trees, and how beautiful life ought to be under them! (*A shout: "Yoohoo!"*) I must go, it's already time. . . . See that tree, it's dried up, but the wind moves it with the others just the same. So it seems to me that if I die, still, some way or other I'll have a share in life. Good-bye, my darling. . . . (HE *kisses her hands*) The papers you gave me are on my table under the calendar.

IRINA I'm going with you.

TUZENBACH (*Uneasily*) No, no! (HE *goes away quickly, then stops by the avenue of trees*) Irina!

IRINA What?

TUZENBACH (*Not knowing what to say*) I didn't have any coffee this morning. Tell them to make me some. . . .

[HE *goes out quickly.*

IRINA *stands lost in thought, then goes to the back of the stage and sits down in the swing.*

ANDREI *comes in with the baby carriage;* FERAPONT *appears.*]

FERAPONT Andrei Sergeich, they're not my papers, you know, they're the government's. I didn't think them up.

ANDREI Oh, where's it gone, what's become of it—my past, when I was young and gay and clever, when I had such beautiful dreams, such beautiful thoughts, when my present and future were bright with hope? Why is it that, almost before we've begun to live, we get boring, drab, uninteresting, lazy, indifferent, useless, unhappy? . . . Our town's been in existence for two hundred years, there's a hundred thousand people living in it, and there's

not one of them that's not exactly the same as the others;
there never has been in it, either in the past or in the
present, a single saint, a single scholar, a single artist, a
single person famous enough for anybody to envy him or
try to be like him. . . . They just eat, drink, sleep, and
then die. . . . And some more are born and they too eat,
drink, sleep, and so as not to die of boredom they fill their
lives with nasty gossip, vodka, cards, affairs, and the
wives deceive their husbands and the husbands lie and
pretend they don't see anything, and a kind of inexorable
vulgarity oppresses the children, and the divine spark
within them dies, and they become the same pitiful,
absolutely identical corpses that their mothers and fathers
were before them. . . . (*To* FERAPONT, *angrily*) What
do you want?
FERAPONT   What? Papers to sign.
ANDREI   I'm sick of you.
FERAPONT   A while ago the doorman at the courthouse
was saying—in Petersburg last winter, he says, it seems as
how it was two hundred degrees below zero.
ANDREI   The present's disgusting, but on the other hand,
when I think of the future—oh, then it's so good! I feel
so light, so free: Off there in the distance the light dawns,
I see freedom, I see my children and myself freed from
laziness, from vodka, from goose with cabbage, from
naps after dinner, from all this laziness and cowardice. . . .
FERAPONT   It seems as how two thousand people were
frozen to death. He says people were terrified. Either it
was Petersburg or Moscow, I don't remember.
ANDREI   (*Suddenly overcome with tenderness*) My own

darling sisters, my wonderful sisters . . . (*Tearfully*)
Masha, my own sister . . .

NATASHA   Who's that making all that noise out there?
Is that you, Andrei? You'll wake Baby Sophie! You know
you ought not to make any noise, Sophie's asleep. You're
as clumsy as a bear. If you want to talk, then give the
baby carriage and the baby to someone else! Ferapont,
take the baby carriage from your master.

FERAPONT   Yes'm.

ANDREI (*Embarrassed*)   I was speaking in a low voice.

NATASHA (*Behind the window, petting Bobik*)   Bobik!
Naughty Bobik! Bad Bobik!

ANDREI (*Glancing through the papers*)   All right, I'll
look them over and sign the ones that have to be signed,
and you can take them back to the board. . . .

[HE *goes into the house, reading the papers.*

FERAPONT *pushes the baby carriage toward the back
of the garden.*]

NATASHA   Bobik, tell Mother what's her name! You
darling, you darling! And who's that over there? That's
Aunt Olga. Say to your Aunt Olga: "How do you do,
Olga!"

[*Two street* MUSICIANS, *a* MAN *and a* GIRL, *come in
and begin to play on a violin and harp;* VERSHININ, OLGA,
and ANFISA *come out of the house and listen silently
for a moment;* IRINA *comes up*]

OLGA   Our garden's like a vacant lot, they walk right
through it. Nurse dear, give the musicians something.

ANFISA (*Giving something to the* MUSICIANS)   Good-bye

and God bless you! (*The* MUSICIANS *bow and go out*)
Poor things! If you've enough to eat you don't go around
playing. (*To* IRINA) Good morning, little Irina! (SHE
kisses her) M-m-m-m, child, the life I lead! the life I lead!
At the high school in a lovely government apartment,
there with little Olga—that's what the Lord has vouchsafed
me in my old age! Sinner that I am, never in my whole
life have I lived the way I live now! . . . A big apartment,
a government one, and I've a little room all to myself,
a little bed—all government property! I go to sleep at
night and—O Lord! Mother of God, there's nobody in
the whole world happier than I am!
VERSHININ   We're leaving right away, Olga Sergeevna.
It's time I was going. (*A pause*) I wish you everything,
everything. . . . Where is Marya Sergeevna?
IRINA   She's somewhere in the garden. I'll go look for her.
VERSHININ   Please do. I haven't much time.
ANFISA   I'll go look too. (SHE *calls*) Little Masha, yoo-
hoo! (SHE *goes with* IRINA *toward the back of the garden*)
Yoo-hoo! Yoo-hoo!
VERSHININ   Everything comes to an end. And so we too
must part. (HE *looks at his watch*) The town gave us
a sort of lunch, we drank champagne, the mayor made a
speech, I ate and listened, but my soul was here with
you. . . . (HE *looks around the garden*) I'll miss you.
OLGA   Shall we see each other again, someday?
VERSHININ   Most likely not. (*A pause*) My wife and my
two little girls will be staying for two months more;
please, if anything should happen, if they should need
anything . . .
OLGA   Yes, yes, of course. Don't even think about it.

(*A pause*) By tomorrow there won't be a single soldier left in town, it will all be only a memory—and of course a new life will begin for us. . . . (*A pause*) Nothing turns out the way we want it to. I didn't want to be a headmistress, and just the same I've become one. It means we won't live in Moscow. . . .

VERSHININ Well. . . . Thank you for everything. Forgive me if anything wasn't what it should have been. . . . I've talked a lot, such a lot—and forgive me for that, don't hold it against me. . . .

OLGA (*Wiping her eyes*) Why doesn't Masha come on . . .

VERSHININ What is there left for me to say to you, in farewell? What's left to philosophize about? . . . (HE *laughs*) Life is hard. It seems to many of us lonely and hopeless—but just the same you've got to admit it's gradually getting clearer and lighter, and plainly the time isn't too far away when it will be entirely bright. (HE *looks at his watch*) It's time for me to leave, it's time! In the old days mankind was busy with wars, its whole existence was filled with campaigns, invasions, conquests, but nowadays we've outlived all that. It's left behind an enormous vacuum which, so far, there is nothing to fill; mankind is passionately searching for it and of course will find it. Ah, if only it would come more quickly! (*A pause*) You know, if only industry could be added to education, and education to industry . . . (HE *looks at his watch*) But it's time I was going. . . .

OLGA Here she comes.

VERSHININ I came to say good-bye. . . .

[OLGA *goes off a little to the side, in order to let them say good-bye*]

MASHA (*Looking into his face*)   Good-bye.... (A long kiss)

OLGA   There, there . . . (MASHA *is sobbing violently*)

VERSHININ   Write me. . . . Don't forget me! Let me go . . . it's time. . . . Olga Sergeevna, take her, I'm already . . . it's time . . . I'm late . . .

[*Moved,* HE *kisses* OLGA'S *hands, then once again embraces* MASHA *and quickly goes out*]

OLGA   There, Masha, there. . . . Stop, darling. . . .

[KULYGIN *enters*]

KULYGIN (*Embarrassed*)   It's all right, let her cry, let her. . . . My good Masha, my sweet Masha. . . . You're my wife, and I'm happy, no matter what happens. . . . I don't complain, I don't reproach you for a single thing. There's Olga, she'll be our witness. . . . Let's start over and live the way we used to, and I won't by so much as a single word, by the least hint . . .

MASHA (*Stifling her sobs*)   By the curved seastrand a green oak stands, /
A chain of gold upon it . . . a chain of gold upon it . . . I'm going out of my mind. . . . By the curved seastrand . . . a green oak . . .

OLGA   Hush, Masha. . . . Hush. . . . Give her some water.

MASHA   I'm not crying any more. . . .

KULYGIN   She's not crying any more. . . . She's a good girl. . . .

[*A muffled, far-off shot is heard*]

MASHA   By the curved seastrand a green oak stands, /
A chain of gold upon it . . . a green cat . . . a green oak
. . . I'm all mixed up. . . . (SHE *takes a drink of water*)
My life's all wrong. I don't want anything any more. . . .
I'll be all right in a minute. . . . What difference is
anything anyway? . . . What does it mean, *by the curved
seastrand*? Why do I keep saying that? My thoughts
are all mixed up.

[IRINA *enters*]

OLGA   Hush, Masha. Now you're being a sensible girl.
. . . Let's go on in. . . .
MASHA (*Angrily*)   I won't go in there. (SHE *sobs, but
immediately stops herself*) I don't go in that house any
more, and I won't now. . . .
IRINA   Let's just sit together for a while and not say
anything. . . . Tomorrow I'm going, you know. . . .
KULYGIN   Yesterday I took this moustache and beard
away from one of the boys in my class. . . . (HE *puts on
the moustache and beard*) I look just like the German
teacher. . . . (HE *laughs*) Don't I? They're funny, those
boys. . . .
MASHA   You really do look just like that German of yours.
OLGA (*Laughing*)   You do. (MASHA *cries*)
IRINA   There, Masha, there!
KULYGIN   Just like . . .

[NATASHA *comes in*]

NATASHA (*To the maid*)   What? Protopopov's going to
sit with Baby Sophie, and Andrei Sergeevich can take

Bobik for a ride. Children are so much trouble. . . . (*To*
IRINA) Irina, you're leaving tomorrow—such a pity! Do
stay at least one week more! (SHE *catches sight of* KULYGIN
and shrieks; HE *laughs and takes off his moustache and
beard*)What on earth—get out, how you did scare me!
(*To Irina*) I'll miss you—do you think having you
leave is going to be easy for me? I've told them to put
Andrei and his violin in your room—let him saw away in
there!—and we're going to put Baby Sophie in his room.
That wonderful, marvelous child! What a girl! Today
she looked up at me with the most extraordinary expression in her eyes and—"Mama!"

KULYGIN   A beautiful child, that's so.

NATASHA   So tomorrow I'll be all alone here. (SHE *sighs*)
First of all I'm going to have them chop down all those
fir trees along the walk, and then that maple. . . . In the
evening it's so ugly. . . . (*To* IRINA) Dear, that belt isn't
a bit becoming to you. . . . It's in bad taste—you need
something a little brighter. . . . And I'm having them
plant darling little flowers everywhere—how they will
smell! (*Sternly*) What's this fork doing lying around on
this bench? (SHE *goes into the house; to the* MAID) Will
you tell me what this fork is doing lying around on
this bench? (SHE *shouts*) Don't you dare talk back to me!

KULYGIN   There she goes again!

[*Behind the scene a band is playing a march;* EVERYBODY
listens]

OLGA   They are leaving.

[SHE *goes away.*

CHEBUTYKIN *comes in.*]

MASHA   Our friends are leaving. Well, let's wish them a
happy journey! (*To her* HUSBAND) We must go home.
Where are my hat and cape?
KULYGIN   I took them indoors. . . . I'll get them right
away.

[HE *goes into the house*]

OLGA   Yes, now we can all go home. It's time.
CHEBUTYKIN   Olga Sergeevna!
OLGA   What is it? (*A pause*) What is it?
CHEBUTYKIN   Nothing. . . . I don't know how to tell
you. . . . (HE *whispers in her ear*)
OLGA (*Alarmed*)   It's not possible!
CHEBUTYKIN   Yes. . . . What a mess! . . . I'm worn out,
I'm sick and tired of it. I don't want to say another
word. . . . (*Irritably*) Anyway, what's the difference!
MASHA   What's happened?
OLGA (*Putting her arms around* IRINA)   This is a terrible
day. I don't know how to tell you, my darling. . . .
IRINA   What? Tell me right away, what? For God's
sake! (SHE *cries*)
CHEBUTYKIN   A little while ago the Baron was killed in
a duel.
IRINA (*Crying softly*)   I knew, I knew. . . .
CHEBUTYKIN (*Sitting down on a bench at the back of the
stage*) I'm worn out. . . . (HE *takes a newspaper out of
his pocket*) Let 'em cry. . . . (HE *sings softly*) Ta-ra-
ra-boom-de-aye . . . / Sit on a log I may . . . What's the

difference anyway? (*The* THREE SISTERS *stand nestled against one another*)

MASHA   Oh, how the music is playing! They are leaving us, one is really gone, really, gone forever and ever; we'll stay here alone, to begin our life over again. We must live . . . we must live . . .

IRINA (*Putting her head on* OLGA's *breast*)   The time will come when everyone will know why all this is, what these sufferings are for, there will be no more secrets— but in the meantime we must live . . . must work, only work! Tomorrow I'll go away alone, I'll teach in the school and give my life to those who'll need it, perhaps. It's fall now, soon the winter will come and cover everything with snow, and I will work, I will work . . .

OLGA (*Putting her arms around both her* SISTERS)   The music is playing so gaily, so eagerly, and one wants so to live! Oh, my God! Time will pass, and we shall be gone forever, they will forget us—they'll forget our faces, our voices, and how many of us there were, but our sufferings will change into joy for those who will live after us, happiness and peace will come on earth, and they'll be reminded and speak tenderly of those who are living now, they will bless them. Oh, dear sisters, our life isn't over yet. We shall live! The music is playing so gaily, so joyfully, and it seems as though a little more and we shall know why we live, why we suffer. . . . If only we knew, if only we knew!

[*The music grows fainter and fainter;* KULYGIN, *smiling happily, brings the hat and cape;* ANDREI *pushes* BOBIK *across the stage in the baby carriage*]

Masha, Irina, and Olga
Photograph by MARTHA HOLMES

CHEBUTYKIN (*Singing softly*)   Ta-ra-ra-boom-de-aye.
Sit on a log I may . . . (HE *reads the newspaper*) What's
the difference anyway! What's the difference!
OLGA   If only we knew, if only we knew!

CURTAIN

AFTERWORD

ABOUT TRANSLATING OF ANY KIND RANDALL JARRELL liked
to quote Chekhov's "When I read other people's translations I am always changing and shifting the words
around mentally and I get something light and ethereal
like lace." In 1953 he chose *The Three Sisters* not only
because it was his favorite Chekhov play; it was his favorite
play. He'd been thinking about it as a play long before
he made up his mind to translate it, and he never really
stopped thinking about it.

He wrote about many writers and cared about many
more, but the one he thought of as being the closest to his
own nature as an artist and a man was Chekhov. At the
time of Randall Jarrell's death in 1965 there were nearly
one hundred handwritten pages of notes for an essay on
The Three Sisters that he meant to write for this book.
On these pages he wrote what he got from reading
Chekhov and about Chekhov over the years: that is, his own
feeling for Chekhov's intentions, and his own way of
looking at this play. The notes were *notes*: rough and
preliminary, but crammed with opinions. Randall would
have edited these and rewritten them, and reedited and
rewritten until he made a finished prose piece about
The Three Sisters. Myself, I could do none of this—least
of all discard one word. I did try with some "changing
and shifting" to get an order of form that would make
them usable to actors especially, and any others who want

to think about the play in detail. Also, for the sake of coherence I contributed some lines here and there in as nearly Randall Jarrell's words as I could.

Working daily for some months with his handwriting and his thoughts has been a fond assignment for me and—though I longed to finish—I am sorry to come to the end of it.

MARY JARRELL

May 6, 1968

About THE THREE SISTERS:

NOTES

I / CHEKHOV AND THE PLAY

IN A SENSE *The Three Sisters* needs criticism less than almost any play I can think of. It is so marvelously organized, made, realized, that reading it or seeing it many times to be thoroughly acquainted with it is all one needs. In it Chekhov gives us a cluster of attitudes about values—happiness, marriage, work, duty, beauty, cultivation, the past, the present, the future—and shows us how these are meaningful or meaningless to people. Values are presented to us through opposed opinions, opposed lives; at different ages in life with different emotions; and finally, on different levels.

Take the ways, for instance, that marriage is presented: so obviously, so tenuously, so alternatively. All the marriages we see are disasters; but Vershinin's goes wrong for different reasons than Andrei's, and Andrei's goes wrong for different reasons than Masha's. Still, Chekhov can lump them into one generalization that we accept when Vershinin says, "Why is a Russian always sick and tired of his wife . . . and his wife and children always sick and tired of him?" Then he uses a generalization from particular experience when he has Andrei tell us, "People shouldn't get married. They shouldn't because it's boring." These are bold truths. And yet, surrounded by bad models (and in Kulygin's case, involved in one), Olga remains convincingly dedicated to marriage as an ideal—woman's role, woman's duty. And Kulygin never loses his faith in its value as a value, or as an "institution" to belong to for its own sake, and continues to encourage the single ones to marry.

"Love and Marriage" is a little ballet for Irina and Tuzenbach of coming together and parting, of going separate ways yet looking over shoulders. First they are on the same side about love. Both of them idealize it and want it, but while his dream of love is Irina, hers is Moscow where she'll meet "the real one." Later, when she gives up her dream, they come together on the marriage level (long enough to be engaged) but not at the love level. Theirs is a poignant pas de deux when, first, Irina truthfully declares it is not in her power to love this homely man and, after that, Tuzenbach's own sensitive drawing back from marriage on those terms. Both of them achieve their maximum substance as human beings at this moment. When he says to her, "There isn't anything in my life terrible enough to frighten me, only that lost key . . ." (the key to Irina's love), and when he puts love ahead of the imminent duel, Tuzenbach is ennobled. The ambiguities here make it possible for us to wonder whether the marriage would really have gone ahead the next day if he had not been killed, whether the "dead tree" allusion of Tuzenbach's meant he *knew* (by willing it) that he was going to die.

Chekhov was nearly forty when he fell deeply in love with the actress Olga Knipper. He wrote Masha's part for her, and, significantly, love and marriage are examined in this play more than any other. The fact he had not married all this while is an indication of sorts, but of course, the stories tell us over and over in fiction what he often told his friends in letters. At age twenty-five he wrote, "I am above marriage." Ten years later he wrote, "Very well, I'll marry if you wish it. But here are my conditions: Everything must remain the same as before—that is she must live in Moscow and I in the country, and I'll make visits to her. The kind of happiness which continues day in and day out, from one morning to the next, I cannot endure. When people tell me the same thing in the same tone of voice every day, I become furious. . . . I promise to be a splendid husband, but give me a wife who, like the moon, will not appear in my sky every day." In a letter to his brother Misha, advising him on Misha's marriage, Chekhov wrote that the absolute essential was "love, sexual attraction, to be one flesh."

When the play was finished he and Olga Knipper were married, but in the months beforehand he delayed it by every possible tactic until she made it plain he could not hold her without it. Shortly after, he wrote his sister (five years later than the other letter about his "conditions" for marriage) and said, "That I'm

married, you already know. I don't think the fact will in any way
change my life or the conditions under which I have lived up to
now . . . everything will go on as before. At the end of July
I'll be in Yalta, then in Moscow until December, and then back
in Yalta. That is, my wife and I will live apart—a situation, by the
way, to which I'm already accustomed." Partly accustomed, yes;
and the marriage went ahead along the lines he'd laid down earlier,
but not as easily as he'd assumed. He did get much writing done
by himself in Yalta where he had to stay at times in the milder
climate on account of his tuberculosis, but also he got bored and
lonely. Among many letters to Olga (they wrote every day) he
once said, "I keep waiting for you to order me to pack and travel
to Moscow. To Moscow! To Moscow! that is not said by *three
sisters* but by one husband." In *The Three Sisters* many voices
tell us what he'd summarized in one sentence in 1898 in the
story *About Love*: "The one incontestable truth about love is
that it is a mystery and all that is written about it is not a solution
but a series of questions that remain unanswered."

THERE IS A REAL GEOMETRY TO *The Three Sisters*. It has an
ideological, character, and chain-of-events organization that
develops with an inevitableness akin to Greek tragedy. After making
his logical skeleton Chekhov invents and *invents* plausible disguises
that keep the play from having the Ibsen-well-made surface and
the symbols from having the Ibsen starkness. Indeed, having so
many symbols and leitmotivs prevents the most important of any
of them from sticking out or being too differentiated from the
rest of the surface. While the underlying organization is extremely
plain, parallel, and symmetrical, it is masked by a "spot-surface"
or expressed in terms of these "spots" themselves.

A visual counterpart of this very method uncannily exists in the
work of the painter Vuillard. In certain of his indoor and outdoor
scenes of French domestic life, the foundation areas on the canvas
are made less emphatic by the swarms of particles that mottle the
walls with rose-printed paper, the rugs with swirls, the lawns
with pools of sun and shade. From such variation and variegation
comes his cohesion. Vuillard commingles plaids and dappled things

as non sequitur as the jottings in Chebutykin's notebook. He
alludes to a mysterious darkness by leaving a door ajar. He baffles
the viewer by a woman's ear glowing red. What does she hear?
In the same way, Masha's eccentric line "By the curved seastrand
a green oak stands/ A chain of gold upon it . . ." baffles us.
What *does* it mean?

These Vuillard "spots" are found in bizarre, grotesque, homey
touches in a speech, a mannerism, a trait, an incident that add up to
several dozen possibly. Solyony, Chebutykin, Kulygin, Natasha,
and Ferapont are covered with them; Olga and Irina and Vershinin
scarcely have any; with Masha and Tuzenbach they are used
sparingly but memorably. Chekhov made such imaginative and
original use of the indeterminacy principle on the microscopic
level (the opposite of Ibsen) while maintaining on the macroscopic
level firm causality. The more his themes and characters were
contradictory, inconsistent, and ambiguous, the more the play got
a feeling of the randomness and personalness of real life.

VUILLARD SPOTS

Act I

SOLYONY. With one hand I can only lift sixty pounds, but with
both hands I can lift a hundred and eighty—two hundred, even.
From that I deduce that two men aren't twice as strong, they're
three times as strong as one man, etc.

CHEBUTYKIN: For falling hair: Two ounces of naphtha in half a
pint of alcohol, etc.

SOLYONY: . . . you'll die of apoplexy or I'll lose control of myself
and put a bullet through your head, my angel.

MASHA: By the curved seastrand a green oak stands, etc.

SOLYONY: Before he'd time to get his breath/ The bear was hugging
him to death, etc.

FERAPONT: How's that? (*Deafness.*)

ANFISA: Irina, darling, now you be a nice polite little girl.

MASHA: The love-sick major, etc.

SOLYONY: Because if the station were here, it wouldn't be way off there, etc.

SOLYONY: Here chick-chicky (*repeated*).

CHEBUTYKIN: Male and female created He them!

KULYGIN: (*Repeating the gift of the book and using Latin tags.*)

KULYGIN: The rugs must be taken up for the summer, the moth balls, *mens sana in corpore sano*, etc.

CHEBUTYKIN: With newspapers and combing his beard.

KULYGIN: C-minus in deportment, etc.

SOLYONY: Cockroaches.

FEDOTIK: Photographs, gift, top.

MASHA: (*Again*) By the curved seastrand, etc.

Act ii

FERAPONT: The forty pancakes.

The rope over Moscow.

MASHA: The wind in the chimney.

CHEBUTYKIN: (Knocking on the floor.)

For eight months, not a kopeck, evidently he's forgotten.

MASHA: Ever since morning I've been laughing.

CHEBUTYKIN: Balzac was married in Berdichev.

FEDOTIK: Giving the crayons and penknife to Irina.

Showing her a new kind of solitaire.

Telling her she isn't "going out" in the game so she won't get to Moscow.

CHEBUTYKIN: Tsitsikar—smallpox is raging there.

SOLYONY: Fry that baby in the frying pan.

TUZENBACH: What's become of the candy? Solyony ate it.

VERSHININ: My wife's poisoned herself again.

MASHA: Mixing up Irina's cards and spoiling her game.

SOLYONY: Ah, be not wroth, Aleko.

CHEBUTYKIN: Chekhartma-cheremsha.

TUZENBACH-ANDREI-CHEBUTYKIN: "My New Porch" song.

Solyony's perfume.

SOLYONY-ANDREI: Argument about two universities in Moscow.

MASHA: The Baron's drunk (*waltzing to herself*).
Troika with bells, carnival people's voices.
KULYGIN: O, *fallacem hominum spem!* Accusative of exclamation.
Accordion in street, nurse singing.

Act III

Sound effects with fire: gathering of clothes, ringing, etc.
FERAPONT: Moscow, the French were flabbergasted.
MASHA: (*Goes out angrily with her pillow*).
KULYGIN: (*Hides behind a wardrobe*).
CHEBUTYKIN: Smashes clock.
KULYGIN: Zero-minus in deportment.
SOLYONY: More perfume-sprinkling: "T'would annoy the geese, I
fear."
More chicky-chicky, etc.
KULYGIN: I'm satisfied. I'm satisfied. I'm satisfied.
MASHA: Bored, bored, bored!
ANFISA: Don't throw me out.
IRINA: I can't remember what window is in Italian.
OLGA: He (*Tuzenbach*) looked so homely I wanted to cry. (*She
cries.*)
MASHA: (*About Natasha*) She walks like the one who started the
fire.
OLGA: (*About Masha*) The silliest one in the family, that's you.
OLGA: (*When Masha is confessing her love affair*) Anyway I don't
hear you. I don't hear what silly things you are saying.
MASHA: Like Gogol's madman—silence—silence.
CHEBUTYKIN: Knocking on the floor again.

Act IV

FEDOTIK: Oh, stand still!
RODE: Good-bye echo. Good-bye trees.
KULYGIN: Your Polish wife will call you *kochany*.
CHEBUTYKIN: He puts a newspaper in a pocket and takes a news-
paper out of a pocket.

Gu-Gu-God-fearing man.

Ta-ra-ra-boom-de-aye . . . / Sit on a log I may, etc.

KULYGIN: With a moustache, or without a moustache, I'm satisfied.

KULYGIN: Nonsense. Nonesuch.

All the yoo-hoos in the act.

KULYGIN: *Ut consecutivum* anecdote.

"The Maiden's Prayer" at the piano.

MASHA TO CHEBUTYKIN: And she loved you? (He): I don't know.

MASHA: Is my man here?

Chebutykin's old-fashioned watch that strikes.

CHEBUTYKIN: Piff-paff.

Noticing the swans and geese flying south.

SOLYONY: Before he'd time to get his breath/ The bear was hugging, etc.

Perfume sprinkling on his hands.

Tuzenbach's straw hat. Tell them to make some coffee, as last words.

FERAPONT: Petersburg or Moscow it was. Two hundred degrees below zero.

Two thousand people froze to death.

ANFISA: A little room, a little bed—all government property, etc.

AN ESSENTIAL PART OF THE PLAY is the meaning of life as opposed to the meaninglessness of life. Chekhov shows us what people say, believe, believe under their acts (unconsciously) until *The Three Sisters* becomes a poll of answers about his values and ultimates. How *many* answers there are and how paradoxical Chekhov thought they were can be seen immediately if they are listed as follows:

THEMES

MEANING	MEANINGLESSNESS
Specific meaning: Knowledge, the meaningful past, Moscow, father.	"What's the difference?" nonsense, stupidity, silliness, crudeness, provincial present.
Remembering this.	Forgetting, denying, departing.
Happiness: through love, dreams, work, progress, ("If only"-dreams).	Unhappiness: frustration, boredom, "work without poetry," loneliness, empty dutifulness.
Satisfactions: work, progress, duty.	Despair at lack of progress or slowness of it.
Fate or lot: accepting this, "We must live," "We shall live."	The life we reconcile ourselves to, nihilism, "What's the difference?" "It's all the same."
Dreams-wishes: dreams are necessary.	Tiredness, exhaustion, headaches due to weariness in waiting for dreams to come true, giving up on dreams.
Love.	Lack of love.
Youth.	Age and aging.

IN A CERTAIN SENSE *The Three Sisters* is as well-made as an Ibsen play in that everything is related to everything else, except that Chekhov relates things in a musical way, or in a realistic-causal, rather than geometrical-rhetorical-causal, way. The repeated use of Wagnerian leitmotivs occurs not only for characters but for themes, ideology, and morality. Diffusing the themes required more concentration, he wrote in letters when he was working on *The Three Sisters*, than for any other play. He perfected it to relax the essential structural framework the play is built on. In the exchange of themes, overly defined edges of characterization and situation are blurred and, to him, more realistic. In particular,

Chebutykin's "What's the difference?" is his own special leitmotiv that, however, is borrowed by nearly everyone at sometime or other, just as themes of fatigue, happiness, boredom, etc., are shared.

Loneliness (hardly a value or a philosophy) becomes a sort of ghost that haunts Andrei all the time, Irina until she gets older, and Solyony under cover of his Lermontov personality. Loneliness pervaded Chekhov's own life in similar ways. He wrote someone, "I positively cannot live without guests. When I am alone, for some reason I become terrified, just as though I were in a frail little boat on a great ocean." Though he kept people around him a lot of the time, there was an essential distance from, removal of everybody else from Chekhov in life. He joked and played jokes and behaved frivolously as a regular way of getting along with people. Even when he was so in love with Olga Knipper, it was hard for him to stay close, and he'd write her "silly" letters that she sometimes scolded him for. She wanted him to talk of the meaning of life once, and he wrote her (à la Tuzenbach's "See it's snowing" sentence), "You ask: What is life? That is just the same as asking: What is a carrot? A carrot is a carrot, and nothing more is known about it." For years he wore a seal ring with these words: "To the lonely man the world is a desert."

He keeps us conscious of the loneliness underneath the general animation. At the birthday party in Act I, there is Vershinin's line about the gloomy-looking bridge in Moscow where the water under it could be heard: "It makes a lonely man feel sad." Later on we hear again when Chebutykin tells Andrei about being unmarried, even if marriage is boring: "But the loneliness! You can philosophize as much as you please, but loneliness is a terrible thing, Andrei. . . ." With the "good-bye trees" and "good-bye echo" and the embraces, tears, *au revoir*'s and farewells, loneliness has built up like entropy as the good social group—that partly kept people from being lonely—has been broken into by the inferior outside world. The organized enclave of Act I, after being invaded by the relatively unorganized environment, loses its own organization like a physical system and runs down to almost nothing . . . Andrei.

The musical side of Russian life, and Chekhov, comes into the play in every act: Masha whistles, the carnival people play off-stage, Chebutykin sings nervously after the duel. Specifically, Act I opens with Olga remembering the band's funeral march after the father's death and Act IV ends with the band playing a march as the brigade leaves and Olga has her last, summarizing speech. The "yoo-hoos" beforehand have imparted a faintly musical nostalgia to the scene, too. In Acts I and II there are guitar and piano and singing. "My New Porch" is a song everyone knows like "Old MacDonald Had a Farm," so that when Tuzenbach starts it off, even lonely Andrei and old Chebutykin can carry it along. Masha and Vershinin's duet becomes a witty—but entirely different—parallel of this formula. The camaraderie at the bottom of the first is countered with the romantic insinuation of the second. "Unto love all ages bow, its pangs are blest . . ." leaves nothing in doubt, and when Masha sings a refrain of this and Vershinin adds another, they make a musical declaration of love. This is an excellent preparation for Act III when, after Masha's love confession, it would have been awkward for Vershinin and her to appear together on stage. Their intimacy is even strengthened, in our minds, by his off-stage song to Masha which she hears, comprehends, and answers in song before leaving the stage to join him.

There was always a piano in Chekhov's house, and having someone play helped him to write when he got stuck. Rhythms came naturally to him, and just as he has varied them in the lines of *The Three Sisters*—from the shortest (sounds, single words) to the arias and big set speeches—similarly there is a rhythmic pattern like that on a railway platform where all the people know each other and little groups leave, say good-bye, meet.

To ME, Davchenko's comment on the lack of spontaneity of this play is really a tribute to its extraordinary solidity of construction. How frail, spontaneously lyric, and farcical *The Cherry Orchard* is in comparison. Chekhov said of it, "I call it a comedy." It was the work of a dying man who had strength to write only a few

lines a day, whereas *The Three Sisters: A Drama in Four Acts*
is his crowning work. It is the culmination of his whole writing
life. *Uncle Vanya* is the nearest thing, but nothing equally long
(none of the short novels) is as good as *The Three Sisters*.

II / THE SETTING

WHAT PEOPLE REMEMBER FROM *The Three Sisters*, if they have
forgotten everything else, is Irina's "To Moscow! To Moscow!
To Moscow!" But few of us know, as audiences at the Moscow
Art Theatre in 1900 knew, the all-or-nothing cultural contrast
between living in Moscow or living in a provincial Russian city.
As for Moscow we can rely somewhat on our imaginations, but
for the Protopopov world that is the setting for *The Three Sisters*,
our imagination comes off nowhere and only Chekhov's own
words can give us the knowledge of it that we need. Here is
Chekhov's description of a provincial city of a hundred thousand
people, or more, like the one where the Prozorov household lived:

> I DID NOT KNOW ONE HONEST PERSON in the entire town. My father
> took bribes and thought they were being given him out of
> respect for his spiritual qualities. In order to be promoted from
> one class to another, students went to board with their teachers,
> who grossly overcharged them for it. The wife of the military
> commander accepted money from the recruits at enlistment
> time and even allowed them to entertain her, she was once so
> drunk in church that she was totally unable to get up from her
> knees. Doctors accepted money too, at recruitment time, and
> the town doctor and the veterinarian levied a tax on butcher
> shops and inn. At the district college there was a brisk trade
> in certificates granting military exemptions for the third school
> year. The higher clergy accepted money from their subordinates
> and the church elders. At the town council, the citizens'
> council, the medical board and all similar boards, the cry, "You
> have to give thanks!" followed every petitioner, and the
> petitioner would return to give thirty or forty kopecks. And
> those who did not take bribes, dignitaries of the Department of
> Justice, for example, were haughty, extended two fingers for a
> handshake; distinguished themselves by their coldness and

narrowness of judgment, played cards a great deal, drank
copiously, married rich women, and undoubtedly had a harmful,
corrupting influence on society. Only from some of the younger
girls was there a breath of moral purity. The majority of them
had lofty aspirations and honest, pure souls, but they had no
knowledge of life and believed bribes were given out of respect
for spiritual qualities; on marrying, they aged rapidly, let
themselves go, and sank hopelessly into the mire of a vulgar,
plebeian existence.

In the shops, the tradesmen used to unload their rotten meat,
musty flour, and left-over tea on us workers; in the churches,
the police shoved us around, in the hospitals, the doctors'
assistants and nurses fleeced us, and if we were too poor to
bribe them, they would feed us from dirty dishes in revenge;
in the postoffice the pettiest clerk felt he had the right to treat
us like animals. . . . But what struck me most of all in my new
position was the total absence of justice, the very thing
popularly expressed by the words: "They've forgotten God."
A day rarely went by without swindling. . . . We always had
to ask for the money we earned as if it were charity—standing
cap in hand by the back stairs.

from My Life, *1896*

III / The Characters

Olga	Tuzenbach
Irina	Solyony
Masha	Natasha
Andrei	Fedotik
Chebutykin	Rode
Vershinin	Ferapont
Kulygin	Anfisa

Olga

And this life was making her grow old and coarse, making her ugly, angular, and awkward . . .
from The Schoolmistress, *1897*

Properties: The past, papers to correct, uniform, dream of Moscow, dream of marriage, headaches, exhaustion, headmistress post, government apartment, Anfisa.

How she makes life meaningful: By living up to the code of *noblesse oblige*, i.e., noble rank requires noble conduct. By teaching from a sense of duty, not desire. By carrying on the household after the father's death, just as she'd stepped into the mother's place after the mother's death. By dreaming of Moscow —not so much the physical city, as Andrei did, but more Moscow as their past—where, if they could just get back to it, she feels sure a young woman of her age and of good family would not be teaching school and having the strength and youth "squeezed out day by day, drop by drop," but be married and stay home all day.

OLGA IS THE MORALLY SUPERIOR WOMAN IN THE PLAY, just as
Tuzenbach is the morally superior man. Her long introductory
speeches are those of the custodian of the family memories. And
she, more than the others, believes in the rehabilitation of their past
in Moscow. Partly she is having to take the place of the father
now, but she is not an authority or power figure; she is simply the
oldest sister acting in a gently supervisory manner. When she
flies out at Masha, we know this is due to the irritability and
headaches caused by her work; still she has the right amount of
correcting-older-sister tone. She has an essentially warm, caring-
for-others, womanly nature—not as self-interested as Masha and
Irina—and wants to see good in life, tries to take what comes as
God's will, and is still hopeful that it is God's will they go to
Moscow. When her headache passes, we see her at her best, being
hospitable, announcing lunch, mothering Irina, and assuming
domestic responsibility.

In Act I she is the hostess. She wants things to go smoothly in
their (the Prozorovs') home. Her incident with Natasha and the
belt shows Olga wants to befriend Natasha and spare her from
the critical comments of Masha and others. She is not trying to
be interfering and would happily give Natasha her own belt if
she had one. The "wrong" belt was just one of the aesthetic
clichés, almost with the force of morality—like a woman covering
her head in church—that any woman would help another with.

In Act II Olga's psychosomatic weariness and headaches are
acute and drive her off the scene and straight to bed.

In Act III we see her disinterestedness established. At the time
of Natasha's first speech on entering Olga and Irina's room, the
stage directions for Olga are: (*Not listening to her*). When Masha
begins her declaration of love for Vershinin, all of Olga's lines
have to do with not listening and she even retires from sight
behind a screen. When Andrei wants to talk out "what it is you've
got against me," Olga very decidedly says, "Let it go now, Andrei
dear. We'll settle things tomorrow." This genteel procrastination
is used by Masha in Act I when she is depressed and wants to
go home and says they'll talk about it "afterwards." Irina, too,
has a version of it in Act IV when Masha is upset and crying over

Vershinin's departure and Irina says, "Let's just sit together for a while and not say anything. . . ." In its dispersal among the sisters, it seems as if this tendency were a euphemism of manners, taught by Mother and the environment to postpone troubling matters as long as possible (on the chance of avoiding them entirely).

In Olga's case this trait is a furthering of the gentility we already know her for and coincides with the shock she experiences from Natasha's rudeness to Anfisa. In the Natasha-Olga quarrel Chekhov is opposing ruthlessness with gentility. It is not the rebellious and spirited Masha nor the mercurial and emotional Irina whom he selects to do this—for they might not be able to control themselves enough to keep their voices down and make the ladylike protests Olga makes. When Olga says that the *least* rudeness, even an impolite word, upsets her and that she doesn't have the strength to bear it . . . and that everything is getting black before her eyes and she is ready to faint, it would be ludicrous to have these lines shouted. Olga would no more raise her voice in this discussion than Natasha would lower hers. This becomes an excellent means of clarifying in a very specific way our knowledge of the gulf between the Prozorov world and the Protopopov world.

Olga's headaches are gone in Act III and also her dreams of Moscow. She is still tired and drained by her circumstances and by her high ethics in giving to others (not only charity for the fire victims but counsel and comfort to her family)—giving, giving, and receiving so little. Surrounded as she is by persons with "lower aims" (adultery, drunkenness, gambling, unkindness, even adolescent emotionalism) than hers, it is hard for Olga, for a while, to see only good in life and accept all this as God's will. In her benevolent counsel to Irina to marry the Baron, Olga thinks of marriage for herself once more and says aloud her little, last, childlike prayer that love would not be necessary, God dear, just any decent man who proposed, ". . . an old man, even. . . ." Marriage, any kind at all, that would take her away is crucial to Olga since the quarrel with Natasha. This was her particular climax when, after such rudeness and the vision of more, Olga sees that the Prozorov enclave of cultivation is simply a barbarian household (with Andrei its one helpless, cultivated slave) and that she has to leave it entirely.

A delicate manifestation of Chekhovian, drawn-from-life writing in the play is the appealing bond between the in-laws Olga and Kulygin. Not only is their mutual exhaustion from their similar endeavors at the school Kulygin's biggest conversational point with her, but their shared loyalty to marriage is of even more significance. All the marriages we see are disastrous. Still, these two continue to think it desirable and both of them have many remarks about marrying. Rooted in the past as Olga is, she holds fast (against the beginning fad to the contrary) to the idea that woman's place is in the home. Unlike Irina who *wants* to work and Masha who is so marriage-weary, Olga thinks marriage gives a woman status, is what she was placed on earth for, and that to be husbandless is to be homeless, which, indeed, in the end is Olga's fate. Kulygin's attitudes are different, but it is rather striking that, in the midst of his own precariously difficult marriage, he can still think of that institution as a source for happiness and come out with such a sentence as, "I often think if it hadn't been Masha I'd have married you, Olga dear. You have such a generous nature. . . ."

In Act IV Olga has escaped from even her "tired" remarks. And this helps to make her seem better off and accustomed to her life. With no more lines about marriage, or "I suffer, too," we feel she has become reconciled to life on this level. She has changed out of her psychosomatic misery and her wanting to give away everything to an essentially calm and disinterested person resigned to an impersonal life. All this prepares us for her final speech. Throughout the play she has served her *noblesse oblige* and it has served her. As someone has said, "What we give ourselves to, we become." So now she is the appropriate one to speak last and sum up the play. Whereas in the beginning her present was made endurable by her dreams of the past, in the end her speeches are all linked to the future, a future not of secular progress like Vershinin's, but a religious future. When she puts her arms around her sisters to say some sentences of consolation, Olga has her big aria about remembrance. Partly she is saying they *will* pass and be forgotten, but also, that in the end, remembrance exists, and not forgetting. She tells them that some meaning is destroyed, but some holds out bravely, means to persist, *must* persist, making an enclave of meaning in the middle of comparative meaninglessness. Finally, she says that when we can't manage to get meaning into our lives, meaninglessness is accepted as meaning that we don't understand (divine). With this she sums up Masha's and Irina's last lines where they've said "we must live . . ." just as she sums up that half of the play that is meaningful, sensible, and hopeful.

IRINA

The endless plain, all alike, without one living soul, frightened her and at moments it was clear to her that this peaceful green vastness would swallow up her life and reduce it to nothingness. She was very young, elegant, fond of life; she had finished her studies at an aristocratic boarding-school, had learnt three languages, had read a great deal, had travelled with her father—and could all this have been meant to lead to nothing but settling down in a remote country house in the steppe, and wandering day after day from the garden into the fields and from the fields into the garden to while away the time, and then sitting at home listening to her grandfather breathing? But what could she do? Where could she go? He goes on: *It would be nice to become a mechanic, a judge, a commander of a steamer, a scientist; to do something into which she could put all her powers, physical and spiritual and to be tired out and sleep soundly at night. . . .* Further along: *And this constant dissatisfaction with herself and everyone else, this succession of bad mistakes that loom up like a mountain before you whenever you look back on your past, she would accept as her real life, her destiny, and she would expect nothing better. . . . And indeed, there is nothing better! Glorious nature, dreams, music, tell one story, but reality another. Evidently goodness and happiness exist somewhere outside of life.* The story ends: *A month later Vera was living at the iron works.*

from AT HOME, *1897*

PROPERTIES: White dress, suggestive of a girl's communion dress, wedding dress, or party dress; Italian words, birthday presents, teaching certificate.

HOW SHE MAKES THE PRESENT MEANINGFUL: By strong family attachments, by planning work, by dreaming of Moscow. (The dream of returning to Moscow is divided among Olga and Andrei and Irina. Olga wants to go back to the good past; Andrei wants to be in the intellectual life of the city; Irina has happy associations with the good past there but mainly anticipates finding the good future: a more beautiful life, work with poetry and with sense, and someone to fall in love with.)

IRINA IS THE AUDIENCE'S OWN YOUTH, hope, beauty, and happiness; and she has their empathy from first to last. In Act I she is surrounded by approvers who keep her sheltered, dependent, and girl-like. What she really wants is for work and love to transform her into a grown-up but, not having gotten this grown-up life yet, she is in a continuation of a child's life with the child's satisfactions gone. The family's staying together is strong in her, and her dreams of Moscow incorporate Olga, Andrei, and Masha, too, "every summer." In the early part of the play Irina wants to keep the family close around her and the brigade close around them. She knows as well as we that, despite her work dream, she is not at all ready to go it alone. Her uneasiness in Act II is apparent whenever she is alone on the stage, and when she says "They've all gone. There's no one left." it is a premonition of her fate in Act IV.

Irina's climax in Act III is in the form of heartbreak and disenchantment. Her stage directions repeatedly tell her to sob and cry. Again, it is significant that, as one of a genteel upbringing as well as the sister closest to Olga's refined sensibilities, Irina is not directed to give way to a loud, hysterical scene in competition with Natasha's. Her speeches are strong, explicit, and quite moving when they are not made indistinguishable by high-pitched shouting. They go well with tears and sobs and, if unhurried, stir the audience's emotions. When violently played, her lines handicap our belief in her maturing moment when she decides to marry the Baron according to Olga's advice. Still clinging to her dream of Moscow, Irina finishes Act III half grown-up.

Irina, open and enthusiastic, is ideally suited for the crisscrossings of others' traits. It happens at once with Vershinin whom she scarcely has anything to do with, really. In his first long philosophical speech he says something about "supposing there are only three people like you. It's plain that you won't be able to get the better of the darkness and ignorance around you . . . their life will choke you." Just minutes after this Irina says to the Baron, "For us three sisters life hasn't been beautiful, it's choked us the way weeds choke grass." How delicately we are shown by this that Irina is an impressionable young girl borrowing big thoughts from the big ones. What we can't know until we know the end of the play is that this is the genesis of her serious and final speech three acts later. After the years have passed and so much happens to her, she comes to find out for herself what Vershinin meant by life's being beautiful in the future because of the people who dream about it now and work for it to happen. When we hear what she says the second time (in Act IV), it is no longer a girl's mimicry but a woman's conviction.

Irina and Masha illuminate each other by their contrast. They are as far apart, of course, as the white of Irina's dress is from the black of Masha's—as far apart as hope is from despair, as virginity from adultery, etc. Even their speech rhythms—Irina's legato and Masha's terse, staccato—differentiate them. And yet, if there were no other lines in the play but what Irina and Masha say to each other, we would know these two were sisters just as well as Chekhov knew he had brothers.

See how the nursery warfare persists! In Act I it is the unhappy, manless Olga who "understands" Masha's gloominess at the birthday party with "a man and a half" while the happy, plan-making Irina, full of herself, is unmoved by Masha's depression and even vexed by her wanting to leave, so that she says (*discontentedly*), "How can you be so . . ." (so full of *your* self on *my* birthday). A year or so later, in Act II, Masha tells Irina (who now has her first grown-up job) how thin she looks, how young and like a little boy. That this is belittling on Masha's part we see from Tuzenbach's mildly defensive, "It's the way she does her hair." Still, in the next sentences Irina and Masha unite against the common enemy, Natasha, and in another minute are laughing together over Chebutykin. The significance is more profound when later in the act Masha displaces her anger (over Vershinin's wife's sending for him) on Anfisa, first, and then Irina. "Let me sit down," she says, and then crossly musses up Irina's game. "Sprawling all over the place with your cards. Drink your tea!" she says. And Irina says, "Masha, you're just mean." And Masha says, "Well, if I'm mean, don't talk to me. Don't bother me!" While Vershinin has caused this explosion, it calls attention to Irina's sexually unawakened state, and Masha couldn't have been more impatient with her if the cards had been dolls she was playing with. This seems to be a reenactment of Irina's incomprehension of Masha's moodiness in Act I, and it is a tightening turn of the key in the machine of Masha's tears-and-depression in Act I which was sexually based then, too.

In Act III, after Vershinin and Masha are in love and Kulygin wanders in with his untimely but touching "My darling Masha, my precious Masha . . ." Irina takes hold in a mature fashion worthy of Olga when she says to him, "She's worn out. . . . Let her rest, Fyodor dear." And in Act IV Irina conspicuously copies Masha's leitmotiv "fate" when she says she is fated not to go to Moscow. Later she has grown so much in sympathy toward Masha and the love affair that it is she, Irina, who volunteers to go and find Masha and bring her to Vershinin to say good-bye.

Irina's arias are the most overwhelming in the play. Work, beauty, belief, happiness are her predominant themes and belong as she does on the side of meaning (what there is in life that has meaning). Her leitmotivs of loneliness and leaving and frustration and forgetting are an interlacing of negative themes from the side of meaninglessness. Here again, Chekhov is schematically unschematic and seeking to disguise the actors in order that we might think they are people.

The Three Sisters is not just about a family, it is one; and if an audience only meets it for an afternoon or an evening, how *can* it catch all those family jokes and allusions? For instance, we hear Irina's slightly absurd first speech about work: "A man must work, must make his bread by the sweat of his brow, no matter who he is—and it is in this alone that he can find the purpose and meaning of his life, his happiness, his ecstasies. Oh, how good it is to be a workman who gets up at dawn and breaks stones in the street, or a shepherd, or a schoolteacher who teaches children, or a locomotive engineer! My God, it is better to be an ox, a plain horse, and *work*, than to be a girl who wakes up at twelve o'clock, has coffee in bed, and then spends two hours getting dressed." We see that this is spoken to Chebutykin, and that he listens; but if only we knew—the way the family knows—what a monument of laziness he is, this would be a small, favorite, comic bit like something in *The Marriage of Figaro* that audiences would wait for and smile over.

As it is, though, it has a fine surface success in showing Chebutykin's best (grandfatherly) side. Our hearts ease about him when he calls Irina his darling, his "own little girl" whom he's known from the day of her birth and carried in his own arms. The affection and companionship between the youngest one and the oldest one in the family add human warmth and sweetness that are rooted in the past. It is important to see how much Chebutykin counts with Irina at this stage, in contradiction to Tuzenbach's saying to him earlier, "You don't count." Olga and Masha, of course, have written Chebutykin off as "silly" and "shameless" and, with their grown-up eyes see his irresponsibility and moral deterioration. Irina has not (yet), and he is still quite often her "dear Ivan Romanich."

Upholding all this, invisibly until we look for them, are Chebutykin's and Irina's parallel phrases. Usually the meanings are at variance, but the words are duplicates and have the effect of that phrase "singing the same words to a different tune," i.e.,

Irina's "Life's gone by and won't ever come back" and Chebutykin's "Life's gone by like lightning," her, "You say life is beautiful. Yes, but what if it only seems that way?" and his only "seeming" to exist, to be a man, to break the clock, etc. What is more truthful and natural than that two people who are used to being with each other will talk like each other? But what is astonishing is Chekhov's carrying this to its limits in Act III when, under catastrophic circumstances, Chebutykin and Irina use many identical words for their entirely dissimilar revelations.

Chebutykin says, ". . . I've forgotten everything I ever did know, I remember nothing, absolutely nothing. . . . Last Wednesday I treated a woman at Zasyp—dead, and it's my fault she's dead. Yes. . . . Twenty-five years ago I used to know a little something, but now I don't remember a thing. One single, thing. Maybe I'm not a man at all, but just look like one. . . . Maybe I don't even exist, and it only looks like I walk and eat and sleep. (HE *cries*) Oh, if only I didn't exist!"

And Irina says, "Where's it all gone? . . . I've forgotten everything, forgotten. . . . I don't remember what *window* is in Italian, or *ceiling*. . . . I'm forgetting everything." And farther on, "Everything is getting away from any real life, beautiful life, everything's going farther and farther into some abyss. . . . I am in despair, I can't understand how I'm alive, how I haven't killed myself long ago. . . ." With the same means that Chekhov holds them together he breaks them in two.

Causally, Irina has not heard Chebutykin's speech and so is not alienated, specifically, by that. We must infer that simply by growing up more she sees more and begins to draw away from him. An intimation of this distance is certainly intended by having Chebutykin break that clock. Irina is the only one who comments on it. With one of the shortened speeches she will use increasingly to him in the last half of the play, she says only, "That was Mother's clock." With it in "smithereens" and Chebutykin quite unmoved, there is a diminution of (1) the material evidence of Mother and the past and (2) Chebutykin's love for the mother and his position—by this association—of special family member.

In Act III, joke as he will and sentimentalize as he does—his
protective ambiguities continue to be spectacular—Chebutykin
is not as close to Irina as he formerly was. Or, the reverse:
Chebutykin is the same "incorrigible" person, but Irina is not as
close to him. When he talks of coming back in a year to be near
her and leading a "new life, sober and respectable," Irina's answer
is again in Olga's key, "Yes, you really ought to, my dove.
Somehow or other you ought." Here, his furtiveness about the
duel echoes his "being up to something" about the samovar in
Act I. Irina is packed and ready to marry the Baron and leave the
next day; but at this moment she is uneasy (shivers) and is
remindful of her apprehensiveness in Act II at being left alone.
Accountably she does not answer Chebutykin's speech about her
being "my treasure. . . . My wonderful girl. . . . You have gone
on far ahead, I'll never catch up with you. I'm left behind
like a bird that's too old to fly. . . . etc." Curiously, Irina speaks
to him just once more before the end when he has told Olga
first about the Baron's death in the duel and then tells her. All
that she says is, "I knew, I knew. . . ."

In Act IV Irina has come to the end of her dream of Moscow,
and she, who never used it before, uses Masha's phrase, "It's fate."
In declaring she will marry the Baron, even without love, she
approaches Olga's disinterestedness and grown-up attitudes about
duty. When the Baron is killed in the duel, she has nothing left
of the present but her dream of work. The dream of work *has*
materialized along with her independence of childhood and the
family organization so that she can say ". . . work, only work!
Tomorrow I'll go away alone, I'll teach in the school and give
my life to those who'll need it, perhaps. . . . I will work, I will
work . . ."

She is grown now, but there is a pathos in her (and the
others), necessity for illusions, dreams-are-necessary. Partly we
see this in her last lines; partly we see her courage, the feeling
that even if one hasn't managed to find a meaningfully occupied
life (that is of some use to oneself and the world), one will
try again.

MASHA

In the story My Life *(1896) about another Masha, a talented
singer who deserts the hero who—uneasy about her—keeps
saying, "Lovely, wonderful Masha. My dear Masha. . . ."
Chekhov writes: "And Masha looked as though she had wakened
from a long sleep and was astonished to find herself, so clever,
so educated, so refined, cast away in this miserable provincial
hole, among a lot of petty, shallow people, and to think that
she could have so far forgotten herself to have been carried away
by one of them and to have been his wife for more than half
a year. . . ."*

PROPERTIES: Literary quotations, tears, hat, pillow, whistled phrase,
musical phrase for Vershinin, black dress, book, cup, cape and
hat.

HOW SHE MAKES THE PRESENT MEANINGFUL: Masha is so *angry*
at the complete frustration of her present that she makes it even
worse for herself by giving up the piano, hardly talking, not
wanting to be with people (even her family), and continuing
to wear black after the father's death.

MASHA IS THE MOST FRUSTRATED AND ANGRIEST OF THE SISTERS because she is the most exceptional, intelligent, gifted; a large thing
compressed into a small space. She suffers more from the status
of women in those days because of her temperament and her
abilities. She needs "work" the most but never says a word about
it and is absolutely idle. Irina and Olga have suffered in the
provincial environment, too, but they sublimate in their dream of
Moscow and in beliefs in personal worth. There is a force in
Masha: *Accept no substitutes.*

She has the masculine bluntness and strength Andrei lacks.
Just as the demands on Andrei are overwhelming, the demands on
Masha are insufficient. How sympathetically these lines tell us
what she is like:

You really don't know how dull and stupid it is to go to bed at nine in the evening and lie there in a fury and with the consciousness that there is nowhere to go, no one to talk to, and nothing to work for because it makes no difference what you do if you don't see and hear your work. The piano and I are the two objects in the house existing mutely, wondering always why we have been placed here, since there is no one to play us.

(They are not in the play but from a letter Chekhov wrote from Yalta to Olga Knipper in Moscow at the same time he was writing *The Three Sisters*.)

When the play begins Masha sits for a quarter of an act without saying a word. Then quoting a line of poetry to herself and humming to herself, she puts on her hat and starts to leave. Her birthday speech to Irina is a long one for her but breaks into her own personal terse, staccato rhythms. These make for a peculiar character type, not as general as Irina's "young girl" and narrower than Olga's. She hasn't the arias nor leitmotivs of Irina, but more of an interchanging, intermingling of anger-boredom themes. These disappear while she is in love and in Act IV are replaced by sorrow.

Masha wants Moscow as much as Olga and Irina do, but hers is a different sort. Theirs, and Andrei's (until he takes a wrong turn just the way Masha did), is a somewhat likely possibility, something good to look to in the future, and a means of changing their lives. Because she had cut off her future by her marriage to Kulygin, Masha could have none of this. At best she could migrate there in the summers. So, her Moscow is the past with the orderlies in it, the officers in uniform, who were the "nicest, decentest, best-mannered people," and high-ranking, trilingual Father overall. No wonder she wears black with all that gone. She cries because she is depressed on Irina's birthday, but partly her tears are for the injustice of her irreparable misfortune.

Masha is the audience's own anger and frustration so far as the Prozorovs and Natasha are concerned. We want helpless, cultivated Olga and Irina (and Andrei) successfully to resist Natasha and the Protopopov world. We want the sisters and the brother to do something for their own happiness. Masha is the only one who does, and we are glad she has the love affair. We accept all her anger, too, as we wouldn't in other circumstances. The other person in the play who has the stage direction (*angrily*) is the other woman of action, Natasha, who keeps fighting-for the way Masha keeps fighting-back.

A human, all-too-human trait Chekhov gives Masha is her repeated displacing of her anger on innocent bystanders. In Act I when Solyony has vexed her about philosophizing women, she answers him sharply and has sufficient residue to say (*angrily*), "Don't sit there sniveling!" to Olga who has just been giving her sympathy! Again in that act, when Kulygin tells her about going to the outing and to the principal's, she answers him, "I'm not going." and in two minutes is (*sternly*) threatening Chebutykin, "Nothing to drink today. Do you hear? . . . Don't you dare!" along with (*angrily*), "Oh damnation, damnation! for another evening to sit and be bored to death at that principal's!" A dazzling example is in Act II when Vershinin is called away to his wife. Masha gets so furious that her anger lands on Anfisa, the old servant, then Irina, the younger sister, and then ricochets off hapless Chebutykin.

Here, Natasha says (*sighs*), "Dear Masha, why must you use such expressions in conversation? . . . Forgive me for mentioning it, Masha, but your manners *are* a little coarse." And what happens to Natasha for this? Nothing. Tuzenbach can hardly keep from laughing at what has happened. But Masha is simply above Natasha and on a different level of being. We know her opinion of Natasha. She could demolish her in one swoop, we feel. Actually she never speaks to her during the whole play!

This seems planned, since Masha is having a love affair just as Natasha is, and a collision between them could become a violent, yelling scene, and all that the play has told us about the enclave's accustomed genteel behavior in contrast to the environment's vulgarity would be undone. This is true also of the Natasha-Prozorov quarrel in Act III when Olga represents the family in shocked low tones. Pitting Masha against her there would again have been too risky.

Being in love represses none of this but adds to Masha what had been suppressed before: animation, gaiety, "life" in place of mourning-for-life. Vershinin and she are two-complainers-about-unhappy-marriages who love Moscow. As soon as she meets him she takes a drink (getting a C-minus in deportment from Kulygin), then goes on to quoting Gogol, waltzing with herself, and behaving in her usual free style, but cheerfully. In Act II her stage directions over and over are "MASHA (*laughing*)." Vershinin is Masha's Moscow: he is a commanding officer as Father was, forty-three years old to her twenty-four-five-six; he makes speeches and, as Kulygin once had, has ideas fresh to her, persuasively beyond her. And Vershinin becomes her happiness. Although he believes "there *is* no happiness" (happiness as a permanently available, God-given right), he is—Masha says he is—the happiness she got "in snatches, in shreds" and then lost.

The enclave criticizes Natasha's actions as anything from petty to ruthless and always as without spiritual cause or feeling. It simply closes ranks around Masha. When Masha is cross, they treat it as one of her depressed times, when she boils inside or feels irritable. Her love affair is not "held up" (even by Kulygin!) but seems viewed as another inevitability, like Andrei's gambling, that the provincial environment is really to blame for.

In Act III Masha has stopped hiding anything. She no longer takes care (Act II) that Kulygin doesn't overhear her and disregards his feelings openly. Her own feelings for Kulygin are dead when her confession of love for Vershinin is made. After that, when she parodies his "satisfied, satisfied, satisfied" with her "bored, bored, bored," it is the corpse's angry first thrust forth three times from the grave.

There is a resuming of her "coarseness" in Act IV when she talks like Marfa, the cook, and tells how she has come to feel about happiness.

Because Kulygin has been so good about the affair, it is going to be worse for Masha after the play ends. She can still feel intellectually and aesthetically superior to him, but not morally. That her dull, wooden pedant was so "good" makes relations with him impossible. Her speech at the last is much the shortest, which is a partial resuming of her terse speeches in Act I but also is significant in that she is morally the least imposing of the sisters, having expressed her frustration in action as the other two have not.

Thoughts and words she learned from Vershinin survive in her lines throughout Act IV. His doctrines—that there is no happiness now but only work so that happiness and progress will come in the future, and, that it *does* matter to have existed—exist in her ". . . we'll stay here alone, to begin our life again. We must live . . . we must live . . ." has, as last, a hint of reconciling in it. Different from Olga's and Irina's ". . . we shall live," Masha's says we must manage to get satisfaction out of what we tried before to avoid as unsatisfactory.

ANDREI

When you dream of playing a part, of becoming known, of being, for instance, examining magistrate in important cases or prosecutor in a circuit court, ("a famous scholar of whom all Russia is proud"), you inevitably think of Moscow; here nothing matters to you; you get reconciled readily enough to your insignificant role, and only look for one thing in life—to get away, to get away as quickly as possible. And in his mind Lyzhin hurried through the Moscow streets, called on acquaintances, met relatives, colleagues, and his heart contracted sweetly at the thought that he was only twenty-six, and that in five or ten years he could break away from here and get to Moscow, even then, it would not be too late and he would still have a whole life ahead of him.

from ON OFFICIAL BUSINESS, *1899*

PROPERTIES: Violin, fretsaw, English book to translate, candle and book, papers to sign, Ferapont, key to cupboard, baby carriage, cottage cheese, cards, mortgage.

HOW HE MAKES THE PRESENT MEANINGFUL: By playing the violin, fretsawing, dreaming of translating a book from English, dreaming of being a professor at Moscow University, dreaming of being in Moscow, reading, gambling, dreaming of the future. By soliloquizing. *When they tell you there are lots of remedies for a disease, it's incurable.*

ANDREI HAS A SENSITIVE, SWEET THOUGH COMMONPLACE NATURE that had too great demands on it by the Father. Now, the sisters more or less expect Andrei, as a man, to do what they as women are not allowed to do (carry on where Father left off) and what Andrei is too weak to do. In Act I when the sisters introduce Andrei to the new battery commander from Moscow as "our scholar" and a "universal expert," he sweats and has to wipe his face and wants to be let alone. Though he reads and does mention translating a book from English, he never makes literary remarks or even "scholarly" ones. It turns out the plan for Andrei to be a professor was really Father's idea; and it soon stops being a plan and turns into a dream. During the speech in which Vershinin talks about the importance of the cultivated individual (when Masha takes off her hat and says, "I'm staying to lunch."), Andrei walks off!

The truth is, in Act I, Andrei is a joke about a violin, a fretsaw, and one of the local girls. He's a joke that has gone on in some form as part of a harmless, and not so harmless, three-against-one game that began in kindergarten or before, and that "Andrei is always going off by himself" to get away from. And yet, Andrei is a Prozorov as much as the sisters, the weakest Prozorov, but part of what they are part of and included with them—and by them—in the plan to go to Moscow.

When he tells Natasha not to mind the teasing, he says, ". . . they mean well. They have such kind hearts—my darling . . . They're all such kind-hearted people, they love both of us. . . ." We know Andrei has had kindness and love in this family, and he is on that side of things that is against rudeness and cruelty. In his rapturous proposal he dreams, and we dream with him, that it will be as he says in his marriage. Instead, we are all slapped in the face by Act II. He'd sought refuge in Natasha from the others who made him feel lonely and shy; then, Natasha becomes the worst of all. Then he seeks refuge in poor, deaf old Ferapont, who

wouldn't object, tease, make Andrei feel inferior, even if he
could hear, and he can't hear.

Andrei is a loneliness figure—lonely with people and lonely
without them. He tells his feelings in long soliloquies to deaf
Ferapont and to his only friend, the unvaluing, newspaper-reading,
"What's the difference?" Chebutykin. (Who can feel inferior to
Chebutykin?) This eccentric uncle figure who loved the mother
and has always been around the family is in no way a forbidding
father figure and is the logical friend for Andrei—worthless
enough to excuse one's own worthlessness.

Andrei doesn't put "If only" into words so that it becomes a
noticeably pervading theme in the play, as the others have. ("If
only I were married"—Olga. "If only I worked"—Irina. "If only
this life were a rough draft"—Vershinin. "If only I didn't exist"—
Chebutykin. Etc.) But Chekhov makes him the personification
of these words, and by intuition we come to know Andrei on
one level by his: "*If only* I were married to Natasha; *If only*
I weren't married to Natasha; *If only* I were in Moscow at the
University; *If only* they understood me, didn't make fun of me;
If only I were young again; *If only* it were the future;—Really,
if only everything were different!"

While in Act II Andrei's relations with Ferapont are kind and
sympathetic, Act III starts with a nervous Andrei, unable to meet
even Ferapont's demands. Instead of calling him "Ferapont, old
man" in friendship with an inferior, Andrei insists that Ferapont
make his inferior status plain by calling the county board member
"your honor." This is a frightening litmus-paper indication of
Andrei's own depreciation. As Irina says, "How petty our Andrei's
become . . . at the side of that woman."

Our bad expectations about Andrei build up in Act III with
the gambling debts, the underhanded mortgaging of the house (he
is too cowardly to talk it over with the sisters first), and the
boasting of his appointment to the county board by his wife's
lover. During the fire he does nothing to help either the men
fighting it or the women assisting the victims, and remains in his
room playing his violin. In this act the distance between the three
sisters and Andrei becomes great. Teasing and overexpectant as

they were with him formerly, still he was "our brother" and they had an affectionate trust that he'd turn out all right in the long run. It is different, now. Irina and Masha have talked about his gambling losses and his general decline. Olga has been silent toward him. Andrei is well aware of their disapproval, their justified disapproval. When he does rise up in his own behalf and Natasha's, they evade any discussion with him. "Let it go now, Andrei dear," Olga says. "We'll settle things tomorrow." But what is left to settle? Andrei's weak nature, indecisiveness, and his real incapacity to use the present are taking on a certain shape the sisters have seen before—they know it well—the shape of indifference, unconcern, and undeniable laziness that resembles Chebutykin more every day. He even sentimentalizes, like Chebutykin, "My dearest sisters, darling sisters, don't believe me . . ." in Act III, and again in Act IV, "My own darling sisters, my wonderful sisters . . ." Just as they have given up on Chebutykin, they have relinquished all the hopes for Andrei— and Andrei knows it.

Act IV is a study in abjectness. It begins with Andrei at his humbling task of pushing the baby carriage. Masha sets the tone with her speech about the bell, raised at such cost, that falls and breaks. That Andrei is like such a bell seems right, but her "for no reason at all" seems a little hard on him. Or does it?

He does raise himself a millimeter above Chebutykin when he says, "In my opinion, to take part in a duel, to be present at one, even in the capacity of doctor, is simply immoral." But he will not act. Andrei has sat through his days "sawing away" while his plans turned to dreams and his dreams faded. Now he just has words: soliloquies. His present is proven as meaninglessly lived as Chebutykin's, but he hasn't found Chebutykin's trick of nihilism. He is still back in the dream stage, the childlike "if only" stage. In his last soliloquy he does admit the difference between the Prozorov past and the Protopopov world of the present, but absurdly dreams that the future will somehow clear away all the "laziness, vodka, goose and cabbage, naps after dinner, cowardice" that is Andrei's existence. He no longer makes any case for

Natasha. He knows now that she is an animal; but he knows, too, that he is the one in the trap.

The sisters are leaving, Chebutykin is leaving; Andrei says, "I'll be the only one left," wishfully forgetting Natasha, just as she later says, "Tomorrow I'll be all alone here." quite forgetting him. In these last minutes Andrei is reduced to someone interchangeable with Ferapont to push babies. After Natasha reprimands him for talking too loudly, Andrei speaks in a low voice and signs the papers. He has no further word, just pushes the baby carriage. This cynical, almost brutal wiping-out of Andrei is as final as ending up in the family graveyard, where, as Astroff says, late in *Uncle Vanya*, "There's but one hope for you and me. The hope that when we'll be sleeping in our coffins, we might be visited by dreams, perhaps even pleasant ones." A few dreams visiting the completely defeated, utterly abject Andrei are the only remnant of the enclave's strong father, cultivated sisters, and weary, once dutiful brother.

CHEBUTYKIN

But now nothing mattered to him anymore. He neither ate nor drank, but lay motionless and silent on his bed. "It's all the same," he thought, when they asked him questions. "I shan't answer. . . . It's all the same."

from WARD NO. 6, *1892*

PROPERTIES: Newspaper, random quotations, samovar, drinking, knocking on floor, washing hands, combing beard, notebook, old-fashioned watch, speeches, jokes, "always doing something silly," walking stick, "What's the difference?" The devil is a "property" Chebutykin calls upon in his speeches from time to time, and this characteristic is contrasted with the others' calling upon God in their speech.

HOW HE MAKES LIFE MEANINGFUL: He doesn't. He finds the present meaningless, just as Masha has begun to and Andrei will later on. He philosophizes that "meaning" is impossible, and this theme is remindful of Vershinin's "happiness is impossible" but, of course, is more extreme and sinister.

THERE IS A COMIC WORTHLESSNESS ABOUT CHEBUTYKIN that the enclave takes for granted, along with his oddness, and the fact that there is something wrong with him, and that he does such "stupid, silly things." Insofar as he stands for nondreams, nonwork, nonevaluation, nonexistence, Chebutykin is a one-character Theater of the Absurd; and his two newspapers are a perfect symbol of his being distracted from distraction by distraction.

In the play, Chebutykin represents the complete devaluation of values. "What's the difference?" is his personal leitmotiv and also a general leitmotiv standing for meaninglessness, senselessness, and hopelessness that, now and then, infects the others. For him, it is the way he has managed to reconcile himself to existing: "What's the difference?" equates everything. As the play progresses, he repeats it more and more until we see it *is* a piece of dramatic organization Chekhov means us to be conscious of.

"What's the difference?" "It doesn't make any difference." is people's regular desperate denial—the more difference it makes, the more surely they say, "It makes no difference." to try to cheer themselves up, to bridge the awful gap between what they want and what they get. (It is worth noticing the climaxes of one kind or another that provoke this phrase from each of the sisters, Andrei, Tuzenbach, Vershinin, and Solyony.)

Chebutykin's forgetting goes right along with "What's the difference?" It is his further breaking down of values and the good system of things, and is his way out of being responsible for his acts. An extraordinary example of this is his answer to Andrei about what to do for asthma: "Why ask me?" he says. "I don't remember, Andrei boy. I don't know." And consider his "I don't remember . . ." when Masha asks if her mother loved him.

In Acts I, II, and IV his nonremembrance and nonemotion protect him from intolerable guilt, but in climactic Act III Chebutykin has his last flurry of normal attitudes. He reveals a worse thing about himself than we could have suspected, in that he is actually to blame for the death of his woman patient the week before. And then a rather touching confession about his (and the others') "cheap low pretense" at the club that, coming on top of the first and real and terrible cause of his miserableness, makes him "feel inside all twisted, all vile, all nauseating. . . ." These are the last manifestations of full humanity in him and the very opposite of "What's the difference?" Here Chebutykin borrows the leitmotiv "If only" from the hopeful, life-does-have-meaning side, in his longing, weeping, "If only I didn't exist!" Here he acknowledges that there *is* so much difference between what is good and what is bad in human existence that he is unable to pretend that there is none, and wishes for the nonexistence in which there is no difference between nothing and nothing.

In Act IV, in both his words and actions, Chebutykin has recovered his equanimity. He again takes refuge, as he formerly did, in saying, no matter what happens, "What's the difference?" Three out of four speeches consist of this concentrated essence of Chebutykin: the disgusted, helpless assertion of the meaninglessness of existence.

Tuzenbach is dead and Irina and her sisters weep for him, and Chebutykin (who has indifferently let the Baron die) exclaims, "The Baron's a good man, but one baron more, one baron less— what's the difference?" He then concludes his part of the play by twice singing his trivial, complacent theme song of the fourth act, "Ta-ra-ra-boom-de-aye . . . / Sit on a log, I may . . ." and by three times repeating "What's the difference, anyway?" From his breakdown in Act III, though, we know that this is as much of a denial as Kulygin's thrice-stated "I'm satisfied."

VERSHININ

Those who will live a hundred, two hundred years after us and who will despise us because we have lived our lives so stupidly and so without any taste—Those, perhaps, will find the way how to be happy.

Astroff: UNCLE VANYA *(1899)*

PROPERTIES: Uniform, wife and daughters, letter.

HOW HE MAKES LIFE MEANINGFUL: By philosophizing about the
future. Saying to himself and others that the present is necessarily *meaningless* except as an interim: a bad prelude to a good
future. This is Vershinin's "theme," his "Vuillard spot," and
his one, long, four-act aria.

VERSHININ'S PHILOSOPHIZING IS A PLAUSIBLE EXCUSE for Chekhov to
have much talk about ultimates. But, actually, when people are
unhappy, frustrated, trying to justify a bad existence, or made
to question something that goes against them, they *do* talk about
ultimates and the meaning of life. When people are happy, they
forget to.

Vershinin's many big speeches of imaginative, well-phrased
philosophizing make his surface show up well, and his more
troubling depths have to be inferred. He does have them, of course.
Think of telling people the first time one meets them, "I often
think if it were possible to begin life over again . . . If only the
first life . . . were a rough draft . . . I believe that each of us
would try above all not to repeat himself—or at least would create
a different set of circumstances for his life, would manage to
live in a house like this, with flowers, with plenty of light . . .
Well, if I could begin life over again, I'd never get married. . . .
Never, never!" Naturally, we infer, as Masha does, that he's given
up on love and personal happiness. "If only I could make you
see that there *is* no happiness, that there should not be, and that
there will not be, for us." Although Tuzenbach and Masha then
defend happiness, Vershinin is unmoved and says more firmly
than ever, "We aren't happy, we never will be, we only long
to be." This is the life Vershinin lives, instead of the life he dreams
of; that is to say, the frustrations we reconcile ourselves to, this
is the life Vershinin lives. It is a life going on year after year
that is partly starved, keeps wanting (as in Act II) a cup of tea—
just a little cup of tea—that it doesn't ever get.

We see the most of Vershinin in the first half of the play, and
his main change is between Act I and Act II. He is excited by
the new acquaintances and this new place that seems better to

him than Moscow, so that he is affable in his early speeches, and his spirits are up in Act I (just the reverse of Masha) and come down in Act II (as hers rise). There is a charming interplay between his enthusiasm for the enclave (the Prozorov establishment just the way it is) and the three sisters' enthusiasm for him as a Moscow substitute. They are novelties for each other, each admiring the other's weather and situation and depreciating his own. The "gloomy bridge" that the lonely man feels melancholy about, and, of course, the big speech about living life over again, imply that being lonely is Vershinin's regular state that the excitement of the moment has overshadowed.

His wanting to come again that evening, his saying, "I feel so good here at your house!" show a touching eagerness to be adopted by this home away from home. He immediately links himself to the three sisters, but *not* to Andrei. Notice that Vershinin can't summon up the least conventional empty compliment for poor Andrei's poor picture frame. And when Masha says to Andrei that Vershinin was never angry when teased about being the love-sick major, "never angry, not even once," Vershinin cheerfully repeats, "Not even once," making himself part of the girls' teasing, especially Masha's, instead of coming to Andrei's defense with even a mild "Well, I did used to get annoyed sometimes, etc." This completely identifies him with the superior three sisters. Vershinin never acts as if their brother were their equal. In his speech about the need for intelligent people (however few there are) among the hundred thousand inhabitants of this "obviously crude, obviously backward place," he says, "Suppose there are only three people like you?" Why doesn't he say four? Poor, weak Andrei.

Of course, the small, superior enclave itself, in the midst of the inferior present, is ideal for Vershinin's philosophy of the beautiful future to come. Simply by existing, being defeated and choked out, it magically makes the future. His belief that cultivation can multiply, that industry and education will—in time—make secular progress for mankind, is Vershinin's religion substitute and parallels Olga's belief that in the future man will make spiritual progress. These are Chekhov's personal views that Vershinin holds, and he also gave them to Astroff in *Uncle Vanya*. That Chekhov was entirely serious about them is shown in a letter to Diaghilev in 1902:

> Modern culture is only the beginning of an effort in the name of a great future, an effort that will continue perhaps for tens of thousands of years, in order that humanity, if only in the remote future, may come to know the truth of the real God, that is, not guess at it or seek it in Dostoevsky, but know it just as clearly as we know that twice two is four.

Act I is a vivacious novelty for Vershinin, but Act II is bored habit so far as the town is concerned. All the intellectuals seem equally uninteresting to him. He's depressed and talks about Russians who have such lofty ideals but low aims, about Russian husbands who are sick and tired of their wives and children, and about their wives and children who are sick and tired of them.

He has fallen in love with Masha, and in Act III he says, "I want like the devil to live." He has found in love something to sing about, and he and Masha sing snatches of song back and forth to each other in the midst of the hubbub of the fire and in the crises in the other lives around them. But how love affects him— other than this—we don't see. He makes no revelation about himself in Act III as the others do. Is there nothing to reveal? Or is there something held back that no one fully knows? Vershinin seems an incomplete character whom Chekhov made that way to simulate an incomplete person. We get some idea of what Vershinin is like from what Masha says about him: "At first he seemed strange to me, then I felt sorry for him . . . then I fell in love with him, fell in love with his voice, his words, his misfortunes." He is primarily someone who speaks beautifully. He reads and then likes to think and talk about what he's read; also, though, as Tuzenbach said in the beginning, "He goes around calling on people and telling them he has a wife and two little girls. He'll tell you that." Yes, he has fallen in love with Masha, although how much can you be in love if you believe happiness is impossible? We have to believe love brings us happiness (and Masha believed this) if we thoroughly believe in love.

In Chekhov's story *Three Years* (1895) the character Laeptev says, "All hopes of personal happiness must be left behind and one must live without desires, without hopes, not dreaming, not expecting, and to avoid this boredom one was already tired of cultivating, one could become interested in others' affairs, others' happiness, and age would come on imperceptibly, life would come to an end—and nothing more was necessary." This might very well be Vershinin's course after he leaves the Prozorovs.

KULYGIN

To see and hear how they lie . . . endure insult, humiliation . . . and to lie and smile . . . all for a crust of bread, for the sake of a warm corner, for some lowly rank in the service [teaching] that is not worth a farthing . . .
                    from THE MAN IN THE SHELL, *1897*

PROPERTIES: Notebooks, Latin quotations, uniform, shaved-off moustache, grades, numbers, jokes, Order of Stanislaus, false moustache, the institution of marriage.

HOW HE MAKES THE PRESENT MEANINGFUL: By work, by looking up to the principal, by being good to Masha, by sticking to routine, by denying unhappiness.

KULYGIN IS A SIMPLE, LOWER-LEVEL ORGANISM with a lower-level expectation in life. The side of Kulygin that bores Masha is his repetitive, routinized, wooden specificness. He is the only one in the play who consistently utters numerical expressions: "Your clock is seven minutes fast," "Thirteen at table," "I worked until eleven," "Everyone who graduated from the high school in fifty years," "At four o'clock we go to the principal's." Persons of this kind often enunciate with particular clarity, and their t's and s's are exaggerated.

His jokey and good-humored side goes along with his timidity—if I joke and am willing to seem absurd, they won't hurt me; nor do I want to hurt them. (This is a point of interest when we

compare how Kulygin has made *use* of being laughed at with
Andrei's being so injured by it.) He is almost psychotic about
avoiding trouble, scenes, and anger; this is one of his strong leit-
motivs that is echoed faintly but surely in Olga's "We'll talk
tomorrow. . . . We'll settle things later." and in her response to
Masha's confession: "I don't hear what silly things you are saying."
Superficially these seem mostly due to Kulygin's timidity and
Olga's refined sensitivities; but—as we have come to expect—
Chekhov is asserting that there are varying amounts of both
these qualities in both characters.

Another refuge for Kulygin is routine. When he quotes the
principal's "That which loses its routine, loses its existence," he's
told us a great deal about himself. We see why, having found the
routine of Latin declensions, academic life, and the institution
of marriage, he cannot break away from any of them. Routine,
being the opposite of chaos to Kulygin, must be preserved, and
any threat to routine he denies. How terribly dissatisfied a man
must be to need to repeat so often: "I'm satisfied, I'm satisfied,
I'm satisfied." Doesn't it sound much more as if it took three
pushes to push down all his resentment and dissatisfaction? His
denial, denial, denial is like Hopkins' "Not, I'll not, carrion comfort,/Despair, not feast on thee; . . ." Kulygin is so frightened
of any admission of aggression that in the earlier acts he constantly
says Masha's disposition is good (!) and that she is a wonderful
wife. In Act III when Masha wants to send him home and be
rid of him, he suppresses his resentment saying, "I'll go in just a
minute. My good and wonderful wife . . . I love you." This is
a mixture of saying what isn't so, along with saying that she is his
superior, better than he, and he's lucky to have her. His "I love
you" is true enough, but it is said to damp out, not to admit the
existence of, his legitimate distress. If I always say *I love you,*
you won't hurt me. The more uneasy Kulygin becomes about
Masha, the more he says, "I love you" until it becomes like the
wistful appeal of a wooden cuckoo clock repeating itself every
hour. It is, of course, Kulygin's peculiar way of saying I don't
resent, I haven't changed (about our marriage) even though you
have. I'm giving you the opportunity to change back simply by

saying, "I love you, too" ("I love you" after all does expect an answering "I love you, too.") Masha's "*Amo, amas, amat*, etc." is so terribly witty because it displays—even to him—the wooden, pigeonholed, repetitive, pedantic, occupational deformation of *his* nature.

Kulygin is half-ridiculous and partially like Belikov, who taught Greek in the story *The Man in the Shell* (1897) and about whom Chekhov wrote: "To see and hear how they lie . . . endure insult, humiliation . . . and to lie and smile . . . all for a crust of bread, for the sake of a warm corner, for some lowly rank in the service [teaching] that is not worth a farthing . . ." The difference between them, and this must be stressed when the lines call for it, is Kulygin's *kindness*. This kindness—a human trait Chekhov treats with warmth and respect in all his writings—actually strengthens the absurd side of Kulygin. Against a background of kindheartedness, the humor can stand out and be funnier than if he were made an unrelievedly foolish figure.

Irina gives us the seed of this in her sentence to Vershinin about Kulygin, "He is the kindest of men, but not the most intelligent." Then in Act III when the sisters have been "wronged" by Andrei's mortgaging their house for gambling debts, all are condemning Andrei but Kulygin. He knows that what Andrei is doing is wrong. Although Kulygin has been giving people C-minuses and zeros on their deportment earlier in the play, when real morality is at stake, he doesn't judge Andrei (nor later, Masha). Masha has just said that Andrei is not a decent person and that what he has done is revolting. In one of the few sentences in which Kulygin dares to disagree with her, he says, "Must you, Masha? What's it to you? Poor Andrei's in debt to everybody—well, God help him." This scene is a preliminary glimpse of how he is to act in the important scene with Masha. Without being shown in this earlier scene Kulygin's generosity of nature to Andrei (who was no threat to him), the audience could have ambiguous responses to the later one. Knowing Kulygin's timidity, we could interpret his tolerance of her behavior as "going along" with the situation out of fear to do otherwise. It is allowable to think of this as some of his motivation, but mainly Chekhov

wants us, and wants Masha, to credit him for showing her the
forbearance that he showed Andrei. Sometimes this small, serious
trait of kindness in Kulygin is lost under the avalanche of absurd
ones he has. But the more we reread the play, the more apparent
is Chekhov's systematic concern with this, and the many other
contradictory, uncalled-for, unstereotyped means he uses to
mitigate the well-made, pen-and-paper, intellectualized type of
character. The most human of characteristics is, after all, something
blurred, left undefined, or hazy that, just when we think we
have typed a person, puzzles us.

Chekhov's consistency is further borne out by forcing Kulygin
to witness Masha's grief and tears at Vershinin's departure (to
make certain he can't deny this situation). Then, the stage
direction for him is: (*Embarrassed*). What he says to her is, "It's
all right, let her cry, let her. . . . My good Masha, my sweet
Masha. . . . You're my wife, and I'm happy, no matter what
happens. . . . I don't complain, I don't reproach you for a single
thing. There's Olga, she'll be our witness. . . . Let's start over and
live the way we used to, and I won't by so much as a single
word, by the least hint . . ." This speech shows him capable of
meeting reality with real decisions when he can't do otherwise.
When he accepts something less than ideal, it is because he is
constituted to be able to do this. Then, how immediately he seeks
out his old comfort, i.e., the joke (moustache joke) that makes
Olga laugh and makes Masha, too, stop crying long enough to
agree about. Soon, Masha is somewhat recovered and able to
talk of going home, and Kulygin's instant obligingness about
getting her hat and cape proves him as satisfied as he needs to be
about his present.

Earlier in Act IV, before the incontestable truth about Masha
and Vershinin is exposed to him, we witness Kulygin's successful
adjustment to his worst fears. Justified and logical as it is to resent
his situation, he embarks on his long anecdote about "*ut consecutivum.*" Being germane to his Latin-academic routines gives him
such comfort that it keeps him from allowing himself to express
resentment or give in to the wreck of his marriage. Instead, he
actually says (compared to "*ut consecutivum*") that he's been lucky

all his life, and that he's happy, and that he's even gotten the Order of Stanislaus Second Class. That this can cheer him up for his private failure with Masha, and permit him to pour his heart into his public success, and constitute his happiness, is touching; but we believe it, we believe it, we believe it.

TUZENBACH

See that tree, it's dried up, but the wind moves it with the others just the same. So it seems to me that if I die, still some way or other I'll have a share in life. Goodbye, darling. . . .
TUZENBACH, *Act IV*

PROPERTIES: German name and Orthodox faith; aristocratic, cultivated St. Petersburg background. Guitar, piano, songs; knowledge of serious music. Cognac (instead of vodka). Uniform, stylish civilian clothes.

HOW HE MAKES LIFE MEANINGFUL: By responding to beauty in music, Irina, nature. By wanting "to share in life," to work with workers, to attend the University with Andrei, to arrange the concert to help the fire victims, to marry Irina. By being good-humored, "decent," believing he is happy, and not demanding answers about the meaning of life.

TUZENBACH IS THE MASCULINE COUNTERPART of Olga's moral superiority and the masculine counterpart, too, of Irina's delicacy, tenderness, and expectancy about life. This links him to those two more than to any others in the play. Indeed, being as cultivated and refined, himself, as the three sisters, he is on as close and comfortable terms with the family as Chebutykin and Kulygin.

Born under a brighter star, Tuzenbach would have been born handsome and not ". . . so homely . . . I absolutely wanted to cry," as Olga says; and Irina would have been able to marry him for love and not for duty, as she finally concedes to do. As it is, they share similar backgrounds and temperaments, they are united in their goals, and Chekhov has given them all the lyric speeches in the play. Many of these are extraordinarily beautiful—and Tuzenbach's are often profound.

When *special care* is taken to have Tuzenbach immediately recognizable as a homely man, his decisions, his devotion to Irina, his managing to be happy, and his death all gain interest. He is an ugly Lensky and when the audience, too, cannot find it in their "power to love" the honorable, tragic Baron, their sympathy mounts with their guilt. The "homeliness" that he alludes to once, and Olga twice, is the one unfavorable quality Chekhov gave him to counterbalance all his virtues. It is what his whole part turns on, and if a merely commonplace-looking Tuzenbach is used, his decisions to resign from aristocratic, wealthy St. Petersburg first, and then the Army, seem foolhardy; his devotion to Irina, doglike; his happiness, a simpleton's; his death, as Chebutykin characterizes it, ". . . one baron more, one baron less—what's the difference?"

Interpretations that make Tuzenbach ridiculous or comic, i.e., stuttering or lisping or lower-class, are not justified in the text. He should simply have the sort of face that is kind but ugly and that cancels him out as unattractive to women, because all his actions are just the reverse.

Now, when an obviously unfortunate-looking man casts away his birthright and status to work among laborers; when he can dream that a beautiful girl like Irina—everyone's darling—can love *him*; when he can believe that constancy and honor are enough; and when, in spite of being the physical opposite of all his aesthetic tastes, such a man manages to think of himself as "happy," we are intrigued. Aren't we?

When such a person says to Irina the ethereal (and perfect for her) lines about "You're so pale and beautiful and enchanting. . . . It seems to me your paleness brightens the dark air like light," we infer our own "If only . . ." for Tuzenbach. In direct ratio to his appearance will be the audience's despair at Irina's conceding to marry him—and soon, the audience's admiration of her spiritual growth.

Of interest in Act IV are Tuzenbach's only complaining lines in the play, when he says, "What senseless things, what idiotic things, suddenly for no reason start to matter in your life! . . ."— the "senseless things" being an imminent duel and an imminent marriage to a woman who has told him it is not in her power to love him. (Chekhov, in an advanced stage of tuberculosis, wrote Olga Knipper before he went to Moscow to join her, that everything was at last in order for their marriage, "except one trifle . . . my health.")

When Irina cries and tells him so passionately, "Oh, what is there I can do? I never have been in love in my life, not even once. . . . I've dreamed so about love so long now, day and night, but my soul is like some expensive piano that's locked and the key is lost." We are moved, and the Baron rises even higher in our esteem when he tells her, ". . . There isn't anything in my life terrible enough to frighten me, only that lost key, it tortures me. . . ."

His saying, "Say something to me" seems at one instant to be asking for so little and so much. And the real distance between them is so plain in her "What is there to say?" Still, Tuzenbach's hope dies hard, it would seem, when he turns back to her, after starting off for the duel, and calls her name. If only she'd had it in her power to call him back, or say anything except that blunt "What?" All he can do is invent a request for some coffee.

SOLYONY

Gentlemen, who remembers the description in Lermontov?
from THE DUEL, *1891*

PROPERTIES: Perfume, literary quotations, resemblance to Lermontov.

HOW HE MAKES LIFE MEANINGFUL: By looking like and behaving like and pretending to be Lermontov (the worldly, unscrupulous, malevolent "friend" of Lensky who takes his fiancée, kills Lensky in a duel, and then abandons the girl).

SOLYONY IS A MENACINGLY AGGRESSIVE, ANTISOCIAL, INTELLECTUAL MAN who is shy, panicky, and jealous inside when he is with people. As he says about himself, "When I'm alone with anybody I'm all right, I'm just like everybody else, but . . ." He demands Tuzenbach's entire attention, just as he devours all the candy. He probably falls in love with Irina (inasmuch as his type is able to) because of Tuzenbach. Chekhov convinces us again and again of Solyony's infantile insatiability and pushing of every relation to its limits.

Through his identification with Lermontov, Solyony's inferior, young loneliness is converted (in his imagination) to superior, artistic loneliness. There is in this a curious partial resemblance to Masha in that he always sits by himself, thinking about something and saying nothing. However, Masha's superior, artistic loneliness is true, while his is false; and her anger is against fate, and his is sadism. When Masha speaks, she relates; Solyony erupts with aggressive remarks designed to attract attention, i.e., his first line: "With one hand I can only lift sixty pounds, but with two hands I can lift a hundred and eighty—two hundred, even. From that I deduce, etc. . . ."

He is a great source of bizarre, grotesque texture for the play. Whereas Chekhov presented Olga and Irina to us through their arias (Moscow, work, marriage, etc.) and through the Wagnerian style of leitmotivs, Solyony got none of these. Instead, Chekhov has covered him with little systems of oddness all connetced by their carefully chosen "rightness" for him. Chebutykin and Kulygin are highly specific types, too, who have these Vuillard spots, but Solyony is the concentrated example. His spots range from crude, awkward, childish sentences: "Chicky, chicky, chicky" and "Cockroaches" and others; upward to his spontaneous but heavily aggressive "joke" to Chebutykin that warns us of the duel: "In two or three years either you'll die of apoplexy or I'll lose control of myself and put a bullet through your head, my angel." And on up the scale to the self-revealing misquotation of Lermontov in Act IV, when he says, ". . . Remember the poem? 'But he, the rebel, seeks the storm/ As if in tempests there were peace . . .'"

Solyony hardly has a speech that is not grotesque, and Irina and Olga haven't a single one that is. His remarks, usually lumped by the others into "stupidities," are often wit manqué and wit. He, alone, gets the better of Natasha. Solyony's sentence, "If that child were mine, I'd fry him in a frying pan and then eat him," so unexpectedly, grotesquely expresses our own dislike of Natasha that we laugh and our sympathy is all on his side; and it is again later, when Natasha is trying for propriety and says, "Excuse me, Vasili Vasilich, I hadn't any idea you were in here. I'm not dressed," and he says, "It doesn't make any difference to me."

Tuzenbach—his complete opposite—is the only person Solyony feels close to, or comfortable with, and feels safe in his aggression toward, which, oddly, is partly an expression of affection. His mildest hostility is in his sentence about vodka's being made of cockroaches, with which he shocks Irina like a little boy showing a little girl a live spider. The duel, of course, is the carrying to the limit of this same impulse. It is thoroughly adult behavior in which he feels none of his usual adolescent or childish lacks. On the day of the duel he feels not simply *like* Lermontov; he feels that for once, he *is* Lermontov.

Solyony is victorious, but he sits among graves. Tuzenbach is gone, Irina going. The third duel for Solyony is not apt to be his last. We can imagine him reduced to soldier's rank finally, with his isolation complete. Solyony's quarrelsomely leaving the room in anger and frustration to be alone is a good symbol for his whole life. He walks out on humanity and kills off his last echo of a connection with it.

NATASHA

PROPERTIES: Green belt, Andrei, babies, things about babies, the rooms, the fork, the candles, nightgown, Protopopov's troika, the servants, the forks, the trees.

HOW SHE MAKES LIFE MEANINGFUL: The present is entirely meaningful to Natasha as the base she works on. Her dreams

are not ideals but direct preludes to action—get a better room
for the baby, drive out the sisters, get rid of the trees. She is a
woman of action whose whole life is a complete animal success
and human failure.

NATASHA HAS THE IMPLACABLENESS, SINGLE-MINDEDNESS, AND DE-
STRUCTIVE SUCCESS of the animal shrew. (How interesting that we
use the same word for such a woman and a little animal that
kills and kills insensately. How much unconscious, or implied,
knowledge of this type is in our name for it.)

She is not only a type, but a new, created-by-Chekhov type:
the female human animal. She is so like many women—the
essence of many—that we not only recognize but can't believe she
didn't exist before. She has the funniness of a monster, yet
everyone realizes so well that she is entirely without self-knowl-
edge, and she is an absurd success. Her type is worthy of
Molière or Cervantes and is akin, of course, to such wives in
folk tales, yet purely invented by Chekhov. Natasha to herself is
good and right, since she has no disinterestedness and can never
compare her actions and another's as if hers were another's. She
is entirely reasonable, with all humor, sentiment, and human
feeling lacking, and is worthy of a war machine in the Department of Defense.

In Act I we see her in an unfamiliar, overawing situation in the
society of the cultivated enclave. She says, "I'm just not accustomed to being in—" But how quickly in Act II and to the end
the Prozorov household stops being "society" and becomes merely
the niche, the habitat of this successful animal! Natasha's completely
victorious "What do we have to have that old woman for, too?
What for?" makes us see (as is intimated in dozens of other
ways) that all human kindness, decency, immemorial tradition,
"She's been with us thirty years," are helpless against Natasha.
If others are ineffective because of distance, uncertainty, she is
completely effective because of her lack of any distance, uncertainty—as effective and sure as a wolverine, shrew. To keep Anfisa
and take care of her, Olga *must* move to the government apartment at the high school.

Just as Olga is elementally incomprehensible to Natasha, Olga's counterpart, the Baron, is lost on Natasha, too. Compare what he says about the trees, "I'm happy. It's as if I were seeing for the first time in my life these firs and maples and birches, and they are all looking at me curiously and waiting. What beautiful trees, and how beautiful life ought to be under them!" with Natasha's "Tomorrow I'll be all alone here," (mentally she's rid of Andrei, too) "First of all, I'm going to have them chop down all those fir trees along the walk—then that maple. . . . And I'll have them plant darling little flowers everywhere—" The new, manipulable flowers are like Bobik and Baby Sophie as compared to the hierarchical trees that oblige respect for past established values and cannot be manipulated as we please.

While the rest of the characters are frustrated in Act II (Vershinin gets no tea, Tuzenbach gets no candy, Kulygin gets no evening in congenial company, Rode gets no evening of dancing that he'd taken a nap to prepare for, the carnival people get no party), Natasha is the great opposite. She gets her troika ride with Protopopov.

Protopopov, from the first mention of him, is so dislikable Masha doesn't want him invited to the birthday dinner, even though he's sent a large cake. Irina had not even considered inviting him. As Natasha's masculine shadow, he stands for the same successful vulgarity of the town as she, but, aside from his laughable name, he does not have the funniness and particularity that make us accept Natasha as—however terrible—reality. Protopopov is just a statistical fact of existence.

In Act IV Natasha's desires are accomplished, or are about to be. Her husband minds the baby while Protopopov sits in the living room. All the Prozorov friends and members of the family leave or are driven out. Andrei, who has frequently remarked about her "noise," can be reprimanded for waking the baby with loud talk, Irina can be corrected about her belt, the trees can come down, and Natasha is *there*, a matriarchal Genghis Khan.

RODE

PROPERTIES: Noisy goodwill, gym class at the high school, companionship with Fedotik.

RODE AND FEDOTIK START OUT AS AN APPARENTLY INSEPARABLE BOBCHINSKY-DOBCHINSKY COUPLE, but instead of being identical twins they are fraternal and different.

Rode is innocently stupid, loud, and repetitive, but still a congenial member of the enclave group. The Prozorov family group somehow is not only a little bigger, but a little better, because of him. His absurdities, foibles are lovable rather than dislikable.

In an affecting end when he is tearfully embracing Tuzenbach several times and kissing Irina's hands twice, he has a tiny apotheosis when, with his one piece of imagination and unusualness in the play, he calls good-bye not only to people but to trees and, finally, with a child's wit, "Good-bye, echo."

FEDOTIK

Like wit and the comic, humour has in it a liberating element. But it has also something fine and elevating which is lacking in the other two ways of deriving pleasure from intellectual activity. [This is] the ego's victorious assertion of its own invulnerability. . . . It insists that it is impervious to wounds dealt by the outside world, in fact, that these are merely occasions for affording it pleasure.

Sigmund Freud: HUMOUR *(1928)*

PROPERTIES: Gifts, guitar, hobbies, camera, solitaire.
HOW HE MAKES LIFE MEANINGFUL: By giving gifts, having hobbies.

WITH THIS VERY SPECIALIZED EXISTENCE FEDOTIK is essentially generous, sweet, and happy. When he can't go to the carnival party, he responds only, "What a shame. I was counting on spending the evening, but if the little baby's sick . . . Tomorrow I'll bring him a toy." Even the farewell is expressed in terms of gifts and photography. The sorrow of parting from his friends is replaced by "official" annoyance of a photographer—"Do hold still." He adds enormously to the pleasant, sweet funniness of the play, giving a sense of niceness to the Prozorov group.

In his one appearance without Rode (during the fire) he adds extraordinary charm and life with his laughter and dancing when he says, "Burnt to ashes! Burnt to ashes. Everything I had in this world!" Again, the climactic Act III has caused or revealed a change. In Fedotik's case his hobbies seem to be merely a satisfactory substitute for something else—something serious, so that when he loses them and is stripped clean he responds joyously and beautifully with the superiority of a human being over circumstances.

FERAPONT

"Oh, Lord," he went on with anguish. "To have one peep at Moscow! To see mother Moscow if only in my dreams."
                                                  PEASANTS, *1897*

FERAPONT IS AN EASYGOING, NATURAL, FAIRLY FOOLISH OLD MAN. His incredibly distorted facts, parodying Chebutykin's newspaper facts, are, somehow, no less trivial and far more amusing. Both characters' non sequiturs flower and pebble and dapple the Vuillard household scenes.

Ferapont's deafness is a convenience for Andrei to say his soliloquies to, that tell the audience his private feelings and his public contacts with the county board and the Protopopov world. Ferapont's litmus-paper reactions to Andrei's moods are another convenience for revealing Andrei's changes, i.e., in Act II the good-humored Andrei calls him, "Ferapont, old man," while in Act III bad-tempered Andrei demands that Ferapont call him "your honor." This is further indicated—and at length—in the second half of the play when Ferapont seems more insistent and has a moment or two of superiority to Andrei when he, Ferapont, actually has to reason with him to get him to sign the papers.

The most important, strange, imaginative function of Ferapont is to parody Andrei's (and the sisters') Moscow dreams. His are the dreams of a big old dog who also dreams of magical Moscow. If his seem to discredit Moscow faintly, they also make it seem inevitable—that is, if doggy old Ferapont has them—that dreams *are* necessary, though his are more absurd than the others'.

Through Ferapont we see in Act IV Andrei's terrible fall in position when he, as a baby-wheeler, is replaced by Ferapont, the humbler one of the two humble servants. In the end, Ferapont and Andrei indistinguishably, absolutely similarly take care of the two children (one Andrei's, the other possibly Protopopov's) as commanded by Natasha.

Ferapont and Anfisa help give the feel of the Prozorov external family group, its servants, friends, and relatives. Both are pleasant, natural, mild and add to the pleasantness and humor of the play except when, through Natasha, they are treated badly.

ANFISA

PROPERTIES: The Prozorovs, Ferapont, later Olga, the government apartment.

ANFISA IS THE LITMUS PAPER from which we read indications about the three sisters, just as Ferapont is Andrei's litmus paper. In Act I, we see from Anfisa's behavior a continuation of the family group as it had been in former days. She treats Irina as a little girl, and in her mind the three sisters are the children they once were. In Act II this is extended and her position is so absolutely, immemorially established that, when she complains about Vershinin's leaving his tea and Masha gets angry at her, she not only is not afraid, but doesn't respond as a servant and, instead, makes an affectionate, good-humored response as though she is an important relative with a position that cannot be endangered. In

Act III, when she begs Olga not to drive her away, we are
astonished and think how absurd. But then, when Natasha quarrels
so violently in an attempt to get her thrown out, we realize that
Anfisa is right (she's heard what Natasha surely has said before),
and our knowledge of this is learned from her. In Act IV, in
one of the most charming, happy, delightful changes in the play—
something that partially counteracts the terrible changes—we
see Anfisa at last entirely assured, happier than she's even been,
singing a little aria of pure bliss about her humble happiness-
situation in the government apartment with Olga.

* * *

One ought to say about the whole minor group of Ferapont,
Anfisa, Fedotik, and Rode, within the major group, that if these
characters are removed, the play will be more terrible and
unpleasant; a good deal of sweetness, charm, humor, and human
inconsequentiality will disappear; and also, the feeling of the
Prozorov extended family as a social group—the little enclave
capable of fairly happy, good, continued existence unless destroyed
—will disappear, too.

IV / THE ACTS

ACT I: *Beginnings*

TAKING PLACE AT NOON ON A SPRING DAY before the first leaves
come out, Act I is one of beginnings. Irina, the young girl whose
birthday it is, is beginning her new year quite recovered from
the death in the family and filled with happiness at the expectations
of going back to Moscow soon. We see Baron Tuzenbach's
beginning declarations of love for her. We see a friendship
beginning in the meeting of Colonel Vershinin and the social group
who, as Moscow speaking to Moscow, are immediately at ease
with each other and like each other at once. With Masha's "I'm
staying to lunch," we have the first intimation of her love affair
with Vershinin. While there is mention made that their brother
Andrei is beginning studies in Moscow to be a professor, he has
actually begun—by his proposal of marriage that day to Natasha,
"one of the local girls"—something quite different.
　In this act occurs the establishment of a social situation that's
mostly very pleasant; mostly there are happy expectations,
mostly they are friendly and well-off. The Prozorovs and their
extensions—Anfisa and Ferapont, the family servants; Chebutykin,
the longtime family friend; Vershinin and the young officers
who knew the family or of it—*all* make a little, foreign, cultivated,
highly organized cell inside a provincial, crude city. The family is
a father-organization that has lost its father. General Prozorov
represented the days when they were governed, had their life
and ideals prescribed for them, and revolt, or breaking free for a
little space, was their only necessity. His censorship they obeyed,
or fooled. With it gone they can say anything; but in this
terrible freedom the vacancy of grown-ups who governed them
has to be filled by themselves, the new grown-ups. They had a

paradise in which they had only to follow the rules. Now they
have to make the rules they follow—and they long to be in
that earlier existence with Father. Moscow is their past, but just
as definitely it is their future.

They are surviving partly happily, partly unhappily, in the
midst of their uncultivated environment when the only son, who
is the family's weakest element, introduces into it a powerful representative of the environment who manages to dominate him
completely and, in the long run, to drive out the other members
of the father-group. In the affectionate joking and teasing of part
of the family by the rest are the first hints of anything troubling
underneath the pleasant surface, and then we begin to see that
Irina *is* partly troubled by life, that Masha is very much so, and
that Olga is extreme and psychosomatic.

ACT II: *Continuations, Frustrations*

AFTER ACT I'S SPRING, NOON, Act II is between 8 and 9:30 at night
in cold winter weather with the wind howling in the chimney.
Act II begins with the continuation of the proposal: Here Natasha
and Andrei are after a year or so of marriage, and the direct-
ness of their condition has a slap-in-the-face force. Here, also,
is the continuation of Vershinin and Masha, of the "happiness"
and "future" and meaning of life. The Andrei-Ferapont relationship
is now fixed so that change can be indicated by change in it,
i.e., Andrei's demanding to be called "your honor." There is
a continuation of Tuzenbach's work-longing; with Irina there
is the first dissatisfaction with her work. Act II is preparation for
a party as is Act I, but a much more troubled preparation, which,
when in full swing of beginning, is canceled out by Natasha
(the provincial city element inside the little foreign cell, itself
inside the provincial city), the element that's begun to destroy,
grows and grows, and finally does destroy.

At the start of tea with singing, the little group is almost as
pleasant as in the first act, but now needs the drunkenness,
obliviousness, as in Act I it didn't. Being undermined by Natasha,
the group continues more hectically with drinking and quarreling,
and comes to nothing in a dreadfully anticlimactic, damped-out

way. Solyony's declaration of love to Irina is unpleasant nothing to Irina, and results in unpleasant nothing to Solyony. The threat about successful rivals brings out in the open the unpleasantness toward Tuzenbach and Irina that finally kills Tuzenbach. Olga's exhaustion leads her straight to bed. The exhausted Kulygin doesn't get his evening in congenial company, and won't accompany Vershinin who (still tealess) has had nothing to eat all day, has to go out all alone. The act ends with most of them, and the carnival people, frustrated in some way; all, except Natasha, who gets her troika ride with Protopopov. Her temporary driving away of most of the family in Act II is foreshadowing what will happen permanently later. The stage is empty at the last with Irina alone, saying yearningly, "To Moscow! To Moscow! To Moscow!"

ACT III: *Climaxes*

JUST AS THE TWO PRECEDING ACTS, this one is a large *social* thing (Act I birthday dinner and Act II Mardi Gras preparations that are canceled). Act III is carried along by the arrangements necessitated by a social disaster, the fire in the town. The whole household is either taking part or avoiding taking part in it. We hardly notice what time of year it is. Under such unusual circumstances the unusual can be said or asked, and the extraordinary truth about most of the characters comes out at this extraordinary time.

With all the climaxes in Act III: Olga and Natasha's quarrel, Chebutykin's and Masha's confessions, Andrei's exposure, and Irina's breaking down, the first announcement is made of the brigade's leaving which will result in the departure of Vershinin and the military attachments of the Prozorovs.

ACT IV: *Conclusions*

THE SPRING AND BIRTH BEGINNINGS OF ACT I have proceeded to the fall's prelude to winter, with the swans and geese flying south, departures, death, and conclusions.

The enclave's allies are leaving, the last remnants of the father-organization are gone. Natasha has complete victory in the house. Irina and Olga have been driven out, and Masha no longer enters the house. Natasha has all the rooms she wants, she can chop the trees down, and she has Protopopov there every day. Natasha, by being introduced into the family-society of *The Three Sisters*, destroys it, just as Yelena's introduction into the family-society in *Uncle Vanya* disrupts it. But Yelena leaves, and that society reforms and tries to go on as before. Natasha has broken to pieces the Prozorov society whose fragments go on as best they can.

What to make of a diminished thing, how to get partial satisfaction, get along, make life on a lower level of expectation? They now regard this existence as necessary, their fate, their lot (like growing old) rather than as something escapable (like leaving for Moscow). Not living in Moscow is accepted.

Olga does this with her impersonal schoolwork and being headmistress. No further mention of headaches and tiredness from her.

Irina plans to be satisfied without love, but with work away from home, and with marriage to a good man whom she doesn't love. This makes her feel happily anticipating again. When Tuzenbach is killed, the marriage part is removed, but she still sticks to the work ideal. Masha, after the partial satisfaction of the love affair with Vershinin, has to settle for continuing life without him but with Kulygin.

Chebutykin leaves for retirement, and Andrei surrenders in complete, abjectly nervous defeat.

In Act I Olga has the first lines and she recalled the band playing at the father's funeral. In Act IV Olga has the last lines to speak, and the band music accompanies her. As *The Three Sisters* ends, Olga puts her arms around the other two and makes a long speech that sums up her sisters' last words and one half of the play itself: the half that is about the meaning of life. She ends this speech by repeating the two Russian words that in an entirely literal translation would be *If knew, If knew!* and that in ordinary American English are *If only we knew, if only we knew!* Chebutykin once more sings his nonsensical little song and then

says twice over the two Russian words that have ended three
out of four of his last speeches, words which sum up the meaningless, senseless, hopeless half of life. "What's the difference?" Olga
repeats, "If only we knew, if only we knew," and the play is over.